ONE DAY FIANCE

LAUREN LANDISH

Edited by
VALORIE CLIFTON
Edited by
STACI ETHERIDGE

Copyright © 2021 by Lauren Landish

All rights reserved.

No part of this book may be reproduced in any form or by any electronic or mechanical means, including information storage and retrieval systems, without written permission from the author, except for the use of brief quotations in a book review.

ALSO BY LAUREN LANDISH

Big Fat Fake Series:

My Big Fat Fake Wedding | | My Big Fat Fake Engagement | | My Big Fat Fake Honeymoon

Standalones:

Drop Dead Gorgeous | | The Dare | | The Blind Date

Bennett Boys Ranch:

Buck Wild | | Riding Hard | | Racing Hearts

The Tannen Boys:

Rough Love | | Rough Edge | | Rough Country

Dirty Fairy Tales:

Beauty and the Billionaire | | Not So Prince Charming | | Happily Never After

Get Dirty:

Dirty Talk | | Dirty Laundry | | Dirty Deeds | | Dirty Secrets

PROLOGUE

CONNOR

Ten Years Ago

The vaulted marble ceilings aren't soundproofed. I know that personally because I dropped a pen in here and it sounded like a pistol shot that had everyone looking at me.

That's what makes this room at the Metro Museum of Fine Art difficult—how damned *quiet* everyone is. I'm the youngest patron in here . . . well, if you don't count the two boys who are with a woman who's definitely their mom in the middle of a school day.

Honestly, the two blond boys look like they'd rather be anywhere else right now. Shoveling up dog poop in the back yard might be preferable. Even shoveling up the neighbor's dog's poop.

But Mom is a trooper. Despite looking like she's about to scream in frustration from talking to the two breathing brick walls that are her children, she's continuing to soldier on.

"And this one is of Robert I, King of Scotland," Mom drones, reading the placard. "He was famous for . . . Timmy!"

"What?" Timmy, who's looking at his phone, asks. Mom can't see it from here, but I can just make out the picture on his screen. He might be studying something, but it sure as hell isn't art except in the eyes of a plastic surgeon. Obviously, puberty is trembling in his loins. "Come on, Mom, can't we just go? Seriously, I'll Google what I need to get the assignment done!"

"Yeah, Mom," the younger one, who's too young to worry about his brother's interest in girls but obviously finds art intolerable, whines. "You promised us McDonald's if we came for two hours, and that was like, five whole hours ago!"

Well, that's pretty much impossible unless they arrived at eight in the morning, which I seriously doubt. But I can see Mom's about to give in, and for some reason, I decide to intervene. Sliding over, I lean against the brass railing that keeps patrons from touching the displays and clear my throat. "Your mom's right, you know. This is fascinating stuff."

The kids look at me like I've lost my mind, and I can see Mom giving me a wary eye too. I'm being helpful, but I'm also a stranger. Her mama bear instincts are tingling.

But she's got nothing to worry about from me. "I'm serious. I mean, look at this guy here, Robert I. Or as most people call him, Robert the Bruce. Forget *Braveheart*, this guy was a bada—" I catch myself. "A leader and warrior. Now I don't know about you, but I think sword fights, winning against overwhelming odds, and literally becoming king of all you survey and all that is pretty cool."

"Really?" Timmy asks, lowering his phone a little more, and I nod.

"There's a famous story about him. After struggling for over a decade for his crown and Scottish independence, he had a chance at the Battle of Bannockburn to finally push back the English threat. Even though he was outnumbered, he led his army into battle. During the fight, he found himself alone, his armor ripped up, his shield gone. His forces were on the edge of fleeing. All he had was his battleaxe. Suddenly, a mounted English knight in full armor charged at him, lance pointed right at his heart. Now imagine, you're standing, exhausted, muscles weak because you've been fighting your butt off, and the medieval equivalent of Iron Man on a tank comes charging at you."

"I'd probably crap my pants," the little one says, and I laugh.

"Me too. But Robert stood his ground, dodged, and took the English knight down. That's what this picture here is showing. The sight was so dramatic that his forces rallied, pushing the English back and winning the battle."

The boys are entranced, and Mom silently mouths 'thank you' to me. I give her a nod, but for the boys, I shrug. "Now, I know that's not as cool as *Naruto*, maybe, but in some ways, I think it's cooler. Because this guy was real."

I walk away, and a moment later, Mom catches up with me. "Thank you."

"You're welcome," I whisper, glancing back at the boys who are eagerly reading about the next picture. "You might let Timmy use his phone to find interesting info and have him share it with you and his brother instead of the other way around. It'll keep his fingers and mind busy and save you from exhaustion."

Mom looks like she might swoon and ask me for a 'personal tour', but I'm not here to entice a married woman. My target is the woman in the corner of the room who's watching all of this while keeping a watchful eye on the patrons and the art.

"Do you think you could . . . you know, give me a hand?" Mom asks me. "Just ten minutes, please?"

I look over at the two boys, knowing it's ten minutes I don't really have but relenting anyway. I talk the boys through two more paintings, including the one they were apparently here to see, until the mom reluctantly says they have to go. As they leave, she silently mouths 'thank you' to me again, and I give her a nod and a shrug like it was nothing.

But it was more than nothing. It was my way in, my foot in the door, so to speak. An opportunity I couldn't have planned any better. I feel a presence behind me, and I turn to see the woman from the corner giving me a smile. "Bravo. I love when someone can get the next generation excited about art history. Do you volunteer here? Or go to school nearby?"

There are a couple of ways I could play this. I could turn on the charm. If my goal were to have this woman's ankles around my shoulders and her screaming my name tonight, that'd be the best play.

And while that admittedly sounds enticing, it's not my goal. So I shrink down a little, wilting into my shoulders and walking the line of shy and confident. "No, just a fan of classical portraiture. Especially the English masters."

"I'm sure you've heard about the new exhibit coming, then?" the woman asks, ready to nerd out a little with a fellow art geek.

Perfect.

"Yes, I can't wait. I'm excited to see the Rossetti piece in person," I reply a little shyly, like I'm nervous about talking about a famous picture of Venus in the nude. Truthfully, I don't give a rat's ass about Dante Gabriel Rossetti or his work, even if it is the most famous piece in the traveling exhibit.

What I care about is that it's in the prep room with the piece I *am* interested in.

"I just hope I can get back when the crowds won't be intrusive," I comment, sighing. "You know how it is. Really studying a piece, appreciating all the small details, is hard with others around."

The woman looks me up and down, assessing me. I play more into the role that I'm trying to portray, that of a legitimate art fan in a nondescript hoodie who couldn't hurt a fly. To that point, I push my fake glasses up on my nose and flash an awkward smile as I slick my gelled hair over, though I know it hasn't moved a centimeter since this morning.

The woman considers for a second, then gives me a little smile. "I do think your volunteer tour deserves a little reward. Come with me."

Damn, this is working smoother than I thought! But the easiest way to get to an art nerd's heart is by being a fellow art nerd. They'll talk about brushstrokes for hours.

I get it, it's like gearheads with their cars and compression ratios, or cooks with their spices. But I see the mechanics, the details, not the affection they so often glorify. I'm motivated by something a lot different from the passion that drives their interest.

I follow the woman into a back hallway, acting like I don't know where we're going already and haven't mapped out where the closest exit points are. Truth is, I know the map of this building like a video game nerd knows a *Halo* level. We take a right turn and reach the prep room. When the door's closed behind us and we're alone, she whispers reverently, "Here it is."

I cover my mouth with a hand, feigning a gasp. Venus, in all her nude glory . . . if somehow a Greek goddess were a pale-as-cream, auburn-haired Brit with semi-ecclesiastical overtones. But I still act like it's the greatest thing since grilled cheese sandwiches. "It's beautiful."

"It is, isn't it?" the woman asks, obviously agreeing wholeheartedly.

I look at the art as though it's magical, and truth be told, it is one of the greats. Rossetti's skill and accuracy in things like the texture of Venus's hair is amazing, and I can see why people are drawn to it. I shift my feet, looking at it from different angles but actually stealing glances at the tables and walls around us.

There it is . . . my mission. It's not even part of the upcoming exhibit but is back here waiting for cleaning and reframing. Which is perfect since that means people won't ask questions at first, assuming some other department has it.

It's small, no larger than a piece of notebook paper, but its value has nothing to do with its size. It's desired, and that's all that counts.

It's time for phase two of my plan. Placing my hand over my chest, I tap a button on the Bluetooth headset taped to my chest, calling a preprogrammed number on the phone in my back pocket. Seconds later, the direct line to the prep room rings.

"That's weird," the woman says, surprised. "Nobody ever calls here."

She suddenly looks uncertain, knowing I shouldn't be back here, so I give her the push she needs. I hold up my hands out wide, then pointedly put them in my pockets. See? Harmless.

"It's all good, I'll stand right here, won't touch anything. It's just . . ."

I look back to the painting with a bit of shine in my eyes, and she whispers, "I know . . . I'll be just a second."

As she scurries off to answer the call, I think, *Good, a second's all I need.*

Quick as a fox, I grab the small canvas from the nearby table and slip it under my hoodie, letting it lie flush against my back in the special pocket I wore in case I was successful. I'm already bent over to examine the signature in the corner of the Rossetti piece when she gets back.

"Sorry, they must have hung up."

I shrug, straightening up. "It's okay. I was enjoying the moment, just me and the goddess of beauty here."

She smiles, but that uncertainty is creeping back in. She's remembering that her job isn't to have art nerds in the unsecured back areas of the museum. I've overstayed my welcome, which serves me just fine because I've accomplished my mission.

Or most of it.

Just one last phase . . . the clean getaway.

"Do we need to get out of here before I get you in trouble?" I ask softly, looking around like someone might've shown up in the few seconds she was on the phone.

"Yeah, probably so."

"I understand. Thank you for showing me the piece, though. You made my day, my month, probably my whole year."

She has no idea how true that is, but the warmth is back in her voice. "Well, you made those kids' day, so it seems only fair."

One more aw-shucks smile as I duck my head, and I follow her back down the hall to the main display galleries.

"Thanks again," I say as she peels off, and I walk through the rooms, slow and steady, pausing to read a few wall plaques here and there and making sure I don't look suspicious in the slightest. I even see the mom and kids out front, eating their promised burgers, and offer them a wave as I head down the street.

Even if they remember me, it'll be as the nerdy art guy who was friendly and kind.

Not the guy who just stole a painting worth thousands of dollars.

CHAPTER 1

POPPY

He clutched at the large bulge in his jeans, squeezing it like a promised treasure. "I'm going to put this in you," he says, "and you're going to like it."

Ugh. Rereading the sentence, I swiftly repress the urge to gag and instead jab the *Delete* button with my finger, breathing through my mouth, only until I get back to a point that I don't feel like it's utter trash.

"Great," I say as I realize where I am. "Four hours of work and a grand progress of . . . fifty words?" I pull up my word counter and double-check. "Fifty *fucking* words? Fiddle-dee-FUCKSTICKS!"

Ugh, even that's more words than I've written in the last fifteen minutes. I thump my fist into the middle of my forehead, resisting the urge to click *Undo* on all my deletions. Yeah, it's terrible, but at least it's something. And something is better than nothing.

Or at least that's what I'm trying to tell myself as I get up from my kitchen table 'office' and walk over to my fridge, where I grab one of my pre-made sippy cups of black iced tea. I'm tempted to grab one of the wine coolers that I've got in there instead, but the calendar stuck to my freezer door reminds me that I've got a deadline.

As if I needed any more pressure. After the success of my first book, *Love in Great Falls,* I got cocky. And when Bluebird Publishing House came to me, offering not just a per-book deal but an actual *advance*, I took it.

That was two advance checks and dozens of talks with my agent ago. Now I've got a deadline looming, and as my Great-Aunt Hannah used to say, it's time to piss or pounce. But that's a lot easier to say when you're not suffering from the inner fear that your follow-up second book isn't remotely in the same galaxy as your first.

I flip off the freezer calendar like it's the one that's done me wrong and this isn't all self-induced stress. "Way to put pressure on yourself, Poppy. Hello, looming deadline." I take a long drink of tea and look back at my laptop, the mostly white space of my current page staring back at me. "Or dooming lead line."

Ugh. If I'm talking to myself, I know I'm losing my shit. A little yipping sound from the couch reminds me that I've at least got *someone* to talk to.

"Why can't I write like J.A. Fox?" I ask my couch as I approach, looking over the top at my two fluffy white Pomeranians, Nut and Juice. They're brothers, pups that I got from a neighbor who suddenly realized her own Pom wasn't sick but pregnant. I told her I'd take one to help her out but somehow ended up with the two runts of the litter. Now, the two, who really do look like a pair of pom-poms, are much bigger, healthy . . . and noisy.

Nut, who's currently trying to turn his brother into a sister, stops his tussling to look up at me, grinning his doggy grin. Juice, who's underneath, also looks at me for about two seconds before deciding to go all UFC on his brother and flip him, sending the two tumbling off the sofa and back to their nearly constant playful battle.

"Shoulda known I couldn't depend on you two," I tell them as Juice pounces away from Nut.

My pups ignore me as always, and I stretch my tense shoulders, catching a whiff of my ripe, aged cheddar smelling armpits and gag again. "Whew, shit on toast!" I gasp, quickly lowering my elbows to my sides. "I stink."

It's one of the perks of being a writer. Yes, I call it a perk. I can sit there and not have to worry about personal hygiene when I'm trying to hit a certain deadline. Hell, most days, I can spend the day wearing what I want. December, and I want to work wearing a Snuggie? I can do it. July, and I want to work wearing nothing but panties? Can do that too.

But when the smell's gotten bad enough to knock yourself out, I should probably pause for some self-care. "No pauses," I argue with myself. "You're procrastinating. You don't have a hot date."

Yeah, but for real, when the stench gets so bad that even Nut and Juice give me ugly looks, I really should at least wash the hot spots—pits and pubes—because you know it's awful when dogs, who literally greet each other by sniffing each other's butts, start shunning you.

And I do have an afternoon writing session at the library. If my dogs are turning up their noses at me, then the writing friends I'm meeting will definitely balk and spray me down with copious doses of body spray. The last time my friend Aleria did that, I sneezed for days. She tried telling me it was my body ridding itself of toxins in that weird hoodoo-voodoo voice she does, but I'm pretty sure the only toxin I'd been exposed to was the stinky stuff she sprayed me with and the pizza rolls I had for lunch.

None of that matters, though. If I don't get some progress made on my book, I'm dead meat. I laugh out loud, thinking that I'd smell worse then. But that's not exactly a compliment, nor a positive thought.

I start back toward the table when my phone rings, and I look down, my heart stopping and then sprinting when I see who it is. Speak of the devil, it's my agent, Hilda.

I don't want to answer the call. Hilda's nice, but she's not going to like to hear that I've been doing little more than wearing out my keyboard for no reason for the past week . . . but I've got to keep her updated on what's going on.

"Hilda, hey," I greet as I answer nervously. "What's up?"

"How's my favorite writer doing?" Hilda asks, sounding wary but optimistic. "Almost ready to turn in your next masterpiece yet?"

I rub the middle of my forehead, hoping that I can miraculously wake up my brain this way and failing. "Uh . . . well, about that . . . have you ever been constipated? Like for a whole week? Where you try and try to push it out, but it won't go, or well, won't come out? Well, I'm like that . . . but just with my writing."

Yeah, I have quite the way with words. It's a gift, I'm told.

Hilda thinks so too, if the *ew* in her voice is any indication. "That's disgusting," she says, and I wait for the other shoe to drop. "And concerning. Poppy, you've got a deadline coming up, and while I can keep them off your back a bit if you're turning in work, right now it's . . . you've given me nothing for two months now."

"I know."

"There's a lot riding on this," Hilda continues as if I don't know and tell myself that every time I get stalled. "Your reputation is your biggest asset. Publishers will always work with someone who puts out copy, but eventually, they're going to give up hope when you don't do that, and then you know what happens."

Gee, thanks. As if I didn't know what happens at that point. I definitely needed that.

"Hil, you know—"

"But I have something that I think might help. Get you out of the house and inspired, ready to kick this book's ass."

"Huh?" I ask, suspicious of the dangling carrot Hilda is holding out. It's not that I don't trust her, but I know she'll do anything to get me to the finish line, whether it's good for me or not. She's an agent first, and if I don't succeed, neither does she.

"Look, I just got news that a sudden spot opened up at J.A. Fox's workshop dinner. Apparently, someone forgot that, yes, sex does lead to babies, even though she writes accidental pregnancy books all the damn time."

Whoa. I mean, I feel bad for the author, but . . . the Fox Dinner. J.A. Fox is the Grand Dame of Romance Writers. The GOAT, in my opinion. And for the past few years, she's held workshop dinners with fledgling romance authors, talking about her illustrious career, giving writing advice, and signing copies of her latest new release. Right now, it's *The Art Thief*, which is already a *New York Times* bestseller. Not only that, but she's going to showcase the rare painting of a beautiful woman called *The Black Rose*, the art that inspired the novel.

I might have been fangirling a bit—fine, a lot—when I heard about the dinner.

"Normally, you wouldn't be up for something like this, but I fought for you to get the spot because it's local to you . . ." Hilda quickly corrects herself. "I mean, I know what a huge fan you are. I thought it'd be a good reward for finishing your manuscript. Maybe that's not a good idea if you're this far behind, though? Hmm."

I'm so excited that I don't worry about her little slight at the beginning or take offense to her dwindling faith. I've always wanted to meet J.A. Fox and have always looked up to her writing prowess. Whether she knew it or not, J.A. Fox was my inspiration, my mentor, my guiding light in the dark. Every time I didn't think I was good enough, I'd remind myself that if J.A. Fox could do it, so could I. And I've got my own WWJD when it comes to writing. What Would J.A. Do?

"Enough waxing poetic, Poppy!" I whisper to myself before speaking up. "Hilda, OMG! Of course, I can do it. This'll be just the boost I need to finish. You're the greatest, I actually love you after all . . . if I can go to this workshop."

"Hmph!" Hilda says with a full *harrumph*. "You don't love me, you just love my agent benefits. But you should be loving me for putting up with your craziness and making it sound cute and eccentric to the publishing company."

"You know I already love you for that. You're amazing!"

"So you say. But if a catering hall chicken breast with no seasoning is what it takes for you to appreciate me . . . *voila*. This will be a once in a lifetime chance, and maybe a little of J.A. Fox's magic will rub off on you and you'll be able to finish," Hilda says, obviously not ready to let up on the pressure quite yet. She'd probably make a Marine drill instructor sweat. "Make sure you show up on time looking fabulous . . . well, at least shower and fix your hair, 'kay?"

Ouch, she knows me that well. Or maybe she can smell me through the phone? I might be rank enough for Verizon to carry the signal.

"Okay, I'm gonna be on it," I promise her, crossing my heart even though she can't see me. "Look, I want to finish at least a chapter, maybe two, and then I've got an appointment. And I'll shower. Definitely shower."

"With body wash?"

"Of course, I promise," I tell her, trying not to hop up and down in excitement. I'm getting to meet J.A. Fox! "Look, lemme get to pounding my keyboard, and then I'll scrub myself fully. Promise!"

"You'd better."

We hang up, and though I just promised, when I check the clock, I see that writing will have to wait. I've barely got enough time to take care of Nut and Juice before it's time to get on the road to get to the library on time. But I do grab a quick shower first, scrubbing down with some cinnamon scented body wash just like I promised and getting dressed.

I don't do anything fancy, just some jeans and a baggy sweatshirt for comfort and to cover the *bewbies* before I let Nut and Juice out into the front yard. I'd prefer the back, but my 'back yard' is about the size of a picnic table with just enough space for a small barbecue and no grass. So front yard it is, but my babies know the invisible fence.

Looking around the neighborhood, I feel that I got pretty lucky. I live in a townhome complex that's quiet and cute, with little two- and three-bedroom places lining the street. Each place has a neatly manicured lawn in front, with plenty of parking and cute mailboxes that let you express your personality. It's not a cul-de-sac, but there's only one other street at the end of the block, and those are cul-de-sacs. The exit to the neighborhood's the other way, and most days, you can go for a walk, jog, or bike ride in the middle of the street with no problem.

I didn't realize it when I moved in, but it's mostly a female residential area. There are few younger women like me who've bought their first place on their own, boss babe style, and quite a few divorced women who downsized after their split. I can understand that because there's no maintenance, it's safe, and it's close to a nearby park for custody changes.

Or so Renee from four houses down tells me. She gets her kids two weeks a month, and they're pretty good kids. Her son, Kyle, even offered to walk Nut and Juice last summer, and he did a good job, all things considered. Like Nut's tendency to pull on the leash and Juice's preference to lie down and not go anywhere, but they absolutely demand to stay together and not be walked separately.

There are also a few older women like my neighbor, Helen, who interrupts my daydream where J.A. Fox raves about my work at the workshop luncheon, telling me I remind her of herself when she started out.

"Watch where the hell you're going with that thing, you blasted dingbat!"

At first, I think she's talking to my dogs, but when I look, I see Nut doing a number two and Juice peeing on the round rock that I buried my spare house key under, so all's normal there.

I turn to see who she's yelling at and find my next-door neighbor, a single woman in her sixties, pointing at a truck. It appears as if she's moving out, with moving men moving in and out of the house hastily. Helen's a cranky old woman with the voice of a leather-lunged truck driver, but she's always been nice to me and loves to gossip about the drama inside our complex. With a few tweaks, I've used her on several occasions as inspiration for some of the colorful women in my stories.

"Helen!" I gasp in surprise. "What's happening, you're moving? You never said anything."

"Too fast to even scoot next door to share the news," she says as she comes over, grinning. "You know how I went to visit my new grandbaby last month?"

I nod, remembering the hundreds of photos I flipped through with Helen of her new granddaughter, who is admittedly adorable, but newborn pictures all pretty much look the same. Squishy and puffy-eyed, sleeping, or screaming balls of limbs curled around a round, tiny belly. Cute, but . . . *not*, at the same time. At least, not when they're unrelated to you. "Yeah."

"Well, my daughter called last week. Told me there was a little house in her neighborhood for sale. It's perfect for me—a little one-bedroom bungalow, walking distance to my baby . . . my daughter too. Big enough that I'm not banging off the walls, but not so big that I'll tucker myself out cleaning it on a regular basis. So I snatched it up. Closed in one week and sold this place to an investment group. So, *boom*," she says with a snap of her fingers, "I'm blowing this popsicle stand."

Her comment hits me harder than I thought. I've always enjoyed talking with Helen and have always treasured her advice. But at the same time, I get it. She wants to be with her first grandchild, which she always wanted. So instead of saying anything bad, I just reach out and give her a hug.

"I'm happy for you, Helen. I'm gonna miss you, though. Do you know who's moving in?" I ask, looking over. Her townhome's one of the bigger units in the neighborhood, three bedrooms with plenty of space. It could attract a fast-moving single person, a work-from-homer like myself . . . or a family with kids.

I'm personally hoping the former. Or at the very least, no rowdy kids or partying young adults. I'm behind schedule already.

Even worse, the looks the husbands give me when they realize that the book they sneak-read and totally deny came from my mind. I even had one guy tell me he'd read his ex-girlfriend's copy and that I obviously knew how to give killer blowjobs, so how about I practice with him?

Nope, don't need either scenario. I want a nice, quiet neighbor who'll make it easy to focus when it's my writing time.

Damn, I'm picky. No wonder I want Helen to stick around.

"I've got no idea, but you'll be fine, dear," Helen says reassuringly. "You're so quiet and easy to get along with."

Maybe Helen's losing her hearing because I know I spend a lot of time talking to myself and yelling at Nut and Juice. But I guess in the scheme of loud kids and partying neighbors, I'm not that bothersome.

"Well, one more hug," I tell Helen, who laughs when Nut grabs her leg and gives her a 'hug' of his own. "Nut, stop that! You can't hump every leg you see!"

"Well at least he thinks this oven can still bake something," Helen says with a chuckle. "Best of luck, dear."

I wave, shooing my dogs back into the house and running out to my car. I'm already running late.

CHAPTER 2

POPPY

*W*3AS.

It's probably not the best acronym in the world, but it works for us. Besides, I think as I run up the stairs to the second-floor study room of the Great Falls Public Library, *Women Who Write Awesome Shit* doesn't look very polite on the room reservation forms.

Whenever someone asks, we just call it 'wheeze', like the sound a two-pack-a-day smoker makes. It's a weird assembly of women, but they're my tribe.

There's Aleria, who is only thirty but is by far the oldest soul of our group. Blonde and often barefoot—and possibly naked—beneath her floaty skirts, she loves to fit social commentary into just about everything she says, does, or writes. She's big on nature magic, inner power, and a lot of 'crunchy granola' stuff like meditation, crystals, and kombucha. More than once, we've caught her trying to cast spells over the group, which she says are protective spells against the 'evil magics the patriarchal capitalist system uses to leech our feminine power', also known as shitty publishing contracts like the one she got tricked into as a newbie romance author.

So of course, she writes indie paranormal romance with some pretty creative sex scenes and groupings that can open your mind to unique possibilities even if you'll never, ever meet a vampire, a werewolf, and a faerie at the same time.

Daysha's sassy but the most no-nonsense of us. Highly educated with a bachelor's from Spellman and a master's from Columbia, she keeps us in line. You always have to be prepped for Daysha because if you ask her for an opinion, she's going to tell you exactly how she sees it. Offended? Tough shit, which she admits can get her in trouble, but more often than not, she doesn't really care. Daysha's specialty is dark romance.

Jasmine's our resident sarcastic, snappy weirdo who bounces between Sci-Fi and Sci-Fi erotica. Younger than anyone else and still in college, she changes her hair color with just about every book she writes, often as a hint to her theme for her upcoming book. Like when she put a book in a *Matrix*-like universe, her hair was a bright neon green. As I walk in, I see that she's still rocking her natural blonde, which probably means she's between books.

The loudest of our group, though, is Becca. She's pretty much our group cheerleader, which is funny because that's largely how she put herself through college, on a cheerleading scholarship. Her time around both the 'in crowd' and 'out crowd' means she knows exactly how to overreact to everything at all times. The Space Deer coffee place is out of her favorite blend? Catastrophe. There's a category-five hurricane in some far-off country? Equally catastrophic.

But Becca's true talent has to be as a professional shit stirrer. She knows exactly how to get people worked up, and if she ever transitions to Hollywood like she says she wants to, she's going to become a director. She's that much of a puppet master, and her rom-coms are just as twisty. I could totally see her writing and filming twenty seasons of the same show and still managing to keep it fresh and surprising every week with stuff like 'OMG, Jason slept with who?' and 'He died from a coconut hitting him on the head'.

"Hey, ladies," I greet as I come in, hugging all around. I swear Aleria sniffs me as I hug her hello, so it's a good thing I showered and washed my hair.

"Are you making the most of your 86,400 seconds today?" Aleria asks in her usual airy tone. It's her way of gently reminding me to choose wisely and not fuck around on my deadline or I'll find out what the publishing company really thinks of me.

"Well," I admit, sitting down and pulling my laptop out of my bag, "I don't know about that, but I've got great news today. My agent got me a spot at J.A. Fox's upcoming workshop."

What I love about my Wheezers is that there's no real jealousy. Instead, it's cheers all around, with Daysha adding on, "Okay then, you lucky bitch, better get to work so you can show her what you've got. Twenty minutes, ladies? Go."

It's a sprint session, one of the tools we use during our meetings. Twenty minutes, just type, and to hell with spelling, grammar, or any of that. Just crank.

My problem, though, is that as I stare at my keyboard, no words come to me. I've been stuck at this same love scene for *Trouble in Great Falls* for going on a week. I've written, deleted, and re-written this fucking thing so much that I literally have pains in my forearms, and for what? Nothing good, that's what!

The main problem is with my two main characters, Amber and Ryker, and the stupid things that keep coming out of their mouths. Half the time they're talking like robots, and the other half, I'm wondering why the fuck I should care about them. And if I don't care about them, the readers damn sure won't.

The sex scenes are causing me special trouble, and I can't help but wonder if it's because I haven't had actual sex with anything but my bedside buddy in almost a year. Seriously, even my *memory* of sex is getting hazy.

And that's a problem. As an author, you're supposed to either know or research the topic that you're writing about. Quite frankly, watching Pornhub to get inspiration isn't doing the damn trick any longer.

Besides, do people really do weird stuff like have sex on treadmills when the couch or floor is right there? I mean, rug burn's a thing, but falling dick- or tits-first onto a whirling conveyor belt sounds way less sexy and is a good way to end up as a dirty meme on the internet.

"I think I need to have sex."

Silence reigns around the table, all typing stopping instantly, and I look up to realize, to my total petrification, that I said that out loud.

"Shit."

"Uh, that's a hard limit. Even I don't mix that into my sex scenes," Jasmine says with a shiver. When I don't laugh, she asks, "So, what's up?"

I lean back, groaning. "I didn't exactly mean to say that out loud. But what's up is that I'm stuck! I need to find a willing subject to let me do some research with him."

"Nope," Daysha says as she points at me and Jasmine. "We're sprinting. We can discuss Poppy's coochie meow-meow's lack of petting in six minutes."

No one argues, simply sticking their heads back down. Daysha's just that sort of super-focused person . . . but I'm left tapping my keyboard aimlessly. This is the worst case of writer's block I've ever experienced! I can't even write a decent scene to get my *own* juices flowing.

I know that beyond my lack of sex, the deeper reason I can't write is that I've heaped so much pressure on myself by taking that advance contract from Bluebird. I've got to deliver a knockout book because my entire career is riding on it.

Between the stress and my lack of bathing, I've broken out in hives several times over the past week, and my sleep cycle's ten kinds of fucked up. Suddenly, just to twist the thumbscrews a bit more, my mind comes up with another fresh worry. What if I go to this writer's luncheon with my idol and a bunch of other authors, and they laugh me out of the place?

"Time," Daysha calls, interrupting my self-induced stress dialogue. "Now, back to what's really important, Poppy's lack of cooter-loving friends."

"Well, here's the problem," I tell them, turning my laptop around, showing them the past few pages of drivel I've written since I last deleted everything. "I'm struggling."

Becca squints and flops back in her chair when she realizes the scene I'm on. "Oh, my God, PULEAAASE tell me you're not STILL stuck on them boinking?"

Jasmine grunts and runs her hands into her blonde curls in exasperation with me. "I've written a space battle, a time warp, and a G-type star literally making our heroine explode in orgasm in the time you've been pecking at your keyboard!"

"Easy for you to say!" I growl, suddenly defensive. "You don't have a six-figure contract riding on your story being good enough for a possible Netflix option, an agent reminding you at every turn that expectations are going to be astronomically high for revenue, fans emailing you to tell you how they want the story to go, and characters that sound like robots saying shit like 'put your big dick inside me so I can feel you breed me, baby.'"

Jasmine rolls her eyes skyward. "Yes, yes, remind us how we're all peons and you're the chosen one with a big fat paycheck on the way."

"I didn't mean that, I'm sorry—"

Jasmine grins and boops her nose, adjusting her glasses that turn her from sex bomb back into girl next door cute when she wants. "Girl, I'm teasing, but please tell me you're kidding about that dialogue, right? That's *bad*, Poppy."

Aleria clears her throat pointedly. "I could make it work," she offers with a shrug, "in the right situation. A succubus, maybe? But only constructive criticism, Jasmine. We all agreed."

Jasmine tilts her head as if to say 'did you hear what she wrote? Someone's gotta tell her.' I get it, but right now, I'll take any help —constructive or not. "What do you suggest, Aleria?"

"Well, you know I have a focus candle that could probably help you find an anchor in the characters," she says, turning to the large satchel she always carries with her. "Some sage and hemp could—"

"You are *not* burning that around me," Daysha says. "Besides, I really don't think that's going to help Poppy at this point."

"Not only that . . . the shit don't work," Jasmine mutters under her breath.

"Excuse me?" Aleria asks, losing her calm center in favor of a bit of neck swirling.

Daysha snaps her fingers, cutting off the debate-slash-sermon in its tracks. "Focus, people."

Aleria mutters, "That's what I'm trying to help Poppy do."

Daysha ignores her and focuses on me. "Pops, you said you need to have sex. So do it. Pick up someone hot, give him a fake name, and do the dirty in all sorts of ridiculous positions, with toys and props and whatever else you think your heroine or hero might like. Test it out. Consider it research."

"Ooh, fun!" Becca says, nodding. "You know, I heard of a great new app for that, and—"

"Just pick up some rando?" Aleria asks, horrified and shaking her head. "No way. It would desecrate Poppy's female magic! You can't let just anybody into the glorious hole of your center being."

"Did you just say glory hole?" Becca asks, grinning. "That does not mean what you think it means. But I should put one of those in my next book. *Eye Level with Mr. Mystery.*"

"Uh, no. I'd like to *constructively* say that's a horrible idea," Daysha says, taking Becca seriously, "and does anyone have other ideas?"

My friends offer up plenty of advice, most of it conflicting. Make the guy more alpha. Make him a 'simp'. Tie her up. Peg him. Talk dirty, be totally clean . . . and the list goes on. Some of their advice is real life and some strictly for the pages of books.

But it's all in fun, which does help, surprisingly. We all write in different subgenres, so while some of the ideas are downright laughable, we have fun with it. I feel like I haven't done that in a long time.

"You know," Daysha says, "you could have her hold a gun to his head and tell him that if she doesn't get off before he does, she's going to set him off another way. Ooh, if he's handcuffed and she's the bad girl, that could totally work."

"Fuck, girl. There's dark and then there's *dark*. It's *Trouble in Great Falls*, not *Game of Sopranos*," I reply.

Jasmine adds, "She's right, but I do like the forced hardness angle. What about a little something-something slipped into his bloodstream? I'd go with nanites, but that's me."

"Microscopic robots do not a good orgasm make," Aleria says primly, making us all crack up. But it's all good. We all know the struggle and the game of getting noticed in the crowded romance market. Besides, half of what they're saying isn't real advice but a valiant effort to help me relax. They're hoping that maybe that'll unknot the block in my head and alleviate my stress at having to reach a publishing deadline.

Not that it's particularly helpful. I do get a few good laughs, but every time I glance at the page, I go back to blankness. Still, the emotional support and encouragement lift my spirits enough that as I walk out of the library, I feel slightly better and think maybe I'll finally get something done tonight.

Honestly, the best advice probably came from Aleria in the end. We were packing up our stuff, and she looked at me, patting my shoulder. "Sometimes, the energy takes us in different paths than what we expect," she said. "So for now, skip the scene and move on. If your energy isn't sensual right now, then write the other parts and come back when you're feeling it. After all, they invented Control-X and Control-C for a reason."

She's right, and I should have done it earlier, but I'm stubborn. Writing dick to vag shouldn't be the thing holding me up. I need to work out the character's emotional build-up and then what the a-ha moments are to progress Amber and Ryker's relationship to the next level, and then the sex part will come naturally.

"Hah . . . come . . . naturally!" I giggle to myself. "Come sooooo good!"

A guy walking his dog looks over at my outburst, and I stare back a little too hard, daring him to say one word to me. What? Can't a woman talk to herself without people looking at her like she's bananas? B-A-N-A . . . dammit. Now I'm spelling out bananas like I'm a Gwen Stefani impersonator.

I'm a riot. Okay, probably not, but in my overloaded, overstimulated, coffee-laden brain, I'm a genius with a stellar sense of humor. I just hope the fans agree.

CHAPTER 3

CONNOR

*I*n my Ford King Ranch pick-up truck, I turn the corner in a remote section of Maplewood as I make my way to meet up with my connection, Juan Pablo.

Despite all my years of being a thief, stealing items in all sizes, shapes, and colors, I feel a whiff of anxiety. Thieves are the sort of people who like to work unrecognized. But this is different. This time, I need to make sure that the right people know my name and what I can do. There's a lot riding on this meeting, and I need to be able to show that I've got the skills needed to work my way up the ladder in the organization. I've worked for a lot of people over the years, but this gig is *The One* that'll open doors.

And if it doesn't go well? a little voice inside my head asks me, but I quickly shove it back down. There isn't time or space to let that sort of doubt creep inside. Not with the consequences of failure. *Clean snatches with invisible getaways* . . . that's always the mission objective.

This one has to be no different.

I'm at a stop light when I get a series of texts and phone calls. I ignore them, knowing exactly who it is, but they keep coming and coming.

Fuck. I can't have this distraction tickling my mind when I walk into a hot zone, I think to myself. I need to be focused and clear-headed.

I should just turn the phone off, or silence it at least. But some remaining loyal speck of decency in my dried-up dirt stain of a heart feels like I need to answer because I've been ignoring her for weeks.

She's my mother, after all.

Irritated and annoyed at my conflicting emotions and knowing that I don't have time for this, I let out a growl and pull over into the nearest parking lot.

The next time it rings, I answer. Before even a single sound can emerge from my mouth, I'm immediately run over by a verbal barrage from my mother, Debra Bradley. "Oh, so now you want to talk to me, huh? After weeks of ignoring me? I'll have you know, I was in labor for forty-two hours to bring you into this world, but I can still take you out of it!"

I've been hearing this for years. When she finally takes a breath, I ask her nonchalantly, "Are you done? Because I'm sitting in a pretty shady parking lot with a guy giving me the eyeball like I'm pissing on his turf by breathing his oxygen."

There's no guy, of course. I'm not in *that* bad a part of town. But still, I appreciate the little sharp intake of breath, and I know I've taken some of the wind out of her sails.

A bit softer, Mom launches into her real message. "Connor, you should be ashamed of yourself. You have checked out on your family. Your sister is getting married, and I would really like it if you would meet her fiancé, Evan, before the wedding. She wants your approval, Connor."

I grunt noncommittally, but my mom's disappointment is harder than the anger. This is exactly what I wanted to avoid. The fact is, my family relationship is a toxic dumpster fire. It's been that way for far too long, and it's not totally my fault, either.

My younger sister, Caylee, wanting my approval and not my dad's, is evidence of this and lighter fluid on the long smoldering issue. It sends fresh heat and fury rising in swirls in my gut.

Obviously, my father has, yet again, fallen down on the fucking job. But if no one is vetting this Evan guy, it'll fall to me.

It always does.

Damn the little bit of heart I've got left. Because while I'm a no-good bastard, time and time again, when the shit hits the fan, I'm the guy who'll step up and do what my family needs. Especially when Dad can't . . . or won't.

"I need details."

Mom sounds happy I'm going to step in, but I know she's a bit bitter that Dad isn't doing this. "Also, to let you know, Audrey will be at all the wedding get-togethers with Ian." Her eye roll of annoyance is audible even through the phone. "Just a warning."

If my relationship with my family is a dumpster fire, my mother's relationship with her sister, Audrey, is a nuclear fucking wasteland. I don't know what started their war, but me, Caylee, and my cousin, Ian, have been pawns in it since we were born.

We're not so much children as achievements to be bragged about and failures to be embarrassingly and scathingly pointed out. Honor roll? Worth a tagged Facebook post. Caylee gets elected homecoming queen? Of course, that's worth more than a few comments.

And as expected, Audrey nearly hired a skywriter when I was arrested for shoplifting as a teen. In her mind, I was a threat to the public and should've been locked up and castrated so I couldn't potentially pollute the gene pool.

Ever since, Mom has been on a mission to prove to Audrey that I'm not some bad seed asshole. Problem is . . . I am the bad seed, despite what my mother thinks. It's why I stay away, it's why I ignore her, it's why I interact with my family as little as possible.

But Caylee will never forgive me if I don't come to her wedding. Especially if I can't explain that it's to keep her safe from my world. And while I can hurt my family, there's still that speck of humanity inside me that doesn't want to break my little sister's heart like this.

But right now, I've got to focus. "Look, Mom, I'm heading into a meeting. I'll call you back later." I know she thinks it's with the sketchy dude in the parking lot, and I intentionally don't clarify that for her.

"But Connor—"

I never hear the rest of what she has to say as I hang up, frustrated yet still putting my phone on 'airplane mode'. This isn't what I need right now. I know I'm gonna have a decision to make soon, and it won't be fucking easy. If I do the right thing and ghost my sister's wedding, that's going to be a bridge torched beyond repair. I might as well be dead to Caylee.

Honestly, severing that relationship might be for her own good, but she's been left too often, mostly by Dad, and I won't be another man to do that to her. Neither will Evan if he knows what's good for him. And I haven't met him yet, measured him in my eyes and determined if I need to shake his hand, break his wrist, or bury him in a shallow grave.

I have to go to the wedding to check him out, but I don't know if I have it in me to sit there and play the part of a good little boy. Not even for Caylee's sake.

My phone beeps as my timer reminds me that I need to fucking move, and I drive, pulling up five minutes later at an abandoned warehouse in the industrial part of town. It's actually not as bad as it could be. Most of the surrounding buildings are in use. It's just this one that's only used for . . . temporary situations.

Outside, I see my contact, a tall, black-haired man with this kind of European vibe going. Maybe it's the artisanal cigarette he's smoking, one I know is going to smell like shit, not that he cares. Maybe it's the way his jet-black hair is slicked back, or maybe it's that his suit is just a little too tailored and form fitting so he looks out of place, not only in Maplewood but in the States.

But regardless of whether he looks like a gigolo or not, Juan Pablo is a man you don't want to fuck with. "JP," I greet him as I pull up and get out. "How's it going?"

Juan Pablo takes a deep drag from his cigarette and exhales, a dragon's breath of stinky whitish gray flowing from his mouth and reminding me to keep discreetly upwind of him. "Goddamn, you Americans and your pick-up trucks."

I shrug. "Call it a character defect," I reply, leaning against my truck's side panel. "What's happening?"

JP unbuttons his suit pocket and takes out an old-school manilla envelope, handing it to me. I open it up, taking a look at the laminated card inside, credentials for the job, obviously, along with five or six sheets of paper, clearly intelligence on the job itself.

"There's a dinner coming up," JP says as I look at the papers. It's not an insult—he knows I can read just fine—just his way. "Some big shot book writer's giving a talk."

I flip through the pages, nodding. "Tell me about the art."

"See, she's going to have the target on display," JP says, pointing to a picture in the back of the pages. "The credentials will get you in. You're one of the private security guards. You do your thing and bring the piece back to me."

I nod, looking through the pages more, and something sticks out to me. "Replacement?" I ask, and JP nods.

Damn. I've worked hard on my reputation. I'm no basic smash and grab guy, and the people who hire me are looking for discretion. I'm not the kind who leaves behind evidence of any crime taking place . . . except for the missing items. But replacement's a whole different ballgame. Stealing's like pulling off a magic trick without people noticing that the rabbit you pulled out of the hat wasn't actually under the table the whole time.

Replacement's more like getting people to believe a kitten is a rabbit just because they're both white and fluffy.

But JP shrugs as if lifting a piece in the middle of a dinner speech filled with nosy patrons is going to be easy. "You can do it?"

It's a subtle challenge. "I'll need to prep more, some additional measures," I tell him calmly. "I'd like to get out of the hotel before anyone notices something's amiss."

"I can help you there," JP says, disappearing inside the warehouse. He comes out a minute later with a sort of half bag, half case similar to ones I've used before for framed pieces. The outside is fairly nondescript, but the inside is made of a silky material that will protect the art. "Here's the replacement."

I take the bag from him, whistling when I open it up and see what's inside. *The Black Rose* isn't the most famous picture in the world, of course. That'd be the *Mona Lisa*, probably. And even I wouldn't take a shot at lifting that chick.

But *The Black Rose* is definitely up there, especially over the past few years ever since the dinner's speaker, J.A. Fox, picked it up at an auction and started gushing over it regularly. It's definitely valuable, but it's the fact that it's an easily recognizable collector's piece that really drives its value.

And this fake looks remarkably good. "My compliments to your forger," I murmur, even as my trained eye starts to see the minute flaws. At first glance, it's hard to tell, but they're there. Tiny discrepancies in color tone, imperfections in the artificial aging process, but most importantly, it doesn't quite have the 'soul' that the original has.

Not that I give a damn. Art is my work, not my passion, and I generally find the idea of people paying millions of dollars for globs of color on canvas when others are starving or dying from lack of medicine the most callous of diversions.

But regardless, I can see the technical skills and the beauty of the work. It'll do, if I do my job right.

"How the hell did you guys manage this?" I ask casually, almost like a backhanded compliment to JP and the organization he belongs to. But I really want to know. Who can produce work this good, this fast in this area? That'd be a resource I wouldn't mind having in my back pocket.

JP shrugs. "I don't know, I'm just an errand boy like you. Mr. Big has a network of errand boys, all of us doing whatever he needs."

He wiggles his fingers in the air like a puppet master pulling strings while inwardly, I scoff. JP is no mere errand boy. He's Mr. Big's right-hand man, handling jobs like this regularly. But he likes to seem small so people underestimate him.

I won't make that mistake, and I definitely don't underestimate his boss. Mr. Big is a mystery wrapped in a comic book-style enigma, a man who is whispered about by everybody and known to almost nobody. But like an invisible octopus, his tentacles wind through and around every kind of criminal activity in our area. There isn't a bookie in town who'll sneeze without asking Mr. Big for a tissue.

But he's especially known for art theft. Forgery, stealing, smuggling . . . if it's art or art related in the United States, you know he's involved.

And though I don't take well to being called an errand boy, this isn't the time or place to argue semantics.

"It'll work?" JP, who's not half the expert in art that I am, asks after another moment. "No one will know?"

I take another look at the piece, humming to myself. I know it's fake, obviously, but I can count on my fingers the number of people in this state who might be able to reach the same conclusion. The head curator at the museum might, one of the professors of the Art Department at the university, and maybe a few others. But even they'd need to be looking carefully.

"It'll do," I tell him, standing back up and putting JP's papers back in their envelope. "Someone'll figure it out eventually, but not before I'm long gone and Mr. Big has his greedy hands on the original."

"Don't think you're in a position to say what's greedy and what's not," JP warns, his eyes narrowed. "This is a notable job for you. Do this, and Mr. Big will be pleased and he'll make it worth your time. But not if you're insulting him."

The threat of consequences is crystal clear. Whoever Mr. Big is, he's a man with eyes and ears in all sorts of places. And people who talk bad about him quickly find themselves, at the very least, frozen out of the criminal underworld and exposed to law enforcement.

Nobody talks about those who *really* piss him off. Mainly because so few facts are known about people who disappear the way they do. But I know if I fail this mission, it might be *my* bodily fluids used as pigment in someone's forgery. That's Mr. Big's touch of melodrama.

It's a lot of pressure, and a lot of people would crack or walk away.

But I'm up to the challenge.

"I'll contact you after the dinner," I tell JP simply, sliding the forgery of *The Black Rose* back into its case. Conversation complete, I get back in my truck and drive off, my mind already going through a mental checklist of what I'm going to need to get this job done.

THE BALLROOM'S SET UP NICELY AT ONE OF THE BEST HOTELS IN town. Actually, now that I think about it, my high school prom might've been here. Not that I went. I was already well down the path to hoodlumism by that point. But I have been here before for various events, usually corporate or social ones when I was little and my parents were still trying to have me make the right impressions in the right circles.

So . . . safe to say, it's been a while. But my prep went flawlessly, and as I check my black cuffs for any sign of dust, I feel comfortable. Still, slacks and a button-up shirt aren't my typical first choices for workwear. Despite what Pierce Brosnan may have shown the world in *The Thomas Crowne Affair*, stealing shit in a suit isn't easy. And if I have to run, I prefer to do it in athletic shoes, not slick-bottomed Oxfords.

I do a final scout around the perimeter of the room, mentally confirming escape routes and identifying the power grid location. Everything's as I anticipated, and I'm able to make my final preparations without being interrupted. I give a few of the other security guards hard looks, but we're all muscle for hire and no one's looking to chat about our childhoods or make friends to drink a beer with after this gig. Communication is short, simple, and professional. We're all on the lookout for various dangers. Never mind that the major risk in the room is . . . me.

Finishing my perimeter check, I move to the stage, closer to my target. I've already been onstage, stashing the fake behind some conveniently placed curtains, but I want to check everything once more. Frankly, too often, jobs go south because someone decided at the last minute that a vase just *has* to be moved or that a projector screen can't go *here*, it has to go *there*, and the operator's caught unprepared.

That's not me. I'm good because I prepare with an obsession bordering on OCD. Still, even my cold heart skips a beat as I see the artwork up close. *The Black Rose*. In person, it's a beauty, the portrait of a sad woman who has the weight of the world on her shoulders. It pulls at my heartstrings because it's with bitter humor that I can empathize with this unknown woman. I know how you feel, lady.

No time for that, I tell myself. I'm here to do a job, and the sad lady here's just going to have to deal with her new life away from the public. I finish my walk-around, mentally adjusting my timing as I see how things develop and more staff start to filter in.

It won't be an easy job, I knew that, but pulling this off in a room full of people with several other guards keeping watchful eyes is going to be the trickiest job I've ever done. But I can do it.

I have to do it.

A side door opens, and a middle-aged woman in a black dress walks in. Her grey hair is pulled back in a French roll and her glasses have rhinestones along the sides. She walks with an air of sophistication, but the smile on her face seems warm and genuine. She's among her kind, and everyone in the room is a fan of J.A. Fox. After all, according to my prep work, she's the author hosting the dinner tonight. She walks directly toward the stage, talking to the woman at her side.

"Everything's all set?"

"Yes, ma'am. Books ready, a box of Sharpie fine-tip, blue ink pens open, and *The Black Rose* on display."

I melt into the background, becoming invisible and looking for all the world like one of the staff the attendees will overlook. I'm like that special green paint Disney uses to hide doors in plain view, only dressed in black, not baby shit green.

"Show them in," J.A. Fox says.

The woman nods at the guard closest to the door, and he silently opens the door. A small crowd of authors walks through the doors, looking eager and excited while at least keeping enough self-control to not rush the stage like Beliebers at a JB concert. A few gasp excitedly when they lay eyes on J.A. Fox, a few others wave as though they're old friends, and most simply walk in as though they're exactly where they're supposed to be.

All right, Connor, I think to myself, *it's showtime.*

CHAPTER 4

POPPY

My nerves are on fire, my brain screaming 'oh, my God, oh, my God' over and over again, and my stomach is threatening to give my buttered toast and coffee breakfast a repeat viewing.

Lunch? Yeah, I didn't eat that at all.

But I stand outside the double doors of the ballroom like a statue, consciously not letting my feet tap or my body bounce around like a rubber ball in a concrete room. I do let my hand drift up to needlessly adjust my lucky earrings, the gold acorns my mother gave me when I turned sixteen that have become a constant companion when I need a little boost. They worked for my first meeting with Hilda, and hopefully, they'll work today.

Otherwise, J.A. Fox might look at me the same way some of the other women in the wide hallway are . . . with undisguised interest, confusion, and an occasional sneer of disdain. I get it. I do. I feel like a poser with these women, some of whom I recognize by sight, some by the names on their pinned tags, and even some from television interviews. And I'm just . . . Poppy Woodstock, author of one measly book that they've probably never heard of, much less read.

I smooth my red dress down my thighs. It's a dinner, and while it's not a formal event, I'd wanted to look nice so I took a few hours to go shopping and to relax. I have to say, I like what I feel.

It hugs my curves in a classy way, reaches the tops of my knees, and has a simple wide ballet neck that shows off my collarbones.

Elegant simplicity, the boutique saleswoman had called it, except did I mention it's cherry red? Some people think I shouldn't wear red because it clashes with my dark red hair, but I disagree. It's not like I'm going to be unnoticed with my bright mane of wild hair. It could be slicked back in a tight librarian bun, and I'd still stand out.

So I might as well embrace it. And I do feel extra adult with my black leather satchel at my side holding my laptop for the workshop portion of the event.

Or I feel like I have a chance at fitting in until I see two women gossiping behind their hands, both of their eyes locked on me. I recognize them and know their names, or their pen names, at least.

And just like that, I'm struck with a fresh case of nerves wrapped up in a barbed wire bow of Imposter Syndrome.

Breathe, Poppy. Or maybe go make friends with them. Show them how friendly you can be. They're not going to suck your blood. This isn't a vampire coven.

Jeez, I'm going to have to share that one with Aleria. She'd probably be able to make a good story out of it.

I'm still considering going over when the doors open, and with a relieved sigh, I realize I don't have to approach the mean girls. I don't care how old they are, women like that always were and always will be 'mean girls'.

Walking into the ballroom, I'm struck. Not by the overt opulence —it is a hotel ballroom, after all, and has the usual bland beige walls and unoffensive abstract art hanging at intervals around the room. What has me on my heels is the reality that I'm here— J.A. Fox's famous workshop dinner. This is the place where serious connections can be made . . . if you can back up your stuff.

The front of the room is set up for dining with several long, white tablecloth covered tables set up in a U-shape so we can all face

J.A. Fox onstage while she speaks. The floral centerpieces are small and tight, giving a sense of richness while not obstructing views, and the place settings gleam with gold edging on the plates, crystal glasses, and gold flatware.

Toward the back of the room, there are smaller round tables set up with four workstations per table. *That must be for the workshop portion*, I think, patting my bag once more. I did manage to get one more chapter done after skipping the sex scene like Aleria suggested, but I need today and J.A. Fox to help get my juices flowing again. My writing ones, obviously . . . I'm not discussing sex scenes with J.A. Fox, that's for sure. It'd be like talking to the Queen of England about blowjobs. She's probably done it before, but I do not need that visual in my head.

Shit . . . too late.

Before that imagery gets so embedded that eye bleach won't remove it, I see her . . . the one and only J.A. Fox. She's wearing a black dress, and her gray hair is smooth and sleek. She looks almost grandmotherly, like she could bake a killer pineapple upside down cake, but inside her head is a brilliance unmatched in the current romance genre. Hell, in any genre. She's created a market all by herself, decades in the making, and is still creating unique, interesting stories.

She's standing by the famous art piece that inspired her latest best-seller. *The Black Rose* is smaller than I'd thought, not much bigger than a piece of printer paper. Maybe I just assumed it was large because of its importance? Together, the sight is a dream come true, and I feel drawn toward it like a tractor beam drawing a cow up into an alien spaceship.

I'm so lost in J.A. Fox being real and right in front of me that I trip over my scrambling feet. The hiss of a giggle behind me slices through my gut, but before I can blush in shame—or hit the ground face first—I hit a hard body and arms wrap tightly around me.

"Oh," I exclaim too loudly. Another giggle, this time with an accompanying chorus of cleared throats, sounds out behind me. But when I look up into the bluest eyes I've ever seen attached to a man who's just as appealing, the symphony of pity from the other authors disappears as I focus on mapping the flecks of brown and gold at the center of these eyes.

It has definitely been too long since I've done my own 'research' on sex because my body, that wanton, thirsty hussy, perks right up at the feel of his body and his eyes focused on mine. He's so close I can smell the mint he must've eaten earlier, and my ovaries, the dried-up peach pits in my gut, start doing a hokey pokey as they come to life and start turning themselves around.

"Who are you?" I ask breathlessly.

At my girlish question, he chuckles too, and the moment is broken. I belatedly realize what an idiot I look like—tripping over my own feet and falling into some stranger before staring up at him with lustful, worshipful eyes like I'm ready to have his babies right here and now.

I struggle to upright myself, my knees not quite ready and buckling ever so slightly. To my horror, the hot stranger catches me . . . again. "Careful now."

"Guess she takes 'head over heels' a bit literally, huh?" someone stage whispers behind me.

Finally vertical and steady, I clear my throat and try to salvage some dignity. "Sorry. I got a little star struck there."

"It happens. I sometimes have that effect on women," he says with a cocky smirk that somehow still looks charming. "Just don't break anything."

"No. No, I meant . . . not you . . ." I argue stupidly, going pale. He doesn't believe my lie, but I stick to my story. "By her. That's J.A. Fox," I whisper like he doesn't know that. If he's here, he must've been invited and know who she is, right? Male romance authors are unusual, and now that my head is on straight, I'm instantly curious who he is. Speaking of straight—oh, God, is my dress okay? I check to be sure it hasn't crept up my thighs or a boob hasn't popped out. All good, thankfully.

"Sure. She's . . . who'd you say?" he says, glancing over his shoulder at the Grand Dame who's thankfully unaware of my misfortunate blunder and greeting other guests warmly.

It's only then that I realize something. He's not dressed. Well, I mean, he has clothes on—unfortunately, because I felt those muscles up close and personal—but he's not dressed up for the dinner. He's wearing all black . . . like a staff member.

Way to go, Poppy. Not only did you literally fall into someone and make a fool out of yourself, but it's a staff member who has better things to do than keep you from splatting on the floor. Like . . . his job.

"Oh, fuck. You're not an author, are you?" I blurt out.

I watch his smile melt and his face turn to stone. It should make him seem cold and lessen his attractiveness, but the clench of his jaw only serves to make him look fierce and hard, something I didn't know could be so panty-melting.

"Sorry, I didn't mean that to sound rude," I try to apologize.

But the moment is gone, and without excusing himself, he walks away. I can't help but keep my eyes glued to him, all confidence and swagger as he moves toward the stage, quietly saying something to another man dressed in all black. Like a good reader, I use my context clues and realize that not only is he not an author, but he's not staff. He's security.

And I'm a total dork, and a bitch too.

A woman onstage taps the microphone, the telltale thump garnering everyone's attention. "Please find your places, and we'll begin." I'm thankful to see that there are ivory place cards on each plate so I don't have to find a place to sit on my own. I see my name and sit down, hanging my bag on the chair behind me. Some of the other authors have set their bags and briefcases down in the workshop area by their nameplates, but I'm too paranoid and can't let my laptop, my manuscript, my baby, be that far from my reach.

J.A. Fox steps to the microphone. "Welcome, everyone!" she says in a posh British accent that sounded so perfect and fancy the first time I heard her do an interview with Oprah. I sit up straight in my chair, wishing I could pull out my laptop to take notes as she speaks, but there's not really room with my plate in front of me. And it's not a college lecture, so it's probably not appropriate.

"I appreciate everyone taking time out of their busy writing schedules to come eat a bite with me today," she says, looking around. "Hopefully, we'll have full bellies, fresh ideas, and flowing inspiration by the end of our session. If you could, while the staff bring out our repast, stand and introduce yourself for everyone. Thank you."

J.A. Fox nods to the woman on the far left of the table, and she stands up, speaking with a clear, confident voice as she's obviously done this before. "I'm Louisa Magnum, author of the bestselling *Oakhurst Family* series."

Oh, I know that one even if I didn't know the face. The woman next to her stands up, and introductions continue around the table, each name seemingly more impressive than the last. Finally it's my turn, and I manage to introduce myself, though not without difficulty. "I'm Woody Popstock. I mean, Poppy Woodstock. I wrote *Love in Great Falls*."

Okay, that went well. I mean, I got English words out of my mouth, and I did it without projectile puking. I'm taking the win. But I'm not going to risk it by eating the chicken and potatoes a server set down in front of me.

After introductions finish, J.A. Fox takes the microphone again. "Please, feel free to eat. A bit of dinner is the least I can offer so you'll let an old lady blabber on."

With that encouragement, I try to at least appear to be enjoying the food, picking up my fork along with everyone else. I nibble at my salad, pretending to enjoy lettuce, tomato, and ranch dressing while the Grand Dame gives a speech.

It's actually interesting as she gives lots of insight on how she found inspiration for her latest book in the famous painting at her side. Listening to her warm up and bring us into the swirling galaxy of disconnected thoughts that coalesced into an entire story that captured the hearts of many is nothing short of amazing.

"And of course, I'm obligated to tell you that having a good editor is essential," J.A. says, earning laughs. "If not, my book would go on and on and make absolutely no sense."

It gets laughs around the room, and she continues on, delving into some of the technical aspects of writing that only fellow authors could embrace. As fascinating as it is, I keep finding my eyes drifting off to the right side of the stage . . . to him. The sexy man in black who looks like he'd make a lead character in anyone's book and easily turn it into a best seller just in describing his incredibly good looks. Chapter One–his eyes, with Chapter Ten (inches) being . . .

I get away with my stolen looks twice, but when the hairs along the back of my neck tickle, I glance over to find him staring openly at me. He winks, and I blush, forcing my eyes back to center stage but all the while considering that maybe he's the inspiration I need just like J.A. Fox is talking about. A sexy guy, with just the right amount of cocky to be a bad boy and enough kindness to catch me when I fall. I reframe my hero, Ryker, adding a bit of ruggedness to his hair and seeing if there's a place I could have him catch my heroine when she falls.

Reality inspiring fiction, and why the hell not? They say even *Romeo & Juliet* was inspired by reality.

Too soon, the Grand Dame wraps up her speech and dismisses us to the workstation tables. I understand that we should mingle and mix to talk to everyone, but my nerves ratchet back up when I see one of the sneering women from earlier sitting at the table where my name card awaits.

Thankfully, the other two women smile warmly as we each pull out our laptops. One's a regency romance writer, while the other's strictly LGBTQ+ fiction.

"Open a new document, please," J.A. Fox instructs. "Sprint write the basic premise of your current work. No complete sentences or literary greatness needed. Just plot, character names, dark moments, and resolution. I'll give you five minutes."

Panic wars with excitement. I'm doing this, here in this room of greatness, and I want to watch the magic unfold. But when I see every pair of eyes click to their screen, mine do the same as I quickly tap out the basics of *Trouble in Great Falls*. Here, in fresh form, it actually makes sense.

The hard part's in turning two hundred words into three hundred pages.

"And time," J.A. says. "Now, please move a few lines down and write a single sentence about what your main concern is with your story. If there's nothing" —she pauses dramatically— "then you're a better writer than I am."

We laugh and get to work. I write about my struggle, not with my story but with expectations from myself, from Hilda, and from the publisher and how they've led to a near-complete mental blockage. It feels good to purge that onto the page, and my hopes that someone of the Grand Dame's caliber might be able to help me rise.

"Excellent. Feel free to work or discuss among yourselves. Find inspiration in each other, help guide each other through your concerns if you're willing to share. Meanwhile, I'll invite you up one at a time."

My inner fangirl squeals, and I have to press my feet to the floor to keep from kicking them in excitement. I'm going to meet *the* J.A. Fox one on one. My life might be complete after that. Put a fork in me because I'm done, bucket list complete, and I'm able to die a happy woman.

There's a little conversation around our table as I chat with the two nice authors. "You know, I had the same thing the first time I had to do a guy-guy scene," Yasmina says. "I mean, it's hot and all, but I didn't *know* it, you know?"

"So what did you do?" Winnie, the regency author, asks.

"Went to a gay bar in my town and told the bartender my problem. He told me to take a table, and for the next six hours, I bought drinks for men who happily told me all I ever needed to know," Yasmina says with a laugh. "Trust me, those recordings more than broke up my writer's block."

"Yeah, but I kinda know how Tab P goes in Slot V," I point out.

Winnie giggles. "Maybe that's your problem? There are other *slots*, you know. Slot A, slot M, slot H."

The mean girl author, Elizabeth, raises a brow at Winnie's list and speaks for the first time since we sat down at the worktables. "H?"

"Hand jobs, dear," Winnie explains. "Shall I define the others too?"

Ooh, seems I'm not the only one picking up on the 'it's bitch o'clock somewhere' vibes from Elizabeth, our fellow author. And Winnie is playing too with sharp, quick wit.

We try to keep writing a bit, but as I do, I can't help but watch as each author is escorted up to the stage. They get a good amount of time to chat, maybe five minutes or so. They then take a photo, receive an autographed copy of *The Art Thief*, and talk about their stories.

I can't wait for my turn.

Not soon enough, the assistant taps me on the shoulder, and I get up to follow her, sliding my laptop into my bag for the trip to the front of the room. This baby's my life.

"So nice to meet you," I say, holding my hand out and fighting to keep my voice on an even keel. "I'm sure you hear this all the time, but I started writing because of you."

She shakes my hand and smiles warmly. "Poppy, lovely to meet you as well. I really enjoyed *Love in Great Falls*." My jaw falls open, and her eyes dance. "Of course, I read it. I think probably everyone here has." She laughs at her own words, and I'm still gaping like a fish out of water. "There's a new name in town, and she's bloody good."

Belatedly, my brain clicks on, and I find words, though not the ones I mean to say out loud. "I think I just peed myself in excitement!"

Even the assistant laughs at that, and I hear a deep-voiced chuckle morph into a clearing throat behind me. I turn to see who it is and find the sexy security guard. Of course, he heard that.

"Unless there's something you're having trouble with, could I ask that we not discuss what happens in *Trouble in Great Falls*? I'm anxious to read it myself and don't want to be spoiled by knowing the plot."

Blinking, I try not to be disappointed. I was hoping that she'd have some great insight to help me, but now, I can't say 'My characters are cold fish with no connection.' That'd surely ruin her reading of it. Oh, my God, she's going to read it!

"Of course. Can I just ask what you do when you have writer's block?" I ask carefully. "I'm having a brick wall of a time right now." I bang my head on an invisible wall in front of me to illustrate my point because words are hard, even for authors, when confronted with a greatness like the Grand Dame.

She purses her lips as she thinks. Finally, she chuckles. "You've got the sophomore slump, dear. That's all."

"That's what I'm worried about, though," I admit. "I've got so many people expecting me to hit a grand slam, and I'm scared I'll strike out. Oh, wait . . . do you know baseball?"

J.A. smiles softly. "Close enough to cricket that I understand. You remind me of myself when I was starting out. Just find yourself and ignore the others. You're going to be fine. Just listen to your heart."

"Time's up," the assistant says politely. "We need to do the photo and autograph, Ms. Fox."

I'm disappointed, but I understand. This is a dinner and workshop, not an all day gathering. Following instructions, I set my bag down on the table and move to J.A. Fox's side. The assistant holds up the tablet, counting down for the photo. "In three, two, one . . ."

For some reason, the sexy security guard behind her catches my eye. He barely moves, but I see him glance up at the ceiling for a split second and then . . .

The room goes dark.

There's an instant of utter stillness and silence before all hell breaks loose. High-pitched voices scream in shock, and movement shuffles all around me. I feel hands grab my shoulders and instantly think I'm going to be kidnapped but instead find myself pushed out of the way unceremoniously.

Of course, they're here to protect the celebrity. I'm just a body in the way.

"Ugh," I huff out as I fall to the ground. This time, nothing stops me, and I sprawl out on the hard floor, my dress definitely riding up my thighs now, but the darkness at least means no one sees.

"Everyone stay calm and be quiet," a deep voice orders, and the room goes silent again. Someone's taking charge, at least. When a deep-voiced man tells us to be quiet . . . we do.

A moment later, the lights come back on. Security guards have surrounded J.A. Fox, a tall blonde on one side and a bald one on the other side, and they're both glaring at me like I did something. Yeah, little ole me . . . I flipped off the lights, ruined my photo op with my idol, and dropped myself to the floor so I could flash everyone my goodie bits.

Everyone begins talking at once again as I start to pick myself up, saying they were so scared, but everything seems to be okay. The security guards have decided there's no threat—though the blonde guy is still looking at me suspiciously like I might dive at J.A. Fox if given the chance. *The Black Rose* is still atop its stand, and the lights seem to be fine now. After checking that I'm uninjured, the assistant directs me to head back to my workstation.

It's not until a moment later when I sit down that I realize something vital. Not only is the sexy security guard gone, but so is . . . my bag! With my laptop inside!

No!

CHAPTER 5

CONNOR

I hustle through the back hallway, sweat prickling at the back of my neck.

That was almost a total fuck-up. The lights went out as planned, but that's when the shit hit the fan. With my mental timer clicking down to zero, the bag from JP turned out to be junk.

First off, it wasn't silk. Instead, it was some silk-like artificial fabric, and as I reached in to take out the replacement painting, the damn thing literally split in half. I was able to get the replacement up without a problem, but I then had to think on my feet.

Not able to carry the piece out in plain sight, I grabbed the nearest bag, shoved *The Black Rose* inside as carefully as I could, and melted into the blackness backstage. My path was clear, and I was able to move unobstructed as everyone else went fumbling for the circuit breakers. Two minutes later, I was out the back of the ballroom area, my black shirt jammed into the bag to reveal the fashionable T-shirt underneath, moving down the hallway looking like any unconcerned hotel patron.

Two minutes after that, I strolled out the side entrance, past the pool, and one quick hop over a bush later, I melted into the foot traffic a block away from the ballroom. About as clean as you could ask.

But I hate when things don't go to plan. I research and plan for everything, but this was one I hadn't considered. That is a failure on my part, despite the success. Now, as I drive toward the drop off, I slam my hand on the steering wheel, disappointed in myself and knowing that this will be a hard-learned lesson I won't repeat.

Seriously, what kind of bag was that? Who plans to steal a painting and then gives the thief a case that falls apart?

And how stupid was I to not even check it? *Now I've got a complication*, I think as I glare at the black leather bag in the seat next to me. Shit. Whose bag is it?

I replay the scene in my mind, looking for details. The assistant had a black bag, but it was smaller, more a purse than a bag. This is like a satchel or a bike messenger bag. And then it hits me . . . the clumsy but hot redhead. I shake my head, laughing to myself.

Guess today was not her day.

JP's waiting for me in the dark when I pull up to the same warehouse as before. I'm ultra-careful, making sure that my case failing was the only 'surprise' tonight. Once everything's clear, I put my truck in park. Leaning out, I whistle, and JP steps out from behind a stack of crates. "Hey. You alone?"

My hackles rise in warning. That's not a good question to ask someone in my line of work. It means there's no trust. "No, I've got my friends Smith and Wesson with me," I tell him darkly.

I actually don't have a gun. It's too big a risk. I get picked up with stolen artwork? I can plead that I'm an unwitting courier and will likely get off with minimal aggravation. But add in a possession charge and shit gets serious.

But JP doesn't know that, and instead he laughs easily. "Relax, man. I just can't see in the windows of that pickup of yours."

I don't bother looking behind me at the truck's windows. I know exactly how dark the tint is because I chose it, so I just shrug. "You alone? I'm supposed to be handing this one over to Mr. Big himself."

JP rolls his eyes. "Yeah, and I'd like to hand something over to Selena Gomez in person too, but you know how paranoid he gets. Always thinking the Feds are on to him . . . like they give a fuck about art."

JP might not think anyone cares, but I happen to agree with Mr. Big. Feds definitely care about art and art thieves. But trust isn't a one-way street, and I'm not okay with not meeting who I'm working for after this amount of time and risk. I like to know exactly who is calling the shots and paying me, and so far, this boss remains elusive.

"So we're rescheduling?" I ask, giving the warehouse another scan. If Mr. Big is nervous, I'm not comfortable either. I even give JP a suspicious look.

JP scoffs. "You must be crazy, man. I'll take the piece and hand it off. We can do a meet and greet another time. Next job."

"Or I can do the hand off," I suggest firmly. "I've got some . . . customer service issues to discuss with him."

"No. You know how this goes. You do the job, I get the product, and then it goes from there. Bitches, gripes, and complaints go to me."

I want more information about JP's process, but if I ask now, he's going to get even more heated. And working for Mr. Big is the big time, hence the alias. He's the leader of the entire art black market and not a contact I can risk.

JP's got me by the short hairs, and he knows it. Reluctantly, I open the truck door and pull out the leather bag. JP's brows furrow. "Where's the other bag?"

"Like I said, I've got customer service issues," I tell him, reaching in to pull the two halves of the junk case out. "I had to go with what was available."

"Dammit," JP mutters, seeing the case. "I'll deal with that."

"Yeah, well, I've bought better bags at the grocery store. So here you go, I did what I could with what I had. You're welcome." The sarcasm is lost on JP, who stays all business.

JP nods and takes the bag from me. Opening the flap, he slides out *The Black Rose* and whistles. "Looks the same as the other, yes?"

I grunt in response. If he can't tell the difference, it's not my damn business. JP pauses and looks in the bag again. "What's this?"

He pulls a laptop out of the leather bag and my heart stops. "Shit. I didn't realize that was in there."

I reach for it, but JP holds up a hand. "Relax, I'll trash it."

"No," I tell him quickly for some reason. "I'll take it."

"What are you thinking? You can't go back there. Clean getaway and stay gone. Speaking of, with whatever heat Mr. Big has going on, you probably want to lie low for a while too. I'll hang on to this," he says, looking at the laptop. It's not a question. Instead, he flips it over, looking at the stickers on the bottom and whistling softly. "My kid could use one of these. This thing looks nice. He'll love it."

Kid? I didn't know JP had a kid. I store the info away in case I ever need it. I'd like to get the laptop back to Red, but JP's right. That's a rookie mistake, one I'm way too experienced to make.

I shrug, wishing I could do more but knowing at least someone will appreciate the laptop. "Then we're good?" I ask, checking off the art handoff and the unexpected laptop issue. JP nods, but I add, "I expect to meet the boss man soon. I've proven myself, my skills, and loyalty. I should know who I'm working for."

JP rolls his eyes again, waving a dismissive hand. "He'll see something in the stars that tells him he's safe, and then he'll probably invite you over for dinner and scotch. He's just paranoid. You understand?"

No, I still don't, but I nod anyway and climb back into my truck. "See ya for the next one."

I pull away, going to make my other meeting of the night. Everyone who lives in the shadows and who plans on maybe seeing the next few years outside of prison needs people they can

ONE DAY FIANCE

trust to make it work. For me, my 'fixer' is Hunter. I've known him for a few years now, and he's one of the best there is.

"You got a place for me?" I ask as I pull into the garage and get out. Hunter's already moving, going around to the back of my truck to swap out the plates. I know they're clean because he's trustworthy and even more careful than I am.

"Yeah, here's the keys," he says, reaching into his pocket and tossing them to me. "It's not your usual speed, but it'll be good for you. You can play house in a nice place like an actual human being, not some hole in the wall."

He's talking about my actual home, a place I haven't been to in way too long. After a job, I always spend a while decompressing and making sure the coast is clear before I go back home. Plus, it lets me keep touch on what's happening on the market, who's looking, who's buying, and who's stealing what. I like to stay caught up, know who the players are.

And despite giving me shit, he's the same fucking way. He floats from place to place so much, I don't even know where his real home is, though I'm sure he's got a home base of operations somewhere. By his age, he must. Not that he's remotely old, but he's got nearly a decade of hard-won experience on me, and I'd damn sure better have some cushy digs by the time I'm pushing up on forty.

"Whatever it is, it'll do. I just need a waystation to handle operations."

"This'll more than do," he says as he roots around in his pocket and pulls out a slip of paper with the address and other important info on it. It'd be really stupid to get caught because I trip my own damn home alarm system. "Enjoy the sweet digs for a change, man. Maybe treat it like a vacation instead of going from one job to the next. You can afford a few weeks of downtime after this one.

I shake my head. "Wish I could, but Mr. Big was a no-show."

Hunter pauses in attaching my new license plate and looks up at me. His gray eyes are stormy as he scrubs a hand across his blond beard. "Well fuck. Maybe no vacation then. What happened?"

"Don't know," I admit, leaning against my truck. "Cold feet, basically. Got the payday, funds are transferred, but no face with the name. I don't like it."

Hunter hums and goes back to bolting on my new plates. "I know. You like to be in control of everything and have everything planned the way you like it. Not everyone falls in line, Connor."

"Yeah, and because of that, I work with people like you," I remind Hunter, who grunts. He finishes up my front plate and knocks on the hood when he's done. He knows better than to pat it and leave potential finger or palm prints. "Thanks for this. I'll be in touch."

"Watch your ass," Hunter reminds me, standing with his arms crossed and a serious look on his face. I dip my chin in acknowledgement as I back out, disappearing into the night. I find the address on the paper, doing a quick drive by in the quiet neighborhood. Even in the dark, I can tell that Hunter was right. This place is swanky compared to my usual hideouts. Normally, my first stop is to the nearest all-night store to buy fifty bucks' worth of roach and rat traps.

Not this time. The townhouse has a small yard with a private driveway and even a cute mailbox with what looks like a firetruck on it. Driving past, I take ten minutes to patrol the neighborhood, just getting a feel for things.

Seeing nothing amiss, I go back and park, grab my go bag, and use the key Hunter gave me to open the door. I wait until the door is closed and locked before turning on a light. The living room is minimally furnished with a couch and a tv on a stand, and I can see through to the kitchen. I know the fridge will be stocked with my favorite beer and some frozen food, courtesy of Hunter. Beyond that, I'll have to take care of things myself tomorrow.

Not a problem, but not tonight. I'm too damn tired. Instead, I arm the alarm system and head down the hall. I do a quick check of the bedrooms and bathroom before stripping for a shower. I pull on a pair of shorts and fall into bed, dreaming of the sad-faced woman from *The Black Rose*.

At some point, her pale face morphs into a blushing, freckled one and her hair shifts, turning bright red. The redhead who fell into me, who is probably freaking out about her missing laptop, looks so sad, like I ripped out her heart. I feel bad about that, but there's nothing I can do about it now.

CHAPTER 6

POPPY

"Miss Woodstock?" a tall, blond man says from the doorway across the room. The clerk at the front desk doesn't even look up as I move past her, studiously keeping her eyes on the screen in front of her though her fingers are typing in slow motion.

Then again, considering the ass-blistering tirade I gave her about ten minutes ago, she probably doesn't want to be anywhere near me right now. I'm not saying that I've been living up to the stereotype about redheads being fiery tempered . . . but the clerks should be wearing fire department coats at this point. I'm not proud of it, but I am desperate and freaking the fuck out. Especially after the last two hours of being ignored by the security guards, a suggestion that perhaps I 'forgot' my laptop or where I put it, and then being summarily dismissed to the police station, where I'd expected to get help but instead found myself sitting and waiting for an officer to 'have time to talk to me'.

"Yes. Thank you for seeing me, Detective," I reply, keeping my voice as calm as possible. As I pass through the doorway and into the office area beyond, I feel his eyes on me, especially on my ass. My dress felt sophisticated and beautiful at the dinner, but now I feel too exposed and vulnerable.

Maybe it's the officer's covetous gaze, or maybe it's that my bag is really missing, but tears spring to my eyes again.

Why, oh why didn't I do the smart thing and back up my work on a thumb drive or in a cloud or *somewhere?* I guess I'd been so dismissive about the piss-poor quality of what I'd written and on the verge of deleting it all anyway that I didn't want it to seem 'final'.

"I'm Detective Jax Carter. Please sit down and tell me what's brought you in tonight," he orders.

"Okay, I went to the writer's workshop hosted by J.A. Fox," I start for what has to be the third time. I told the hotel staff and security guards, I told the patrol cops they called, and I told the clerk out front . . . do I really need to do this again?

"Right," Detective Carter says, glancing at a piece of paper. Okay, maybe he does have the patrol officer's report. "Says here that you're a writer?"

"Yes," I say as evenly as I can. "Anyway, there was a blackout, and I was pushed to the floor."

"Yes, I see that. The security team was a bit alarmed . . . and I have to say, rightly so," Detective Carter says. "Apparently, Ms. Fox is a bit of a celebrity."

"It's not like I was charging at her like a bull," I continue, trying to stay calm at his implication that I did something wrong. "After the lights came on and the guards realized I wasn't a threat, they helped me up from the floor." Under my breath, I mutter, "Showing the whole room my Spanx in the process."

Dammit, that wasn't quiet enough, and *now* he's interested. "Go on."

"So I went back to my workstation and realized my bag was missing. I'd set it down on the table onstage for the photo, and when the lights came on, it was gone," I conclude. "The security guards helped me look, but it had vanished. I think the other security guard took it."

Detective Carter taps his fingers together, leaning in to listen . . . or maybe get a view of my cleavage, I'm not sure which. "Other security guard?"

ONE DAY FIANCE

"There was a security guy standing on stage. He looked up right before the lights went out, and then he was gone when the lights came back on, and so was my bag." I hold my hands out wide like the connection is obvious.

He smiles condescendingly. "This security guard? Did anyone else see him?"

"They're all contractors, according to J.A.'s assistant. No one even knew his name . . . something that started with a C or a K, one guy said . . . Chad, Kyle, Cole . . . something like that. Apparently, they all came in for a one-time gig."

"Helpful," he says dryly. I swear I think he's doodling random check marks on the report now.

"So, what do you need? The model type, the color?" I ask, trying to get us on track to do something, anything that might result in getting my laptop back. Isn't this sort of like a kidnapping? The first four hours are key.

"And what exactly was on this laptop that would make it worth stealing?"

"My manuscript!" Detective Carter looks perplexed, so I add, "Of my book. Like you said, I'm a writer."

Humor lights in his eyes, and he's almost laughing as he asks, "What kind of stuff are you writing about that someone would want to steal your manuscript? I've heard of superfans, but stealing a story seems a bit . . . overboard. Are you sure there wasn't anything else in the bag . . . or on your laptop?"

I can see the way he looks at me, and I unconsciously cross and uncross my legs, trying not to shift around too much. I feel tears threaten, and I feel so small and ridiculous that I want to curl up and disappear.

Maybe this is a sign that this book isn't meant to be. I've had enough trouble with it, but I kept pushing. Maybe this is fate's way of telling me to just give it up.

Seeing my distress, Detective Carter seems to decide he's done enough to put me in my place and leans forward, offering me a tissue. "It's okay, honey. I'll see what I can do for you."

That sounds about as authentic as a two-dollar Rolex and doesn't ease my mind in the slightest. The condescending 'honey' irritates me too, but instead of going off on him, I take the tissue and roughly swipe under my eyes.

"Why don't you tell me what the book is about? Maybe that'll help."

"It's a romance, the sequel to my first book," I continue, trying to calm myself.

"Romance."

Judgment is already apparent, the corners of his mouth twitching as he fights a smile. "Like lady porn? All heaving bosoms and unsheathed swords? Or are we talking the red room whips and chains type?"

Somehow, his disdain for my work is the spark needed to push me from being weepy to being pissed off again. Fire flames up in my gut, not embarrassment because I'm not embarrassed about what I write. What's wrong, in a world where people treat each other like shit on a regular basis, with writing about women empowering themselves, men who have good hearts, and love that always ends in happily ever after?

What's so *fucking* wrong with love?

Okay, so sometimes, the characters are works in progress, needing a little help and growth to go from bad boys to good guys, or from traumatized to strong, but that's real life.

So no, not embarrassed. In fact, as the fire builds and the anger grows inside me, I square my shoulders again, staring at him. What gives this . . . man . . . Detective Jax Carter the right to be so cavalier and rude about something that means so much to me, writing it off like my heart and soul spilled on blank white pages is nothing more than drivel and sex?

Fuck this guy.

"You know what? Forget about it. Thanks for absolutely nothing, *asshole*," I bite out harshly and intentionally loudly. I want everyone in the room, though there's only the clerk up front and one other officer several desks away, to hear me. "I'll have my agent be in touch about the police report so we can file a loss claim."

I'm talking out of my ass. I don't know what the publisher or Hilda is going to do about this, but I'm going to need their support if I have to deal with shit like Jax Carter. Because all I can think about is slapping that smug smile off his face and pinching his oversized head straight off his body right now.

I offer up a silent little thanks to my dad. Mom might have given me my red hair, but Dad's the reason for my short temper and fighting spirit. And I'm ready to fight for myself now, standing up and glaring at the detective.

Detective Carter looks shocked, probably at my language and possibly at being called out. He's probably so used to being the biggest swinging dick in the room that he's stunned when a *woman* dares to call him out on his shit.

He stands up too, trying to regain the height advantage and not show embarrassment from my outburst. "Miss Woodstock, wait—"

"Too fucking late," I snap. Nope, he's lost my cooperation. I don't even slow, bitch-walking my way right out of the office, my heels clicking on the tile.

The clerk flinches as I pass her, and I'm sure she heard every word of that last bit. Good. I want everyone from the lowest patrolman to the chief of police himself to hear how unhelpful, judgmental, and rude Detective Jax Carter is.

"Miss Woodstock? Is everything okay?" the clerk asks, probably reveling in someone else getting some of my ire after I freaked out on her earlier. Hell, maybe appreciating that someone knocked me down a peg or two as well.

"No, it most definitely is not. If that's what you have to work with every day, I am so sorry for adding to the shitshow earlier. You have enough to deal with."

The clerk's brows jump up, but there's a bit of 'you got that right, sister' in her eyes, and I feel like my apology is at least accepted.

As for Detective Carter's half-assed request for me to come back to his desk for more questions, I ignore the fuck out of that.

My phone dings, reminding me that it's now nine in the morning. Last night feels like it was a decade ago, and my addled brain is aching from the lack of sleep. I've pretty much stress eaten every sweet, salty, or otherwise 'junk' item in my pantry, and as I stagger to the kitchen to suck down another cup of coffee, the streaky raccoon that looks back at me from the reflection in the machine reminds me that nope, I haven't even washed up since getting home.

I've just wept, raged, walked circles in my living room, and raged some more. Nut and Juice finally gave up on me and flopped down in the corner to sleep, and maybe I passed out for an hour or two, somewhere in between my double stuffed Oreos and my salt and vinegar chip binges.

But whatever. I've got to do this . . . I've got to call Hilda. Still, I procrastinate, not wanting to do it. I go to the bathroom to pee and then wash my face so that at least I don't make this call worse than it has to be. I fake smile at myself in the mirror, aiming for a confidence boost, but the cookie crumbs crowded around my gums dash that hope too. I don't bother with toothpaste but at least scrub away the grossness with a wet toothbrush. But with that done, there's no putting off the inevitable.

With trembling fingers, I dial Hilda's number, and she picks up on the first ring. "You're welcome."

"Hilda . . . it's gone."

Hilda, obviously expecting me to answer with a happy 'thank you' and some gushing, pauses. "What?"

Quickly, in one long, semi-coherent rush, I explain what happened. Hilda listens, and her first question is a punch to my gut. "And you didn't back up the file?"

I groan, another round of fresh tears threatening though I've surely got to be cried out by now. "Hilda, I know it's bad, and I did go to the cops, at least. And I'm going to fix this. I don't know how, but I'm going to."

"You'd better," Hilda says. "Look, I can talk with Bluebird. Maybe they'll give you a little more time if you have to start from scratch . . . but there's not going to be any more advance checks until you actually turn work in, you know? Whatever's in your bank account, that's it."

"I know."

Hilda sighs. "I know I shouldn't need to ask this, but you're okay bill-wise?"

"Oh . . . I'm okay," I assure her, even though I'm going to have to be careful. I've got the advance funds in the bank, but most of the profit from the first book went to buying this townhouse. "I'll figure it out, Hil."

"Do that. But when you get a replacement laptop, pick up a flash drive and make it a habit to use it from here on," she says with some force in her voice, but then she softens. "I'm glad you're safe. If you need anything, call. Okay?"

"Okay. Uhm, bye for now?"

"Call me this evening and tell me about your new computer," Hilda says before hanging up. A yip from behind me tells me that Nut and Juice are up, and when there's a growl and yip in reply, I realize they're going at it for round 6329 or whatever it is.

"Quiet, guys," I growl, looking over at them and trying not to yell. It's not their fault my head is pounding. "Momma really doesn't need that this morning."

Juice looks at me, and I swear those two have knocked a few brain cells out of each other in their tussling. But before I can repeat myself, I hear folks outside making noise and then the rumble of a big diesel engine.

What the hell? I go to my living room window and look out to see a gaggle of the neighborhood's divorcee residents gathered on the sidewalk outside next door and a big black truck parked in the driveway.

Damn, a new neighbor already? That was quick . . . but what's with the Desperate Housewives Welcoming Committee?

I step outside, closing my door behind me to keep Nut and Juice inside, and approach the group. One of the ladies moves aside, and in an instant, I can see why they're being *so* welcoming.

There's a man standing there. I can only see him from the back. He's pulling something out of his truck, but what I see is tall and broad and tapered in that sexy upside-down triangle shape. He's wearing jeans and a black T-shirt, a simple combo that on him could melt the sidewalk, from the looks of things.

Ah, the mating dance of the suburban divorcee, I muse as I get closer. *Next step will be bringing over a cake or some cookies. After that . . . a casserole. All to get a taste of that eggplant.*

Why can I funny in my head and not on paper? Before I can think about that and lead to thoughts of my missing laptop, I crane my neck to get a better look at my new neighbor's ass, which seems vaguely familiar in a pair of well-worn Levi's that make me consider taking out stock in the jeans.

"Jeez, you're really getting hard up if you're recognizing asses," I murmur to myself, "especially when you need to be handling this crisis and not . . ."

The guy turns, and shock hits me hard.

I know that face.

I *do* know that ass . . . and that asshole! It's the security guard with a C or K name who stole my laptop!

Before I can even process, my body is moving totally on instinct-fueled rage. I run across the yard, hopping the little knee-high border fence between my yard and Helen's former yard, and launch myself at the man's back with a Valkyrie screech promising death and dismemberment. Not necessarily in that order.

"You rat bastard son of a bitch!"

I land on him hard, my shoulder right in his low back, and he takes a startled step forward, dropping whatever he was carrying before spinning in circles, this way and that. "What the fuck?" he asks, trying to twist me off.

But I'm a bull terrier, hanging on and growling with grit and determination. This man has my goods, and I'm not leaving without them.

"Poppy?" Jane from a few houses down says questioningly. "You know him?"

"Yes, I fucking know him," I growl between clenched teeth.

He tries to reach behind himself to pull me around when I shift, climbing up his back and starting to pummel his head and shoulders with a fist. "Where is it? Where is it?" I yell with each punch. "Where is it?"

He switches to reach over his shoulder, but I'm a spider monkey, not letting go even though my punches seem to have no effect. His back and shoulders are rock hard, thick with muscle, and his skin's so warm . . . *No! Poppy, focus!*

I squeeze my thighs around his waist, climbing higher to go for his face. Fuck it, even a superhero's gotta protect his eyes. "I'm gonna kill you . . . filet you open like a fish and gut your insides and then choke you with your own intestines."

Yup, I do have a way with words on occasion.

But words don't win fights like this, and suddenly, I'm flipped neatly over his shoulders. I have about a blink for my mind to suddenly go *wheeeeeee!* before I'm dropped back-first onto the grass. I'm stunned as my breath is knocked out of me, and the moment's loss of focus is all he needs. He scrambles, half cartwheeling over me and pinning my shoulders with a thick forearm across my chest while his knee pins my hips down. I writhe and wiggle beneath him, still yelling and cursing a blue streak.

"What the fuck, woman?" he roars from inches away.

I blink in surprise, the reality of the situation hitting me. I attacked him. He threw me over his shoulder like I weigh no more than a rag doll. His thigh is between mine. Our breath is mingling hotly between us.

He stole my fucking book!

The fury of hundreds of sleepless nights, of writing and deleting incessantly, of questioning myself endlessly, of creating something born of my soul, only to have it ripped away, ignites in a mushroom cloud of destruction, demanding justice. I bring my knee up sharply, slamming him right in his junk.

He grunts in pain, falling over to the grass beside me in the fetal position. "You kicked me in the fucking ballbag," he snarls.

"You deserve that and so much worse," I tell him, still wheezing from having the wind knocked out of me by the hard ground. We lie next to each other, too hurt or tired to keep trying to draw blood at the moment.

One of my neighbors, Jane, or at least I think it's her, calls out, "Okay, folks. Show's over. Looks like Poppy's got this one well handled." To me, she says, "Let me know if you need a shovel and an alibi. We women gotta stick together."

I barely know Jane, but in this moment, she becomes a much closer friend. I'm going to bring her cookies next time I buy a batch.

Everyone must comply and wander back into their houses because by the time I prop myself up on an elbow, there's only the sound of my panting breathing and the asshole's moans of pain.

"Where's . . . my . . . laptop?" I demand.

"What laptop?" he says, but the pain must be subsiding because he's starting to stretch out. His legs are impossibly long next to mine, and I'm reminded how hard and wide he felt over me, pinning me down. If it'd been a different situation, that could've been awesome.

I roll myself up, thankful for the handful of sit ups I did three weeks ago in a fit of creative movement that was supposed to unblock my writer's block. To no surprise, it didn't and only made my stomach sore. I really should do more, but this isn't the time to debate my lack of a fitness routine. For now, I manage to sit up and bend a knee, getting ready for round two. Because it's coming . . . I can feel it in the air between us.

"My laptop. The one you stole last night," I explain as if he could've possibly forgotten what he did yesterday. "You were right there, the lights went out, and then poof . . ." I flash my hands like a magician doing a bad trick. "No laptop and no you. I know you stole it, Chad, Kyle, Cole . . . whatever your name is. And I want it back!"

I point an accusing finger at him, one with now-chipped red polish. Damn shame what a roll around in the grass will do to a manicure because I just got my nails done yesterday morning.

Not wanting to listen to more bullshit from him, I start round two, jumping over to pin him beneath me and slap at his chest. He blocks the blows at first, arms up to protect his chest and face, but when he realizes that despite my spitfire tendencies, I'm more of a weak kitten than a badass pit bull, he lets his arms fall to his sides. His hands rest on my thighs, which straddle him again, this time from the front, and he starts to laugh at my piss-poor attack, his flat belly bouncing beneath me in a not-unpleasant way as my hands start to sting from slapping his rock-hard chest.

"I didn't take anything," he says between laughs.

"Yes, you did!"

"Prove it!"

"I can't! I already talked to security and the police, but I need my laptop!" I hate the hint of a whine that's entered my voice, but I'm desperate. "If I don't get it back, I'm done."

His hands tighten on my thighs, and I can tell he's trying to control himself. I have no doubt that he could throw me off him easily, but he's not. Instead, he seems to calm and looks up at me with something approaching compassion in his eyes. "Look, I'll buy you a new one. Whatever you need. Deal?"

I blink in surprise. That's actually nice, but it won't solve my problem. "Not good enough. I need *my* laptop. It has *my book* on it."

He tilts his head, squinting in confusion. "Book?"

Is he playing dumb or something? I glare back down at him, nodding. "Yeah, like you didn't know that when *you stole it.*"

He opens his mouth like he's got a rebuttal on the tip of his tongue, but a buzzing sound interrupts, garnering both of our attention. He holds up a single finger, telling me to hold on a minute as if I'm not in charge here, pinning him to the ground. Reaching around my thigh, he pulls his phone out of his pocket and glares at it.

I wonder if he glares at everything because that seems to be his most common expression in the two days I've known him. Glaring, lying, laptop-stealing, sexy, strong . . . ahem, asshole of a man.

God, I'm such a mess. But I'll be even more of a mess if I don't fix this and get my laptop back.

He rolls his eyes, huffing in annoyance. Wow, a new expression . . . and the tally goes up to three. Four, if I count that flirty smirk he threw at me when he caught me last night.

"What's wrong?" I ask before I can stop myself. "Did I crack it?"

I should have, but instead he just grunts, shaking his head. "Nothing."

"Of course you'd say that. Obviously, something's wrong."

"My mom is overbearing." It's the slightest insight, but it's like pulling teeth to get even that much. But before I can try to pry that crack open, his phone rings again. He looks at it, and in the movement, I can see that the screen still says *Mom*.

"You gonna answer that?"

"No."

Yes! He may not have realized it, but Mr. C-K-I don't know your name just handed me leverage on a silver platter.

Before he can do anything, I reach down and pinch his nipple through his shirt, twisting it sharply. He yells and bucks his hips, half throwing me off as he curves away from me, giving me the perfect chance to grab his phone. I lunge and snatch it, scrambling to my feet and sprinting around his truck in an instant, but he's hot on my heels.

"Give it!"

I keep him opposite me as much as I can, a standoff of inches around the bed of the truck. "Or what?"

I hold up the still ringing phone, and he demands, "Don't you dare."

His phone buzzes again, and never being one to do what I'm told, I hit the button and answer on speakerphone.

"What the hell, Connor?" a worried older voice says over the phone as the guy looks worse than when I kneed him in the balls. "You're not even answering my calls now? Did you see my text about Caylee? Your sister is worried sick about you."

Connor. Now I know his name. And his sister's.

"Oh, I'm so sorry. Connor's not available right now. Could I take a message?" I ask in a faux-sweet customer service voice.

"Oh . . . I didn't realize," the woman answers. "You must be Scarlett. I've been telling Connor we'd love to meet you for ages. You'll be at the dinner tomorrow night, right? He told you about that? And the wedding?"

I look at Connor, who looks so different, vulnerable and almost pleading even as he tries to look angry at the same time. I've definitely got him by his *real* balls here, and I smirk. He shakes his head slowly, mouthing 'no' sharply.

"Scarlett?" I ask as if I'm confused.

On the other end of the line, the woman slowly says, "Connor's fiancée?"

Desperately, Connor yells out, "I told you she can't come, Mom. But I'll be there."

It seems like even that promise is painful. But honestly, it's a little disappointing for me too. Even though I shouldn't regret that he has a fiancée named Scarlett, I do.

But Scarlett can have her lying, stealing fiancé, and good luck to her.

"Why isn't she going?" I mouth to Connor.

He glares . . . again. I glare back, not budging an inch. Nope, you might be able to pin me to the ground like I'm a feather, but I've got the advantage here.

At least, I think I do until Connor lunges around the corner of the truck, and with a wingspan that would make a basketball player jealous, he grabs my wrist in an attempt to get his phone back. He struggles, but we end up both holding it, fighting for control of the device. "What's up?" I whisper again. "Why isn't she going?"

"She doesn't exist. I made her up to get my mom off my back," he admits reluctantly, almost blurting it out but still whispering quietly so his mom doesn't hear. Shocked, I let go of the phone, and he snatches it back victoriously. "Mom, I'll have to call you back, 'kay?

I'm not done, though. Before he can hang up, I yell, "Absolutely, I'll be there. I wouldn't miss it for the world. *Connor* is helping me out with a little laptop problem right now, but I'm sure we'll have it straightened out in no time and will be there for dinner."

I see him flinch when I use his name. Or maybe it's that I just promised his mom that I'd be at this family dinner. Whatever it is, he can suck it because I'm going to use this opportunity to get my laptop back. I know he has it. He all but admitted it, because who would offer to buy a new laptop if they weren't feeling guilty for stealing the original? Only some Daddy Warbucks kind of guy, and though my hair is red, I'm not getting Orphan Annie vibes when Connor looks at me.

"That's awesome, dear! So glad to hear it," Connor's mom says just as quickly since she's probably used to her son hanging up on her, if I'm catching the vibes right. "Okay, I'm going to go before Connor disagrees. Tootles!"

The line goes dead, and Connor looks at the device in his hand as if he can't believe what just happened. Slowly, so slowly I can almost feel the secondhand ticking by as he moves, his eyes lift to mine. Cold fury burns in their blue depths, the gold flecks flashing like sparks. I smile and offer a little finger wave. "Hey, fiancé. Now, about my laptop."

CHAPTER 7

CONNOR

*H*ow did I lose control of this situation so damn quickly? Two hours ago, everything was cool. I woke up, drove out to a storage locker I keep to grab a few personal items, and then swung by a twenty-four-hour big box place to get the other things I need.

I sigh, not sure how this could have happened. Controlling the uncontrollable, predicting the unpredictable, adapting and overcoming is what I do, but I've been totally thrown off my game by this five-foot-three redhead with the mouth of a sailor and the impulse control of a toddler on a sugar rush after a night of watching the sun come up.

Frustrated, I grab a bag out of the truck and throw it her way. Thankfully, she catches it, though it doesn't have anything too important inside. I move lightly, knowing the house has already been set up with most everything I'll need, but I still like to have my own clothes. Reaching in, I pick up a box and head toward the open door in the small one-car garage.

She doesn't follow, so when I get to the door, I turn and call out, "You coming? Seems we've got some shit to sort out."

I feel like it gives me some control again, and instead of getting angry, I wait. She rattled me, sure. But I've learned that when shit happens, you can't react like you're in the toilet bowl. You have to keep your mind going. It's like chess. You might be forced to sacrifice a pawn to protect your king, but you should always be adjusting and playing several moves ahead.

Sexy Red doesn't strike me as the type who thinks more than five minutes ahead a lot of the time. Feeling like she's still got me under her thumb, she slings my bag over her shoulder and comes in, stopping in the doorway to look around. "Helen had pretty wallpaper with flowers in here. What happened to it?"

"Landlord must've taken it down," I answer, looking at the freshly painted white walls. Truthfully, I have no idea what Hunter did to this place after the last owner moved out. I probably won't even be here long enough to use this kitchen, much less remember it. When another job comes through, I'll be gone.

She doesn't need to know that, though. I set the box on the small kitchen table, and she does the same, setting my bag on the table and giving me a look of challenge that's ruined by a curl that's escaped her messy bun and hangs down in front of her right eye. It makes her look cute and sweet, two things she definitely is *not*.

Playing my next move, I walk past her wordlessly, back straight and jaw tight. Outside, I lean against my truck, wondering exactly what the hell I'm doing playing with this girl.

What are you doing, man? No strings, no messiness. You know the drill. You're too close to a major breakthrough to risk fucking it up with some crazy she-devil who lives next door.

My mind remembers how she felt, both clawing at my back and when she was pinned underneath me, but especially when she was straddling my waist, and my animal side says she's definitely what I've been missing. She's not cute and sweet but instead fiery and sexy . . . a very appealing combination to me.

Which means I should climb in the truck and drive away. There's nothing I need in the house, and even if there were, Hunter could get it for me later. I consider it carefully. I could leave, forget about the laptop, forget about the redhead, and stay on mission.

But I'm intrigued. And attracted. And maybe a tiny bit guilty, the littlest shred of remorse. I didn't mean to put her in a bad spot. I just needed a bag, and hers was right there for the grabbing.

And I do know where the laptop is, or more like who has it. Getting it back from JP won't be easy, but I can probably figure something out.

I pick up the last bags from the store, steeling myself. I might see life as a chess game, but I'm also smart enough to know I'm not half as in control as I want to be. I know I'm going to need every bit of skill I possess to navigate this conversation. About the laptop . . . and about my mother.

I carry the bags inside, where my neighbor has helped herself to a box, unpacking my few personal items. "That's none of your business," I snap, setting my bag on top of the one she's trying to unload and effectively pushing her out of the way with the movement.

"Ooh, yeah . . . I'm really gonna damage these," she says, pulling out an old Rubik's cube I fidget with when I need to go all Zen and think about things. She picks up the other item she's pulled out—an oversized insulated coffee mug that keeps my lifeblood hot for hours. Turning the mug in her hand, she reads the words, "I might look calm. But in my head, I've killed you seven times." She smiles like it's funny and not the damn truth. Hunter gave it to me after a rough job, and it's a favorite. "Jeez, I'm engaged to Mr. Sunshine, aren't I?"

"We're not engaged," I growl as I pull the mug from her hand, setting it in the sink for a scrub down before my morning refuel, and she sets the Rubik's cube down on the stack of boxes. "We need to talk."

"Ya think?" she sasses, hand cocked on a thrown-out hip. "Let's start with . . . where the fuck is my laptop?"

"Nope. Start with your name."

Her eyes narrow, and she brushes that lock of hair back in a bratty move, huffing out, "Like you don't know." When I look at her expectantly, she freezes. "Wait . . . you really don't know?"

"I really don't."

"Then why'd you steal my laptop?"

She thinks this is about her computer and not her bag. I might have a way to salvage this. "Long story."

"A-ha!" she shouts triumphantly, pointing a finger at me. "You admitted it. I should call the cops on you."

Dammit, but I had to take this particular risk. When her declaration is matched with zero movement, I realize that I've still got plays to make. She doesn't trust or like the cops, perhaps? Interesting. Maybe Sexy Red's got a bad girl side to her. I look at her expectantly and she gives in.

"Poppy Woodstock."

I snort. I've been jumped and am talking to a walking meme. "Of course. Poppy." I look her over, taking special note of the mane of red hair. It's not poppy colored, at least not the orange-red California poppies I'm thinking of, but something about her seems vibrant and lively like a field of her namesake.

"That's right . . . Connor," she reminds me. "So now that we both know names, I want to know why you stole my stuff!"

With a sigh, I pick up my phone again and click a few buttons. "What do you eat on your pizza?" I ask as it rings. "Might as well, you know?"

"Isn't it early?"

"Never too early for pizza."

"Good point," she says easily, as if what I just said makes perfect sense and isn't a dodge to try and gain some more time. "Sausage and jalapeños."

Totally not surprised. I'm also not surprised that she's quick on her feet . . . another point in her favor. I'm the sort of person to stockpile personalities, quirks, habits, and routines about people the way most folks study for college exams. It's a skill I've perfected over years of practice and has come in handy more than a few times.

I order the pizza, giving the address I've already memorized. "It'll be here in thirty minutes."

Going over, I pull out a beer from the fridge and offer her one. To my surprise, she takes it from me without a word about the before-noon hour, but before she gets it too far away, I twist the top off. She smiles in appreciation and I lift one shoulder an inch.

I'm not a total cretin.

I'm not a gentleman either.

Never had a need to be.

"Sooo . . ." she drags out, rocking from her toes to her heels, "about my laptop?"

I sip at my own beer, trying to decide how I can explain this without mentioning *The Black Rose*. In the end, being 'partially completely honest' seems like the best angle. "I took it. I gave it to a guy."

"You gave it away?" she sputters. "You know how important that laptop is?"

"Well, it was nice," I admit, thinking about how JP reacted last night, "but relax. I can get it back. I think."

She spits out her own sip and barks, "You think? What the fuck does that mean?"

"It means I think I can get it back," I repeat more slowly. "I know who I gave it to, and I know his plans for it."

She steps forward bravely, or with zero regard for her own safety —I haven't decided which yet—and growls up at me, "I need it back. It has my manuscript on it and I'm on a deadline."

I hold my hands out up, showing I mean no harm. At least not right now. "Tell me about the manuscript."

She sags heavily, wind dropping out of her sails in a heartbeat. "I'm an author. The J.A. Fox dinner was a big deal for me until it all went to Satan's asshole when you showed up." She glares at me again before continuing, "That manuscript is my baby, one I've worked on for months. There's blood, sweat, and tears in those pages. I have to finish it and turn it in by the beginning of the month or I'm done-for. Dead woman walking."

She drags a thumb across her neck, but I don't think she means literally unless she's got a really fucked-up publisher with mob ties. Hmm, I wonder if that exists? I mean, it could. Mobsters read ... probably.

After all, Mr. Big is an art aficionado and a man who can kill without remorse.

"And you didn't have a backup?" I ask, lifting my eyebrow. "Nothing on the cloud?"

"After the cloud hacks the past few years?" She scoffs but then softens. "Dammit, I know. Trust me, I know!"

"Whoa, whoa ... I got it." I tap my bottle to hers, acknowledging that I hear her. "I'll do what I can to keep you among the living," I joke dryly. "We'll get it back."

She makes a face, twisting her lips and squinting her eyes at me brattily. "Promise?" I dip my chin to seal the deal, but that's not enough for her. She holds out a fist, her pinky sticking up. "Pinky promise or your dick is mine. And not in the fun way," she threatens, "but in the snip, snip, chop, chop way."

I don't laugh, not at losing my dick, but it's a close call. But I do want to think about her wanting my dick in another way, and a chuckle tries to escape. I cough to cover it, wrapping my pinky around hers and shaking in agreement.

"That's my laptop situation. Now, how about you tell me about your mother situation since I'm going to meet her at dinner tomorrow?"

I choke on the drink I just took, spitting half of it out as the other bit goes down the wrong pipe. Wiping at my mouth, I growl, "You're not going to dinner tomorrow."

"Yes," Poppy declares evenly, "I am. Your mother is expecting me. Well ... she's expecting Scarlett, your fiancée. Why'd you lie about that?"

This is dangerous. I mean, it's already dangerous to even let her know my name and not be on the road to the nearest Holiday Inn. I should just feed her a line of bullshit. Hell, I lie so often that sometimes the lies seem more real than the truth.

But somehow, there's something about Poppy Woodstock that has me doing the totally wrong thing . . . and telling her the truth. "My family's got lots of shit going on. And Mom is . . . a lot. She gets all up in my business, which I just can't have. Honestly, she's like you."

"Cute and perky?" she suggests with a faux-innocent blink of her bare, pale lashes.

"You're not cute," I growl. "Either way, my sister's getting married, and it'll be this whole dog and pony show with the aunts and uncles and cousins. I'm not going."

"To the wedding? Your sister's wedding?" she asks, horrified.

"No wedding, and no dinner either." I answer darkly. "Every family's got a black sheep, right? Well, that's me. In fact, I'm like a radioactive black sheep."

"Doesn't matter, we're going." Stubborn doesn't begin to describe her, and that's coming from someone who's been described as stubborn as a mule more than once. "She wants you there!"

She doesn't get it. I'm not going for their benefit, not mine. "Did you not hear me? I'm radioactive. My mom doesn't know who I am, what I do. She thinks I'm a good guy, wants to show me off to her sister, my Aunt Audrey. And those two . . . they've had a pissing match for years. Their kids are just soldiers in their war, and I have zero interest in competing with my cousin, Ian."

Poppy smiles, her teeth flashing white before she tries to cover it with her beer bottle.

"What?"

She shakes her head, taking a big gulp. But under my hot gaze, she melts and her laugh bubbles out. "I'm trying to imagine you" —she gestures from my head to toes— "competing with someone named Ian." The insult hits me sharply, but then she says sadly, "Poor kid. With a name like Ian, he never had a chance."

Wait, she thinks I'm better than Ian? She doesn't know him, and all she knows of me is that I'm a lying, stealing thief, but somehow, that brings me ahead as the winner in this imaginary contest?

I grin cockily and agree. "He really didn't."

Somehow, it forges a little bond between us, and Poppy relaxes, taking another sip of beer. "So tell me about you, and tell me about Scarlett since I'll be playing her tomorrow."

Oh, God, Scarlett. That's a whole other bundle of shit to deal with, and I'm glad when the doorbell rings before I can reply. Still, it makes me jump a little, and I chastise myself that I didn't hear the car pull up outside. *Don't get distracted, Connor. It might not always be a pizza.*

I take the pizza from the delivery guy and set it on the counter. Sliding a slice onto a plate, I hand it to Poppy and then plate one for myself. She sits at the table, and I realize that she moved the boxes while I was getting the pizza.

She's helpful and willing to pitch in. I store that information away too.

I hope that's true because in the scarce moment it took me to get the pizza, I've realized that she's right. If I don't show up for the dinner now, my mother will never quit calling me. And Caylee will never forgive me.

A little part of me that hopes for redemption at some point says I can't let that happen. I have to try, at least.

"Okay," I say as I sit down heavily in my chair, my appetite for sausage and jalapeños lost for now.

Poppy freezes, her mouth full of pizza. She mumbles, "M'kay, wut?"

"Dinner. You can go. Just that, though, not the wedding. One day. You'll be my one-day fiancée." I'm making it sound like I'm doing her a favor, but we both know the opposite is true. She's the one giving me half a chance to try and have a future with my family . . . potentially.

She proves me right when she open-mouth grins, showing me the half-chewed pizza. "Cool."

"If . . . you can eat with your mouth closed," I deadpan.

Her mouth clacks closed, and she chews before swallowing thickly. "Okay, mom and aunt, sister and cousin. What else? Give me the whole intel brief like I'm Jane Bond going in for an operation."

I set my pizza down, staring at the small puddle of grease on top. "I wasn't always the bad guy, actually started off pretty decent." She looks at me wryly, but I keep going. "But I got into a bit of trouble when I was a kid, nothing too serious. Pickpocketing, petty theft . . . stupid shit, but just enough to embarrass them. Things got tense after that. I left the day I turned eighteen, and that's when I . . . got really good at what I do," I say carefully.

"Like bag snatching?"

I nod, letting Poppy continue to think all I stole was her laptop, probably assuming it was J.A. Fox's or something. I'm not going to divest her of that assumption. She's already too close, too tied up in a bad situation. "Anyway, to try and get some breathing room, I made up Scarlett. They think because of her, I turned my life around, became an upstanding citizen, a business consultant with a sweet, kind-hearted, patient fiancée."

Poppy levels me with a playfully evil smile. There's no sweetness in the way she bares her teeth, but the light in her eyes tells me she's joking. "Well, if you can play upstanding, I can play sweet. What about your dad? You didn't mention him."

"Sore subject. He'll be there," I admit through gritted teeth. "In body, at least, but he's been absent for a long time. He probably won't speak to you."

That's the long-story-short version. My dad checked out on our family years ago when his father died unexpectedly. We all dealt with it in different ways, but Dad never got out of the hole he fell into. But that's probably something that won't come up in our dinner and doesn't need to be discussed.

"Grumpy dad, getting info is like pulling teeth . . . wonder where I've seen that before?" Poppy says, and that zings. She taps her chin thoughtfully, gazing into the distance. Her eyes clear and zero in on me. "And again, I haven't forgotten about my laptop.

Speaking of, I need to get moving. I've got to go buy a backup laptop for work, though I don't know what I'm going to do without the first chunk of my writing. Should I start over completely or continue from where I left off?"

She doesn't seem to be asking me but rather trying to decide for herself, so I wisely stay quiet. Watching her process is fascinating. She seems to be talking to herself, not silently but out loud, actually turning her head left and right as though arguing with herself. It's a weird and interesting sight, like she's legit got the classic cartoon 'angel and devil' on her shoulders.

"What'd you decide? Did the left shoulder or right shoulder win?" I tease finally. "Or is it a secret?"

Poppy shrugs her right shoulder up, looking at it from the corner of her eye. "I'm going to keep on keeping on, trusting you to come through and get my laptop back. So something cheap it is."

I'm surprised. She has no reason to trust me other than desperation, but it feels like more than that. I can't help but question her instincts if she's putting her life, which is what she called her manuscript, in my hands. "Okay then. Go get your temp laptop, and I'll make some calls."

She gets up, setting her empty plate in the sink before heading to the front door. I follow her, more of a gentleman than I would've guessed. To justify the action, I take the opportunity to look at her ass in the very nicely fitting yoga pants she has on.

"What time tomorrow?" she asks. "The dinner."

"Six o'clock." I dimly remember that from the voicemails my mom has left. "If you no-show, there'll be no hard feelings. I'll still get your laptop."

She looks at me for a long moment, and I can't decide if she's reading my soul or memorizing my face. Either is uncomfortable as hell, but I stay as still as a statue, not flinching. Finally, she nods, and in a surprising move, she boops my nose.

"Six o'clock. I'll be ready."

I'm so stunned by the boop that all I can do is watch as she walks across the yard. Her hips sway back and forth to a rhythm I can feel in my cock, hypnotizing me.

She gets to the small fence between our yards, and I'm curious what she'll do considering she came over in a flight of rage earlier. She doesn't miss a step, taking a single running step before leaping over it gracefully, looking almost like a dancer in the air before she lands.

Well, spoke too soon because as she takes her first step on the other side, her foot slips a bit in the green grass and she stumbles.

I start to move toward her, but she steadies on her own. She looks back over her shoulder to check whether I saw that, so I lean on the doorframe, arms crossed over my chest and a smile on my lips. I'm sure that from here, if she wanted to, she could see the full bulge in my jeans. But she's looking at my laugh, so instead she glares, turning back around. Losing the hip sway, she stomps the rest of the way to her door, slamming it shut behind her.

"Nut juice!" she calls out, and I do a double-take, laughing out loud at the odd curse. I watch her living room curtains before evaluating her whole house in a moment, mentally assessing the access points and safety concerns. She locked the door after going in, which is a plus. I wonder about the front window, though. There are no blinds, just gauzy curtains. I'll have to talk to Poppy about that.

Shifting my attention, I scan the street looking for anything unusual. But it's a quiet neighborhood, very suburban and polite. Hunter chose just about the safest place to drop my bad seed.

Seeing nothing, I turn to head back inside. Only then does it all hit me.

Shit . . . I'm going to dinner with my family and taking a fake fiancée!

CHAPTER 8

POPPY

*I*t's two minutes until six, and I'm in my second-best polite outfit, standing by my front door, trying to decide.

Should I go over to Connor's? That might come off as being too pushy, and I pushed my luck really hard yesterday.

Should I wait here for him to pick me up? Yeah, no, that'd be a good way to get ghosted, if I'm reading him right.

Do I stand outside by his truck? That screams 'desperate stalker' way too much.

What is the protocol for a not-a-date, fake fiancée, dinner to meet the family? The more I rack my brain, the more I'm certain one doesn't exist. I should write one.

I shake my head, deciding there's probably not a lot of need for this specific situation. Only I would find myself mixed up like this. But ironically, it seems to have done a little bit of good. Going by memory and my written notes, I was able to actually pound out a whole supporting chapter today on my new laptop, saving it to my also new external flash drive.

I'm not making the same mistake twice.

Nervously, I peek out the front window and see Connor exiting his front door. He glances toward my place, and I'm so fucking glad that I'm not standing outside where he can see me right now. He doesn't deserve to know what the mere sight of him does to me.

But right now he looks . . . overwhelming. In a black suit, with a white dress shirt and black tie, the look could go blah and bland, but on him, the classic look is like a sexy dream in the flesh with his day-old scruff of stubble that I want to scratch at. Or maybe feel scratch along my skin.

I wish I weren't so affected by him, but my traitorous body responds to his like plucking an overtight string, making my hips shimmy with desire while my heart thumps a driving jazz beat in my chest.

No, Poppy. Horny or not, this is not okay. No matter that the bad boy cleans up well . . . really well. Just because his slacks look nice enough to run your hands over and the buttons on that shirt look like they'd be perfect to unbutton with your teeth, you can't. No matter if he's got his sleeves rolled up to show his thick forearms and his jacket is thrown over his shoulder, highlighting the gleam of a fancy watch on his wrist.

"I wonder if he stole it?" I ask myself to try and throw ice-cold water on my horniness, and it helps a little. The ugly thought breaks me out of my reverie, reminding me that while he might be sexy as sin, the devil tempts in lots of ways.

Making up my mind and mostly in control of myself, I open my door, calling behind me. "Be good, boys. Mommy will be home soon."

Outside, Connor's heard me and is giving me a curious look. "Nut and Juice," I explain, but his brows jump up his forehead in shock, and I hear what I just said a second too late. "My dogs. They're white Pomeranians. Get it? Nut juice. It seemed funny at the time."

"And now?" he asks dryly.

"It makes me smile," I admit, "at least until I have to call the little escape artists back. Nothing like walking around the neighborhood yelling, 'Nut Juice!' to get some awkward looks and a reputation as the neighborhood weirdo."

I expect him to smile or laugh because that's some funny imagery right there. And it did happen a few times when Nut and Juice were puppies and I didn't have them trained. But instead, he frowns. "Are you the neighborhood weirdo?"

"Uhm . . . yes?" I answer uneasily. "I mean, look around you. This might be a single woman-heavy neighborhood, but it's about as standard operating beige as you can get. Folks get up, go to work at eight, and get back home at six for dinner and the news, maybe an evening of chauffeuring kids around if it's their night. Some might be extra-wild and go to Zumba class at the Y, but most of the active people join the neighborhood walking group where they bitch about their office drama and comment on people's gardening skills, or the lack thereof, as they circle the neighborhood. Me, I work at home writing romance novels, and I go days without showering if I'm in the writing groove, wear pajamas most days, get food deliveries at all times of the night, and have dogs named Nut and Juice. I'm not exactly invited to the pool parties for fun times."

I stop, surprised at the vehemence and tinge of bitterness in my voice. It's never bothered me until this moment, or at least I've pretended so well that I've fooled myself. But under Connor's piercing gaze, the eyes of a man who'd be even more shunned by the neighborhood than I am, I realize that maybe it bothers me more than I admit.

"Hard worker, focused, able to prioritize, creative," Connor says, rephrasing my self-describing words and turning them on their heads. "I'm not finding the problem."

His reframing of the laundry list of my flaws heals something I didn't even know was broken, bringing a smile to my face. Reflexively, I reach out and punch him lightly in the chest, making him smile a little.

"Sexy. You forgot sexy," I brag-chastise, twisting left to right in my dress. I'm not fishing for compliments, but he'd damn well better agree.

I wasn't sure what the dress code for 'family dinner' is, so I played it safe in a red circle skirt that hits mid-thigh and a slim-fitting silk blouse. I chose a matching jacket that I can leave on if it's chilly or take off if it seems appropriate. In my heels, I'm feeling large and in charge next to Connor.

"And sexy," he says quietly. The word comes from deep in his throat, rough and scratchy in a way that makes my skin vibrate even though he's a solid two feet from me. But his eyes flow over me appreciatively in a way that brings my focus solidly to him, and I stop my girlish twirling, freezing in place. I get the sense that he's being genuine and is as surprised by his admission as I am. After a too-quick moment, he growls, "We should go. Get in."

He broke first, but instead of feeling like I won, I feel like he was able to wrench back control faster than I could, making me the loser in that battle. But I will win the war. The one for my laptop, I remind my libido. That's what this is about.

My insides tighten, trying to argue that a little poke and play couldn't hurt and would probably feel *really* good. If anything, I bet he could clean out my pipes and clear my writer's block while leaving me feeling fully sated.

But I refuse to listen to the horny bitch and walk to the passenger side of Connor's big truck. Putting my hand on the door handle, I pause, looking over at him with a smile. "You're not kidnapping me, are you? We're going to dinner with your family?"

His eyes narrow, and I wonder what about that joke slipped in a bit too deep. The kidnapping or the family dinner? Or maybe it's that I committed him to this charade and dinner when he obviously didn't want to go in the first place. "Get in the truck, Poppy. Or don't. Your call." He walks around to the driver's side, getting in and starting the roaring engine. Fuck the gentleman act, it seems.

"Guess I'll get the door myself then," I say, knowing he can't hear me over the growl under the hood. I climb in, literally since his truck's on some big ass tires that have me showing a hell of a lot of thigh just to get in, and buckle up.

"Do you have any sense of self-preservation?" he asks, hands tight on the steering wheel. He looks at me, and I realize his asshole act outside was because he *wanted* me to storm off and go back to my house, cowering in fear of the big, bad man next door.

Because if I did that, he'd be off the hook. Oh, he'd still peel off into the night, but it sure wouldn't be to go to his family's for dinner. But with me here, he's got no choice. And that scares him. Hell, I might even scare him instead of the other way around.

"Of course," I answer, though I'm not entirely sure that's true. Right now, I'm starting to scare myself because I'm not leaving this truck short of a pistol in my face. "But I am also willing to do anything to get my laptop back. And I figure if we go to dinner, I'll find out more about you, and I can leverage that to get my laptop back," I say, explaining my not-well-thought-out plan of desperation. And then I shrug. "If you kidnap me and sell me to the highest bidder, then my publisher won't find me and the book won't matter anyway. Either way, let's go."

Dark humor, but nerves are starting to bounce around inside me like wasps, stinging and sharp. But it thaws Connor some, and he gives me a nod. "Fair enough."

I thought we might have a little conversation on the way, him filling me in on more details and maybe even planning some information in case folks ask those landmine questions that happen in every 'fake relationship' story I've ever read . . . but those are the only two words he says for the entire drive.

I, on the other hand, ask questions—lots of questions. About his family, about his stealing, about how he got good at it, about who has my laptop, about his sister. I'm a regular chatterbox, peppering him with questions to show him that I'm not going to give up and that I want to do this.

And not once does he speak, not a single answer, no matter how easy or outlandish the question. So I resort to talking to myself, a frequent habit.

"I'm just curious, you know. It's in my nature to learn about people, their experiences, their lives, what makes them who they are," I comment as we make a right turn. "Sometimes, they end up as characters in a book, but mostly, it helps me imagine the world from different perspectives. It makes me a better author, I think. Maybe a better person too. I'm a good listener."

He grunts at that, and considering I've been talking for almost forty minutes straight, that does seem a little less than true. But I am a good listener and a good observer. For instance, Connor might not have said a word, but he's reacted to plenty of my questions. I see his teeth grit when I get too close to a button, his lips twitch when he thinks what I said is amusing, and the way his eyes cut over and his Adam's apple bobbed when my skirt shifted as we drove over a pothole.

Finally, at a pause in my rambling, he clears his throat, and I wait for him to share some massively informative detail or answer one of my hundreds of questions. "We're almost there. Two-minute warning to back out."

Instead of changing my mind, I take a tip from Aleria and place my hands on my thighs as I close my eyes. "Universe, if you're not too busy dealing with the tides and the earth's erosion, could you spare a moment to watch over me and Connor on this dangerous mission to see his super-scary family? Thank you. Peace, love, light, and donuts. Love, Poppy."

I open my eyes to see Connor staring at me from the corner of his eye in shock. "Did you just pray to the universe that my family dinner goes well? And offer donuts in exchange?"

"Everyone likes donuts," I say with a shrug. "Even Mother Nature." He blinks rapidly like he doesn't know what to say to that. Just to really tweak his brain, I add, "I tend to rotate the prayers and wishes. Always want to cover my bases, and I figure that it'll at least give me an in if there is someone up there listening for me to explain myself when it's my time."

"Huh." A minute later, he turns into a driveway that surprises me. I don't know what I was expecting, but it wasn't this. This house is massive, more estate than homey. I'd call it a McMansion except the property's too big for such a trite description.

He parks, and I see the first clear vulnerability in Connor's armor as he squeezes the steering wheel and lets out a rough sigh. "You okay?"

"I should be asking you that," he says, but he doesn't. Instead, he gets out and comes around to my side, opening my door this time. I offer a smile of thanks, but he only mutters under his breath, "Let's get this over with."

We're greeted at the door by Connor's mom, a tall, beautiful woman who carries herself with grace. "Why, hello . . . it's so nice to meet you, Scarlett!" she greets me, air kissing both of my cheeks. "I'm Debra, but please call me Mom. Where has he been keeping you?"

"Oh, he keeps me tied up in the basement," I tease. Connor stiffens at my side, but Debra laughs, her blue eyes sparkling with amusement. "But seriously, it's nice to meet you."

"We're so lucky to have you here," Debra says. "I promise we're not nearly as bad as he says we are."

She glances at Connor with a smile, and I'm sure she means it to be a joke, but it comes off a bit too truthful. To ease the tension, considering Connor hasn't said much, I tell her, "He hasn't said much. Guess he's the strong, silent type."

To seal the comment, I snuggle into Connor's side, doing my best to sell our 'fiancé' situation. Unfortunately, Connor's stiff and straight, like he's got a corn cob stuck up his ass. I'm about to elbow him when Debra laughs lightly, though it's one of those polite, that wasn't funny, fake ones. "Okay then. Let me get Dad and Caylee. They're in the office."

Once she's gone, I push away from him with a glare. "Hey, buddy, I can't do this alone. You have to play along if you want to keep up this charade." I point from him to me. "Buy in a little."

Connor sags slightly, looking like even that small interaction nearly exhausted him. "I'm here, aren't I?"

"Not enough," I warn. "Keep this up, and they sure as fuck will know I'm not Scarlett."

He shrugs, and I think he might be on the verge of saying fuck it to the whole fake fiancée thing minutes after walking in the door.

I definitely didn't consider that as a potential play-out of tonight's act.

Before Connor can reply, Debra comes back with an older version of Connor trailing her. Next to him is a young woman who definitely takes after her mother in the tall, elegant, and pretty departments. I swear, did these people hit Copy+Paste and create their kids, one in each of their image?

"Okay," Debra says when Connor doesn't say anything, "so this is my husband, Robert, and our daughter, Caylee. Everyone, this is Scar—"

"Poppy," I interrupt, smiling sweetly. "Sorry for the confusion."

"I thought your name was Scarlett?" Caylee asks curiously. She seems to have her brother's number more so than his parents and is looking at me carefully.

I run with it, giving a pretty good, embarrassed grin as I lean back into Connor's side and gaze up at him bashfully. "Well," I drawl out, "it's sort of a thing that only King Con calls me. You know, because of the . . ." I gesture to my red hair, making the nickname connection obvious and also making it seem more like a bedroom name than a pet name in the hopes that they'll leave it. I mean, who wants to hear their son called King Con around the dinner table when it instantly brings up thoughts of dick size and wild monkey sex?

"Oh," Caylee says, easily satisfied and backing away from that verbal bear trap.

"Where's the groom?" Connor interrupts, trying to move things along and check the boxes he's got in his head for this visit. "I thought I was going to meet him."

It's the right move, redirecting the conversation to a topic he knows his sister will want to talk about so that she doesn't focus on us. Or the pretend us, at least.

"Evan will be here any minute. I came out early to talk to Mom about last-minute wedding details, and well" —she smiles generously— "he's pretty much done with all the wedding talk. I might be a little obsessed." She holds her finger and thumb up an inch apart, grinning at me. "I'm sure you know how it is."

Actually, I don't. I'm seriously the sort of woman who'll have my wedding on a last-minute whim if and when it's my time, but I've got a role to play. "Of course. We're taking things one day at a time, though, not on the edge of *The Day* like you are." I take a cue from Connor, keeping the focus on Caylee. "You must be so excited."

Caylee squeals happily, her feet doing a tappity-tap dance on the wood floor as she finds a new ear to bend. "I can't wait. You have to come. You'll get him to come, won't you?"

Her eyes implore me, nearly begging, and I look to Connor, who clears his throat. "Tonight, Caylee. I came to dinner. I'm meeting Evan. Let's leave it at that."

Connor's voice isn't unkind, just matter-of-fact, but I see the disappointment in Caylee's eyes. She offers a shaky smile to her brother, though. "Yeah, I'm glad you're here. I just thought . . . maybe . . ." She trails off.

The front door opens, and a male voice calls out, "Babe? Where you at?"

Caylee immediately brightens once more and runs for the door. Through the frame, I watch as she jumps into the arms of a blond man in a suit. He spins her in a circle, her knees bent to keep her feet off the ground, as he kisses her with a loud growling smack. Obviously, it's Evan.

"I missed you today," he tells her sweetly like a hero from a Hallmark movie. He's definitely got eyes just for Caylee. I can see that even through my crack.

She beams as he sets her down, and they come into the big room, Caylee excitedly tugging at his hand. "Evan, this is my brother, Connor. And his fiancée, Poppy."

Evan moves forward instantly, an easy smile on his face and his hand outstretched to Connor. "Good to meet you. I've heard a lot about you, man."

"None of it good, I'm sure," Connor quips back, taking his hand in a firm yet polite handshake.

"Let's eat," Mom says, stopping that train before things can run off the rails. I get the feeling that Connor's right. Whatever Evan's heard, it probably wasn't good.

We go into the dining room, which despite the size and formality of the decor, is laid out with a homey casualness that tells me that even if Connor comes from a rich family with issues, their noses aren't so far in the air that they can't smell their own farts.

"How was your day, Evan?" Debra asks, opening a bottle of wine. "Ready for the big day?"

"Everything's ready," Evan says with relief. "My boss verified that my vacation is approved, and they even threw me a surprise wedding party in the break room." He turns to Caylee. "The gifts are in the car, and Janice wrote down the list as I opened them so we can do the thank you notes to everyone correctly."

Caylee smiles and pats his hand. "That is so sweet of her."

"She made the cake too, and though I didn't tell her, I am really hoping our wedding cake is tastier." Evan pauses dramatically, already grinning at his own joke before he tells it. "She made a fondant 'ball and chain' decoration. Cute idea, but in execution, it looked like dog turds made of chocolate. Kinda killed the *yum* factor."

Soft laughter rings the table, at least from most of us. Connor merely snorts, his lips twitching while Robert says nothing, like he didn't even hear the joke. But everyone seems to just let that slide as food's passed around and plates are filled.

"So, Poppy, what do you do?" Caylee asks. "Connie never told us."

"Connie?" I quip, giving Connor a raised eyebrow. He glowers but doesn't correct his sister, which tells me more than ever about them. "Well, I've done a lot of things, to be honest. But I'm an author working on my second book, *Trouble in Great Falls*."

"Is that so?" Debra asks, but a second later, her eyes widen. "Wait . . . you're *that* Poppy Woodstock? I read your book! Connor, how did you find yourself a gem like her?"

"I'd say he stole me more than anything else," I tease Connor, who growls, though I'm not sure if it's at my tease about stealing or his mom's implication that he could never score a find like me. "Seriously, how could I have resisted this big glowery look of his? And I take it as a personal challenge to massage away that frown line on his forehead." I play the odds and gently run my finger along the line in question, feeling victorious when he doesn't flinch away but instead stares directly into my eyes, allowing it.

"Good luck with that," Caylee says. "Connor's had that since I was a baby, at least."

"Speaking of babies . . ." Debra says, and I have to snort as Caylee puts on an expression that makes her look so much like her brother it's scary.

"Mom, repeat after me," Caylee says, taking Evan's hand. "Wedding, honeymoon, and then, sometime in the future, babies." It sounds as though they've had this conversation before. "But if you keep asking, I'm going to be forced to tell you, in detail, about all the ways we're 'practicing', and neither of us wants that. Keep your nose out of my uterus, and I promise I'll tell you when there's something to tell."

"Caylee," Debra gasps. I swear if she had on pearls, she'd be clutching them.

But Caylee shrugs, "You're the one who asked about the potential results of my sex life at the dinner table. You get what you get."

I make several mental notes, wishing I could write them down because Caylee is character inspiration come to life and sitting across the table from me. I'm in writer heaven.

Small talk continues, with Caylee getting asked a lot about the wedding without another mention of babies while Caylee and Debra both toss questions my way about me and Connor. Connor answers most of them, but I deal with more than my fair share as well. It's fun, vibing with Connor and trying to weave my truth into the fictions that Connor may have told his family.

Thankfully, his lack of communication with them leaves me plenty of holes to slip my facts into. One strange thing, though, is how Robert Bradley doesn't say anything. In fact, Connor's father has been silent since I shook his hand, and even then, I think he only offered it out of social habit.

Since then, he's appeared distant, merely sipping on his drink and shifting food around his plate. Connor isn't really all that much better except when someone speaks to him directly, though I've seen him giving that patented glare to his dad a couple of times. They're obviously not close, and Connor said as much when we were talking about what to expect tonight, but I didn't expect this degree of ice between the two men.

Actually, it's not just between them. There seems to be a thick wall around Robert Bradley that keeps everyone at arm's length. He's practically an island in the room with his own family. Ironically, as much as that seems to bother Connor, he's doing the same thing to his mother and sister.

We're mid-meal when the doorbell rings. Connor instantly tenses up at my side, and I don't understand why. I look at him questioningly, and he seems to be consciously choosing to relax. His shoulders drop incrementally, his jaw unclenches, and he takes a deep breath.

"Who's that?" Robert says, his first words since sitting down.

"I'll go see," Debra says, getting up from the table. She goes into the foyer, and moments later, we can hear her surprised greeting. "Oh, I wasn't expecting you for a few more days. We were right in the middle of dinner."

Another female voice says, "Good. I'm starving. I'm sure you've got *something* worth eating."

The tension around the whole table ratchets up at that voice. Well, I don't get more tense, but that's because I have no idea what the hell's going on. I seriously feel like I just got dropped into one of those dinner theater mysteries, except that I have no character cards, and so far, there's no body on the floor. But maybe that part is still coming? I eye Connor and then his father, deciding they're the too-easy suspects. I slide my eyes to Evan, the nice, polite newcomer, and decide he's either the victim or the murderer of the yet-to-happen pretend death.

An older woman and a young man appear in the dining room doorway, Debra's face is stony as she leads them in. "Audrey, Ian, this is Poppy, Connor's fiancée. Poppy, this is Connor's aunt, Audrey, and his cousin, Ian."

Ah, the whole picture becomes clear now. If this were a dinner mystery theater, I could now clearly declare 'the game is afoot!' This is the aunt and cousin Connor told me about. Interesting that he's not the only one who seems to hate them, but everyone in the room is noticeably more tense now, even Robert.

Audrey looks a lot like her sister, if you dipped Debra in glitter and then told her to go Rodeo Drive on everything. Her outfit's clearly designer, her jewelry's flashy, her makeup is pristine, and her hair is a shade of blonde that only comes from an entire day in the salon chair.

And Ian is somehow just as I pictured him to be—slick and polished looking, a guy who you can tell lives on Daddy's money and thinks his shit doesn't stink. I've written characters like him before. They always end up being the bad guy or the annoying as hell character who gets put in his place on a constant basis and serves as a distraction from the real bad guy. Funny to think that I'm sitting here with an actual criminal at my side as my fake fiancé, but Ian seems to be the villain in the room.

Audrey pulls up a chair without asking and begins criticizing the dinner she hasn't even tasted yet. Not that she was even invited to. "Pork roast and potatoes? How quaint and . . . basic. Ian, when was the last time we had a roast? It must've been in that little chalet restaurant in Switzerland, right?"

Ian nods, though I don't think he's even listening to his mother. His eyes are locked on me. I'm the outlier here, the newcomer who grabs interest, and with my red hair, I'm used to attention. Connor, however, places an arm across the back of my chair possessively like Ian's sniffing around his territory a bit too much. "Good to see you, Ian. What're you up to these days?"

Before Ian can answer, Audrey jumps in, bragging about her son. "Oh, Ian purchased another five properties this year. That brings it up to fifty now, I think." She looks to Ian but doesn't wait for him to respond. "He's quite the real estate tycoon. Real estate investment is the only way to go these days," she tells me arrogantly. "It's the smart money."

"That's true," Connor says generously. But then, he sends the bomb he set himself up for. "All you need is Mommy and Daddy's money to buy property and a management company to do all the work. It's a foolproof gig, if you can get it."

It hits home, and Audrey makes a sound of huffed displeasure. "Well, it's better than being a *thug*."

"To-may-to, to-mah-to," Connor says, refusing to be drawn in at Audrey's level. "We're all stealing in our own ways. I'm sure the people Ian buys from think he's quite the con man, buying their houses for bottom dollar, slapping a couple of hundred bucks' worth of paint and some polish on them, and then renting them back out at top dollar. At least I'm honest about what I do."

Not thinking, I place my hand on Connor's thigh and squeeze. "What you did, sweetheart. You're reformed now, remember?"

It feels good to remind Connor of the story he told me he'd shared with his parents, of a fiancée who helped him find the straight and narrow and become a business consultant.

I wonder what it would it take to make Connor's lie a reality.

He looks down at my hand on his leg. His very muscular, thick thigh that I want to squeeze again. As I'm trying to decide if he wants me to remove my hand, Connor covers it with his own, holding me in place. "Yes, reformed. But let's be real . . . business is a cut-throat world, and we're all crooks to some degree."

He sounds more dangerous with that statement than with any other I've heard pass his lips. So why do I stay in my chair, sitting at his side primly with my hand on his thigh, and not run from the danger in the room? Because he's tracing my fingers gently, slowly, almost reverently as he utters the growled threat.

He might be a crook. He might be dangerous, for all I know. But that touch tells me that he's not dangerous *to* me . . . but he might be dangerous *for* me. In a good way.

It's a very subtle and very intoxicating difference.

Debra tries to break the awkwardness and returns to a seemingly safe topic . . . weddings. "Oh, Poppy . . . I didn't get to see your ring. May I?"

"Oh . . . uh . . ." I stammer, clenching my hand under the table as if that could make a ring suddenly appear. "Well, I don't have it tonight. It's—"

"At the jewelers," Connor says quickly. I give him a look, lifting one brow as if to say, 'Is it that easy to lie?' His answer is to blink slowly and take a casual sip of his wine like he's handing the rest to me.

"Yes, sorry about that. It's at the jewelers. Connor said I could get the ring of my dreams, so they're custom-designing the wedding band to go around the solitaire and getting it all sized for me because once I put that baby on, I'm never taking it off." I smile sweetly at Connor, doing my best to make it look like I've got heart bubbles in my eyes.

See, I can do this! I tell him silently. *But you've gotta work with me.*

"That's so sweet," Caylee gushes, clearly vibing on the romance of the whole evening. She's got love, so her brother has to have love too, right? "Custom rings?"

"He's probably making layaway payments on it," Audrey quips under her breath, but I'm sure she intentionally said it loud enough to be heard. Ian chuckles, smirking at Connor like his mother got one over.

Debra, with some surprising bite of her own, sugar-sweetly asks, "Isn't that what Harold had to do with your ring?" Then she waves a hand, "Oh, silly me, I forgot, you bought it yourself, didn't you?"

Jeez, this family's a soap opera in the flesh.

Audrey looks like she sucked on a lemon covered in warhead powder. "I did. Because I married for love. Not for money."

She looks from Debra to Robert with disdain, and next to me, I can feel Connor vibrating like a racehorse about to burst out of the gate . . . except I think what he's holding back from is letting his rage explode all over this room.

Caylee saves the day as she rolls her eyes and huffs loudly. "Could we not? I'm getting married in one week, and I really don't need World War Three breaking out between the two of you between now and then. Let's call it a draw, retire to your respective corners, and you can pick up this fight again after the wedding."

It seems like Connor's not the only one tired of whatever this battle is between his mom and aunt. Caylee's right. She's got a lot on her plate, and dealing with childish adults shouldn't be one of them.

Debra tilts her head at Caylee, giving in though I can see the continuing words of anger she'd like to spit at her sister sitting on the tip of her tongue. Audrey starts, "Of course, dear. You know we're all here for you. It's your day—"

"Good," Caylee says, cutting her off. "Now, Connor . . . you'll be there, right? I need my brother there for my wedding. I'm only doing this once, you know?"

He's shaking his head before she even gets the question out. "Caylee, no. Dinner, that's all I promised, and I'm here."

He seems to conveniently have forgotten that it's me who agreed to dinner, not him. My heart twists as I see the disappointment in Caylee's eyes. But a million points for Evan as he looks lovingly at her, wishing he could take this pain away. Audrey looks triumphant, especially as Debra takes a heavy drink of her wine. And Robert looks resigned, as if he never expected more from his bad seed son.

"Of course, he'll be there. We both will." I don't squeeze Connor's thigh this time. I flat-out pinch him, daring him to disagree. When he makes a sound of shocked pain, I do it again, pinching up higher, dangerously close to the Jolly Green Giant's beanstalk zone and reminding him that I fight dirty. "Isn't that right, babe? We wouldn't miss Caylee's wedding for anything in the world."

As the words pop out of my mouth, Connor's glare turns up to level eleven. Huh, who would've thought he had more intensity than the glares he's already given me? Certainly not me, but the proof is right there in his gaze.

Uh-oh.

I might be in real trouble now.

CHAPTER 9

CONNOR

*I*f looks could kill, I would murder Poppy where she sits at my family's dining room table. In fact, like my coffee mug suggests, I'm thinking of at least seven ways to do it right here, right now. I could probably bury her curvy, sexy little body out back in the treed part of my family's property and no one would be the wiser.

Not that I've ever done that. I might be a thief, a bastard, and a lying shit who walks out on everyone and everything, but I'm not a murderer.

But she's tempting me. In multiple ways, which scares the hell out of me because no matter how hard I try, I cannot control or predict this woman. All I can do is adapt on the fly and see if it leads to disaster or not.

This time, though, as much as it pisses me off, it seems to be the right thing to say because Caylee shouts and claps, "Oh, my gosh! Thank you so much, Poppy! And you too, Connor! It means so much to me!"

She claps again, and I can see how happy she is. I'm not exactly close to Caylee these days, but once upon a time, we were thick as thieves. No pun intended. And for some reason, it means something to her that I'm there. Even if she doesn't need an asshole like me fucking up her happy day.

"Excuse us for a minute," I tell the table before I drag Poppy into the hallway. She stumbles after me, trying to keep up with my long strides in her heels. I whirl, backing her into a wall and looming over her. Getting right in her face, I demand, "What the fuck was that?"

Her eyes cut back to the dining room, where I'm guessing they're listening closely to every word we say. But I'm doing this on purpose. I'm being the asshole so that we can end all of this now before someone gets even more hurt. When her eyes return to mine, they're flashing with warning as she whispers, "It's your sister's wedding. Did you see how happy she is? You have to go."

"No. I don't. I don't *have* to do anything," I argue, not bothering to keep my voice down. I want them to hear me. It'll suck, of course. But it's better that way. For us all, Caylee especially. As much as I hate to hurt her, she needs to know that she can't count on me, not for this. I stand up straight, stubbornly unwilling to debate something that's not even an option.

"Connor—" Poppy pleads quietly, and I fight to let it roll off my back.

I can't let it develop. Not what she's doing. Not what she's awakening inside me. I can't have it. It's not meant for people like me.

Trying to keep ahold of what's threatening to rise inside me, I interrupt whatever puppy dog-eyed plea she's about to unleash. Quietly this time, I remind her, "One day. Just one day as my fiancée. Dinner, that was all I agreed to, and that was only after you stepped in where you weren't wanted."

She flinches, and regret for my words is bitter on my tongue. I don't want to cause her pain . . . and for some reason I don't want to examine too closely, Poppy's pain turns me away from the path I know I should take, hurting her now to save her long-term devastation. "Shit. I didn't mean it like that."

"It's fine. I'm used to it," she says, ducking her head down. Suddenly, the fiery, mouthy spitfire is gone, replaced with someone small and unsure.

What . . . what's happened to her? Did I do that?

"Poppy," I try, leaning down closer, but she ducks even farther away from me. "Pops, look at me."

I don't even realize I'm doing it until my fingers touch the soft skin of her jaw, guiding her chin up and her eyes to mine. My thumb brushes back and forth, enjoying the silky feel of her cheek, and I say something that I've said maybe a handful of times in the past few years. I apologize. "I'm sorry. I didn't mean it like that. I'm the one who's not wanted here."

She licks her lips slowly, speaking carefully. "Connor, I don't think that's true. I think Caylee very much wants you here, and your mom does too. Not just because of whatever weird feud she's got going with Audrey and Ian, either." She shakes her head like she's trying to rattle all the thoughts in her head together before putting them into something logical, but there's no logic in that. So she lets them pour out regardless, imperfect and unfiltered. "I couldn't take it, their talking to you and about you like that. I barely know you, and you stole my laptop, but even I can tell that you're not the monster they make you out to be. Or that you make yourself out to be."

I'm surprised. No, I'm shocked to my very core. Poppy has no reason to defend me or to believe in me. I am quite literally the boogieman in her life, the monster who stole her lifeblood, but yet, she's defending me?

Why?

She seems softer, vulnerable as she looks up at me, waiting for me to disagree with her. But footsteps along the wood floor tell me someone's coming, and I act impulsively, something I never do.

I kiss her. This isn't some polite peck on the lips, either. I claim her, full-mouthed and passionate, no gentle caresses, no slow tasting. I kiss her like I've done it hundreds of times before and she's mine to kiss. Her hands reflexively lift to my chest, and for a second, I think she's going to push me away. She should. I absolutely deserve that and have done nothing to earn her kiss. But instead, her hands curl into my shirt, holding me in place.

I angle my head to get deeper, wanting more, and nip her bottom lip when she doesn't give in. When she gasps in surprise, I take advantage and push my tongue into her mouth.

I don't know what's come over me, but I like it, even as warning bells are going off loudly in my head. Poppy melts for me, matching my intensity without restraint or second thought. Her tongue fights with mine for control, something I refuse to give up.

Between my legs, I'm hard as a rock, wanting this fiery woman's body as well as her mouth. I push into her, our bodies aligned as I press her against the unyielding wall. Poppy's hands wrap around my neck, one leg lifting to rest her thigh on my hip, and I feel warm heat press against the bulge in my slacks.

My God, she wants me too. After all she's seen . . . and she wants me. I hold her leg there, squeezing the taut muscle with my strong palm, and she moans into my mouth.

I swallow the sound, wanting more of her passion.

"Ahem," a too-close voice says. Ian.

Poppy startles and jumps, her mouth leaving mine as she follows the sound, and I definitely want to pop my cousin in the nose for breaking us up. "Oh, uh . . . sorry."

Her apology is accompanied by a small giggle, like a schoolgirl who got caught by the principal making out in the hallway with a boy. But she is no girl, I'm not a boy, and Ian is definitely not worthy of being any sort of morality police. He might not be responsible for the rift between Mom and Aunt Audrey . . . but this apple did not fall far from the poisoned tree, and he's rotten to his core.

"I hated to interrupt the show, but you know . . ." He throws his head to side, indicating that the parents are all one wall away, listening raptly. The way he's looking at Poppy, though, has me furious, his greedy eyes tracking slowly up and down her body like he's noticing things about her that he has zero business noticing.

She's mine, asshole.

I don't know where the thought comes from, but I go with it, putting myself between Ian and Poppy to intentionally block his sightline, and snap sharply, "We'll be there when we're done with our discussion."

My unexpected anger only fuels Ian's interest, and his brow lifts as he smirks, "Discussion? Is that what it's called these days? Maybe you should deal with your mother's temper tantrum over the wedding drama, and I can have a *word* with Poppy. I'd be happy to explain the family history."

I'm certain any 'family history' he'd explain would amount to why I'm a piece of shit. Not that I'd give him a chance alone with Poppy. He thinks he's cute and clever, but he's slick and slimy, virtually licking his lips at whatever indecent image he's creating in his mind.

The mere thought strikes a dark chord in my gut, making me see red before I can even consider why I'm feeling possessive and protective of the redheaded spitfire currently peeking around my arm at Ian.

Strike that . . . the redhead who *was* behind me. Poppy moves deftly and gracefully around my body, one hand on her hip and one finger stabbing Ian in the chest, murder written on her face. "Does that sort of shit actually work for you or are you used to saying whatever you want because of the size of your wallet?"

She pokes him harder, her fingernail definitely causing a dent in the thin skin beneath his expensive shirt and cutting off any lame ass retort he can come up with. "Don't bother answering because we all know the answer, don't we? You couldn't 'explain' a damn thing to me. You're not capable of anything more than parroting what others say. So why don't you run along back to Mommy and let the grownups talk? Like Connor said, we'll be there when we're done with our discussion. However long it takes."

Ian looks at Poppy in shock and maybe a little pain as she digs in hard with her finger once more to send him on his way. Me, I'm in shock . . . and utterly delighted. And it's for the same reason. No one's ever told Ian off before, but she does it easily and without hesitation, cutting him exactly where it hurts the most.

Don't piss her off. She really can get your balls in her purse if she wants.

I store that tidbit away too.

The silence is deafening, both in the hallway and in the dining room beyond. Everyone is waiting for Ian's response. Except, of course, Poppy, who waits for no one and nothing. When Ian doesn't skip himself right back as instructed, Poppy waves her hand at him, shooing him. "Go on. Or I'm gonna step aside and let Connor tell you *in his way*."

I'm not some attack dog she can control, calling off or siccing me on people at will, but the twisted evil pleasure she gives those words is downright sexy as hell. And fine, beating the shit out of Ian would be a fucking dream come true. He's deserved it for a long time.

Too bad today's the not the day I get that chance because though he gives me one last glance, trying mightily to seem unbothered, when I take a step his way, he squeaks and runs back to the dining room.

When I glance down at Poppy, she's got her hands over her mouth, trying to cover the fit of giggles pouring forth. I give her a dark look, changing my trajectory and stepping closer to her menacingly. "You think blowing up my family is funny?"

She shrugs, still fighting her laughter and not concerned at all about the monster in her midst and manages to say, "Not your mom or Caylee." Pointing over her shoulder, she adds, "But him? Yeah, he deserves it. And it was funny."

She's right, but I hold my glare steadily, not willing to lose control again. I'm able to keep it up for a second or two until she makes a fear-filled face, her shoulders hunched up to her chin, and mouths, "Mommy! Help!" Her impression of Ian sends me over.

I can't stop the laugh that rumbles out of me. She's irreverent and wild, a rebel with zero fucks to give doing whatever she wants, which is somehow entertaining and interesting as hell.

Her hand goes to my chest, her palm flat over my sternum and her eyes locked there as well. "What?" I grunt, the laugh dying off instantly.

"Just wanted to feel that laugh," she says softly, earnestly. "I get the feeling you don't do that often."

She has no idea. I can't remember the last time I really laughed. Polite chuckles? Sure. Fake laughs for JP to grease the skids in our relationship? Of course.

But real laughter? I can't remember the last time I felt that sort of pure light feeling. But she pulled it out of me, and I think she could probably do it again if she wanted to. Hell, I might do it just because she asked me to.

"Don't know what you're talking about. I laugh all the time, a regular Chuckles the Clown," I deadpan.

"*Right*," she answers sarcastically, pinching my tie between her fingers and thumb and tugging me toward the dining room. "Then come on, Chuckles. Let's go tell your sister you're going to her wedding."

"We're not discussing that."

She looks at me wryly. "You're right. We're not. You know you're gonna go, I know you're gonna go, so can we skip the whole 'no, yes, no, yes' deal and get on with the important shit? Your mom said there's chocolate cake for dessert, and I haven't had cake in sixteen days. Do not get between me and cake, mister. You hear me?"

"Sixteen days?"

"Out of everything I said, that's what you heard?" she asks, then sighs. "A cupcake is my reward for benchmarks, and since I've had writer's block, I haven't been meeting them. No benchmark, no cupcake. But I'm making a special exception for your mom because nobody tells their fiancé's mom no, especially not about cake. And cake is different from a cupcake, anyway."

"No, it's not." Seriously. Flour, eggs, butter, chocolate, sugar. How is it different?

"Yes, it is," she growls. "A cupcake is a sexy muffin with icing. Cake is . . . cake."

"Cake by the ocean?"

"Now you've got jokes? About cake? Which is totally different from a cupcake." She glares at me, daring me to disagree with her repeat declaration. "Besides, since it's your fault I'm missing benchmarks now, I think it's only fair that I get cake out of the deal." She's being sassy and playing up her anger. And maybe a part of her is mad, but right now, that's not the emotion at the top of her roller coaster.

But the reminder of why she's here with me is sour, stabbing sharper than I would've expected. The laptop. It all comes back to that damn thing and my spontaneous solution to a problem. That's why I plan so much . . . so fuck-ups don't happen. And Poppy doesn't even know why I stole her laptop. What would she think if she knew? That I'm not some petty thief but that I stole *The Black Rose*?

She's digging into a sore spot—my perfectionist tendencies and need to keep everyone at arm's length. The irritation is growing, scratching just below the surface, looking for a way to lash out and inflict the most pain in return. And the hardest part of it all is . . . it's an irritation that I'm starting to think I might like, which only pisses me off more.

"You're really cute when you're angry," I say condescendingly, making it seem like I'm trying to irritate her right back. To add lighter fluid to the fire, I twirl a lock of her red hair around my finger, aiming for mindlessness but laser focused on her every reaction.

I knew pulling that grenade pin would cause an explosion, and it does. Her breath hitches, then goes jagged, her eyes widen and then narrow sharply, and she flicks her head, roughly yanking her hair from my grasp. With her head held high, she stomps right past me, intentionally bumping my arm with her shoulder.

I remind myself, *It's for her own good.*

Mine too, I think. Because her hair felt good, and again, I'm back to full mast in my slacks. I turn around, squeezing my eyes shut as I slowly count to ten and recenter myself.

It works until from behind me, I hear Caylee ask, "Did he say yes?"

I grind my teeth painfully as I wait for Poppy's answer, knowing I won. There's no way she's going to see me for anything other than exactly what I am and recognize that she needs to stay far, far—

"Yep, he'll be there. We'll be there. It's just one more teeny-tiny day, a few hours, really, but it's the most important one for you and Evan, and we wouldn't dream of missing it."

What the fuck?

But the damage is done. I hear Caylee's squeal and fast footsteps. "Thank you, Poppy!" Caylee says in a high-pitched voice. Before I know it, Caylee is in the hallway with me, happiness pinging off her like neon disco lights. She throws herself at me, hugging me tight. "I knew you wouldn't let me down, Connor. I don't think I could walk down that aisle if you weren't there."

Poppy's head peeks out of the dining room, and I look at her over Caylee's head, where she's still snuggled into me. I don't think she's hugged me in years. Poppy licks her fingertip and draws it through the air, giving herself a winning tally mark.

I'm going to kill her.

Or maybe kiss her again.

Maybe kiss her and then kill her, my mind suggests. It's a lot less Tim Burton that way.

CHAPTER 10

POPPY

"*And* then . . . oh, my God, Connor looked like . . . mmm-mmm!"

Around the table, I'm getting a mix of looks. Daysha looks amused while Becca's a little confused. "Connor?"

"You remember!" Jasmine says, hushing her. "The hot security guard, the guy who stole her laptop?"

"Oh . . . I thought . . . never mind," Becca says, grinning now. "Right, hot security Connor. I'm with you. Go on."

Go on. How in the hell do I do that? I feel like someone stuck a stick blender in my head and tapped the power button for a quick 'bloop'. I'm able to make some coherent thoughts, but half the time, I feel like I'm just swirling and trying to still make sense of everything.

"So anyway, after I jumped him—"

"You go, girl!"

"Not like that!" I correct Becca, who pouts. "I jumped on his back and beat the shit out of him. Or well, I tried. But he threw me to the ground."

Aleria doesn't look happy at that. "He violated your person?"

"Al, she did jump on him," Daysha says. "Rule in life. You start shit, expect shit. That's true for everyone."

"And I did end up kneeing him in the nuts," I point out, making Daysha give me a double-take.

"Oh, no, you didn't." She laughs. "That's cold."

"Yep," I affirm, grinning. "And he basically admitted to stealing my laptop."

"What did you do?" Jasmine asks. "Call the cops on him?"

I glare at Jasmine, my eyes asking if she entirely slept through the part about how unhelpful the police were with the whole missing laptop issue and how much I wanted to kill Detective Carter with my bare hands.

"Right, right. No cops. So, what did you do?"

"Uh, well . . . his phone rang, so I swiped it and told his mom that I'm his fiancée."

Around the table, the response is unified and simultaneous. "You *what*?"

"Well, I figured that if I called the cops, I wouldn't get anything," I try to explain, trying to give a reason for my instantaneous decision. "I mean, even if he ratted on his guy, it's not like that guy's going to just admit it, and so on and so forth. But anyway, he agreed to get my laptop back, and I didn't want to let him out of my sight. Plus, I need leverage, so I went to dinner with his family and pretended to be his fiancée."

"You . . . to the guy who stole your laptop?" Becca asks, confused again. I swear, how does she keep her characters straight when I'm only talking about two people—me and Connor—and she can't keep up.

"Well, it sounds weird when you say it like that."

Daysha snorts. "It is weird, woman!" she grins. "But go on."

"So, at dinner, they're all giving him shit, and they don't even know he's a thief!" I tell the hushed group. "So when the wedding came up, I said yes."

"What wedding?" Aleria asks. "Wait . . . you're marrying the guy who stole your laptop?"

"What?" I ask, shocked. "No! His sister's wedding. He got mad and dragged me into the hallway, and that's when we kissed."

"Kissed?" Jasmine asks with a raised eyebrow. "The laptop thief neighbor?" At least she's got it all straight. And now Becca is nodding, apparently thankful for the Cliff Notes.

"Okay, kissed doesn't begin to describe it," I admit with a happy sigh. "I've never been kissed like that, like I forgot my own name in a drunken haze."

I sit back, still in utter awe of the memory of last night.

I feel their eyes on me until finally, Daysha sighs too. "That's the best kind."

"Wait, badass Daysha has a big streak of gooey romance in her?" Becca teases. "Ooh, I gotta know more because I thought you were all whips and chains, 'take what I give you, my sweet slut', and emotionally damaged savior types. This is news!"

"One story at a time!" Aleria begs. "I have to keep them straight. But we're totally coming back to that."

Becca snorts. "You said coming."

Wanting to move on, I jump in before an argument can spring up. "So we're going to the wedding next weekend."

Aleria looks totally unfazed while the other girls look like I'm nuts. "What about the laptop? Your book?"

"Connor says he's working on it," I admit, pulling out my current replacement. "In the meantime, this'll work."

Jasmine scoffs. "Girl, you'd better get to 'working on it' yourself or Hilda is gonna skin you alive."

"I know! What do I do?" I ask the group, frazzled again. "About the laptop and book? About all of it! What sayeth the W3AS?"

We've been talking and even laughing at some of the outrageous things that have happened since I saw them last, but I'm serious now. I need their help and advice. The four women sober instantly, ready to stand steadfastly by my side.

Daysha sits up and fixes me with her light brown eyes. "Okay, focus. This Connor. He might be hot as hell, babe, but I don't trust him. Nothing personal, but he hasn't exactly given you a reason to trust him."

It definitely makes sense. And Daysha's always got her head screwed on nice and tight. "That's true, but I have a gut feeling about him. I feel like . . . there's more to him than what he lets people see."

"You should trust your gut instinct. Sometimes, the primal self knows things the intellectual mind hasn't figured out yet," Aleria says in all seriousness.

"Yeah, well, my gut's saying you want him all up in *yours*," Jasmine tells me. "And that can affect the accuracy of your instincts."

Also a valid point.

"Did he even say why he stole your laptop?"

"Uhm, no, actually." The girls look at each other knowingly, and even Aleria looks concerned. "Look, he didn't know about my being an author or about the book. I mean, it is a pretty good laptop, you know? He said that he gave it to someone."

"That doesn't even make sense," Jasmine says. "I mean, you're there in the middle of a whole room of bigwig writers, the whole thing. There was a whole room of fancy shit. Computers, books in progress, fancy purses, jewelry, and even the damn *Black Rose*! Why your laptop? Makes no sense."

"Exactly. Like I said—don't trust him," Daysha concludes as if Jasmine just argued her case for her. "Now, the second issue. You need to work at the same time you're figuring out this laptop deal. That's priority one. Write, write, and write some more. I don't care if you shower, shave, shit, or anything else. Hell, I'll have food delivered if that'll help because you need to write like you've never written before, starting now."

Daysha's right, and a good friend. She would make sure I'm fed if that's all I needed to get this book done. She would also come stay at my place and spank me with a ruler every time I pause if that's what I needed. I could do with the former and hope it doesn't come to the latter.

We get to work, and I have to say I'm in a rhythm that I haven't felt in a long time. I still haven't dropped back to the sex scenes yet, but the chapter I'm working on right now? Oh, it's flowing like water.

Finally, Becca closes her laptop. "There. Sprint one done. Now Pops, I know you need to work, but we need to address the elephant in the room. The not-book one. Tell me more about that kiss."

"It was . . ." I start before shaking my head in disbelief. "It was the best kiss I've ever had. Is it crazy if I want to kiss him again? Even after he stole my laptop?"

"Yep," everyone says at once.

"Yes, totally crazy," Jasmine repeats. Seeing my crestfallen expression, she reaches over and shakes my shoulder before I can drop into a deep pout. "Hey, that's not a bad thing. I've known you're crazy for as long as I've known you. Doesn't surprise me in the least."

"I don't know . . . this could be a bad idea," Becca says, but she's quickly hushed by everyone else.

"Poppy," Aleria says, "the universe wants us to find happiness. To follow our hearts and make connections along our journey. There is a purpose to this moment, this craziness, as you call it, and though you might not see it yet, it will all be revealed when the time is right. Understand?"

"Yes, follow your heart, just make sure to bring your head along for the ride," Daysha warns a bit more cynically, but then she shrugs, giving in. "I guess you never know. It might be the ride of a lifetime."

CHAPTER 11

CONNOR

The coffee shop is rather busy, but that's actually a good thing. When everyone's off in their own world, nobody's going to notice me as I settle onto a stool at the bar top in front of the big window. From here, I can see the world outside go by.

It's your typical weekday morning, with men and women in suits mixing with college students in much more relaxed outfits. There's the occasional worker in a uniform of one kind or another, a delivery driver, a postal worker, or even the occasional restaurant worker adding distinct bits of color to the mix. Everyone flows by, only aware of themselves, their own agendas and plans, oblivious to each other and their surroundings for the most part.

It's honestly fascinating, though I feel so outside of that type of existence.

I take a sip before setting my cup down with the coffee shop's logo facing the street and then subtly watch as a man at the bus stop across the street gets up to head to the shop. He enters, orders, and comes over to sit down next to me. Taking a sip of his drink, he groans. "Getting so hot out there, I'm going to have to switch to some vanilla iced latte shit like I'm a sorority girl named Madison."

"Nah, black coffee only. No substitutes."

All the proper security protocols complete, Hunter gives me a glance. "Wasn't expecting to hear from you so soon, Connor."

We've traded code and counter code, so he's able to speak more freely, though we're still, and always, aware of our surroundings. There's a reason we use this particular chain of coffee shops for these meetings. They like to use polarized windows for privacy, which give us not only a view of the outside but ghostly reflections of the shop around us.

"Couldn't be helped. I need your input on something."

Hunter looks at me in surprise, his brows jumping up before they furrow. "My input?"

I grunt, thinking maybe I shouldn't have called for this meet and greet. But more than being a resource that provides me with a place to stay when I need to lie low and occasionally help me with gigs when it's a two-man job, Hunter is about the closest thing I have to a friend. And though this is well beyond the scope of our usual conversations, I'm hoping he'll be a good sounding board and help me think with my head instead of my dick.

He recovers his usually stoic expression and offers a second run at a reaction. "What do you have? Hit me with it."

That's more in line with what I expected him to say, but I take a slow sip of my coffee, enjoying making him wait. "I met someone."

His insulated cup claps against the Formica bar top, his eyes going wide as he stares at me in shock. "You what?"

"It gets worse." I look out the window, purposefully focusing outside because I don't want to see the reflection of his reaction. I already know what it's going to be, anyway. "I met her on a job. The dinner."

"Son of a bitch, Connor," he hisses, sounding not only angry but disappointed. "You fucking know better than to do shit like that! What does she know?"

"Nothing," I sigh. "Remember I told you there were some complications?" In my peripheral vision, I see him nod. "She's one of them. I needed a bag and grabbed the closest one I could remember. It was hers, and I didn't know it, but her laptop was in it."

"So what? She can cry it out and go buy a new one. Or you can make a secret donation if you feel that guilty," Hunter says coldly. "There's no going back."

"She's my neighbor. She knows it was me."

Hunter sits up straight at that, facing me fully after looking around the room. I know he sees what I see . . . every exit, every person having their mid-morning caffeine hit, and every risk factor in the room. But as far as danger goes, there are only two possible threats . . . him and me.

"You're serious."

"Dead fucking serious," I tell him. "You put me right next door to her."

"Fuck me. Of all the . . ." Hunter trails off, pinching the bridge of his nose. But he recovers quickly. "Well, what does she really know?"

"Nothing about the job. She thinks I'm a petty thief who stole her laptop, that's it," I reply, and Hunter relaxes a hair. "But I need it back. It's got something on it she needs."

I'll give this to him. Hunter doesn't ask what or question what I'm thinking further. He just focuses on the important matter at hand. "Where is it?"

"I gave it to JP. He said he was gonna give it to his kid."

Hunter laughs darkly.

"I need a meeting with JP. Tomorrow. Anywhere, anytime. I need to talk to him, and you're the only person I know who might be able to make that happen."

Hunter scoffs. "That's not how this works and you fucking know it. JP calls you. It doesn't work the other way around."

"Make it work," I warn Hunter evenly, draining the rest of my coffee. "Or I'll track him down myself."

Hunter stares at me, taking my measure. "You've been doing shit for JP for months, working your way up. And you're willing to throw away a shot at the big leagues for some piece of ass."

I stand, my boots thumping loudly on the floor. For reasons I don't understand, and really don't want to understand, my hand is around Hunter's neck in an instant to stop him from saying anything else about Poppy. Deep in my gut, I know one thing for sure—if Hunter says one more insulting word about her, I'll kill him right fucking here. He can draw his last breath among the spilled remains of his coffee, for all I care.

"Set it up, Hunter."

His eyes bulge as he nods, his chin digging into my hand. At his agreement, I let him go. Turning to walk out, I realize that everyone in the entire coffee shop is staring at us, and I can see at least two people already reaching for their phones.

Quickly, I switch into a character and laugh, throwing my hands out. "My bad, folks. He said Backstreet Boys were better than N'Sync. Can you believe that shit? N'Sync forever, man."

A few people titter uncomfortably, but someone quietly sings, "It's gonna be *may*."

Hunter clears his throat uncomfortably but covers for us with a horridly off-key attempt. "Backstreet's back, all right. Forever *and ever*."

I force a smile to my face, hoping it looks natural and congenial. I'm not known for faking nice and harmless anymore, but I can still pull it out when I need to. Thankfully, it works, and hands fall away from phones, but eyes from all over the room follow me as I walk out the door.

I'm only a few stores down when my phone buzzes in my pocket.

H: Consider it done. I'll text with time and place. Hope she's worth it.

Me fucking too, man.

Me too.

Maybe the universe is trying to tell me something, but after a week of stellar weather and flawless skies, the clouds decide to open up. It's not a drizzle, either. It's raining cats and dogs and soaks everything in town.

But I made a promise, and I have an appointment. Hunter texted me the meet info, and I know I'm putting everything in jeopardy by calling JP like this. I no-show this, it's not just Poppy that I'm hurting. I'm hurting myself because you don't make a man like JP stand around for a no-show. It's not a good investment in your retirement plans.

Turning up the collar on my jacket, I adjust my baseball cap to shield my eyes and speed-walk out to my truck, hopping in only to find Poppy sitting in the passenger seat already. "Where are we going?"

"Son of a bitch!" I yell, shocked and surprised . . . and a little scared. How'd I miss her? And does she know how close she came to getting unintentionally punched between the eyes? "How'd you get in here? And nowhere. Get out."

"A lady never tells her secrets. And yes, you are. And no. I'm sticking on you like Gorilla Glue." She presses her palms together with an evil smile. "So, where are we going?"

"You're not going. Don't you have to walk Nut and Juice?"

"Already did it," she says, "and they hate the rain." She tilts her head, reconsidering. "But they love their doggie rain boots. Nut's are yellow, and Juice's are red. I considered blue for both because 'blue boots' is kinda close to 'blue balls', and that's funny considering their names, but then they'd fight over them. So I got two colors because they fight enough as it is."

I blink, not sure what the hell she's talking about. I got lost somewhere around rain boots for dogs.

"Where. Are. We. Going?" she repeats slowly and precisely like she's not the one who spent the last ninety seconds talking about her dogs' color and weather preferences.

I growl, sighing in frustration. "*I'm* going to get info about the laptop."

"You mean 'get my laptop'," she corrects. I shrug, not worrying about that grammar point, and she growls back. She probably thinks it's mean and threatening, but little does she know, it's fucking adorable. "I'm coming along."

"No."

"Yes."

I'm wasting time. By the time I could get Poppy out of my truck, the truck might have rusted to dust around us. JP would definitely think I'd ghosted him. But maybe . . . yeah, it's possible. Bring her along, ditch her for a few minutes to meet JP, and she'll be none the wiser. "Fine. But you have to do as I say. These are dangerous people, Pops."

She looks a little nervous at that, but she steels her spine and says, "Let's go."

We drive downtown to the University Art Museum where JP requested our meeting. I'm not surprised. UAM's security isn't as good as it seems, and I suspect JP or someone in Big's organization recruits their forgers from the local fine arts program. Also, he's more interested in the amount of money a piece can bring on the black market, but he's got a good eye. He has to so he knows if something is worth the risk of obtaining.

"Let's check out the 'Techno Landscapes' exhibit," I tell Poppy, knowing that will get us close to the meeting point with JP. Poppy agrees, and we enter the newest of the exhibits. It's a curated assortment with some professional pieces mixed in with the best of the fine arts student pieces.

"This one has good technique," I mention as we stop in front of a painting of a car junkyard. She stares at it, but I can tell she doesn't see what I see. "The way the steel pipe is so straight . . . you can't do that without using some kind of edge to guide your brush. But to do that without blurring your base layers . . . that's skill."

"I see it," Poppy says, looking closely. "I never thought of it before."

"Check out the way they use light and shadow too. Here, the shadows make the still-formed car look slightly threatening and oversized while the light on the crushed vehicle remains in the background give them a sort of angelic feel. It's quite a statement," I add, leaning in. I note the artist's name, filing it away. This is a name I could see having to steal one day.

"You know a lot about art," Poppy says, giving me a curious look.

"Art Appreciation 101," I tell her dismissively, hating the lie but knowing that saying anything more is dangerous. "Same as most people."

"Yeah, well, most people don't get out of that class with much more than an ability to identify a few Monets on sight. But not you," she says appreciatively. "And I happen to think smart guys are sexy."

We're in dangerous territory again. She just can't get it through her stubborn head that I'm bad news for her, but I've got to keep trying to get her to see reason. "I get the feeling that you think everyone, and everything, is sexy. I'm a thief? Sexy. Family drama? Ooh, baby. Obscure knowledge about boring shit? And you're dropping to your knees to suck me off in the middle of Techno Landscapes of the 21st Century."

She blinks in shock at my vulgar words. Time to seal the deal.

"Even now, you're deciding whether you like me talking like that, but your pulse is racing in your neck, telling me everything I need to know."

She flushes, not in embarrassment but in fury. Exactly what it should be. "You think you're so smart? You don't know anything about me! Maybe my pulse is racing because I'm disgusted by your filthy mouth, you animal. Men should be gentlemen. Like in my books."

Gentlemen . . . yeah, that'd be a nice dream for me as well. But life doesn't operate that way, and I left that option behind a long time ago. "If you expect men to be gentlemen, then it only makes sense that women would have to be ladies."

"Are you suggesting I'm not a lady?" she snaps as I look her up and down.

"Not suggesting. Flat out saying it."

"Oh!" she huffs. Her cheeks are nearly the same red as her hair now, bright and splotchy with anger.

"And your books are fiction," I remind her bitterly. "Women think they want some sweet, romantic guy to sweep them off their feet and treat them like a princess."

"I suppose you know better?" she asks sarcastically.

"Some women do want that. But not you, Poppy Woodstock," I tell her in a harsh whisper as a couple walks through the gallery. Thankfully, they catch the vibe in the room and continue on their merry way. "You'd walk all over a guy like that. You need someone strong enough to stand up to you and put up with your mouth. Someone who won't bat an eye when you do something crazy, running off half-cocked when you don't even know the whole story. Hell, when you don't even know half of it."

"And you think that's you? The rough, tough, bad boy who's going to give me what I need." There's hope in her voice, a subliminal admission of the truth in my words. She wants a partner, and in me, she recognizes someone strong enough to be that for her.

But I can't let that hope live. Not for either of us.

"No. I'm going to get your laptop back . . . and then ditch you."

The truth hurts me more than it hurts her, but my reaction is visceral and hidden, a skill I learned long ago. Poppy reacts like I punched her in the heart, her face going red, her eyes lighting with flames of anger, and her hands balling at her side. I consider the odds of her hitting me given her previous attack, but I suspect she's mostly a verbal warrior, so I don't give her a chance to fire back with words that won't be true.

While she's still prepping her argument, I finish with another bitter dose of truth serum. "And I'll move on, and you'll be glad you dodged this bullet."

I thump my chest with a palm, hurting myself at the same time. Because I fucking hate it, hate myself for what I've become. Not a man but a bullet aimed and fired by the people who hire me. Eventually, I'll likely die by their hand too.

For her own good, Poppy doesn't need to be mixed up with me.

She inhales sharply, holding my gaze while she holds her breath.

"Breathe, Pops. You're trying to look mad, but all you're doing is pushing your tits all up in my face." I trace the line of her cleavage with my eyes, licking my lips with hunger for something I know I'll never taste.

She's a connection I can't have, can't risk.

Her chest deflates with a sigh of defeat. "I really was trying to give you a compliment. About your knowing all about the art stuff." She waves her hand around the gallery we're in. "I didn't mean to start a fight. Or whatever this is."

"A conversation," I tell her sadly, though now that I've won, I try to soften her loss with a small dose of humor. "The truth. A fight is fists and blood. And so far, neither of us is bleeding." I hold my hands out to show that they're clean despite knowing that invisible stains mar my entire soul.

"Yet," she threatens with a sly smirk, though I can tell she's forcing herself to play along. "You never know."

She moves on to the next painting, and for some reason, I feel like as hard as I was, as hurtful as I was . . . it's somehow made her resolve even stronger.

What do I have to do to convince this woman that I'm the worst thing to ever happen to her life?

A few minutes later, I see JP in the next room. He doesn't acknowledge me, but I know he's aware that I'm here.

"Poppy," I tell her quietly, "hit the bathroom for a minute. Down this hall, second door. Give me five."

She looks at me in surprise. "What?"

"Don't argue. Do what I say, remember?" I growl. "For your own damn good."

She wants to argue, I know she does. I can see the words on her tongue, but at the serious look on my face, she thinks better of it and struts down the hall. I don't have time to enjoy the show of her hips swaying this time. I've got work to do.

I enter the next room, part of the university's permanent collection, the highlight of which is a collection of landscapes by an artist who grew up in the area. It's a bit of a lens back in time to years when cows roamed in fields that now support an airport.

JP's studying a piece, sitting down on a bench as he looks at a picture of an old church picnic during the Great Depression. "It's a lovely piece," he says. "Nice color," he adds dryly. Given that it's a black and white photo on canvas, I think it's his version of a joke.

"*Sunday Spring,*" I offer. "One of my favorites in this collection."

"You called this meeting. Supposedly something important? I don't believe it's this." He points at the large canvas in front of us, already dismissing it.

"The last job, the laptop I gave you. I need it back."

JP scoffs, side-eyeing me. "No laptop. Gave it to my son. He took it to work."

"Shit. Are you serious?"

JP nods. "Why do you need it?"

"There's something important on it that I didn't realize was there."

JP, ever the financially focused criminal, hums in interest. "Valuable?"

"Not quite, but it definitely has high sentimental value to a certain party," I tell him, shading the truth a little. If JP thinks he can get money out of this, he will. I'd prefer not to do that if I can avoid it. "Look, I'll buy your kid a replacement, an upgrade even, whatever. I just need it back."

JP eyes me for a long moment, trying to figure out how much I'm lying to him. Oh, I know he's assuming some lie. That's the way people like us operate. But it's in the levels of deceit that we build our trust, ironically. After a moment, figuring he doesn't have anything to lose, he nods. "You know Pupusa?"

"Salvadoran restaurant," I reply, knowing the name.

"He just got started there, trying to do it legit," JP says. "He works in the kitchen, name's Manuel. Don't fuck around with my kid."

Or else doesn't need to be said. Instead, I nod evenly. "I won't. This isn't about that. Just the laptop. I know it's a big leap of faith to share that info with me."

"Very much so."

I give him a second nod. "A sign of our friendship."

He nods back, but the truth is unspoken. JP and I aren't friends.

Colleagues?

Maybe.

Accomplices? Definitely.

But I really won't hurt his kid. That's not who I am. Or at least, I try to not be that guy, and in this instance, I can fulfill this promise to JP while fulfilling the one I made to Poppy.

"I'll let my son know you're coming." JP gets up, rubbing his hands together and leaving without offering a handshake. A minute later, Poppy comes back, finding me sitting alone and still studying the landscape.

"Let's eat."

She turns her head, looking at me like I've lost my damn mind. I've intentionally pushed her away, treated her like crap . . . and now I want food?

"Seriously?"

CHAPTER 12

POPPY

*H*e doesn't say much on the drive across town, but that's okay. Because despite all his harshness, all his mean words, the fact that I'm sitting in the passenger seat of his truck says a lot.

I'm still curious, though, when we pull up in front of a restaurant called Pupusa. "We're here."

"I figured," I tell Connor as he gets out, once again not coming around to open my door. It's pretty damn clear what he's doing, trying to push me away. And if I were smart, I'd probably listen to his warnings and stop trying.

We go inside and sit down in a booth. The place is bright with colors, from the orange-red of the floor tiles to the vibrant blue spelling out the restaurant name in a mural along one wall.

Connor looks around while I take a quick glance at the laminated menu, unsure what he's looking for. Finally, I decide that there are things more important than my grumbling stomach.

"Did you get my laptop?" I ask for the tenth time. Yup, I decided that if he's going to try and push me away, I'm going to show him how doggedly stubborn I can be. At first, he didn't answer, but I knew I was making progress when he resorted to grunts. I need some answers, damn it. I *need* my laptop. So I'll keep asking. "Helloooo . . . did you get it?" Make that eleven times.

"No."

"So we're grabbing a quick bite and then going to get it, I presume?" It's a question but also . . . not. If he thinks filling me with tamales is going to get me to leave him alone, I'll prove to him that I can tamale him right under the table.

"I told you I was getting information. I did. Now we're here. Eat."

He grabs a chip from the basket between us and bites into it. The crunch sounds final. But I'm not done, not remotely close to it.

"What information? Where is it? When do I get it back?" I look at the door, grabbing my purse as I slide toward the edge of the booth. "Let's go get it now."

Quick as a flash, Connor reaches across the table, placing his hand over mine. The touch of his skin against mine is electric, and I freeze, my body tingling with the sensation. It's just my hand, but the way he makes me feel, I can't move. "No. We're not going anywhere. Not yet."

I swallow back the shock, searching his face through narrowed eyes. "What? Why?"

Connor releases my hand, his lips twitching up in a half smile. "Anyone ever tell you that you ask a lot of questions?"

"More people than you can imagine," I reply with a snort. "Better ones than you, too." The dig is a leftover snipe from our earlier fight popping back up because I'm desperate to get my laptop back and lashing out.

But Connor doesn't take the bait. "Don't doubt that a bit."

Well, that didn't get the reaction I wanted. "Look, Connor. Whatever I need to do, wherever we need to go, can we please get to it?"

"We are."

"What?" I snap. Connor looks at me, one brow lifted in expectation. It's then that it all clicks together.

"It's here, isn't it? My laptop is here!" I say.

"Shh," he shushes me. "And no. But the new owner is."

Okay, maybe I didn't 'say' that so much as shout it. At least one table looks over at us, a woman giving me a strange look before going back to her conversation with her tablemate. Quieter, I say, "Where?"

"Calm down first," he orders. I do my best, curling in and pressing my hands into my lap, but I'm buzzing with energy and hope, bouncing in the seat. "That'll do, I guess," he says sarcastically. "My contact gave it to his kid who's at work."

Connor gestures to the restaurant around us, and it makes sense now. I could so kiss him, and not just in a 'let's get it on' sort of way. At the least, I wish he were still holding my hand, but when he lays his down on the table, one over the other, I clasp mine in my lap.

Looking around, everyone in the room suddenly becomes the potential possessor of my laptop. Connor said 'at work', so it's probably one of the staff. But all I see is a couple of waitstaff and one bored looking girl standing behind the cash register, examining her nails.

"What's his name?" I demand, ready to pat down search everyone in the restaurant if I have to. I said I'd do anything, and I well and truly meant it. Though maybe paying a ransom would be preferable to kidnapping or assault?

Hmm, I wonder if that would be a good plot arc for my story? Maybe my hero has to rescue the heroine after she's kidnapped? It is called Trouble in Great Falls, *so that would track.*

Now that I'm so close to getting it back, my writer's block seems to have totally crumbled, and all I can think of are story possibilities. Maybe even ideas for a third book? I open my mouth to say something to Connor but stop when a waitress walks up and asks, "Welcome, what can I get you to drink?"

Connor smiles at her, his face transforming as he does. "Two waters, please. And can you tell Manuel I'm here? He's expecting me."

The congenial smile and the polite tone are completely unlike the Connor I know. The waitress smiles back at him like I'm not sitting right here, and a very unexpected flash of jealousy surges inside me.

Pointedly, I lay my hand over his and stoically tell the waitress, "Us. Manuel is expecting *us*."

If I could piss on Connor to claim him as my territory, I would. But it seems unneeded because the waitress's smile falls at the obvious rebuff.

"Sure. Two waters and Manuel, coming right up." She scurries away, and Connor smirks at me.

"Jealous."

As much as I ask question after question, Connor never does. He states facts, opinions, and sometimes opinions as facts.

"Well, you are my fiancé," I tease with an innocent blink of my lashes. "I'm not letting any rando bat her eyes at *my* man."

"Don't remind me," he says, but there's a tiny twinkle in his eye. Or at least, I'd like to think there is.

A few minutes later, the waitress reappears with two waters and downcast eyes. "Manuel said he'll be right out."

I'm prepared to glare at her again, but she doesn't look up a single time before she disappears into the kitchen. Once we're alone, Connor turns back to me. "Tell me how you got into writing."

"What?" I ask, and Connor nods. "Really?"

"You'll hopefully never know the price that I'm paying for this. I won't argue with you about whether I deserve it or not. But I want to know why I'm doing this."

Uhm, wow. That is . . . hot. And now I'm curious what he paid to get the info to get us here. Whatever it is, it obviously cost him dearly.

"Other than my other author friends, I haven't told anyone," I admit. "I guess part of it is the way I grew up. I was awkward, too 'this' or too 'that' as a kid. I was always the kid who never had a group, you know?"

Connor nods as though he understands, but I suspect he has never been awkward a day in his life.

"Yeah, and I just couldn't figure it out. So I watched everyone, trying to figure out how they weren't too much or too little but somehow 'just right'. Over the years, that became me creating entire backstories for everyone I saw. People at the mall . . . they might just walk past me for a split second, but if there were something interesting about them, I'd create this whole narrative in my mind. Who they were, where they were going, what their life was like. Eventually, I started writing it down, and more stories came to me about people who only live in my head."

Connor picks up his glass, taking a sip. "People in your head."

"I'm not crazy, if that's what you're thinking," I tell him quietly. "I just realized that whatever made me not fit in wasn't going to change if I stayed true to myself. So I made my own friends in my mind and put them through hell . . . but only for good reason."

"A happy ever after?" he deadpans. He means it as a barb, but he doesn't understand that I believe it in my heart.

"Yes. Everyone deserves that."

Connor looks surprised, but considering how hard he keeps trying to shove me away, I think he doubts himself and his worthiness of his own HEA. "You think you'll have that?" he asks quietly.

"Happy doesn't mean perfect," I point out. "So by that, I already do. I have real friends who support me, and I support them back. I make a good living doing something I love and am passionate about. I have two dogs who love me unconditionally. I'm living my happily ever after."

"No prince?"

Well, you're pretty Dark Prince-y, I think but don't say. I'd freak him out, and I'm not even ready to admit it to myself. "I'd like that, but if it doesn't happen, I'll be okay. I have plenty of princes in my life, even if they're on pages. Or grumpy assholes who live next door."

It's as close as I'll get to what that little voice is saying, but even that hint has Connor pressing his lips tightly together and glaring at me dangerously.

A few silent moments later, a young teen boy comes out, his white apron dingy and his T-shirt damp. He's wiping his brow with a bandana as he walks our way.

"Sorry to make you wait," he says a little shyly. "You asked for me?"

"Manuel?" Connor confirms, and the kid nods. "Good. Look, I'm a business associate of your dad's . . . a friend."

It sounds like Connor stumbles over the word, but he keeps going. But he's way too slow for my taste, and I can't keep my mouth shut another second. "Where's my laptop?"

Manuel's eyes widen, and then they dart off to the side before returning to Connor even though I asked the question. Connor meets the kid's gaze, and I'd swear they're having a silent conversation, but they just met and things like that take time. Right?

"Who?" Connor demands in a quiet, almost kind voice. A kind demand . . . that's a new one for me.

"It's fine. No worries," Manuel says, looking over his shoulder again, but this time, it's to check out the bored cashier. I can hear it now. This kid's worried, scared. But not of Connor.

"There's blood on your apron, residue on your nose," Connor states matter of factly. "You didn't have a spontaneous bloody nose, Manuel. Who?"

Now that Connor mentions it, I do see a tiny spot of dried blood on Manuel's left nostril, and low on his apron, down by the hem, is a bright red spot. Manuel fidgets with the tied strings at his waist.

"Who?" Connor growls, harsher this time.

Manuel flinches and whispers. "You said you're a friend of my dad's? Can you get the laptop back?"

Connor nods but bursts the kid's bubble of hope. "I gave it to your dad not realizing that it was important to someone." Manuel looks at me in question, and Connor confirms. "Yeah, it's hers. She needs it back, but I'll replace it."

I jump in, figuring that if Connor can be the rock, I can be the pillow for this kid. "Look, I'll buy you a laptop, one of those big jobs that can game all day if you want. Or an Xbox . . . a PlayStation . . . anything you want. I just need *my* laptop back."

Manuel looks more and more excited as I list out all the things I'm willing to buy him. I don't have any idea how I'll afford it, but I'll figure something out . . . if I can just get my manuscript back so I can get to work.

"A laptop," Connor corrects, giving me a hard look. "Only a laptop. We can talk upgrades after we get the original."

Manuel shrugs like that's a more than acceptable deal. "Line cook. Tall guy, built like a tank. In back."

Connor nods. "Name?"

"Derrick," Manuel spits out.

Connor stands and then thinks better of it. "Stay here," he tells me, pressing his finger into the tabletop. An order and demand all wrapped up in one, if ever I heard one. And this one isn't nice.

Connor walks toward the kitchen before I can argue, but I still glare at his back, willing him to feel the painful pinpricks of my gaze. He walks through swinging door, and I look to Manuel.

"You plan on making me do what he said?" I intentionally drop my voice, trying to sound deadly serious. Judging by the smile Manuel tries unsuccessfully to hide, it doesn't work. But he shakes his head anyway. I stand up and roll my neck. "Good choice. You should go talk to her," I suggest, cutting my eyes to the cashier. But the kid shrugs, looking shy again.

Focusing on my own problems and looking as badass as I can, I stomp across the dining room. I steady myself before I go through the swinging door too.

This is not the time to be rash and impulsive, not when there's so much at stake.

Steady as can be, I push through the door to find . . . nothing. And no one. The kitchen is empty, but the back door is open. Slowly, I move that way, acting like the food burning on the grill might jump up and get me. To my shame, I even look back at the swinging door wishing Manuel had come with me to offer a bit of moral support.

When I peek out the door, I see a small group of men gathered in the fenced in alley area and Connor pointing his finger in a tall guy's face. This must be Derrick because he is definitely built more like a tank than a human. For his part, Derrick is grinning impishly, his arms crossed easily over his chest, not at all worried about the man in front of him demanding answers.

"Where's the fucking laptop?" Connor snaps.

"Check your mama's cunt," Derrick says. "It's wide enough."

I expect punches then, but Connor doesn't take the bait. "Don't make me say it again, asshole. The laptop."

"Go fuck yourself."

Connor's jaw clenches, and he lowers his hands to his side. "You're making a huge mistake."

I know I shouldn't do anything, but I can't control myself and suddenly find myself jumping between the two men. "Where's my laptop, asshole?"

Connor doesn't react verbally, but I can sense him moving slightly to restrain me. Derrick's white teeth flash as he laughs and tells Connor, "Better get your bitch under control, man. She's losing it."

"His bitch?" I ask, growling. "He doesn't control me. Nobody does."

"Maybe that's what wrong with you?" Derrick suggests. "I could show you what you need—a real man to take control."

He moves to touch my hair, and I flinch back. But before I'm even halfway back, Connor's moved fast as a blink, grabbing the big guy and spinning him to slam him against the brick wall of the restaurant. Derrick's own size and weight work against him, making the impact hard and sharp.

"Do. Not. Touch. Her." Connor snarls. Around us, the rest of the restaurant staff freeze, shocked that the expected ass kicking they were looking forward to isn't going the way they planned.

"Whoa, whoa, dude. Chill," one of the white-aproned guys says, but he makes no move to step in to stop Connor.

Derrick's grin is gone, his easy comfort replaced with anger and fear in equal measure. Trying to bluster, he 'bro-laughs'. "I didn't mean nothing by it. She's the one that got all up in my face like a crazy bitch."

"I'll show you a crazy bitch," I threaten, pushing my way into the small space between the two men, my fist cocked back. In the tussle, Connor has to readjust and pushes me back with a hand on my forehead while keeping Derrick pinned with his forearm at his throat.

"Let me, Pops. For once in your damn life, stand there and be quiet."

I growl, hating that phrase more than anything. I've been told to shut up so many times in my life that I finally quit trying. I keep to myself because I never tell myself to quit talking. I think I'm a good conversationalist.

"You can bitch me out for that later. Promise. But for the sake of your laptop . . ."

His eyes implore me to play this smart. Smarter than I have been. He's actually on my team, playing a game where I don't even know the damn rules. Not that I like it.

"Fine," I huff, crossing my arms over my chest. But I'm still glaring, one eye on Derrick and one eye on Connor, but not in a cross-eyed way. Just in a focused 'did you know lionesses eat their young and I'm a mother fucking lioness' kind of way.

"My bad," Derrick says, sounding cocky again. "Looks like you do have her under control."

"You really don't know when to stop, do you?" Connor grits out. "Where's the laptop?"

"Gave it to my girl."

"Address?" Connor demands.

"No way," Derrick argues, shaking his head. "You're fucking crazy."

Connor's forearm presses in harder. I can see the tension in his shoulders through the muscles in his back. Derrick's face starts to turn a light shade of purple as Connor's forearm begins cutting off his air.

"You don't seem to understand the shit you've stepped in," Connor says in an almost eerily calm voice. "First, I need that laptop back. Now. And I don't care what I have to do to get it. Second, you stole it from a kid you do *not* want to fuck with."

"Manny?" Derrick says, a laugh trying to bubble up past the pressure on his neck. "The dishwasher?"

The other two guys who've been watching the show chuckle along too. They're willing to laugh at Manuel but not step in to defend Derrick. At least someone around here is smart enough to not fuck with Connor.

"Manuel," Connor corrects. "He's not someone you fuck with. Ever again. Or I'll seem like the fucking Easter Bunny, a sweet surprise, compared to who comes to see you next time. Understood?"

"Whatever you say, man." Derrick doesn't seem convinced.

"The laptop." The reminder is cold and calm. From my experience watching people, I think Connor is nearing the end of his rope. He's someone who, the more you push him, the quieter he gets until he explodes like an atom bomb on your ass. "Where's your girl?"

"I pawned it," Derrick answers.

Connor's lip lifts in a sneer. "You just said you gave it to your girl. Liar. I hate fucking liars."

Finally, Derrick looks like he gets it, and real fear trickles into his face. "I ain't lying."

"Either you lied then or you're lying now. Either way, you're a liar." Connor lets that sink in. "I hear you're a cook too." The subject change seems random until Connor stares Derrick down. "You know what cooks need more than anything?"

Derrick's eyes widen. "No, man! N—"

Derrick's words turn into a scream of pain as Connor grabs Derrick's left index finger with his free hand, twisting hard and fast and breaking it.

The other two guys hiss sharply.

Holy shitballs! Connor did that like it was nothing, without a blink!

Staring wide-eyed at his oddly bent finger, Derrick bawls out, "Pawned it, man! Down on the corner." He starts sobbing, his bravado lost and the bully fully put in his place. "I fucking swear!"

One of the other guys interjects, corroborating Derrick's story. Well, the second one. "It's true. He went down on his break. Came back with a few Benjamins."

Connor pushes off Derrick, who straightens quickly, trying desperately to act like nothing happened even as he cradles his broken hand. Suddenly able to breathe again, Derrick finds his balls, which had crawled up deep into his body cavity. He looks to me, smug arrogance returning to his sneering expression as he gestures wildly with his uninjured hand, scant inches from me. "Guess I did have it wrong. It's not you who needs to be on a leash, bitch. It's him."

Connor moves fast as a flash again, the heel of his hand catching Derrick under the nose and sending the back of his head rapping against the brick side of the restaurant. Derrick drops, blood gushing instantly, and he tries in vain to cover the mess.

"*Fuck*," he hisses, already sounding stuffed up from the blood dripping onto the concrete. I guess his nose hurts more than his finger because he doesn't pay the dangling appendage any attention.

"Don't touch her," Connor reminds him. Derrick didn't, but he came close. Too close for Connor's liking, though I'm not sure what that means. Connor crowds in close to Derrick but talks to the entire small group of men. "And don't fuck with Manuel. He's a good kid. Or you'll *wish* I were the one coming back." The smile that sweeps across Connor's face is pure wickedness, like he can't wait to see what malevolence awaits Derrick if he so much as looks at Manuel wrong. His words might not scare the men, and his beating up Derrick might not either, but that creepy look definitely has them pissing in their pants.

Without waiting for any confirmation from the trio of kitchen dipshits, Connor takes my hand, firmly but gentler than I would've expected from his cold, vicious manner with Derrick.

Following along behind him, we walk through the kitchen, through the dining room where he tosses Manuel a chin nod, and out into the parking lot. He leads me to the passenger side of his truck, opening the door for me. It's not gentlemanly and kind. Oh, no, once the door is open, he virtually shoves me inside before slamming the door again.

Connor gets in and starts the truck, placing his hands on the steering wheel. He's squeezing the leather wrapped wheel so hard, his hands are turning white. Finally, he lets out a deep breath, staring at his hands like they don't quite belong to him.

"Let me have it," he demands.

I blink in confusion. "What?"

"For the shut up comment. Let me have it."

Is that what this is about? He just fucked this Derrick guy up, and he's worried about that comment? "To be clear," I tell him quietly, almost amusedly, "you told me to be quiet, not shut up. Same, but *really* different too."

Connor looks at me in shock. "Either way, I'm sorry. But I just needed you to be quiet for one minute while I got the info we need."

I was taught that an apology isn't an apology if it's followed by a 'but'. In this instance, I'm not sure that's true. Connor does seem sorry, and maybe he's a little bit right. He was definitely the better choice to get the info.

Plus, he said 'we' . . . not him, not me, but we! And that alone makes the 'but' seem like a teeny, tiny three-letter word I can ignore. This time.

"Apology accepted. Now let's go to the pawn shop." I pause, chuckling to myself. "That is something I never thought I'd say, especially on a date."

Connor barks out a rough laugh. "This isn't a date."

I don't argue, but he's wrong. This is so a date. Maybe the best date I've ever been on, which might be sad to some, but I think it shows how awesome I am. Okay, and Connor too. Other than the thief thing, but he's making that right as we drive down the street, so it probably . . . mostly doesn't count.

CHAPTER 13

CONNOR

I'm a jumble of thoughts and confusing emotions as we drive the short quarter-mile down the street to the nearest pawn shop. On one hand, that asshole deserved everything I gave him and more.

Laying hands on a kid? Hell, breaking his finger and maybe his nose might have been a gift to Derrick. If JP had learned about what happened to his son, the consequences could have been fatal.

But was I doing it just for Manuel?

Deep down, I know the truth. I didn't go off until Derrick started messing with Poppy, who is sitting, happy as a clam, in my fucking passenger seat like she didn't watch me turn violent in a flash.

This is just ten kinds of wrong.

The pawn shop's a sad looking affair, with dirty windows and an old-school fluorescent red and white 'three balls' sign. The awning is faded and torn in spots, and the yellow vinyl looks like it's seen quite a few better days.

For most people, these would be bad signs. This is a pawn shop that's not doing a ton of business. But that's a good thing for us. The guy who owns this place isn't a 'pawn star', so he's not going to be moving merch frequently. Hopefully, that means there's a good chance the laptop is still here.

On the bad side, though, I can tell the pawn shop is closed for the day even from here. Still, I get out and go to the door, knocking so hard it rattles. Poppy follows me, peering through the window.

"They're closed. Nobody's here." Poppy states the obvious, but I don't give up that easily.

"They might be in the back, counting up the day's take."

It's a low chance option, but Poppy takes my encouragement to heart, slapping the window hard. She bangs even louder than I was, going so far as yanking on the handle like it's the only thing standing between her and life. I guess it might be if her laptop is still inside because it has her life on it, the manuscript.

But no one comes from the back, and she wears herself out, turning around and sagging against the door in defeat. "Fuck!"

"We'll come back tomorrow," I promise. "We can get it then, and in the meantime—"

I stop as Poppy looks left and right, up and down the street. There are a few cars, a dozen or so people walking, and not much else. But when Poppy looks back at me, there's an evil glint in her eye that worries me. It's a surefire indicator that she's about to do something crazy.

She whispers, though no one is close enough to hear her, "Let's break in, smash and grab style."

For once, my knowledge of crime may actually be useful in *preventing* a crime. Go figure.

"Sure," I deadpan. "We'll have to be fast, though. A place like this has an alarm for sure. Probably calls the police automatically." I squint as though calculating, "ETA of police, based on the closest precinct, is around six, six and half minutes tops. Doesn't leave us much time to search, bust open the display case and make sure it's yours, possibly break into the safe so we can fuck up the video camera footage, and get out clean. Just so you're prepared, it's not as simple as busting down the door or breaking the window."

Poppy rolls her eyes. "You could've just said no."

"You would've argued," I point out with a smirk. "This way, you know I'm right."

"You're *probably* right." She sighs, not yet willing to give up on her wish of getting her computer back today. "We're coming back tomorrow first thing."

It doesn't sound like a question, but I answer it as one. "Promise."

I stop, blinking as I turn away from Poppy before she sees the concern on my face. I'm doing a lot of promising lately. It's a bad habit to get into. I'm not a man who makes promises because I'm not a man who keeps them.

I can't.

But something has changed. Without thinking about it, I open the door of my truck and offer her a hand to climb in. Smartly, she doesn't call attention to it, but she doesn't have to. I already know that I'm walking a dangerous tightrope, but I can't seem to hop off. I've known for a long time that I'm an adrenaline junkie, but I never considered that a person could surprise me at every turn in a way that makes excitement surge in my bloodstream the way a job does.

I drive back to our neighborhood, pulling into my driveway. The rain's stopped by the time we get there, although the steel gray sky says we may not be done with the downpours yet.

"Want to come in?" Poppy asks when we park. "I mean . . . come on over."

I shouldn't. I should just walk up my little patch of sidewalk and into my house. I told her that she couldn't break into that pawn shop, but I could do it easily. I've already been thinking about how I might be able to go back tonight, and the few hours between now and then would be the perfect time to prepare.

But there's something in her face, in the way her hair is still half plastered to her head since the overhang at the restaurant didn't stop all the rain, that has me nodding. "Yeah."

She smiles a little but quickly turns so I can't see it, and we walk next door to her place, where she unlocks the door and opens it up for me. My immediate impression is that Poppy's idea of putting things away seems to consist of piling her crap up, sticking a hand grenade into the middle of the pile, and pulling the pin.

It's not really that bad, just . . . cluttered. Her dining area's clearly her work office, with a full-sized whiteboard covered in scribbled notes and magnets with scraps of paper tucked under them. Next to it is a corkboard that looks like a full-on conspiracy theorist's dream, with pictures of celebrities and random model stock photos connected with bits of colored string.

"Wow," I breathe, part impressed and part scared. This is similar to what I do when I'm planning a job, but I usually keep it in my head. It's safer that way. This is . . . all out there in the open for anyone to see her crazy.

Poppy looks where I'm focused and rolls her eyes, but her laugh is tight, betraying her nerves. "I swear I'm not some weirdo conspiracy theorist. It's my design board for my books. When I make a character, I create a picture that best fits how I picture them. The string is how I can remember their relationship with other characters at a glance. The whiteboard's my written information."

"That's—"

I'm interrupted as twin yapping sounds fill the air, and suddenly, two furry balls of insanity are streaking around the room, dancing around everything before realizing that there's a new human inside. Immediately, I'm swarmed with bouncing, sniffing, and yipping.

"Nut and Juice." Poppy introduces them like I didn't already figure that out.

They're maniacs, but I know how to deal with that. I don't bend down to pet them, but instead, I snap my fingers sharply to get their attention and then hold out a palm. They calm instantly, tongues hanging out and attention locked on me. "Good dogs."

Poppy looks at me in wonder, "How'd you get them to do that? They never do that for me."

I shrug. "I guess they recognize an alpha."

She hums disbelievingly, taking it as a joke. I'm only half kidding.

"I wanna show you something," she says, spinning and going into the kitchen. "Come here."

I don't take orders from many people, but I'm curious to see what she's got up her sleeve. *If she even knows*, I think wryly. Seriously, the more time I spend with Poppy, the more I think she lives her entire life fifteen seconds at a time.

In the kitchen, she kicks out a chair, gesturing for me to sit. I scan the room quickly, noting that the layout is similar to my own place and actually a lot cleaner than her dining area, then lower to the wooden chair.

Poppy digs around in a drawer and pulls out a little bag that looks like a travel toiletry kit before coming over to sit beside me. "Hand?" she says, holding hers out.

I lift a brow in question, not moving a muscle. She growls, cute as can be, and reaches for my hand. I have plenty of time to move away from her, but I don't. I'm too curious about what's she's doing.

It's not until she lifts the hand up and looks at the heel of my hand and starts peering at my fingers that I realize what she's doing. She's checking me for injuries, and her bag is her first aid kit . . . in a blue and yellow vinyl shaving kit bag.

Because Poppy.

"It's fine," I tell her, but I don't move away. Not when I'm enjoying the feel of her fingers dancing over mine, testing and teasing as she searches for any signs of trauma. I'm not used to people taking care of me. It's . . . nice, though warning bells are sounding in my head telling me not to get used to it.

"I'm sure it is, tough guy. But that guy's nose has probably seen more snow than a Colorado mountaintop, and the last thing I want is for you to get some weird infection from his snot and blood splashing into a hangnail or torn cuticle on your hand."

I blink, processing what she said. "That's . . . very specific."

Her lips tilt down, not quite a frown but definitely taking that as an insult. "I told you, I create entire scenarios in my head, taking notes on real ones and pretend ones, adding details and drama at every turn. It's what keeps my life—and my stories—interesting."

"Here," she says, opening her kit and taking out a little bottle of hand sanitizer and grabbing a napkin from the table. She uncaps the bottle and puts a dab on the single tiny cut she's found, letting it ooze in and start to sting before she wipes it away. "And now . . . Neo."

Out comes the Neosporin, and then a Band-Aid to top it all off. When she's done, I flex my hand, nodding. "I think I'll live."

"Very funny," Poppy says, not letting go of my hand. "Connor, what you did with Derrick . . ."

Her voice trails off, and she looks up at me with questions in her eyes. Wordlessly, she takes my uninjured hand and pulls it in closer, laying it on her damp T-shirt over her heart. I can feel the pounding thrum racing beneath my palm, and she's leaned in so closely, I can hear the jaggedness of her breath.

"I didn't mean to scare you," I rasp, trying to focus on calming her nerves after seeing me that way. I shouldn't care, but fuck knows, I do. She already knows I'm an asshole, but I don't want her to think I'm a monster too.

Slowly, I lift my injured hand, praying she doesn't flinch away. When she stays still, I push a wild lock of red hair behind her ear. I freeze when her eyes close and she leans into my touch. "I'm sorry you had to see that."

"I'm not," she whispers as she opens her eyes. She turns into my hand, looking at the bandage before pressing a gentle kiss just above it. Her lips against my skin are so soft I think I might've imagined it, but the feel of her mouth anywhere on me sends electricity shooting through my veins.

"Poppy." It's more of a sound than a word, a rough growl deep in my throat.

She releases my injured hand to cover the one on her chest with both of hers, holding me there. "My heart is racing, but not because I was scared. Or not scared of you. I was scared for you. But I didn't need to be, did I?" She swallows thickly, and I don't know what I say, but it must be the right thing because she goes on. "Thank you for protecting me when I jumped in half-cocked."

Her lips lift as she uses my words to describe herself, but she's pressing my hand lower on her chest to the warm breast beneath.

Totally on instinct, my hand curves, cupping and molding itself to the soft weight, and I can feel the pebble of her nipple against my palm. I knead her flesh, learning and memorizing her responses.

"You're a hot mess, Poppy," I growl honestly, standing up and pulling her with me. I press her against the countertop, caging her with my arms on either side. "But nobody says shit about you as long as I'm around."

She gasps, and I capture the sound with a kiss, pressing my lips to hers to feel the velvety softness. It's scary because the only reason I'm doing this is because . . . I want her.

Desperately.

She moans hungrily, reaching up to cup the back of my head and pull me closer. Her tongue takes the initiative this time, demanding entrance, and we twist around each other, the kiss quickly becoming hot, erotic . . . and very, very serious.

Before was a cover, a necessary tool to hide the drama from my family. This is not a cover or pretend. This is hot, sexy, and most of all, real. Which is what makes me stop, pulling away to hold myself against the other countertop even if every cell in my body is saying to take what Poppy offers and give her what she wants. What we both want.

But I don't do real, ever. It's too dangerous . . . for me and for Poppy.

"I can't. We can't," I pant, my body fighting my every syllable. "I'm no good for you, Poppy."

"Says who? And who says I want someone good for me?" she asks, her voice dripping with desire and lust. "Maybe I want someone bad, very, very bad."

My poor fucking balls.

But I stay pulled back, not moving a muscle. My hands clamp down on the edge of the countertop behind me as she comes closer, my desire warring with my instincts. She's making it nearly impossible to be a good guy here, especially when she kisses along my jaw, her hands curling into the hair at the nape of my neck. I could lift her onto the countertop to pull her jeans down, spread her legs, and feast on her flesh, or bend her over the wooden chair and take her roughly from behind, or tell her to get on her knees and suck me. I think she'd welcome any of those options, or even all three.

But not like this. She deserves better, and though she's all-in right now, eventually, she'll realize that I'm right. And I'll be the asshole who took advantage of her.

I growl in frustration, pushing her back to put a foot of space between us. Instantly, I miss her touch, but I can't give in to the urge to pull her back in. I won't do that to her.

"I want you so bad, but I'm trying *real fucking hard* to do right by you," I admit in a voice that sounds a lot more pained than I've heard in a long time. "Let me do that, at least. Please."

Poppy looks hurt, but I can see her mulling over my words, analyzing them the way she does the ones she writes. I've never felt less adept at expressing myself with a random combination of twenty-six letters.

"I should go," I tell her, taking another step, but it's still not enough. I can smell her, feel her, taste her, and see her, so close but yet too far. Not too far away, but too far above me. She's so good, even in her wildness. She's simply better than me. But I'm trying my fucking best here. "Get some work done tonight. I'll see you in the morning, and we'll go to the pawn shop."

She nods stiffly. As I head for the door, she calls out my name. "Connor!"

I pause, turning back to look at her, hoping she tells me to come back while praying she tells me to go. She looks so fucking sexy, with her red hair mussed from my fingers and her lips puffy from my kisses. I'm surprised I haven't busted out of my jeans already. "Yeah?"

"Nine o'clock. I'll be at your truck."

I grunt an agreement and flee to my house. I do a quick safety check, but there are no alerts. Everything is safe.

Except the woman whose home I'm staring at through the kitchen window's open blinds. In the shadows of my house, she can't see me. But I can see her, going back and sitting at the table, looking dazed and confused. Me too, woman. Me fucking too.

She presses her fingers to her lips as though feeling me still there.

And then she smiles, reaching down to cup her breast through her T-shirt the way I did moments ago. Her head drops back as she finds a stiff nipple and pinches herself.

I don't think, I act. Reaching down, I fumble my belt open and my jeans down, my dick springing forth as my eyes fix on the sight of what Poppy's doing.

I can't hear anything, of course, and the angle of the table and the window don't allow me to see everything . . . but I can imagine. Just like she creates dialogues and scenes for her characters, I fill in the gaps as I take my cock in hand, pumping slowly.

"That's it," I whisper, my thumb smearing the slick precum already oozing from my tip around the head of my cock. "Play with your nipples."

Though she can't hear the order, she does it naturally, one hand massaging her breasts while the other dips below the table to do the same thing I'm doing over here. I can't tear my eyes away, matching her stroke for stroke as we rise together.

In my mind, her plump, luscious lips form words of desire and want as she starts rising up and down in her chair.

I don't know how I do it, keep myself going without rushing back to her, but we go faster and faster until, with a cry that I can actually hear between our two houses, she comes with a shaking spasm and I growl deeply at the sexy sight.

My cock is about to explode, and I ride that edge of pain and pleasure as long as I can before I erupt, hot spurts of my cum splattering all over the kitchen cabinets and floor. There's no trying to hold this back, no trying to save the mess with the power of my release.

My knees unlock, and I have to plant my hand on the edge of the countertop to prevent myself from dropping to the floor. Gasping and feeling my heart pound in my chest, I blink slowly to clear the stars in my vision.

Holy fucking shit.

I can't move for long moments, my body shaky from what I just did. Finally, with weak legs, I find a dish rag and wipe up the mess.

When I'm sure everything is cleaned up, I throw the rag into the laundry room and wash my hands. While I suds up, I look out the window once more to see that Poppy's not in her kitchen anymore. But the dining room light is on.

"Good girl. Get some work done."

I don't know what romantic bullshit ideas she's planted in my head, but for some reason, I blow her a kiss. And then promptly, I shake my head at the ridiculous move. I can't even see her, but I'm going soft-hearted.

What I need to do is take a hot shower and get a good night's sleep so I'm strong enough to resist Poppy tomorrow. And get her laptop back.

"See you in the morning."

CHAPTER 14

POPPY

I'm a little bleary, but so happy and relieved that I don't mind it. After Connor left and I took a few minutes to relieve my immediate tension, I changed clothes and got to writing. And other than stopping to take the boys out to do their business and eat a trio of granola bars, I didn't stop working until three in the morning.

Three whole chapters. I almost *never* get three chapters done in a single writing session. They'll need editing, lots of it, but I can finally feel it. The writer's block is totally dissolved, all the juices flowing, the characters talking, the moments building into overlapping layers.

But now it's morning. And I'm running late, rolling out of bed fifteen minutes ago to scrub the fuzz off my teeth and let the boys out to do their thing while drinking my first cup of coffee.

Connor said we'd go back to the pawn shop, and I need my laptop so I can weave the manuscript and what I've written on this cheap backup together into one master file.

I peek out the window to make sure he's not already in the driveway. I wouldn't put it past him to try to sneak away without me. Hmm, I might have to plant myself in his truck again if I want to be sure I can go.

And I definitely do.

Shit . . . I've got to get a move on. Slugging down the rest of my cup, I hop in the shower, scrubbing down as fast as I can. Yanking on jeans and a T-shirt, I glance in the mirror. My hair is half bun, half rat's nest, but there's no time to do anything for it. Instead, I give myself exactly two minutes to swipe mascara on my fair eyelashes.

I grab my tennis shoes just in case there's a little light breaking and entering at the pawn shop. Because I am not leaving there without my laptop today. With one shoe on and one shoe off, my phone rings. Any other time, I'd ignore it, especially since it's an unknown number.

But there's a chance it's Connor.

"Hello?"

"Hi, Miss Woodstock? Poppy Woodstock?"

Ugh, a telemarketer. I really don't have time for this.

"No," I say slowly. "Can I take a message?"

I'm hopping around, trying to slip on my other shoe and only half listening since I'm expecting another freaking call about my car's extended warranty. Don't these guys ever give up? And has anyone in the history of ever been like 'why, yes, tell me more about your program'? I sincerely doubt it.

"It's extremely important that I speak with Miss Woodstock immediately. It's regarding a matter we discussed previously."

Something about the voice breaks through the chorus in my head, and I pause, my eyebrows knitting together. "Wait, what? Who is this?"

"Detective Jax Carter."

"Are you serious?" I snap, instantly angry that this asshat is calling me after blowing me off when I needed some help. It's only through random good luck that Connor happened to move in next door and I've got any chance of getting my laptop back. No thanks to Detective Carter.

"Yes ma'am," he says haltingly, like he expected me to be thankful he was blessing me with a phone call. "Good morning, Miss Woodstock."

"What the fuck do you want?" I don't play nice and polite. There's no need to, not after how he treated me.

"Ahem, well . . . it seems we might've gotten off on the wrong foot before."

I snort. "You could say that. Or you could say that you were a condescending asshole. But that's probably not why you called, is it? Let me guess . . . my agent called and ripped you a bloody new hole to shit out of, and now you're trying to play nice?"

Detective Carter clears his throat, not quite dropping his arrogant 'take charge' act but definitely taken down a peg or two. Or at least trying to sound contrite. "Poppy—"

I cut him off again. "Deal with Hilda, not me. I have no interest in discussing this matter with you ever again."

"We have a lead," he says, the words rushed out like he knows I'll interrupt him if he doesn't say them as fast as possible.

"What?" I say woodenly, freezing in place. Even my mouth freezes, hanging open and silent.

"Yes, Miss Woodstock. We have a lead, and I'd like to discuss it with you. I'm sorry for how I behaved last time, but this is important. Very important." He sounds grave, serious, and infinitely more professional than before.

But a lead?

He can't have one as good as I have.

Or could he?

Could he have figured out who Connor is too? When I went into the police station that night, I would've killed the thief with my bare hands to get my laptop back. I was that desperate and furious.

But now?

Things have changed. I still want my laptop back more than anything, but the thief is a real person to me now.

It's . . . Connor. My fake fiancé.

I can't let him get arrested before Caylee's wedding.

And I don't think I could let it happen afterward, either. I mean, as long as I get my laptop back, no harm, no foul. And in what I've seen over the past few days, he's going above and beyond in trying to get it back.

I've been silent too long, lost in my own swirling, tumbling thoughts, so distracted that I haven't heard a thing Jax Carter has said, nor the man who's entered my house.

"Poppy, you okay?" Connor says from right behind me.

I jump a foot in the air, screeching like a banshee. "Ahh!" I spin before my feet, one still bare, hit the floor. "You scared the fuck out of me!"

I swat at Connor's chest, hard and unyielding beneath my weak smacks. He grins arrogantly and brushes the back of his hand on his chest, 'wiping off' my hits like they're nothing.

A buzz comes from my phone. "Miss Woodstock? Are you okay?"

I realize Detective Carter is still talking in my ear, concerned from my screaming reaction to Connor sneaking up on me. "Yes, I'm fine. Thank you."

Connor's eyes tick to the phone pressed to my ear. I can see the questions lurking there. So many questions. I've got some too, man. But not now. Now, it's laptop time.

Priorities, Poppy.

For once, I've got to play this smart and not act first, ask questions never. The consequences are too high.

"I'm not interested. Have a good day." I hang up the phone with Detective Carter still talking.

Despite my assumptions, Connor doesn't ask who it was.

He never asks questions.

Usually, that's because I volunteer more information than I probably should. My life's an open book, for the most part. I'll share it with Connor, the teller at the bank, and even my readers when I use it as inspiration. Of course, it's usually boring as fuck. But now, it's not.

"You ready?" I ask instead. "Let me finish putting my shoes on."

I slip the other tennis shoe on, bending down to tie it quickly. When I stand, Connor is watching me closely. And something hits me. I'm late. He could've left me, gone to the pawn shop without me, or even moved on, leaving me behind to handle it on my own.

But he didn't. He's here. He came for me. He kept his promise, and for a man like Connor, that says something. It means a lot. Especially after that kiss.

"Thank you," I tell him solemnly.

"We don't have the laptop back yet," he answers, misunderstanding. But I watch his eyes drop slowly to my lips. He wants me, even if he pushed himself away last night.

I lick them in preparation, hopeful for another taste of his strength and heat. Can't he understand that I'm not scared, that I've seen the dark side of him and I'm not going away? I see the way he wars with the decision in his gaze and wonder if he knows that his own lips have parted and turned up at the corners.

Not a smirk, or arrogance, but hunger. For me. The smoldering desire overwhelms everything else, and the whole world fades away. All that matters is Connor.

But he's not as lost as I am.

He takes a half-step back, swallowing before jerking his head toward the door. "Let's go."

The order surprises me. I wanted him to do what we both want and kiss me. Hell, I wanted him to pick me up, throw me on my bed, and tear my clothes off before ravaging my more than willing body. So I'm disappointed, painfully so. Especially at my core, which is so wet I might as well be swimming in the ocean.

The sharp stab of the lost opportunity breaks the surface, reminding me of what today is about. My laptop. My manuscript. If Connor can focus, so can I.

"Yeah, let's go." I walk quickly out to the living room, where Nut and Juice are now napping on the sofa. I gave up long ago trying to keep them off the furniture, and now, I don't dare disturb them. They always wake up grumpy, but especially so when I'm leaving. So I'm as quiet as I can be while grabbing my keys and purse. Connor follows, leading me out to his truck, and we drive to the pawn shop.

It's sunny today, which makes the place look somehow even grungier than it did yesterday afternoon. Against the bright blue sky, the yellow awning appears even more faded and sad, and the dirty windows are covered in streaks from where the rain ran down.

"I need you to do something for me," Connor says as we park. "Dead serious, Poppy."

The way he just called me Poppy has me nodding and half melting. God, to hear him say my name . . . "Anything."

"Keep your mouth shut and follow my lead."

And there's my little dose of ice water to put me back on track. "No way."

"Oh, I didn't realize you had a plan." He side-eyes me, holding a hand out in invitation to share this magical, mystical, and nonexistent plan. Unfortunately, he's right. I plan out books and stories in slightly messy but organized ways.

Life? About the only thing I'm not diving for that I want is between his legs, and that's because I don't think I can get my head in between his steering wheel and his crotch.

"I'm going to ask for it," I tell him in reply, acting as if I've had a legit plan for hours. "If that doesn't work, then I'll demand it. And if that doesn't work, I'll start smashing shit and throwing anything in arm's reach until he gives me the laptop just to get me to stop."

Connor laughs. It still sounds a little rusty, like it did at his parents' house, but it's warm and genuine and sends little chills down my spine. Later, I'll replay it in my mind and enjoy it, maybe in bed where I can really appreciate it like I did last night. Now, it pisses me off.

"What? You don't think that'll work?"

Connor turns to look at me, lifting an eyebrow and studying me up and down. "Could it? Sure. But I think you'd have better luck showing him your tits than destroying property. Or, you know, there's always the option to buy it. You know, more flies with honey than vinegar and all that?"

"Oh." Duh. I was more than happy to toss money Manuel's way yesterday. Now I'm all kick ass and take names. Why? "I didn't . . . think of that."

"Let's try that first. Just follow my lead." Without waiting for my reply, he gets out and walks around the truck to open the door for me. Gentlemanly, despite the fact that he doesn't think he is.

The inside of the pawn shop's about as worn down and grimy as the exterior. Most of the stuff on display looks like it's barely worth the space it's taking up, let alone what some of the price tags are asking for them.

And it's your usual assortment of pawn shop crap. Cameras, cell phones, a rack of guns on one wall, musical instruments, and electronics.

But I'm only here for one thing, and as we let the door close behind us, the tiny brass bell on the door frame jingling, I see the owner. Pawn Shop Pete, or at least the guy with that emblazoned on the back of his shirt, is probably in his mid-forties with three days' worth of unshaven stubble on his fleshy neck and a few stains on the too tight polo shirt he's wearing. Turning as the door closes, he hits mute on the TV he's got on display that's currently showing a game show. Ironically, the prize being given away right now is a high-end laptop computer.

"Hello, folks!" he greets. "Welcome. What can I help you with today?" Seeing Connor and me fully, his eyes brighten, and he jumps into full sales mode, making assumptions along the way. "Oh! Let me guess . . . engagement rings! Right this way!"

He hops up off his stool faster than I would've thought possible and opens a case, pulling out a tray.

"No, no . . . we're here for—" I try to tell him. But it's of no use. He's made up his mind what we're here for, and he's a man on a mission. Woman and man together equals ring!

Too bad we're not buying what he's selling. I'm here for gigabytes, not gemstones. Besides, as I look at the collection of bands, my brain can't stop making up stories. Each one of these bands represents a potential broken promise, a relationship that was supposed to end in happily ever after, only to fall apart into tears, guilt, and a few bucks exchanged in this shop for the incomplete relief of having to never look at the ring again.

It's fucking depressing. Not that Pete notices as he takes a large, gaudy diamond ring out of the case and holds it up. "This one is perfect. So pretty."

I wave my hands, still arguing. First, that diamond's about as real as pro wrestling. Second, I want *silicon*. "We need—"

"Too big. I understand. Sometimes petite is the way to go, eh?" he jokes with Connor, assuming my protests are likely because of the cost of the large solitaire.

Connor offers an amused smirk as he crosses his arms and leans a hip into the case. Normally, I'd be mad about his potentially leaving marks on the glass, but this case hasn't seen Windex in years. "Go on, you heard the man. Try it on."

What? This is not a plan, this is not a 'lead' for me to follow. It's a waste of time. Precious time. I'm about to argue with him, to just blurt out that I want my damn computer, but the amusement in his eyes stops me. And when Connor flashes a full white smile, I melt and grind my teeth at the same time. Insufferable asshole, he's enjoying this!

Connor nudges me toward Pete, and I stumble over my own two feet.

"It is dazzling, isn't it?" Pete says, misunderstanding the reason for my clumsiness.

"I've got you. I've always got you, you know that." Connor speaks solemnly, like he's making vows, not keeping me from almost busting my ass on this gross carpet that definitely hasn't been vacuumed in years, much less shampooed.

I make a mental note to leave my tennis shoes outside when I get home. Then wash them. With bleach. Or maybe just burn them. I do not want to bring whatever germs are in this place back into my house. Nut and Juice would probably end up with an STD, and then I'd have to explain that to the vet. And something tells me he wouldn't believe that they lay out on my carpets with their legs straight behind them, dicks down, and I might've brought home an antibiotic-resistant strain of who knows what from a pawn shop floor.

Connor picks up my hand and holds it out toward Pete. Of course, Pete's on Team Connor and slides the giant diamond ring on my finger.

"It's gorgeous. Perfect for you," Pete gasps dramatically, trying to make a sale. Based on the amount of stuff in here and the utter lack of customers, he needs it. He starts talking carats and clarity, all utter gibberish to me. All I know is that as the ring slips over my finger, fantasy fills my mind. A fantasy of romance, of giggles and real diamonds . . . of happily ever after.

A fantasy I want . . . but right now, not what I need.

I open my mouth to say so, but Connor interrupts me. "Maybe a ruby? It seems appropriate."

I start to protest again, but Connor puts an arm around my waist, pulling me in tight to his side to press a tender kiss to my temple. And with the touch of his lips to my skin, my arguments flitter away like dandelion fluffs in the wind.

He's playing a part, much like when he played the part of a security guard, but it feels so real.

Seeing Pete's held-out hand, I know I have to take the ring off and give it back. And as ridiculous as it might be, I hate to take it off. I could play this part too.

That of Connor's fiancée. Not fake, but real. Is it really playing, then, or is it something more?

I'm still trying to decide when Pete holds up a ruby ring and my jaw drops. I don't know if it's real or fake, but it's beautiful.

The eye-shaped stone is smaller than the diamond and is nowhere near as obnoxiously gaudy. But the way it sits in its setting is perfect, elegant and bright.

It's unique.

Maybe like I am?

Or how I'd like to be, at least. Aleria would say it's a personification of my goal self, the outer version I'd like to be on the inside. All I know is . . . *Come to mama, baby.*

Knowing he's got a fish on the hook when he sees it, Pete lays on the butter as thick as he can to try and close the sale. "Ah, I have sold a lot of rings in my day, and I know that look. Here, it is only right for you to do it."

He hands the ring to Connor, who takes it delicately, almost cradling it in his large fingers as he studies every bit of it. But there's no need to discuss carats or clarity or anything technical on this ring.

Somehow, despite my earlier thoughts about how depressing this place is, this ring was made for me.

Connor takes my hand and formally slides in onto my left ring finger. "Well now . . . there you go."

Perhaps not the most romantic words ever uttered in history, but it doesn't matter. We're standing in a dirty pawn shop, a sweaty guy looking at us like we're the suckers born just this last minute, on a desperate mission to recover my laptop, but right now . . . we're not.

We're Connor and Poppy, a couple. Getting to know each other, working together, helping each other, and maybe more? Connor looks deep into my eyes, and I look deep into his. I can't be alone in this. There's no way. He's gotta feel the fireworks shooting off, threatening to burn the pawn shop to the ground, even if he said destroying the place wasn't a good plan at all.

Pete claps wildly, breaking the moment. "Oh, yes! I love this moment! You may kiss the bride!" he says gleefully.

"Oh, we uh—" I start, but the words die on my tongue when Connor places my left hand on his chest, right over his heart, and bends down to kiss me.

This one is different from any of the others we've had, softer and sweeter, as he slowly melts me. I feel like he's learning my every nook and cranny. Not of my teeth, but of my soul. Like he's mapping out . . . me.

Whether he realizes it or not, that's a two-way street. With every second we're pressed together, I can feel that his guards are down too, and I can feel his soul. There are no false fronts, no fake lies that he tells the world, tells himself. I can feel the heart of who he is.

When we pull apart, needing air, Connor pins me in place with a dark stare like he's trying to figure out what the fuck just happened.

"Me too," I tell him. I don't know what I'm agreeing to, exactly, but hell fucking yes to all of it. Any of it.

Connor's lips tilt up the teensiest, tiniest bit before he starts listening to his inner whispers and doubts again, going somber. "We'll take it."

Pete's smile is so big I can see it even though I'm still looking at Connor. "Excellent," he says. "Would you like a box? I have more than a few I'll happily throw in for free, and—"

Connor turns to Pete and adds, "And the laptop Derrick sold you yesterday."

Pete's face changes in an instant, flipping through surprise, confusion, concern, and finally landing on uncertainty. "Uh, laptop?"

Connor's voice goes dead serious, cold and eerie like it was yesterday. This isn't 'my' Connor. This is work Connor . . . he's just working for me right now. "Laptop. The one Derrick, the line cook from the restaurant down the street, sold you. He stole it from a friend of mine."

"I don't know any Derrick. But I do have laptops. Right this way." Pete looks nervous, rightfully so, considering Connor has gone from blissed out groom to murderous sounding asshole in a blink.

Connor walks to the case Pete gestures at. "Any of these yours?"

I look into the case, not seeing my baby. Hell, most of these are garbage. Tears spring to my eyes, and I shake my head. I thought this was going to be it! We'd come in here, get my laptop, and I could finish my manuscript. I never considered any other option.

"What am I going to do?" I ask Connor.

Connor turns his attention back to Pete. "Where's the one Derrick sold you?"

"I told you, I don't know any Derrick."

Connor reaches in his back pocket, and I freeze. He gave me shit for going all destructo mode, but he's going to pull a gun? Or a knife? Or whatever the hell he's doing.

Pete freezes too, likely seeing his life flash before his eyes. He's just a poor guy running a pawn shop and trying to deal with everything associated with that. He's probably seen some shit in his time, but he never expected to have the end come at the hands of a guy who he thought he'd talked into buying a ruby ring.

But while what Connor pulls out is big and black, it's not a gun. It's his wallet. He sets it on the counter. Thick with cash, he lays his hand over it securely.

"Here's what I know . . . Derrick, the line cook from down the street, stole a laptop from a friend of a friend. A real good kid. After very little *coaxing*, Derrick said he pawned the laptop to you. And here I am. And here you are." Connor looks around the store. "Now, I'm not going to make any accusations. But I wonder how much of your merchandise is stolen property. Is that ring stolen too?"

Pete shakes his head, his eyes twitching and desperate. "No. I got it as part of an estate sale lot. I swear it."

"And the laptop?" Connor asks again.

"I didn't know."

Connor grins, but there's no warmth in that smile. It's icy, the smile of a man with no qualms about causing untold amounts of violence if need be. "I can understand that. I'm not upset with you. A man's gotta do business. I do a little business myself." He pats his wallet. "But this laptop, it's different. I need it back."

"I . . . I don't have it anymore," Pete stutters, eyes flicking from Connor to the wallet. He wants the money, I can see that plain as day, but he's pretty damn close to pissing himself too.

"Where is it?" I bark, getting in on the plan.

Pete looks at me like I'm crazy. Or maybe like I'm a fluffy-haired poodle playing with the pit bulls. But I can be a Pit bull too! I growl and clack my teeth together, snapping them in a biting motion.

Connor looks at me like I'm crazy too, or at least, he looks at me. But while his face is straight, I can see the laughter in his eyes.

"You heard her. Where is it?" Connor repeats. For some reason, Pete takes the question much more seriously from him.

Men, I think with an internal eye roll.

"I sold it."

"Name. And let's not pretend you don't know or I'll sic her on you. You ever heard the expression 'it's always the pretty ones'? That's her, batshit crazy. She wanted to destroy your whole shop, figured busting windows and cases would get you to give up the computer."

I take my cue like a well-seasoned Broadway actor and grab a golf club from a nearby display. I spin it, trying to channel Harley

Quinn, but it's a messy twirl because I've never even twirled a baton. "What is it you call before you hit a golf ball? Three? Five?" I lay on the ditzy blonde act, even if I'm a redhead. "Oh, yeah, FORE!"

I raise the golf club high over my head, ready to smash it down into the case. Right as I reverse and start to swing it down, Pete yells, "Diana Nichols!"

Connor catches the golf club in mid-air, mere inches from the glass case. "That wasn't so hard, was it?"

He's talking to Pete, but I'm thinking . . . yeah, it was! Not hard to swing the club, but honestly, hard to stop! Later, I would've felt horribly guilty and definitely would've sent a check to cover the cost of the case replacement, but deep down, a twisted little corner of me was kind of excited to smash into the case like a giant piñata.

I wonder if I could add that to my story? If I'm not going to get to do it in real life, that's the next best thing.

Or maybe I can just get an actual piñata and beat the hell out of it in the backyard? That'd definitely get the neighborhood talking. Though after my violent attack on Connor, they might be concerned for their safety, and I do not want to be a line item at the next homeowner's association meeting. Those things are vicious!

"Diana Nichols," Pete repeats, eyeing me suspiciously.

Oh, I guess I can put the golf club down now. I lay it on the case gently, even giving it a sweet little pat.

"Good job," I whisper to the club, patting the head like it's alive.

Connor shakes his head, probably enjoying my little wrinkles to the show. "Tell you what . . . we'll take the ring, and I'll give you an extra hundred for the sale sheet on the computer. I need to find Diana Nichols."

"The ring?" I ask with a smile, glancing down at my hand and noting that it does look pretty sweet with the red stone gleaming there. "You don't have to do that." But at Connor's look, I shut my mouth. Until . . .

"And the golf club," I add happily, deciding it'll make a great souvenir as well as be inspiration for when I write this scene in my book. Hell, it might even come in handy as some protection at home. After I beat up a piñata with it and eat all the candy guts.

Pete looks at me and then back to Connor, who sighs heavily.

"We won't hurt Ms. Nichols. I just need the laptop. We'll pay her for it too, enough that she can get a new one."

"Two hundred," Pete bargains. It's in his blood, I'm sure. He's got a customer, and he's going to drive the best deal he can for himself. "Plus the cost of the ring and club."

"Done."

Pete tells Connor the total, and he pulls a stack of crisp one-hundred-dollar bills out of the wallet. But he holds them firmly until Pete hands over the printed receipt with Ms. Nichols's name and address and the description of my laptop and I verify that it's mine.

Exchange made and information gathered, we head toward the door.

"You're not going to hurt her, right?"

I look to Connor, but he's looking at me, and I realize that Pete is asking me, not Connor. He's the scary monster, but apparently, I'm the one to fear. I might be a touch crazy because somehow, that makes me smile. "I won't hurt her. I promise."

Outside in the truck, I hug my new best friend, Gary the Golf Club, to my chest and stare at the ring on my finger. I'm wiggling like a kid at Christmas, and I know I'm grinning like a fool, too.

Connor says dryly, "That went well."

I look at him to find him glaring at me. But instead of being put off or scared of that dark look, I think it's kinda cute now. "I think so too."

He sighs but puts the truck in drive. "This address is on the other side of town."

We ride in silence until a few minutes later, he asks, "Were you really going to break the case?"

"Uhm . . . maybe?" I venture. "Can we get a piñata while we're out?"

Connor looks at me like I'm crazy, but the idea of beating something up sounds good, really good, and like a great way to release some of this stress that's eating at me . . . about the laptop, my book, and even about wanting Connor even though I shouldn't.

But I've got a hell of a ring and a sweet golf club. I take a look and see Gary's a 3-iron, which is just fine by me. Connor is again silent, but it's almost a comfortable silence now. We're doing this together, and that's the bottom line.

It doesn't take us long to drive to Diana Nichols's house because traffic's good today. Part of me wonders how Diana decided to go into that grungy ass pawn shop, but it doesn't really matter as we get closer to her address.

It's not a good part of town, and the apartment building's the sort where I wouldn't feel comfortable coming and going at night. There's a guy sitting on the front steps, and he looks friendly. Maybe too friendly, like he's looking for repeat customers to do a walk-by purchase.

But Connor looks totally at ease, comfortable in this environment, which surprises me after seeing how he grew up.

"Is this where Diana Nichols lives?" Connor asks the guy, putting a foot up on the second step. The guy leans back, evaluating us before answering. He's probably trying to figure whether we're trouble or not. We're obviously not local missionaries. Or census workers. But Connor isn't willing to wait for the guy to make a judgement call about us and rushes the decision along by reaching into his pocket. The guy on the steps stiffens but relaxes when Connor comes out with a folded-up bill, a five, I think. "Diana Nichols."

"Yeah, this her place," the guy says, pocketing the bill without verifying the amount. "But you ain't gonna see her right now. Ain't home."

"She's not?" I ask, my mood falling. "Where is she?"

"Work," the steps guy says. "She does twenty-four-hour shifts. Won't be home till tomorrow afternoon."

"Where?" Connor asks.

"Everywhere. She's a paramedic. She could be anywhere in town. Dunno if she's got a station or not."

"You've gotta be *fucking* kidding me," I hiss, and the guy on the steps shrugs. He's not bullshitting us, that's just the way it is.

Connor sees it too and sighs. "Come on, let's go home. You can work, and we'll come back to see Diana."

He ushers me back to his truck, and I'm quiet until he closes my door. As he goes around to get in, I let loose with a yell of frustration. "Fuck! We were so *close!*"

CHAPTER 15

CONNOR

*P*oppy is quiet on the drive back to her place. I can virtually see her brain whirling inside her head. I'm trying to decide whether she's listening to the unique genius of her mind, creating storylines and scenarios and characters in her head, or if she's mad at the delay in getting her laptop back, or maybe she's finally remembering that she wouldn't be in this situation if it weren't for my stealing it in the first place.

When we pull up in my drive, she opens her own door and climbs out, and I can feel the silence pressing in on my skin. She's going to leave now . . . and I don't want her to. But instead, she meets me at the front of the truck, pointing over her shoulder toward her place. "You coming over?"

This is a bad idea. I should say no, and I know it. But some strange madness has seeped its way into my brain. When I saw that ruby on her finger, and then when we kissed, it infected me with an insanity that I can't seem to shake from my mind. I don't want to leave her. I can't. She's got me under some crazy spell, so instead, I say, "Yeah."

In her living room, I perch myself on the edge of the couch, edgy and twitchy like a cat that's about to go tearing ass out of the room at the first sound. I feel like a wayward kid who's been called to the principal's office . . . ready to get yelled at for misbehaving. But I didn't skip school or get into a tussle in the hallway.

I'm a thief, something much more serious. And a brute, breaking that cook's nose to get what I want. It doesn't matter that he deserved it or that JP would have done worse. It still speaks to my character and how far I'll go to get my way, like bribing Pete and that guy on the steps. And I'm a liar, but she doesn't even know how deep that goes.

Poppy leans her new golf club against the wall beneath her inspiration board and comes to sit beside me on the couch.

"I'm sorry," I say suddenly, feeling like shit.

"For what? It's not your fault Diana Nichols is at work," Poppy says, not on the same deep, dark dive into my soul that I'm tripping on.

"Not that. For . . ." I let my head drop with a sigh, unable to meet her eyes. I don't want to see the judgment there when I'm baring my soul. I deserve it, but I don't want to see it because it'll be something I memorize to take out and replay when I'm beating myself up. "For stealing your laptop in the first place. It wasn't supposed to be like that. I was just . . . doing my job."

I'm searching for words, trying to be real while protecting her from my truest ugliness. I don't know if I'm looking for comfort, forgiveness, or an escape, but I can feel something inside me reaching for her. Something that wants the hint of what the ruby on her finger teases me with.

Poppy places her hand on my shoulder, her thumb making tiny circles through my T-shirt. I haven't earned her kindness, but I let out a shuddering, needful breath, wanting her touch anyway. It's been so long since I've received any softness from anyone that I can't refuse her kind generosity. I'm even more of a bastard for taking it from her after I've taken so much, but I never claimed to be anything but an asshole.

"I don't know why you do what you do, but you're a good man, Connor."

Her declaration hits me like a punch in the sternum. After all that's happened, how can she possibly think I'm good? I have to show her how wrong she is or this house of cards is going to destroy her when it falls. And it inevitably will.

Desperately, I play the last card I have to hold myself back from the inevitable fall at this point . . . the ugly truth.

"I started down the wrong path young, as a teen. You saw my parents, my house. There were all these rules and expectations. Society rules, family rules . . . I hated everything about it. What to wear, what to say, how to smile even as poison dripped off your every word. It was all so fake, totally useless. So I escaped any way I could, rebelling with stupid shit at first."

Poppy's hand stills but doesn't lift from my shoulder. "Like what?"

"I'd sneak out, not even to do anything wild, just to be out and see if I'd get caught. I didn't. Then I started drinking and smoking, tried drugs, and was generally up for anything that might piss off my parents. Anything and everything I could do to just make them *pay attention*. All I wanted was them to look at me as more than some type of fucked up asset, some toy to be paraded around at the right times in front of the right people. And they . . . didn't even notice. So, I tried other things. Pickpocketing, stealing, you know."

I shake my head, remembering those days. How I'd felt invincible and untouchable. "It was a rush. The truth is that it became what I lived for. The rush of being able to beat the rules, to throw up my middle fingers to the world . . . because rules had never done much for me. And at the time, my world seemed so fucked up. At first, I would sell the shit I stole to friends or a friend of a friend, but eventually, word got out. I got hired for a job here or there, and ironically, I felt like I'd made it. *That* felt like success to me, because people were noticing me."

"I get that."

"The buzz I got from getting away clean was only topped by upping the ante. That's when I got in deep. Poppy, I'm good at what I do, have skills that make it the perfect job for me. And I'm not exactly conditioned to be the sort of person who can sit behind a computer and bang out reports or spreadsheets or what the fuck ever all day. So am I good, Poppy? Fuck no. I haven't been that in a long time, and no matter what good I do in this world, it'll never be enough to balance what bad I've done."

Surely, she must get it now. She has to understand.

But instead, she runs her fingers through my hair, scratching the back of my neck lightly. "I can see that you're good."

I huff out a humorless laugh. "Are you deaf? Didn't you hear everything I just said?" Shit, I've said way too much already. Nobody knows all the things I just told Poppy.

That's all been buried deep in a dark hole inside me for a very long time. But even with all that floating in the air between us, she's as stubborn as a mule.

Finally, I lay it out. "If you want to have a good life, if you want to have the happily ever after you deserve . . . you'd run the other fucking way every time you see me. Because the worst thing of all is . . . I can't keep pushing you away. I'm a greedy bastard."

She pulls my chin up, forcing my eyes to hers. Hers are glittery with tears, but there's steel in their blue depths. "You listen to me, Mister. If anyone should be mad as fuck at you, it's me. But I know everything you just said . . . and asked you inside anyway. Because I see something that you're either too hurt, too scared, or too ashamed to admit. There is still good in your heart. And for whatever you did, you're also fixing it. If you were some turd-nugget bastard, that'd be different. But you're not. You care that I'm freaking the fuck out. Right?"

I snort. "Turdnugget. Is that even a word?"

"Right?" she demands, her fingers on my chin getting tighter.

She has zero sense of self-preservation and no concern that I'm on edge. The edge of what? I don't know, but I know my skin feels too tight for everything bubbling up inside me.

"Yeah," I answer begrudgingly.

"And you're helping me, right?"

"Trying, but you keep trying to get yourself in trouble. B-n-E and assault with a deadly weapon, for starters." The attempt at a joke is a last-ditch effort to thwart the impact of her scooping my soul out with a rusty spoon.

"Har-har," she answers dryly. "And you care about your family. If you were irredeemable, you wouldn't care about Caylee and her wedding. Right?"

"Yeah," I agree less reluctantly this time, knowing she won't let me duck away from her hard-nosed brand of self-help therapy.

I've got walls of concrete, built on a foundation of bedrock, and designed in a labyrinth of a maze, but she's busting through like a bulldozer, going right for my center. It's not an ooey-gooey soft place by any means, but the fire there suits Poppy. Instead of being burned by it, she's acting like the embers of my soul are perfect for making some yummy s'mores.

"You didn't ask me to stop stealing."

Poppy looks at me in surprise. "Why would I?"

"I'm a thief with some obviously tortured feelings about that fact, but you didn't tell me to just stop."

"When, and if, you're ever ready," she says with a quiet, certain confidence, "you will. Or you'll figure out a way to put your skills to work for good." She offers me a brilliant smile, daring me to argue. "Because you are good."

She doesn't know everything, doesn't know half of it, but she's closer to the real me than anyone has been in a long time. I feel like myself, not a weapon or tool to be used by people in power.

With Poppy, it's just us, and I want to fall into that, even if only for a little bit. I give in, taking her hand in mine and kissing her fingertips. "Thank you," I whisper.

She's given me more than she could ever imagine, but I want more. Her kindness makes me desperate for more. Just once. I need a physical way to shut off this emotional storm she's conjured.

I swallow thickly.

"What are you thinking?" she asks softly, sensing the change in my mood.

"That I want to fuck the shit out of you." Maybe by stripping all the feelings out of it, by being crude to the point of insulting her, she'll understand.

But instead, she just grins. "Okay."

My eyes widen. "What?"

"I said, it's about fucking time," she says and then giggles. "Get it? Fucking time. Here or my bedroom? Kitchen?"

She points as she offers choices of where I can take her, where I can have her.

"Poppy . . . you didn't ask me to stop stealing, but I need you to tell me to stop now. Or I won't be able to. I want you too much." I growl the confession, wishing I didn't have a shred of decency left in me. Then, I could fuck her rough six ways to Sunday and not feel a hint of remorse.

"Connor," she says, climbing into my lap to straddle me, her hands on my cheeks so I can't get away from her direct gaze—the one staring into my soul, "if you don't fuck me on this couch right now, I'm going to get myself off. Watch if you want, or don't, but your being all . . ." —she waves her hands through the air, encompassing what I'm guessing is supposed to be me— "is really sexy, and I'm a stroke away from coming already."

I place my hands on her hips and pull her against my raging cock, letting her feel what she does to me. She moans, so I do it again, and again, finding a rhythm that elicits sexy sounds from Poppy's throat. "Are you going to come already?"

Her head falls back, her hair hanging down her back to tickle my hands. I gather a bit of it in my hand and pull gently, testing her waters. She hisses out, "*Yes*."

I can feel her heat through our jeans. Remembering last night, I bury my face into the soft T-shirt covered mounds of her breasts, sucking and biting through the cotton. She cries out, her hips bucking against me as she braces herself on my shoulders, her fingernails digging in.

"Shirt," I growl against her skin, and she nods, letting go to pull her shirt off. The soft, creamy mounds of her breasts almost spill into my face as she leans forward, finding the catch on her bra and shrugging it off to drop, unneeded, between us.

Perfection. Her breasts are perfect lush teardrops on her chest that are capped with pale pink nipples that are already pebbled up and ready for my eager teeth and tongue. I latch onto one immediately, sucking and licking as she thrashes in my lap.

"Connor . . . Connor," she cries out when I find what she likes. I'm not surprised she enjoys a rougher touch, her hips jerking when I stop sucking and bite her nipples softly, tugging and letting my teeth rasp against her silky skin. Her thighs tremble, tightening around my hips, and suddenly, she stiffens when I nip a little harder. "*Fuck*!"

Feeling this woman fall apart for me is heaven in itself, and I hold her secure in my grip as a climax jolts through her, watching her hungrily as she moans. She sags, and I hold her, only releasing her when I hear a twin pair of worried yappings around our feet.

"Guys, hush!" Poppy growls as Nut and Juice dance around, probably worried about their mama. "I'm fine!"

"Protective little monsters," I point out, and she lets out a beleaguered sigh. "I like it."

Poppy smiles then, getting up and tugging on my hand. I nod, dumbstruck, as she pulls me by a willing hand to her bedroom. When we get there, she shoos the whining Pomeranians out, closing her door to give us privacy. They must not be too upset because an instant later, I hear their nails clicking as they walk back down the hall to the living room, probably to go lie in their shared dog bed.

"With my luck, I've got twenty minutes tops until they come looking for me again, or need to go out, or want a treat, so get naked." Poppy goes for the button of her jeans, hastily undoing it and shoving the denim down her thighs to reveal an adorable set of red-striped granny panties with an elf on the right hip.

"It's not Christmas," I murmur as I watch her quick striptease.

"What?" Poppy says, kicking off her shoes and trying to get out of her jeans without falling over. "So help me, if you only have sex once a year on Christmas or some shit like that, I will put twinkle lights on the tree over there or buy some eggnog later, but right now, get naked."

"No, your . . ." I am not going to say panties. Or undies. That word on a man's tongue is just . . . not happening. As I pull my shirt over my head, I settle for, "Elf."

Poppy looks down, realization dawning. "Haven't done laundry, but you can totally stuff my stocking." Her eyes go wide. "Oh, my God, that was so bad. Pretend that didn't happen. Pretend I'm not a writer who gets paid to write sexy dirty talk." She shakes her head, and under her breath, I swear I hear her say, "At least I didn't talk about breeding this time."

"What?" My fingers freeze on the button of my jeans.

"Oh, nothing. Book stuff." When I don't move, she adds, "I'm on birth control. I swear."

Hell, I don't know if I'd stop even if she did start spouting some weird breeding talk. It's not my thing, but if it's hers, I could make it work.

Thankfully, I don't have to, and once I'm naked as instructed, we simply look at each other for a long moment.

"You're beautiful," I tell her, loving the way her whole body flushes in response. "Lie down."

She backs into the queen-size bed and sits down before spreading out. I follow her, taking the two steps to the bedside, and stand over her. Her hair is a messy red halo, her cheeks are pink, and her eyes are sparkling brightly. She wants me.

And I want her. I want to trace her curves with my hands, find all the secret spots that drive her wild, and feel her surround my cock with velvet.

But first, I run a rough hand up her calf, tugging her knees apart and studying the way she bites her lip as I get between them. "What's wrong?" I ask as I see something change in her eyes. "Do you want me to stop?"

"No. It's just . . . nobody's ever looked at me with so much intensity," she says, swallowing. "You make me feel sexy."

"You are sexy," I tell her, climbing onto the bed and between her legs to kiss up the insides of her thighs.

Softly, I tease her flesh, kissing my way up Poppy's legs until I'm almost at her pussy. I inhale her, and the sweet scent makes my head swim

Forget the rush of crime . . . this is more addictive.

Maybe, but for now I kiss her center, teasing and tasting her and listening to her reactions. I slip my tongue into her folds and am rewarded with a burst of wetness that has my cock pulsing precum onto the sheets underneath me.

I memorize every bit of her as I explore her body, my fingers holding her legs apart until I find the pearl at the top. And like the thief I am, I steal it from her with my tongue, wrapping and fluttering, watching with greedy eyes as she cries out, her hands balled up in the sheets as she surges into my mouth.

"Fuck, Connor, right there. Oh, fuck . . . oh, fuck!" she shouts, her eyes rolling up as I stroke her clit and watch her. I bring her up, higher and higher, until I can't hold back any longer.

With a growl of hunger and greedy desire, I let go of her thighs to rise up, nocking myself at her entrance and pressing into her. Poppy cries out, tugging on my neck and kissing me even before I can thrust forward, and our moans are swallowed between us as I fill her.

"More," she gasps as I slip into her, my cock embraced by the tight, slick walls of her grip. "Fuck me, Connor. I need all of you. Let me make you feel good."

I want to make it good for her, to give more than I take because I'm in heaven inside Poppy. But there will be hell to pay for this and I know it. Eventually, she's going to regret this night, but if I do everything in my power to give her the physical pleasure and release she wants . . . maybe she won't hate me when it's all said and done.

I'm burning, my desire for Poppy and anger at myself mixing with who knows what in my veins. But I use it as fuel to give her exactly what she asks for. I pound her, fucking her with every ounce of my strength and clapping my hips and balls against her body.

Take it . . . take it, Poppy, I think as I fuck her hard and deep with demanding strokes. I don't know if I'm punishing myself for being unworthy of her or punishing her for taking me anyway, but instead of my breaking her, she meets me equally, surging up to capture my mouth with a hard, sucking kiss.

We give in.

We tear into each other, hair is pulled, fingernails score my back, hips piston, and my cock surges, harder and thicker than I've ever been. Suddenly, we're on the edge of eternity, ready to hurtle into the dark abyss, and I freeze.

I stare into the abyss, but like a philosopher once said, the abyss stares back as Poppy bucks herself up into me, and I see . . .

Her leap. Not a fall into pleasure, but rather, an absolute wingless flight into floating bliss. It sends me tumbling, spiraling wildly after her.

"Poppy!" I growl, plunging into her. My balls tighten before spilling over, my orgasm carrying me away as I fill her with hot spurts of my seed. She holds me, her legs locked around my waist as she quivers, her own climax sending aftershocks through her body that seem heightened with every jet of my release.

In the silence that follows, I collapse, holding her in my arms as I sag into the sweat-soaked sheets. For damning her, I feel . . . lighter. Like maybe, in all of that, she did shine a little bit of light on my soul.

Poppy curls into me, kissing my chest softly and humming happily until she stiffens suddenly, her body going tense. "What is it?"

Poppy sits up, blurting out, "I need my laptop."

Okay . . . uhm, not what I expected. Then again, I expected tears, anger, and getting thrown out of here, but this is not at all what I thought might happen. "I know. We'll go get it tomorrow night."

"No, no . . . the one in the kitchen," she explains with a happy giggle. "I need to write down my thoughts on this. Right now."

Without another word, Poppy hops from the bed, as naked as the day she was born, and runs from the room. I lie there, stunned. I don't think I can ever say this has happened before, and I'm not sure what to do . . . or even what the fuck is going on.

She said her thoughts on *this*, obviously meaning the sex we just had. Is she going to give me a report card? Like a 'needs improvement' and 'exceeds expectations' type deal? I'm down for feedback, but that's a bit much, right?

But before I decide whether I should get up and get dressed or follow her to the dining area, she's back with her cheap little backup laptop in her hands, almost leaping into the bed to flop down next to me. Yanking the cover open, she starts typing.

I look over, wondering exactly what she's typing about, but she doesn't seem to mind as I start reading her story.

. . . his eyes roam over my body, the searing heat trailing behind like his laser intensity is real. His hunger is a palpable thing, as real and physical as his sexy, chiseled chest, and when he reaches for me, I can't resist even though I know I should.

This isn't what good girls do.

She keeps typing, so fast that her cursor stays ahead of my reading. I'm surprised steam isn't rising from the keys of the cheap little computer, not only because of how fast she's typing but how super hot and over the top it is.

I mean, it's sexy as hell, and I sort of wonder if more men should read romance like this. They might learn a trick or two.

"And . . . yeah, the clit thing," Poppy murmurs, lifting a finger before going off on another speedy rush of flying fingers and smokin' hot words on the page.

"Is this what you usually write?" I ask when her fingers slow a bit.

"Shh, wait one second," she responds, holding up one finger in the universal 'wait' sign.

She taps the keyboard without typing and then reads what she's written aloud. Listening to Poppy's breathy, sexy voice read what she's written transforms the words from being 'lady porn' to a shot of Viagra-laced Redbull straight to my dick. My buddy's rock hard, got wings, and is ready for round two. And maybe three and four.

"Does that sound okay?" she asks when she's done. "It's a first draft, so it's okay if it doesn't."

I roll to my back, taking my cock in my fist and showing her the effects she's had on me. "It sounds hot as fuck when you read it. And it's sexy that you have those filthy thoughts in your head."

She watches me, her tongue peeking out to wet her lips. "Sweet Lord."

"Read it again."

She does, her voice slow and deep, seducing me with her mouth in a way that I've never imagined. Sure, her being sexy and still nude, the smell of sex in the air, and memories of what we just did helps . . . but it's her words that have me hard once more.

"What's next?" I rasp when she reaches the end of the passage. She begins typing again, saying the words out loud as they spill from her mind through her fingers to the page.

She smiles as she types and talks at the same time, eyes flicking to my hand stroking my cock and then back to the screen. "His thick cock grew rigid, his balls pulled up tight to his body. Veins stood out on the marbled shaft as he squeezed the base tight, milking out thick drops of precum to glisten on the tip. Stroking himself to right on the edge of exploding, he grunted and pumped harder and faster, knowing that ecstasy was right there for the taking."

I follow her commands, my hand moving up and down in a blur and squeezing tight.

"Come on me," she says. I'm not sure if that's her saying it or her character saying it in the book, but I angle myself her way. "Let go, cover my pussy with your cream, and then use your cum to get me off."

"*Fuck*," I groan, barely rolling fully to my side before I spasm. My back curls in as my cum spurts, the first shot so hard it reaches Poppy's bellybutton. She must've known it was about to happen because she's already shoved the laptop out of the way protectively.

I keep stroking, aiming myself as I want every last drop to coat her pussy. I give myself one last swirling stroke to gather the remaining cum on my crown and spread it over her clit and lips.

"Want me to rub my cum into you? Mark you all up with it, claim you with it?" I don't know what I'm saying. The words are pouring out of my mouth the way they poured out of Poppy's fingers.

"Yes, yes," Poppy cries out, her eyes tight with fresh want and need.

I rub the slippery mess on her skin, focusing on her clit after a moment and giving her no mercy. "Come for me. Cover me in your cum too, Poppy. Mark me all up as yours."

There's no doubt that we will both wear the proof of this moment tomorrow. I can feel the marks on my back, can see the hickey I gave her, but this is different. This isn't just about relieving a physical need. It's about something else, something just as primal and raw but very different.

When she explodes, I slip my fingers inside her, wanting to bring forth as much of her cream as I can. I want it all. I want it everywhere.

Poppy bucks into my hand, our combined juices covering us and dripping down, soaking everything. But the release is more than worth it as we drop bonelessly to the bed, breathing hard.

"Holy fuckballs. Not yours, but just" —Poppy waves her hand lazily through the air— "you know . . . whoa."

"Me too," I agree.

At least I know I did something right. I hope it's enough for later, when she's wishing she'd never met me. I push that thought away, trying to stay in this moment, with and for Poppy.

Later will come soon enough, there's no stopping it, but for now, I can pretend that this is all real and everything will be okay.

If there's one thing I'm good at, it's pretending and lying.

Even to myself.

"I've got pizza rolls," she says out of nowhere, "unless you want to call for delivery?"

I laugh at the unexpected question. "We greet the pizza delivery driver like this, and we'll have a whole different type of story on our hands. Like 'Delivery Driver Found Dead in Quiet Suburb.'"

Poppy stops, looking over at me seriously. "Really?"

"No," I tell her, raising a brow that she actually might've believed that. "But I'm not sharing you with anyone."

"Good," she says, "because I'm a greedy bitch too."

CHAPTER 16

CONNOR

"Does it sound stupid that I don't want you to leave?"

I hold Poppy in my arms, her forehead nestled under my chin and her arms wrapped around my waist to twine her fingers into my belt loops. "No. But you've got work to do."

She makes a growly sound of displeasure that's fucking adorable and feels sexy as hell against my chest. "I've been working all night with you here."

That's true. She's been typing away for hours. Some of it, I slept through, but then she'd wake me up to read a passage aloud and ask my opinion. It's fascinating how her mind jumps from one thing to another, and then she fills in the details to get the characters where they need to be. I wish someone had done that for me and my life a long time ago, because I'm obviously shit at it, ending up in a place I never imagined.

"I know, but you need to focus, and I'll be a distraction. I'm gonna shower, run some errands, and I'll be back later."

I'm lying to her already. My 'errand' is a meeting with JP, but I don't want to worry her when she needs to meet her deadline. She's already behind because of my actions, and I don't want to delay her any further.

"Okay," she agrees, lifting to her toes to give me a quick kiss. "I'll see you this afternoon." There's a slight edge to her voice, warning me that I'd better get back here and take her with me to Diana Nichols's place on time.

I turn to leave, pausing outside to watch Poppy do a little shimmy back to her sofa to get to work. With Nut on one side and Juice on the other, she immediately begins typing away with a pencil in her mouth.

I don't know why she has a pencil considering she has no paper, but I'm not going to ask about her process. I'm just going to appreciate it for what it is.

I do actually shower, washing and getting fully shaved. After a quick breakfast of black coffee and a protein bar, I hop in my truck to head out. A glance through the window reveals that Poppy's still hard at work, and I give her a little wave as I shift into drive. She's so into her writing she doesn't wave back, but that's what I want.

JP's waiting for me at a coffee shop, not the one where I meet Hunter but a different place. This one is mob affiliated, which makes me wonder again about exactly who Mr. Big is.

"Heard about what you did for my boy," JP says flatly by way of greeting. For a moment, I'm worried. Is JP mad? Glad? Is he the friendly distraction while someone else cracks one of these heavy ceramic mugs over my skull, drags me out back, and makes me disappear into the back of a truck?

But I don't show any of that concern. All I do is sip my own coffee, setting it down on the counter without letting go. In my mind, I play out options—of using my own mug in defense, of escaping out the front door to go right or left on the street outside, of the number of patrons versus mob guys in here. "Yeah."

JP takes a sip of his coffee, one of those tiny-cupped strong things that's as thick as motor oil and seems to be popular here.

"Thanks, man. Manuel says Derrick got fired that night. Boss said they didn't need him stealing from employees and bringing in violence," JP says with a mirthless smile. "Plus, I guess he wasn't much for prep that night. Heard he had some sort of accident, busted his nose and a finger."

"He should count himself lucky," I point out. "It was his left hand, not his right."

"True. At least he can still wipe his ass properly." JP's lips twitch at the idea of Derrick potentially needing someone to clean up his shit, and I think he might've preferred that I go for the dominant hand.

"I promised Manuel a replacement laptop," I point out. "I intend on making good on that."

JP waves me off, sipping again. "No need. I can buy him one. I had been planning on it when you dropped that one in my lap. I figured there was no sense in wasting money if I got one for free. So it's nothing. You paid for it by sticking up for my boy."

It's a relief, and we sip our drinks in companionable silence. "He's a good kid. How much does he know?" I ask carefully.

"Enough to know that washing dishes in a restaurant is cleaner than the life his father leads," JP says. There's the smallest hint of bitterness in his eyes, but it's gone before I'm sure it was even there. "I came here and did whatever I could to give my son the choices I never had. Now he's doing just that." JP laughs quietly. "Although I do wish he'd become an engineer or a doctor, like I wanted. But kids these days, with all their fanciful ideas of chasing their dreams." JP rolls his eyes, but his smile seems genuine, as though he's glad his boy can have the luxury of a dream.

"Want me to go by the restaurant every once in a while? Make sure they're treating him right? I didn't get to eat anything but a couple of chips, so I wouldn't mind checking out the food."

JP shakes his head. "No, I went in for lunch to see my boy. I sat down with him, right there in the restaurant, and got the whole story. Though I have a question, one Manuel said you could answer."

"What's that?"

"The waitress, she called me *El Hombre Conejo*. Care to explain?"

I grin, laughing into my mug. I'm no expert in Spanish beyond knowing the curses that can lead to a bad situation, but I know enough to deduce that they're calling JP *The Rabbit Man*, aka something worse than the Easter Bunny.

"Something I said to scare the idiots there. Don't skin them alive."

JP shrugs, not taking the joke. "Just tape their mouths shut first," JP counters, "then it's no problem."

He sets his cup down and sighs, his face going stony. It's time for business. JP reaches into his suit jacket and takes out a small envelope. "Mr. Big has a job assignment for you."

"Now?" I ask incredulously. Normally, assignments are weeks, if not months, apart. This close together increases the chances of the police being aware of what's going on. "I'm working on something else, but it'll wrap up in a day or two."

JP frowns and gives me a discerning look. "Is that something else about five foot three, redheaded, and quite pretty? She's terrible at playing hide 'n' seek."

The mention of Poppy on his tongue sends ice through my veins and is enough to change my mind. The threat is clear and doesn't need to be spelled out. "What do you have for me?"

Wish I could say no, but I can't help it. This is my job, and I need to do whatever I have to so that I can prove myself to JP and get a meet and greet with the big guy himself. I need that. I deserve that after everything I've done for the man.

Poppy said I'd know when and if I were done, and it's not now. I know that for sure. Especially when the last thing I want is for JP to think Poppy has anything to do with my work. Or worse, might be holding me back from the work Mr. Big wants me to do. That'd put her in danger.

"There's a piece coming into town." Now that I've agreed, JP is relaxed again, sipping his drink.

"What's the timeline?" I ask, and JP pushes the envelope toward me.

"Data," JP says. "We want you to do some research to see if retrieval would be possible. We need to plan this down to the smallest detail. No chances for anything to go wrong. But if Mr. Big says go, the time window is extremely small."

I nod in understanding, taking the envelope and slipping it into my back pocket. "Understood. I'll be in touch."

Business complete, I drain the rest of my coffee and offer JP a nod to say goodbye. I'm still on high alert as I leave the coffee shop, but everything seems fine as I get in my truck.

On the drive back to the house, my mind starts . . . musing. Perhaps this isn't the traditional path people take, but as I look back, I have to admit to myself that I take pride in my work. I've worked hard to perfect my skills and get to where I am, and I'm so close to meeting Mr. Big. That's been a goal for a while, and it's right there, barely beyond my reach.

But with that comes the truth that what I do is risky. JP said he needs this planned down to the nitty gritty so nothing goes wrong, but nobody knows that more than I do. If something were to happen, I'd be the one who pays the price, with hard time or my life.

I'm about halfway home before a thought hits me.

Poppy would pay the price too.

I didn't mean for this to happen, and maybe I should've stopped it before things went too far. But the truth is . . . it already has. It's too late to go back now. Or is it?

It wasn't supposed to be like this. One little run-in at a fancy dinner and a ripped bag have somehow sent both of our lives veering diametrically off-course.

More than that, she's going to get hurt, and it'll be all my fault.

I warned her, but it doesn't make it any less wrong.

By the time late afternoon rolls around, I've got myself half convinced that I have to break this off. I have to tell her that we can't do this anymore, even though it hurts somewhere deep in my chest to decide that. Not my heart, I sold that to the devil long ago, but maybe to the hollow void where it used to reside.

We need to get her laptop back tonight, and then I have to stop this insanity. Whether I want to or not. For her sake.

My resolve is echoed in my firm knock on her door, and I tell myself again . . . laptop and done. But when the door opens, she sends me stumbling backward as she leaps at me and kisses me hard, hanging onto my neck and waist with her arms and legs.

"Hey," she says when I can finally be sure I'm not going to fall down, crushing Nut or Juice underneath me since they're dancing around my ankles and yapping. "I missed you."

"I can see that," I reply, holding her up to feel the press of her body against mine for as long as possible. Her intensity is a powerful drug I could easily get addicted to.

Maybe I already am.

"You've become part spider monkey."

"I prefer tree sloth, but that's because you've got a thick piece of wood for me to hold onto," she teases, wiggling against me and said piece of 'wood'. "I made dinner for us before we go."

Stunned into silence, I let her slide down my body and then follow her into the kitchen. She's cleaned up a bit, and while her whiteboard and corkboard are still in their familiar places, the table itself has been totally cleared. The papers are gone, stashed away someplace, and instead of the mess, she's set up two place settings. A candle burns warmly in the center of the table.

It looks like a romantic dinner date at home.

"You shouldn't have done this," I whisper in shock. "What about your work?"

"I wanted to, and work was fine. I got a lot done. Besides, we're engaged, remember?" She does little finger quotes around 'engaged', but it feels a bit too real with the scene before me. She pulls two plates from the cabinet and sets them down, gesturing for me to sit before she pulls a casserole dish out of the oven. I watch as she serves up two portions of something that smells delicious.

"I made Diana a dinner too," Poppy says when she sets the plate of what looks like a homely but delicious shepherd's pie in front of me. "I figure she'll be hungry after her shift and more likely to be helpful if she's fed."

"Good thinking."

"I cook when I'm nervous, or excited, or both." Poppy sits down, nearly bouncing in her seat.

"Are you?" I ask. "Excited? Nervous?"

Poppy nods enthusiastically, and I notice that her usual messy bun of hair is in a ponytail today. It bounces around on the back of her head, making me want to wrap it around my fist to pull her hair back and thrust deep and hard into her body, making her scream my name. But I keep that to myself, doing my best to remind myself of tonight's goals . . . laptop and done.

As we eat, Poppy tells me about the progress she made on her book today. Her smile is easy, her excitement contagious. Both alleviate some of my earlier guilt for fucking up her life by stealing her laptop.

"So yeah, I was able to get some great action scenes written out," she says between forkfuls of meat and potatoes. "And I created a separate doc that I'm storing the plotted sex scenes in. I gotta admit, I cranked out two of those today like it was nothing. I haven't had such an easy time doing scenes like that in . . . well, ever."

"Glad I could inspire you," I joke. "Your writer's block problem is solved," I summarize, taking a bite of my own shepherd's pie. It's damn good, and while it's a little early for dinner by my normal schedule, it's a great dish regardless.

"Totally!" she says happily. "Once I get my laptop back and merge all of these files, I'll be in decent shape, I think. Hilda would disagree, of course. She won't be happy until she's got a manuscript sitting in her inbox." She tilts her head, her smile twisting into something less joyful. But quickly, she smiles again. "I can do it. I *will* do it."

Her affirmation is for herself, not me, but I nod along anyway, taking it to heart. Maybe I can do it all too—get Poppy's laptop, do the job for Mr. Big, and not break Poppy's heart in the process.

Fantasy? Sure. But stranger things have happened, like someone like her accepting someone like me, just as I am.

But no matter how good Poppy feels about her chances, I'm not feeling as good about mine.

CHAPTER 17

POPPY

*I*t's past sunset by the time we get back to Diana Nichols's apartment building, and the streetlights are on as Connor parks his truck on the street. I notice that he visibly hits the lock tab on his key fob when he gets out, making sure the double beep and flashing lights tell anyone who might be watching that the car's locked.

It's that kind of neighborhood.

But the same guy as yesterday is still sitting on the steps wearing a green T-shirt instead of yesterday's black tank top. He's also got a friend with him, or at least I assume they are by the way they're talking.

"You must be out of your got-damned mind! Ain't no way in hell Lebron's better than MJ!"

"Look at the point totals, man. Lebron's bigger, taller, more points, more rebounds—"

"Championships! That's all that matters!"

As I get closer, the guy from yesterday nods to me and says, "Welcome back," lifting his chin toward the door before going back to his conversation. "Man, you gonna run my blood pressure up trying to tell me MJ ain't the greatest."

I'm not sure if he's giving us permission to go inside or telling us that Diana is home, but Connor tries to shuffle me in with his hand on my lower back.

"Wait," I tell him, spinning out of his reach. I dig around in the bag of food I packed and turn back to the steps-guy to hold out a baggie of cookies. "I made these today. Thanks for your help."

He holds his palm toward me, shaking his hand in a warding off gesture. "Nah, I didn't help with nothing."

The other guy interrupts to ask curiously, "Hey, those some sort of *special* cookies?"

I smile at his interest. "Yes, my grandmother's recipe."

"Your *grandmama* made special cookies?"

"Of course! Doesn't everyone's grandma? These are chocolate chip, my favorite. I sprinkled in a little extra love and chocolate too," I confide with a wink, rubbing my fingers through the air like I'm sprinkling magical fairy dust over the cookies.

The two guys' eyes light up. "Okay, okay," he says, taking the bag of cookies. "One for you, one for me," he tells his friend.

They dig in, munching and moaning in delight as their eyes close. "Fuck, man, I gotta call my momma after this."

"Enjoy!" I tell them and then go back to Connor, whose lips are twitching like he's trying not to laugh. At what, I don't know.

He guides me inside, and we go up the two flights of stairs to Diana Nichols's floor. We find her apartment by following the info from the pawn shop, pausing outside the worn but solid looking door. Right before Connor knocks, I place a hand on his chest. "Wait. This time, let me handle this."

"Excuse me?" Connor asks, and I can see he wants to argue and to protect me.

"You said to let you lead at the pawn shop," I reply quietly, "but this is different. This calls for a gentler touch."

"You almost went berserk with a golf club at the pawn shop. Is that what you call a gentler touch?" he growls. "Besides, I can be gentle."

"Yes, you can, fair point. But she's not going to open the door if she puts her eye to the peephole and sees you looking all tall, dark, and dangerous in her hallway. And it'll be easier to get her to listen to us if you're not looking like John Wick with better hair." I point at his head with finger guns, firing them like *pew-pew-pew* to show how intimidating he appears to be, especially to a woman alone at home. "Let me do my thing, and if it doesn't work . . . well, we won't have to worry about it because it will."

I straighten out my ponytail and do my best to put on a friendly look to show him how it's done.

He sighs, knowing he can't compete with my smile and giving in to the fact that he's beat, hands down, with no need for a recount. "Fine. No golf clubs, though."

I crinkle my brow, giving him an airheaded 'duh' look. "Of course not. I left Gary at home."

"Gary?"

"The golf club."

I think I hear him mutter something about crazy chicks under his breath as he steps off to the side, out of peephole view, to lean against the wall. But in a flash, he softens his features, unclenching his jaw and smoothing his brow. The difference is dramatic, turning him from intimidating to handsome. I'm not sure which look I prefer.

I straighten my back and knock on Diana Nichols's door.

Nothing happens for a long minute.

"I thought she'd be home."

"Maybe you look too intimidating?" Connor deadpans.

I scowl his way but then fix a charming, friendly smile on my face as I knock again. A few seconds later, I hear footsteps, and then a tired, wary voice from the other side says, "What do you want?"

"Hi, Ms. Nichols. My name is Poppy Woodstock. I'm here because—"

There's a harsh laugh from the other side of the peephole. "Woman, you aren't Poppy Woodstock, so get to stepping away from my door."

"Uh . . ." I look at Connor, not for a rescue but because I wasn't expecting her to tell me I'm not . . . me. "I assure you, I am Poppy Woodstock." A light dings in my head. "I can prove it!"

I dig in my purse, the tiny wallet clutch I carry, and pull out my driver's license. "See, I'm . . . me." I hold up the card to the peep hole and then move it down so she can see me.

Smile. Look non-threatening, I remind myself.

"Oh, my God," I hear her hiss, and then I hear a thud, almost as if she bonked her head on the door. Before I can start to ask if I need to call for a paramedic, as ironic as that'd be, the locks begin to disengage. Still careful, she cracks the door. "Are you *the* Poppy Woodstock?"

"Yeah?" I say as I slip my driver's license back in my wallet, a little unsure why she asked it like that. "In the flesh."

"The author?" she clarifies.

My eyes pop open in surprise. "Wait . . . you know my book?"

"*Love in Great Falls*? Doesn't everyone?" she gushes.

"You'd be surprised," I say wryly.

"Oh, my God, I devoured it in like one quiet shift and then read it again the next to make sure I got it all. I can't wait for book two!" She's totally fangirling, eyes bright, smile wide, and hands clasped below her chin.

"Funny story . . . but that's actually why I'm here." Just like in a book, I throw out the hook, hoping she wants more. "I need your help."

"What?" she asks, her brows dipping together. "My help? What, are you writing about a paramedic?"

"It's kind of a long story." I tug, tug, tug on the fishing line carefully, hoping she'll bite. "Can we come in for a second?"

"We?"

I tilt my head down the hall. "This is Connor, my fiancé."

I see his eyes narrow sharply at the label, but I know what I'm doing. If I introduce him as 'the guy I'm with', he's threatening. As my fiancé, though . . .

"Your fiancé!" Diana squeals.

Connor pushes off the wall and steps forward. Diana's eyes trace over him from head to toe, her jaw dropping open and her eyes getting wider and wider. I swear she measures the width of his shoulders at least three times. "Holy shit, Poppy. Now I see where you get your inspiration from."

She's only complimenting Connor's good looks, not flirting with him, but possessiveness shoots through me anyway. I cuddle into his side, placing my hand on his chest to flash my ruby ring.

"Ooh, you lucky ducky," Diana sings enthusiastically through a huge, happy grin. "Got yourself one of the good ones."

At first, I think she's talking to me, but she's looking directly at Connor. He seems to catch her meaning too and pulls me in tighter with his free hand. "Quack, quack," he deadpans. "Hi."

I look at him in shock. "Did you just make a joke?"

He doesn't smile, but his eyes bore into mine before they flick to Diana. Oh, he's playing a part . . . the part of the dutiful fiancé to apparently famous author Poppy Woodstock.

Wait, when the hell did *I* become famous?

I shake my head, falling back into character. The character of . . . me. "I swear I'll explain everything if we can come in for a minute? Please?"

"Yeah, yeah," Diana says, moving back from the door in welcome. "Excuse the mess. I came home from work and crashed."

I look to where she indicates, seeing the couch pillows arranged in a cozy corner of the couch, a blanket haphazardly thrown aside, and a very full glass of red wine on the table. At the foot of the couch is a pile of what looks like fresh but unfolded laundry, but other than that, I've seen a lot worse.

I live in worse. At least her couch isn't covered in Pomeranian hair.

"Speaking of, I made you dinner." I take the brown bag of goodies from Connor and hold it out to Diana. She takes it curiously, peering inside.

"You made me dinner? Why?" Suspicion enters her tone.

"We came by before, and the guy downstairs said you were working a long shift." I shrug. "I know how that is, working so hard that you don't stop to eat. I figured you'd be hungry."

"And that then you'd be more inclined to listen," Connor adds, bringing us back to the point of our visit.

"Listen to what?"

I look around, spying a few casual looking chairs. "Can we sit?"

"Uh, yeah. I guess," Diana says slowly, but she takes several steps into the living room and we follow. She points toward the couch, and Connor and I sit after moving the blanket and the laundry. Diana sets the bag of food down in the kitchen before coming back in to pull one of her chairs over and sit down herself.

This is it. I'm on.

Weaving a story that makes my readers feel something, experience it viscerally as they read the words I've poured onto a page, is not only my job but my passion. But my words have never been more important than right now. And I'm not used to working on the fly like this. I prefer to put my words on paper so I can massage them until I find the right combination.

But this is do or die. If Diana understands and I get my laptop back, I'll be able to write book two in time to meet my deadline. If not, I don't know what I'll do.

I've already resorted to breaking and entering and intimidation. How much further will I go? I hope I don't have to find out.

"Diana, you're sort of right. I have been working like mad on book two."

Diana squirms in her seat, eager already. "What's it called?"

I'm not supposed to say. It's in my contract with Bluebird Publishing. But that's the least of my concerns on what I'm about to reveal. Still . . .

"Can you keep a secret?"

Diana's eyes light up, and she makes a locking motion to her lips as she nods. Not only is she hearing about the story, but she's getting insider information. Nothing could be more irresistible.

"It's called . . ." I take a breath, diving in with both feet and no safety net, *"Trouble in Great Falls."*

"Oh!" Diana's mouth falls open a split second before she covers it with both hands. "No! Not Amber and Ryker! I thought they got their happily ever after."

"Well . . ." I twist my lips, not saying that's not true but definitely implying it. Diana leans forward, definitely interested in hearing more. "Like I said, I'm working on it. But I ran into a bit of trouble.

"With the book?"

"You could say that." I sigh dramatically. "My laptop was taken. With my book on it."

"No fucking way!"

I nod sadly. "Yes, fucking way. And it's been an adventure all its own, trying to track it down, here and there and everywhere. Seriously, I've been from one side of this city to the other. Over the past few days, it's felt like a quest to get my heart back." I place my hands on my chest for emphasis.

"What does that have to do with me?" Diana asks, her face worried. "Why are you here?"

Connor stares at her with dead eyes and raised brows, and even in her overtired state, she figures out the puzzle pieces without my having to give too many details.

Diana's eyes widen, and she gets it. "No way!"

"Way," I confirm. "Diana, it all sounds crazy. I know it does. And it's been through several pairs of hands now, but the laptop you bought at the pawn shop is mine. It has the manuscript of *Trouble in Great Falls* on it. At least I hope it still does."

"The manuscript is on my laptop?" she echoes, then laughs at the ridiculousness of that statement even though it's the truth. "You bullshittin' me?"

"Well, *my* laptop," I correct carefully. "And no bullshit. If you bring it out, I can pull up the file myself, log in under the desktop, all that."

Diana's expression goes from confusion to wonder to 'oh, no, you didn't' in rapid succession. "Wait, you think I—"

Connor leans forward, his elbows on his knees and his expression serious. "We're sure you didn't know, Diana. You just went to a pawn shop to get a new computer."

"Damn right, I did," Diana says, sounding defensive.

"But it's still possession of stolen goods," Connor adds flatly.

Diana sighs heavily, flopping back in the chair. "Go to the pawn shop, Diana. They'll give you a good deal." Her voice is high-pitched and bitter, mimicking whoever told her that. To us, she says, "I start a nurse practitioner course tomorrow. I have to have a laptop to log in."

"Where is it?" Connor demands, and I can see Diana's hackles rising.

"Wait!" I interject, trying to soften things because I don't think Connor meant that to sound so ominous. Or well, maybe he did, but it's not getting the response we need. "Look, Diana. I need the laptop back. I'll even buy it back from you. I know you bought it with hard-earned money, and I respect that. I'll pay you back what you spent and buy you a new laptop . . . but I gotta have my data. Tonight. If not . . . well, let's just say the next time my editor gives me a call, you'll be responding to my house for a murder scene. Mine."

"Poppy—" Connor says, but I hold up my hand. Because it's true. I'd love to have my laptop back. Those keys practically contour to my fingertips at this point, and it's sentimental because I wrote my first bestseller on it.

But I can get by with my replacement . . . if I have all my data.

"I don't know . . ." Diana says slowly.

"Name your price," Connor simply instructs her. "Or if you really need a computer, wait here with Poppy. I'll get you one tonight so you're ready for classes in the morning."

"Please," I plead with her. "Please, Diana. I know it's asking a lot, but . . . I need it."

"Poppy Woodstock . . . Great Falls . . . book two . . . on my laptop . . ." Diana seems to be in shock, muttering to herself as her eyes glaze over, unseeingly staring at me. She shakes her head and sighs. "Out of all the laptops out there, I got this one?"

"May I see it?" I ask, and after a moment's hesitation, Diana gets up and disappears down the hallway. As she's going, I look over at Connor, who holds up a finger, his eyes saying everything I need to know. Stay calm . . . it's not over yet.

She comes back with a laptop, my laptop, and I can't help but squirm in my seat a little. I'll give her virtually anything she wants to get my baby back in my hands.

"Okay, here's what I want," she says, hugging my laptop.

I guess she had some time to wrap her head around this shitshow on the walk to her bedroom and back, I think wryly.

"I want to read the book as soon as I can. Please."

Oh, well that's easy. "Promise, I'll send you an early signed copy."

"Okay. And, in this book or the next, I want a paramedic character named after me."

Connor gives her a dark look. "I mean, it is *Trouble in Great Falls*. I'm sure you could come to an unfortunate end somehow."

I'm not entirely sure if he's talking about a character or the real Diana. Probably an imaginary one. Mostly.

"Uh-uh," Diana tells me, ignoring Connor. "Don't make me the token red shirt who dies five minutes after being introduced. No sending me to investigate creepy noises or hanging out looking for a Dr. Feelgood husband at the hospital. I'm too smart for that." She taps her temple. "You don't need to make me a main character, and I don't need a dose of Prince Charming dick. But I want a few lines, I want to live, and I don't want to be a villain or a stereotype."

"Deal."

"And a dedication?"

"Sure."

Diana takes a deep breath, smiling at how well her negotiation is going. "Last thing. I'm serious about my studies. I need a replacement, not money, and I don't have the time to buy another one."

I glance at Connor, expecting him to argue. But instead, he just whips out his phone and starts tapping. About ten seconds later, he looks up, nodding. "Done. It'll be here at eight a.m. You'll have to take the delivery."

"You don't have to do that," I argue even though I'm glad he is. I could get Diana a new laptop for classes, but I don't have connections that'll get one here by the morning. Maybe by ten P.M. if I pay for rush delivery.

"I told you I would fix this," he reminds me.

"Here," she says, laying my laptop with its cord on the coffee table. "Uhm, I don't want to press my luck—"

"Too late," Connor growls. He's reached the end of his patience with this and is about ready to take my laptop and walk right out the front door without another word to Diana Nichols.

She flinches, and I lay a hand on Connor's thigh. "What is it, Diana?"

"Can you just tell me if they work it out?" she asks, but then she blinks and shakes her head. "No, wait. Don't tell me. I want to be surprised."

I'm glad that someone cares this much about the characters who live in my head. "How about if I say that . . . romances always end in a happily ever after . . . eventually? Sometimes, the journey there is just really bumpy, sending the characters and readers through a bunch of ups and downs before they get to the final resolution."

"Like real life," Diana says wisely.

"Exactly," I agree, shooting Connor a glance. I find him already looking at me with an inscrutable expression.

"Okay." Diana's agreement takes me by surprise, even though it's what I want. It's almost . . . easy. Not that getting to this moment has been remotely simple. "Thank you."

Diana watches me as I take my laptop in trembling hands and open the lid, relief rushing through me when I see my screensaver pop up on the screen, a good sign. "Oh, my God! Nut! Juice!"

"*Excuse* me?" Diana says.

"Her dogs," Connor explains for me. "Pomeranians."

"Your dogs are named Nut and Juice?" Diana asks, fighting a grin.

"That's what I said too," Connor tells her, but I ignore the same old comment about my weird dog names. Mostly because I'm dancing around Diana's apartment with my laptop as my partner.

"Thank you," I gush when I'm finished, coming around to shake her hand. I'd hug her, but my laptop's in the way. "I can't wait to get to work. I have so much to do!" Excitement and happiness are surging through me, creative energy swirling up in a tornado that I know will keep me up all night.

Diana smiles. "I'm glad. I can't wait to read it."

Giving it up, I close my laptop and hug her with one hand, bringing Diana into my impromptu dance party as I vow, "I promise I'll make the Diana character as awesome as you are. Maybe she can rescue someone, rush them to the ER in her ambulance, and be the hero who saves the day!"

Diana dances away from me, shaking her hands wildly before putting her fingertips in her ears. "No! La, la, la, la . . . no spoilers! Just work your Poppy magic and it'll be perfect. But if I save someone tall, dark, and sexy, I promise I'll still be surprised!"

I'm in such a great mood, I almost dance with Connor too. But one stone-eyed look from him lets me know he'll put up with a lot of my craziness, but not dancing to music that doesn't exist except in my heart.

I nod wildly. "We should go so I can get started."

Our eyes meet, the gold flecks in his fiery blues swirling even though his features are still stone cold. But it's the eyes, and the unsaid things contained within, that have me frozen in place. I can see the words forming, words that can't, or won't, escape his lips.

Our mission is accomplished. Or at least, we've got my laptop back. But is that all there is? I certainly don't think so, but does he?

Diana watches us but after a few seconds starts fanning herself. "Ooh, don't mind me over here . . . watching everything. Every. Thing."

The moment of magic is broken. Connor blinks, and I clear my throat awkwardly.

"You take care of her. She's one of a kind, a treasure."

"You have no idea how right you are," Connor says, his voice rumbling and sending shock waves of delight through my entire body. "Come on."

"Thank you again!" I say, heading for the front door. As Connor holds the door for me, I stop, turning around. "Oh, and warm your dinner in the oven on 350 for fifteen minutes. There are cookies in the bag too, my grandmother's special recipe."

Diana grins, her hands going over her chest. "I love cookies!"

CHAPTER 18

CONNOR

I put my truck in park, leaning back in the driver's seat and feeling my strength leave me. "Guess I'll leave you to it. I know you have a lot of work to do."

My arms feel like lead, my gut like stone. Watching her take over the conversation with Diana Nichols, I felt like I was watching a door close for me. She has what she needs, and obviously, my growl first, break bones next, and later, feel any sort of remorse tactics didn't need to be used.

Truthfully, I think she's done with me now that she's got the laptop back, and I want to preemptively give her an out before she awkwardly tells me to go. The laptop is what started this whole thing, and now that I've fixed that fuckup, I feel better about it, maybe less guilty.

Besides, I should work on research for the new job for Mr. Big. I'm actually glad I have that as a distraction now so I can throw myself into work and tell myself that it's for the best. At least, it'll be the best for Poppy.

"Like hell," Poppy says on a laugh, looking over at me like I've suddenly sprouted antennae out of my head and started speaking nonsense. "I mean, I've got work, but I'd like for you to come inside."

"Inside?" I repeat dully, and she nods. "Why?"

"Inspiration, of course. You are . . . my muse." She waves her hands wide in a move reminiscent of a *Price is Right* model.

"And what, exactly, is a muse supposed to do?" I ask, softening to her antics and only slightly affected by my own desire to stay with her, no matter how bad of a plan it is.

Poppy grins, knowing she's got me. "Pretty simple. Sit on the couch and look tough and grumpy and sexy as hell. Preferably naked, but that's up for discussion. If it helps you decide, I'll put a clean sheet down so there's no Nut and Juice hairs on your taint." She somehow makes that sound like a major concession.

"That's much appreciated," I reply, still unsure. "You mind if I . . . read while I muse for you? Uhm, work stuff."

She pauses, only for the tiniest split second, but I feel the hesitation like a shot to my gut regardless. But she still agrees. "That's fine. You can even use my now backup laptop," Poppy offers as she hugs her original laptop tightly. She gets out, and I follow her inside, where she calls out to Nut and Juice. "Hello, my precious babies! Have you boys have been good?"

A fusillade of yaps greets her, and she opens the door wider for them to run out and do their business. I have no idea how she trained them to just use her yard without much more than a short fence border they could easily scale, but they do, rolling around a minimal bit before trotting inside as if they own the place. She gives them each a treat and some loving pets and then kicks a ball down the hallway.

"Go play for a bit. Mama's got work to do," she tells the two, who run off after the toy. She watches them, listening to the rumble of their playing, and then looks over at me. "Want a beer?"

"Yeah," I reply, going over to her couch and sitting down. I toe off my shoes and pull off my shirt, leaning back with my arms stretched wide along the back of the couch. When she comes back, her jaw drops open. "Feeling inspired?"

"Great googly eyed mooglies . . . I'm feeling something, that's for damn sure." She lifts one of the bottles to her forehead, still watching me.

I pat the couch next to me. "Want me to take off my jeans too?"

"No, that'll be fine," she assures me, setting the beers on the coffee table. "You get naked, I'm gonna get distracted, we'll have crazy sex all night, I won't finish my book, Hilda will kill me, and then there will be the whole memorial mess to deal with, and I don't have a black dress that fits to get buried in."

She surprises me at every turn, somehow going from sex to death to outfit selection in one sentence. I guess that's why she's the writer, not me.

"As it is, I could write paragraphs about those nipples, that chest, and that cute little happy trail to Dicktopia." She shakes her head, bringing herself out of whatever scene she's writing in her head. "But I'm going to be a good girl for now."

Primly, she walks over to her work area, setting everything back up after plugging her laptop in. As she gets things where she wants them, I take a sip of beer and watch her quietly. "I understand," I start slowly. "I know that with your laptop back, you're going to be burning the candle at both ends."

"I'll be burning the candle at both ends, the middle, and everywhere else," Poppy confirms.

"Well, I'm just saying . . . you don't have to go to Caylee's wedding," I tell her. "I get it. It was only supposed to be a one-day fiancée thing to begin with, and you don't owe me anything more. Especially now that you have what you wanted." I lift my chin toward her laptop, which is booting up to show a picture of Nut and Juice sopping wet and looking quite rat-like. "I promise I'll go, and I'll make all the right excuses for you. They'll totally understand why you 'ditched' me and the wedding is off."

"No way," Poppy says, stopping her paper arranging to look up at me. "You're going. I'm going. *We* are going."

Damn, she saw through my lie about going myself. She knows me too well and knows I'll bail on my family. "I'm trying to protect them and let you off the hook."

"Protect them from what?" Poppy asks. "From you?"

Poppy gets up and crosses the room to sit down beside me on the couch, but I can't look her in the eyes. "Connor, I know I don't know even a whisper of all the shit you've done and the drama between you and your family. But I'm not stupid, and the truth is easy to see. You're not trying to protect them, you're trying to protect yourself. And I get that, especially after meeting them and seeing them in action. They're a fucking *Bravo TV* reality show in the flesh. But I think your mom is salvageable. Your aunt and cousin, maybe not. Your father? I have no idea. But that's why we need to go. You can't leave Caylee to the wolves with no one to have her back. That's not who you are."

"She has Evan," I point out, and Poppy scoffs. "What?"

"Evan's good, but he's going to have his own stuff to deal with on his wedding day, even if his family is full of saints, which I sincerely doubt. Caylee needs her brother there. She needs you looking out for her, on her side against the rest of them."

I sigh and take another swig of beer. "I know."

I go quiet, remembering back when Caylee and I were close, before everything went to shit, especially with Dad. We used to be friends, playing together in the backyard. Our most common game was called 'river rapids'. Caylee would line up rocks and pebbles into a winding lane while I would dig a hole at the end. Then we'd fill it up with water from the hose, creating a miniature river and pond for Caylee's little pet shop animals to 'swim' in.

We always had our favorite animals, Caylee liking this pink poodle one and me preferring the shark because I liked the logic of a water animal swimming, even if there was the whole fresh water versus saltwater issue.

Even when we got older, both dealing with our shit in our own ways, I always looked out for Caylee. In middle school, long after things had become difficult in our house, she'd had a first boyfriend who was a miniature twelve-year-old version of an asshole. That's probably common, but this one was especially terrible.

When I heard Caylee crying over the stupid prick, over how he'd made her feel inadequate by flirting with another girl, I'd handled that. A visit to his soccer team practice, a short 'conversation', and that was that. They broke up, but he never said shit to her afterward. Caylee didn't know about it then and doesn't know about it now.

Guilt for not truly checking out this Evan guy assails me, but even sharper is knowing the disconnect between Caylee and me is my fault. I'm the one who cut her out of my life. She didn't need to get caught up in my rebellion, especially when it went from mere rebelling to outright criminality.

"So, we're going?" Poppy asks gently, having let me disappear into my memories for a long moment.

"You don't have to." I'm still worried about Poppy, about this connection developing deeper and wider. And about her safety. "I will go."

"I want to," Poppy says in that same soft, gentle voice. "You need some support too. Unless . . . you don't want me to."

I can hear the unasked question, the pain at the thought of not going, of my pushing her away again. She's kept coming back, forcing herself in again and again . . . but even someone as stubborn as Poppy has limits.

Now that we're at those limits, I know something else, too.

I've been dead wrong to keep pushing her away.

"I want you." The words don't come out the way I want, so I clear my throat and say them again, bolder and with more feeling. "I want you, Poppy."

Poppy's smile is worth what's going to come from those four words, and she claps happily. "Good. Then we're going. But first, I write. Now . . . muse!"

I muse my ass off.

There's nothing particularly special about the wedding venue. Riverside Methodist is about as *beige* a church as I can think of, politely unoffensive and one of those places where the football loving members can always count on getting home in time for the early kickoffs.

I'm in my best black suit, the one I normally reserve for the best jobs, but Caylee deserves my best.

"Have I mentioned that you look hot?" Poppy says with a twinkle in her eye as I come out of the men's room.

She looks pretty hot herself in a pale blue halter-style dress that leaves her shoulders and upper back bare. I wonder if she's wearing one of those weird sticky bras or if her nipples are a scant few layers of chiffon away from my touch. I could find out with a bare brush of the fabric, but even the thought is enough to make my suit pants feel a bit tight. "Twirl for me."

That gets my attention away from her tits. "No."

"Twirl, Muse!"

I cross my arms, trying to glower. "I do not twirl."

She lifts a brow expectantly, and with a heavy sigh, I spin. Not a twirl, nothing so dainty, but more of a four-quarter perimeter check even though it's totally unnecessary. At least that's what I tell myself.

"Yay!" Poppy says, twirling herself easily. The skirt of her dress spins out, flashing her upper thighs to anyone who might happen by. I rush at her, helping the skirt down to possessively hide her legs from any eyes but mine. "Don't smush my flower!"

Poppy is looking at the satin belt around her waist where a silk flower with a button center sits off-center just above her left hip. "I made this myself with hot glue, tears, and a button from Nut and Juice's dog bed. Don't worry, I washed it first. The button, I mean. And the tears were because I burned the hell out of my fingers, but it was worth it in the end." She fluffs the flower needlessly. "Or at least it was until that marriage ended in divorce, but hey . . . at least I get to wear the bridesmaid dress again. So, happy ending." Poppy told me about her dress last night when she asked if it was acceptable for the wedding. Apparently, she was a bridesmaid at a cousin's wedding a few years ago and loved the dress, just not the cousin who'd complained about Poppy's red hair standing out in the photos like a sore thumb.

"You look beautiful," I tell Poppy again. "And thank you for coming."

She smiles up at me, cupping my face gently. Her blue eyes sparkle with happiness, and I'm still shocked every time that it has anything to do with me. "I wouldn't dream of being anywhere else right now," she says earnestly. But then she pats my cheeks a bit too hard. "Now, go find your sister while I get us seats. Fair warning, if I see any little old ladies with walkers, I'm gonna knock them down to get to the front row. Everyone knows that's where the best mosh pits are."

"I don't think there will be a mosh pit during the ceremony. It's planned for the reception," I answer dryly.

"Hmm, I must've missed that memo," Poppy says lightly. With a shrug, she adds, "Well, if one happens to spontaneously break out, it definitely won't be my fault. Nope, not my fault at all."

With a kiss so quick I don't even get to pucker, she's off. Alone in the hallway, I take a steadying breath before going to find Caylee.

I wander down a corridor until I find a closed door with a sign proclaiming *Bride* and then knock. Opening the door slowly, I call out, "Everyone decent?"

Caylee answers, "Yes, come in."

The room is sparse, with some suitcases in the floor and two tables set up with makeup and hair stuff. But I don't see anything other than Caylee, not entrance and exit points, alarms, or any of the other things I typically note automatically. It's just my sister, all grown up.

Caylee looks beautiful in her wedding gown, a white, slim-fitting dress with lace along the bodice and hips. Her hair is down in curls, and a beautiful tiara that makes her look like a princess sits on her head.

"Connor!" she cries out, hugging me tightly as she realizes that I'm really sticking to my promise and have actually showed up tonight. "Thank you."

"You look stunning," I compliment her. "Really, Caylee."

"You're not so bad yourself, big brother." She grins, so happy she's nearly in tears. "I can't believe you came."

I sigh, nodding. "I wish I could say there's no way I would've missed it, but we both know that'd be a lie."

Caylee's smile falters as a hint of sadness enters her eyes. But she doesn't give me shit for being absent for so long. Instead, she says, "Poppy's good for you."

I want to argue with her, but she's right. Last night after working and 'musing', Poppy was so exhausted, we fell into her bed. Not for sex but to actually sleep. I'd held her in my arms as she snored softly and had slept more peacefully than I have in years. I want to share that with Caylee, but in the end, I settle with the truth. "I worry I'm not good for her."

Caylee looks at me with pity. "I know. I had the same problems when Evan and I started dating. The peril of having parents we couldn't please, no matter what we did."

There's really no way to reply to that, it's simply the hardhearted truth. "I didn't do a whole lot of people pleasing back then, anyway."

"Yeah, well . . . I kept trying," she says with some bitterness. "You were always the smart one, going the other way when you saw it wasn't going to work no matter what you did."

I snort at her assessment, both that I'm the smart one and that the youthful transgressions she knows about were the better option. I wonder if she'd still feel the same way if she knew just how far I've gone and how deeply I've fallen. But beyond myself, I realize that when I rebelled, leaving my parents' expectations and rules behind, I also left behind . . . Caylee.

"I'm sorry." The words choke me, and I cough, not expecting this to be so damn hard. "I'm sorry, Cay. For then and for now."

Caylee presses her lips together, looking up as she blinks rapidly and fans her face. "Don't do that. If you make me cry before the pictures, I'm going to look like a demon-possessed raccoon with red eyes with a black smudge of liner. Then I'll have to kick your ass."

"Think about coconuts," I blurt.

Caylee looks back at me, surprised. "What?"

"Coconuts," I repeat. "Sunscreen. Sand. Sea. Picture it, smell it, feel it. You can't cry on the beach. It's humanly impossible. Probably illegal too. At least in a handful of countries."

It's Poppy's words coming out of my mouth. I can feel the randomness of them, but they're also from the heart and seem to work because Caylee immediately laughs and dabs her eyes. "Coconuts. Okay then. Thank you. And for coming."

"Close your eyes," I respond, reaching into my pocket. "And hold out your hands."

Caylee gives me a quizzical smile but does what I ask and closes her eyes. With the sun on her face, she looks so ethereal it takes my breath away. It makes me realize how much she's grown up, no longer the knock-kneed, snaggle-toothed kid but a beautiful woman beginning a family of her own.

Taking my hand out of my pocket, I pull out the small shiny rock, second-guessing myself. She might not get it. She might not even remember. But it's too late not to give it to her when she's eagerly holding her hands out, her smile growing brighter by the second. So with a lot of nervousness, I put the white rock in her outstretched hands.

"Here."

Caylee opens her eyes and looks down. She gasps instantly, her fingers closing around the rock as she holds it to her chest. "Connor! It's gorgeous."

I can't help it, I smile at her excitement. "You remember? The backyard river? I was thinking about that the other day, and it seemed like a good memory."

"Of course I get it. We spent every day doing that for years," Caylee says with a happy, wistful laugh. "You know, I hated getting all muddy like that, dirt under my nails and smudges on my face. But if you wanted to do that, I was always in to hang with my big brother."

I blink in surprise. "Caylee . . . I didn't want to do it either. You were the one who always wanted to play with the animals."

We lock eyes, both of us realizing that we'd been doing it for each other. That we would've done anything for each other back then. And maybe we would even now. Laughing, I reach out and truly hug my sister for the first time in a long time.

"Shit," I admit as she hugs me back tightly, "I'm going to cry."

Caylee's laugh vibrates my chest. "Not allowed, buddy. You cry, I cry, and then Poppy will cry because I'll kick your ass so hard."

A fault line in our relationship starts to heal. It's not an instant thing, no *poof* and we're all good again. But it's a start. I just hope I can be around long enough to keep it going, but that's never guaranteed in my line of work.

"Caylee," I whisper when we let go slightly, "even when I'm not here or we don't see each other for awhile . . . I love you, Cay."

Caylee pats my chest, giving me that same megawatt smile I've missed for too long. "I love you too."

"Hold it, just like that!" a voice snaps. I look up to see the photographer framing a sibling moment for Caylee and me. Instinctually, I want to argue and say 'no pictures' or duck away from the lens. People like me do better when we're not photographed. But for Caylee, this time . . . I don't. I face the camera boldly and hold her a little tighter.

She notices, and her smile grows. "She's good for you."

"Not disagreeing." She is . . . despite my misgivings.

"Don't fuck this up, Connor. You're better now, and I think she has something to do with it," Caylee continues as the photographer moves on. "Besides, I've always wanted a sister. And I can't think of a better one than Poppy Woodstock." She sobers, her face going serious. "She doesn't like pink poodles, does she? I'll share you, but I'm not sharing Mr. Peabody."

I hum as though giving the question deep consideration. "No, not a pink poodle type, I don't think. Pomeranians, actually."

"Good, then I want to keep her," Caylee says. "Besides, I want to meet Nut and Juice."

"You know her dogs' names?"

Caylee blushes. "I might've done a little homework on your fiancée too." She holds up her finger and thumb an inch apart. "Just a little Google research and maybe joining her online fan group to get the scoop. She posts pictures of the dogs sometimes."

I look at Caylee in surprise and with a newfound respect. She shrugs it off. "Hey, you checked up on Evan, so it's only fair that I check up on Poppy. We siblings have gotta stick together."

The wedding planner comes in, looking pointedly at her watch. "Knock, knock. Time get a move on." I'm shooed out and go find Poppy, not in the front row but in the second row.

"It's apparently reserved," she whispers. "So when I get up to dance, make sure you follow my lead."

She's kidding. I think.

The ceremony is sweet, though seeing my dad stoically walk Caylee down the aisle has me clenching my fist at my side. He doesn't deserve that honor, not after the way he's been for the past decade. But when Dad places Caylee's hand into Evan's and he turns to sit with Mom, I see him quickly swipe at his eyes.

Huh?

Maybe the old man isn't as empty and unemotional as I thought, though if your baby girl's getting married doesn't warrant some emotion, you're probably completely cold and dead inside.

Evan looks at Caylee like she not only hung the moon but actually created it out of silk and magic. I decide that yeah, he can live a bit longer. Especially as Caylee looks at him with just as much wonder and love.

Relaxing my clenched fist, I take Poppy's hand instead. She looks at our interwoven hands in surprise, but then she leans into me, laying her head on my shoulder. "Weddings are nice."

I'm not as good with words as she is, but she seems to understand the depth of what I'm trying to express. I feel her smile against my shoulder, and then she stays snuggled into me for the remainder of the ceremony.

At the reception, things start off well as Mom looks overjoyed. "Isn't she beautiful?" she gushes as Caylee and Evan spin around the floor for their first dance. Mom sips at a champagne, her eyes twinkling.

"She looks great, Mom," I tell her.

Spying the ring on Poppy's finger, Mom zeroes in. "Ooh, it's lovely! Soon, it'll be your day too."

"Thank you. Uh, yeah . . . soon," Poppy says, her eyes cutting to me.

I laugh a little uncomfortably and put my arm around Poppy's shoulders. "Let's enjoy Caylee's day and catch our breath before rushing into another wedding."

Mom nods absently, dabbing at her eyes. "I know. I'm just so happy."

She looks it, truly delighted at Caylee's big day and the beginning of married life with Evan. Hell, she looks happier than I've seen her in years.

"Oh, there's the Parkers. Excuse me," Mom whispers before taking off to mingle.

Poppy leans in to tell me, "You're handling everything well."

"So far, but the night is young," I tease.

But as if I foretold it myself, as Poppy and I move around, my mood quickly darkens as some of the reasons I have stayed away make themselves noticeable. "Hide the silverware," Justin, one of my cousins, stage whispers as he comes by. "Con-air's around."

"Con-air?" Poppy whispers, and I grit my teeth.

"A nickname I got when I first got in trouble," I reply, not letting myself get baited.

Another relative, who I don't even know, walks by and openly looks me up and down before telling the woman at her side, "He's strictly look but don't touch. Sticky hands, if you know what I mean. Let me introduce you to someone worth your time."

Poppy gapes and almost goes after the woman. I can picture it now ... she'd rip her back by her hair and demand that she apologize to me for what she said. But I don't want to cause a scene. Today is about Caylee.

"No mosh pits, and no fights for my honor among people who have none," I warn Poppy. She narrows her eyes, giving a threatening version of the stink eye to the two women, but she stays at my side.

"Of course. But I may need to make a pit stop later, you know, if they go powder their noses." She says it sweet as sugar and innocent as can be, but something tells me Poppy will introduce them to Paulette the Purse since Gary the Golf Club is at home.

We mingle, some people cordial and civilized, but then I hear a voice that scrapes along my spine like nails on a chalkboard. "Connor! Come see the aunts and uncles."

I breathe in deeply through my nose, turning to see Aunt Audrey along with a few of my other 'aunts' and 'uncles', those cousins from an older generation. Most of them, of course, believe the hype and not the reality about me.

"Hello, Audrey," I say flatly. "Gene, Lisa, Bernie."

"Hello, Con-air," Bernie, who if I remember right, took to that nickname harder than any of my other family members, chortles. "Keeping your nose clean these days?"

"Cleaner than yours," I reply smoothly, staring at the bulbous nose in question.

Bernie starts sniffing and rubbing his nose, trying to 'hide' the nonexistent booger while also wondering if there's something I know that he'd rather I didn't. It's no secret that he's had some indiscretions of his own, both personal and professional.

Next to me, Poppy smirks, and Audrey, of course, notices. "Hello again, Poppy. Ian's around here somewhere, I'm sure."

"I'm sure he is. He probably doesn't get far on that short leash you've got him on, does he?" She winks and then laughs as though she's joking. But Audrey's face pinches in anger.

"So, you're Connor's girlfriend?" Lisa, who's been one of Aunt Audrey's biggest sycophants since well before I was born, says. "I've heard so much about you. What is it that you do again?" It's an obvious setup, but Poppy doesn't take the bait.

"I'm an author, working on my second novel."

Audrey sniffs, clearly still trying to cast shade. "She writes *romance* books."

Lisa gasps on cue, looking like she just smelled a three-day old rotten egg fart. "I see."

"Hmph," Bernie, who probably doesn't know anything about romance books, or knowing his personal history, about romance at all, grunts. "You know what a criminal degenerate this one is, don't you?"

"Trust me, she knows," I growl. Bernie's always been one of the family members most obsessed with my criminality.

Audrey shakes her head sadly, acting as if she's the long-suffering fountain of wisdom and forbearance even though she's just stirring the shit. "I tried to tell her. You know I did. Some people just don't take good advice when it's given."

Gene hums, his eyes fixed on Poppy's figure in her dress. "Such a shame. A pretty girl like you could do so much better than an ugly man like Connor."

He doesn't mean my good looks. He's talking about his perception of my soul—that its ugly, black with sin, and worthless because I don't bow down to what he deems the proper thing to do and be.

Bernie huffs his agreement with Gene and then sips his champagne. Looking at Poppy, he shrugs dismissively. "You'll never get his family money, anyway. Robert and Debra won't support his *lifestyle*."

"What the fuck did you say?" I snap too loudly. The sharp and cutting tone draws attention from people all around us. Audrey looks like she can taste the victory of pushing me over the edge.

I'm not even mad at what he's saying about my parents and me. I'm furious that he's reducing Poppy to nothing more than a gold-digging whore when she's nothing of the sort.

Poppy, who has every justification to go full-on batshit crazy on this group, is a rock, though. Calmly, she lays her hand over my arm before I go ballistic and ruin Caylee's special day by becoming the violent thug my family thinks I am.

"Connor," she says quietly, patting me gently like I'm a lapdog she can control with the slightest command. I don't know what to say about the fact that I instantly quiet, knowing from her overly sweet smile that she's about to slice and dice this guy, and I, for one, can't wait to see it.

Clearing her throat, Poppy's smile takes on that manic glint that I've seen before, the one she showed the pawn shop guy who she insists on calling Gary's 'foster daddy'. "Oh, I'm not with Connor for his handsome face or his family," she says in a fake as hell snooty accent, laughing lightly like that's absurd. "I'm with him because of his *monster* dick." Everyone gasps in shock, but Poppy keeps going, never one to back down from anything. Especially something crazy. Her sugary smile only grows. "It doesn't hurt that he *really* knows how to use it too. Well, sometimes it does hurt, but in the *best* way. You know what I mean, don't you?"

Poppy nudges my Great-Aunt Edna, flashing her a conspiratory look. Edna sputters, hand over her pearls, literally clutching them in horror. "I, well . . . no, I never . . ."

Poppy frowns dramatically. "Never? Oh, dear, how utterly tragic." She tsks sadly. Dropping her voice, she confides, "I tell you what, I'll send you a copy of my bestseller book. Ryker really gives it to Amber good. Think of it as 'girls helping girls', you know." Poppy winks with her mouth open, like she's sharing some great secret. "One warning, though, it does have anal in it. That might be a bit advanced to start out with, but you just see what feels right, m'kay?"

"Anal?" Edna stammers.

Poppy smiles wide, purposefully misunderstanding Edna's reaction. "Ooh, Edna! You naughty minx. Don't worry, if anal sex is what appeals to you, I spell it out in graphic detail. Just remember . . . you know how in real estate, it's location, location, location? With anal, it's lubrication, lubrication, lubrication. Never too much, right, babe?" Poppy asks me.

I reach down and grab a handful of her ass, squeezing vulgarly. "Never too much," I agree.

If she were talking about anal sex with anyone other than my wrinkled Aunt Edna, I think I'd be hard as rock right now, but the ridiculous brilliance of Poppy's mind is sending blood to my own brain instead of south, so I can fully enjoy her special brand of crazy. Admittedly, I'm particularly enjoying Aunt Audrey's face, which looks like she sucked on a lemon coated in years of bitterness.

"Why, I never!" Audrey exclaims, and I smirk, claiming the victory for me and Poppy.

"We know." Deciding I'd better quit while we're ahead, I take Poppy's hand in mine and tell the assembled family group, "Excuse us."

"Oh, yeah . . . excuse us." Poppy offers a little two-fingered wave. "Don't worry about me if we disappear for a bit. I'll be fine, just *fine*." She wiggles her hips in a silly dance, though we're nowhere near the dance floor, making it more than obvious that she's implying that I'm whisking her away to fuck her in some remote corner of the reception before the cake is cut.

I clench my jaw, gritting my teeth to fight back the laugh trying to force its way out as we walk away, leaving the people gossiping in horror.

"You know we just confirmed their beliefs," I whisper when we're far enough away, "that I'm a total degenerate, and anyone who spends time with me must be just as bad."

Poppy shrugs it off like what just happened is no big deal. "No matter how much you grow, some people don't see it. Their mind is made up, and they're unwilling to see that circumstances might be different now."

"Doesn't mean I have to put up with it," I murmur. "And that especially doesn't mean you should have to put up with it."

"Who, the geezer who called you Con-Air?" Poppy asks. "Are you going to see that guy again? He's like a bajillion years old and looks like he made a deal with the Grim Reaper just to see today's sunrise. So who the fuck cares what he thinks? Do you care what a shriveled old prune with zero filter says about you? I sure don't. And hell, maybe a little dick in her ass will make Edna's day. You never know."

I shake my head, partly in trying to make sense of the way her mind works but at the same time trying to shake the image out of my head. "You are amazing."

"I know."

We're about halfway across the room, and I stop, taking her hand and pulling her in close. "Fuck it. Let's dance."

Poppy looks at me in surprised delight. "You dance?"

I lift an eyebrow as if that's a silly question. "The rules are pretty simple. Move your feet, sway, and rub your junk together . . . what's hard about that?"

Poppy laughs. "You're such a romantic. And I'm certain there will be something *hard* by the end."

"Now who's the romantic?" I tease as I pull her close, moving to the happy, celebratory music. And to be nice, I don't rub my cock on her . . . much. But I enjoy holding her in my arms, our bodies in tune with one another as the polite inches between us disappear.

"Mmm, you do know how to move," Poppy says as her chest touches mine.

"Only when I have a good partner," I reply.

The tempo slows, becoming softly romantic, and I pull her in even closer until Poppy puts her head on my chest, listening to my heartbeat. I close my eyes for a long moment, lost in Poppy, oblivious to everyone and everything around us as we barely sway. That's not a safe thing for me to do, but she makes me feel like I'm a normal man falling for a very unique woman. She makes me feel like there might be a future for me, for us.

And even if that's not true, I want to pretend for a moment.

A throat clears next to us, and I crack one eye to see Ian standing there, obviously sent by Audrey. He flashes a cocky grin. "May I cut in?"

Manners require me to say yes. Etiquette requires Poppy to spend a song moving around the floor with him. It's the kind of artificially polite structure my family has thrived on for generations, and Ian fucking knows it.

But he, and apparently Aunt Audrey who is sitting at a table along the edge of the dance floor with a wry smirk as she watches, have completely forgotten a key element to civility.

It only works if everyone plays by the same rulebook. And Poppy and I operate by a totally different set of rules than Ian and Audrey and the rest of the hypocritical members of my family.

"No."

Ian's smile falters, and he glances over his shoulder to his mother, who waves a hand telling him to get on with it while next to me, Poppy looks amused, not moving from my side. Ian's eyes cut back to me. "Excuse me?" he says snottily, likely having never been told no in his entire life. "I'd like to dance."

But Ian and Audrey seem to have also forgotten one more thing. The notion of asking a man to dance with his woman is ridiculously antiquated. And Poppy is not one to take that sitting down . . . or standing up . . . or any other way.

"I see," Poppy says, crossing her arms and giving Ian a withering look of her own. "Don't you think you should ask me to dance? Unless you want to dance with Connor. No judgment if that's the case. Other than the whole cousin thing. That's kinda a sticky wicket."

I snicker while Ian finally gives Poppy his attention. Because this isn't really about her at all. It's about me. It's about taking what's mine. It's about taking the opportunity to show me in a bad light.

His fake smile blooms again as he thinks he's found another way to win against me. "Yes, of course, how *gauche* of me. Please excuse my errant question, and I shall ask you. Would you care to dance?"

He holds his arm out, inviting her to slip her hand to his elbow. But Poppy doesn't move an inch. "No."

Her answer is just as flat and dismissive as mine was. His smile flips completely upside down into a frown. "Excuse me?"

"It's pretty simple," Poppy says. "You asked me a question. A question is, by its very nature, allowing for choice and options in answer. And my choice is to say no. Unless you only asked rhetorically and you're saying that I don't have the choice in who I want to dance with?"

Ian flounders at her logic, or maybe it's the big words like 'rhetorically', and out of the corner of my eye, I see that Caylee's paying attention, grinning. She's on Team Poppy, or Team Connor, or whatever we are.

Ian flushes. "No."

"Exactly," Poppy says. "No. That's my answer, Ian. Now run along back to Mommy and tell her that her scheming is transparent and mean-spirited."

Ian starts to turn, but Poppy calls him back. "Ian? You can tell her no too."

Ian laughs like that's ridiculous and scurries off the dance floor before any more attention can come his way. Poppy watches him, then turns back to me, shrugging. "Can't save them all."

I laugh softly, pulling her back into my arms to continue our dance and looking into her sparkling eyes. "You're amazing."

"Thank you."

I almost stop there. Maybe I should. But before I can stop it, I give her a little pebble of my soul too. One even more important than the one I gave Caylee. "I think you're saving me."

Poppy's smile falters for a moment before she lifts onto her tiptoes to give me a soft, tender kiss. It feels different this time, deeper and more meaningful. And more dangerous, but her lips' accepting mine so openly washes away my concerns, letting hope get a foothold.

After, she giggles and whispers, "I flipped off Audrey while I was kissing you. I know it's juvenile, but it makes me feel better."

I blink and look over to see Ian trying to appease Audrey, who is fuming visibly but too concerned about appearances to actually do anything about it other than shoot us a sneer of distaste.

I flip her off too, giving her a bonus wink. "You're right. That does feel better."

We go back to our seats, enjoying the festivities and the food until it's time for toasts. Caylee, perhaps wisely, doesn't ask me to toast them, but when it's time to throw the flowers, Poppy goes out there on the dance floor with the rest of the single women, ready to play wide receiver. The women are good-naturedly volleying for position, and though I can't hear them, I think there's a fair amount of smack talk going on out there.

Caylee looks over her shoulder one last time, smiling at her guests, and then takes three practice swings. Three . . . two . . . one. The bouquet arcs high into the air, nearly catching on a chandelier, and everyone dives for it at the same time, bouncing into and off each other. It seems Poppy was right about the mosh pit, after all. And there she is, right in the middle of it.

The flowers bounce along the grasping hands to tumble to the dance floor, where the women scramble for it like football players going after a greased fumble. Caylee hikes up her dress and scoots back from the incoming wave of women with a shout encouraging them to 'get it!'

It's a heap of tulle, lace, and pretty dresses, but Poppy squirms over and around them, dodging and weaving before popping up with the slightly crushed flowers in her hands. "Boo-yah!" She holds it up high in triumph, and the other women laugh, instantly realizing that they were going ham over a dozen roses they could buy at the grocery store.

But it's about the symbolism and tradition.

Caylee's clapping, and when she catches my eye, she mouths to me, "I like her. Don't fuck up."

Poppy returns to the table holding the bouquet like a trophy. "I caught it!"

I pull her down, giving her a kiss on the cheek. "Well, you grabbed it off the floor."

"Same difference. It's mine, and you know what that means," she sing-songs happily.

For a moment, the whole thing feels . . . real. Like she's really mine, like we're really engaged, like we're actually going to get married.

It's a great gift from Caylee to me, even if she doesn't know she's giving it.

CHAPTER 19

CONNOR

"Tonight was amazing," Poppy says as we climb in my truck to leave the reception.

Across the console, I take her hand and trace her fingers with my own. I need to touch her, want to keep this feeling of a fairy tale come to life alive inside me for as long as I can.

We're about halfway home when Poppy turns to me. "Connor, pull over."

"What?" I ask, immediately worried. "Are you okay?"

"Pull over up there," she says, pointing to a spot just off the road. I do, noticing that we're in a pretty out of the way turn off. The reception was held up in the hills surrounding town, and right now, we're practically alone with no headlights visible for miles.

I shift into park and turn to Poppy. "Poppy, I—"

My words are cut off as she practically lunges across the center console, kissing me hard. I kiss her back, running my hands through the thickness of her hair to hold her close so I can take her mouth even deeper.

She's my air, my breath, my being, and I can't get enough of her. It'll never be enough.

I can't explain it. It's just . . . Poppy.

I've wanted her all night, maybe even longer. Maybe since I last left her heaven, but I've been trying to be good, waiting until we got back home at least. But the time for waiting is over. She wants me right here, right now, and I'm more than willing to give her what she wants.

"Wait," I growl as she tries to crawl over the console between us and bangs her head on the roof. "Back seat."

Poppy's eyes cut to the back bench seat of my truck, and she grins wide, her teeth flashing in the dim light from the dash. "Meet you back there . . . naked."

I laugh as she dives over the console, going ass over head as she climbs through the cab. I've got my pants undone before I get my door unlocked, yanking my shirt open Superman-style as my feet hit the dirt. Buttons go flying, but fuck it.

Poppy's upright and waiting for me when I get the back door open, and through the miracle of a well-designed dress, she's already nude except for a pair of blue see-through panties that frame her hips deliciously.

I climb in, closing and locking the door behind me, and the dome light dims. We don't need it, anyway. I already know Poppy's body by memory, and I don't want to risk anyone else seeing us from the side of the road. Because she's mine.

"Come here," I tell her, shifting my body around. I don't want to crush her underneath me, so I sit upright with my legs spread wide.

Poppy's petite height comes into good use as she crawls into my lap and settles in on bent legs to press her core against my throbbing cock. I wrap my arms around her, pulling her down again and again, teasing us both with what we desperately want.

She moans loudly in my ear, and I squirm, trying to find leverage in the tight back seat to give her more of a stroke, even through the layers of our clothes.

We don't say anything, but as our mouths find each other, the frantic pace grows softer, more tender. The kiss deepens, but there's no need to rush. We can stay parked here all night if we have to, exploring each other's mouth and body.

Her hand reaches down between us to take me in her hand, her breathy gasp when she finds me rock hard exciting me even more. "For you, Poppy."

She arches her back, giving herself room to work me, and I slide my hands down her body, teasing and plucking her nipples, grabbing her ass roughly, and scratching down the backs of her thighs. Her hips buck instinctually, telling me where she wants my touch. Her panties are a thong, and when I pull them to the side and slip my hand down toward her cleft, I find her soaked.

"For you, Connor."

A spasm of pleasure rocks through me, almost making me come instantly. But I hold off, not nearly ready to be done with her this quickly.

Her hand strokes me up and down, and I match her measured pace with my own finger, dipping into her entrance to feel her heat. She moves to kiss down my chest and rearrange herself in the seat beside me. Still on her knees, she bends forward, her tongue leaving a wet trail over my skin before she swallows me in the dark.

It's heaven. I can barely see her head move in the moonlight that filters through the windows, but that only adds to the pleasure. All I can feel is the sensation of her tongue swirling around my head, her lips on my shaft, and the softness of her hair in my hand as I guide her up and down my aching cock.

"Fuck," I groan.

I can't say anything else, my brain so overwhelmed that I can barely make any conscious sound at all.

I just give myself to Poppy, relishing the pleasure she's giving me until I'm on the edge and tightening my fingers in her hair, freezing her.

"You," I whisper, and she pulls back, climbing into my lap once more. I pull her face to mine and kiss her until she whimpers, needing me as much as I need her. I tug her panties to the side, and there's nothing but soft, slick heat as she lowers herself onto me, both of us freezing as she takes me fully.

In the darkness, we lock eyes. She's undoing me, years of walls falling away like rubble, leaving me vulnerable. She's inside me . . . my heart, my soul. And I can see a direct, open line to her heart too. Whatever walls she has are nowhere near as impenetrable as mine, but I still recognize the precious gift she's offering by allowing me in.

I learned a long time ago to trust my gut, even when my mind says its wrong. And Poppy is the right thing for me . . . it's fast, crazy, and a completely ridiculous idea, but completely true regardless.

She's mine, and the ruby on her finger means something more now. I'm not sure what yet, and that's something I'll have to discuss with her, but all I know is that she's a hell of a lot more than a one-day fiancée, and this is about so much more than a laptop.

Poppy rolls her hips, grinding her clit against me as we kiss again.

I know what this will require. I need to tell her everything, the good and the bad. I'll have to tell her about *The Black Rose*, and maybe even Mr. Big. But I want to be completely bare with her, no fronts or façades, because I've never been that with anyone.

Maybe not even myself.

But she deserves to know the truth. All of it.

I bite back the words that are rising because I don't want there to be any doubt about their honesty when I have to expose the dirty deeds she doesn't know about yet. So I save them, for now. But I can make sure she knows how I feel. I've got to do that. What I can't say, I pour out in my touch, my hands tracing all the places I know Poppy likes, my fingers pinching her sensitive nipples and then gripping her hips as I start thrusting up into her. She rides me, her soft cries of pleasure giving me what I need.

Her whimpers are a salve for my soul.

I buck my hips harder and faster, driving deep. She falls forward, catching herself with her forearms on the back window, and I take advantage, sucking a stiff nipple into my mouth.

"Connor!" she gasps as she hovers on the edge of coming, her pussy tightening around me until it's nearly like a vise. I thrust up, my balls tight and my body on edge, but I wait there in that blissful moment for her. I swat the round globe of her ass, and she falls apart. "*Yesss*" she hisses.

When I feel her orgasm in her quivering walls, I release myself. Maybe I say her name, maybe I don't, but as I explode inside her, I know that I'll never be the same. She's changed me for good and there's no going back.

I hold her close, our hearts beating in time as she sags against me. The only sound is our panting breaths until . . .

A truck passes by, his horn loud and obnoxious and making us both jump like teenagers caught misbehaving.

She laughs when she realizes what it was, calling out, "Glad you weren't a few seconds earlier, asshole. I would've been really pissed if you'd messed up my big O."

"I don't think he heard you," I say gently, running my fingers through her hair and kissing her forehead as my satisfied cock deflates. Slipping out of her is bittersweet, a loss of heaven, but I pray I'll be invited back in . . . forever.

She groans, feeling the loss too.

"Your knees okay?" I whisper, and she wiggles weakly.

"I don't know yet. I lost feeling in my feet several minutes ago, but it didn't seem important at the time," she tells me with a shrug.

I smile and reach for her toes to rub the circulation back into them, but that is most definitely the *wrong* thing to do because she squeals sharply and flails, falling over in the seat. "I'm ticklish! Don't touch my feet!"

She somehow ends up kicking the window, leaving a Poppy-sized footprint right on the glass.

"Oops!" she says with wide eyes.

"You know what that looks like, don't you?" I ask, and she tries to swipe it off. "No, leave it. I kinda like it there."

Instead of leaving it alone, she presses her palm to the glass too. "Now people will wonder what kind of crazy positions you're getting into in the back of your truck. They'll be doing . . . this . . . and this . . ." She holds her hand up one way, her foot tilted the other, and then switches them around, trying to match the two prints at the same time.

"You're crazy," I tell her with a smile.

"You're just now figuring this out?" Her brows are crinkled like I just told her that I learned how to add two plus two.

I chuckle, running my hand up her thigh and staying really far away from her feet.

"I want you to stay at my place tonight," I tell her honestly, the words popping out before I realize I'm thinking them. "I want you in my arms all night."

She blinks slowly, like she's letting my words sink in deep, and then a beaming smile spreads across her face. "I'll have to let Nut and Juice out before we go to bed, and again first thing in the morning, but I think that can be arranged."

CHAPTER 20

POPPY

Smack!

I can't help it, I giggle at Connor's playful swat on my butt. I mean, I did just tweak his nipple when he came in to get me out of bed. But we'd just spent a half hour snuggling, and despite his reminders that we both have deadlines to meet, I didn't want to get up. Not even when he got up and started coffee, coming back to find me hugging his pillow and inhaling his scent like a creeper.

"Come on now, the sausage biscuits aren't going to stay fresh forever," he mock growls, trying to sound strict and utterly failing. Oh, I'm sure to most people he still sounds like a stern, grumpy asshole.

But I know him now, and I know that growl. It's his way of saying, 'Let me feed you and take care of you.' But only with me. To everyone else, that growl is still a warning sign of impending doom.

We unlocked a lot of emotional doors and rocked a lot of foundations inside each other last night, and I think Connor's still uncomfortably digesting some of it. His grouchiness is his way of saying, 'I'm not denying all that happened, I just need a little time to unpack it, examine it, and figure this shit out.'

I don't mind giving him some time, though, because I know what I feel, and I'm a bit more open to happy, lovey-dovey emotions. Okay, a lot more receptive, but he'll get there.

I sit up, shaking out my wild and freshly fucked bedhead. "Okay, okay," I reply. "I might be a little underdressed, though."

Connor isn't wearing anything fancy, just a T-shirt and athletic shorts, but it's a heck of a lot more than the absolutely nothing I've got on. I gesture to my naked body, scanning my own skin. Oops, it looks like I've got a fresh hickey on my right boob and a few fingerprints on my thighs.

Connor looks me over too, seeming quite pleased with himself for the love marks he left behind. "Here," Connor says, pulling his T-shirt off and offering it to me.

My eyes dance over his skin too, taking twisted pleasure in the fading pink lines my nails scored over his chest. I know there are matching ones on his back too. We were rough, but in an amazing way I'd love to repeat.

I inhale his T-shirt, moaning happily before pulling it over my head. I could wear this all day. I twist my hair up into its usual messy bun on top of my head, knotting it in on itself so it'll stay without a ponytailer. Happy with my new morning attire, I get out of bed and follow him to the kitchen, where the delicious smells make my stomach growl instantly.

It's just good rich coffee and sausage biscuits from the oven, but as we sit down with our mugs, his in the seven ways to kill you mug and mine in a plain white one, it feels perfect and homey. My legs are folded up inside his oversized T-shirt, so my knees are near my chin, making it look like I have watermelon boobs, aka big and long. I blow him a kiss over the rim of my mug.

"Good morning."

Connor lifts one brow and takes a sip of his coffee. "'Morning," he growls. "Although if it had been your choice, it would have been afternoon."

I can't keep the smile from my lips, especially after last night.

"What?"

I take another sip of coffee, then pick up my sausage biscuit. "You like me," I brag. "No man shares his Jimmy Dean unless he likes you."

"Meh, you're all right," he deadpans. "I guess."

I take a huge bite of my sausage biscuit, chewing noisily. When Connor doesn't groan in disgust, it only proves my point, and I grin . . . after swallowing my mouthful. "You don't like many people, you said so yourself. But you like me."

The declaration is strong and proud because I'm completely certain. And also, wiggling happily in my chair, making my knee-boobs dance. Because I know for damn sure he likes my body.

I've never felt sexier than when he looks at me.

"Don't get a big head about it," he says with a little snort. "And that chair's pretty janky. You might want to stop that."

"Too late," I tell him, hopping from my completely solid chair and sitting down in his lap uninvited, crowding into his space. He throws his hands wide, making a sound of surprise as he holds his coffee out to keep from spilling it on me. But as soon as his coffee's secure, he wraps his arms around me and we settle into something comfortable, both of us with our mugs, me in his arms, with my bare ass pressed against his soft cock in his shorts. "What work do you have to do today?"

"Prep work," he says in a roundabout way. "And you?"

I groan. "Don't remind me."

"I thought your book was going well?" Connor asks. "The writer's block gone?"

"Oh, it is," I tell him, running my fingers through his hair, "But you have no idea how good yesterday felt. And not just the sex. You know what I really want to do?"

"What?"

"What if we stay in bed all day—naked, of course—and order food in, watch a movie, and take a nap. Just have a day of total chill."

It is a great idea, and we both know it. I can see the temptation in Connor's eyes, though he scowls. "Poppy," he says in a warning tone, "we both have goals to meet."

"Connor," I reply, copying his tone. In my own brighter voice, I tease, "Did I mention that 'watching a movie' is code for fucking? Out of curiosity, for no specific reason at all, how many times can you go in a day? Like full dicking. Though I'm not gonna argue if your dick gives out and we resort to fingers and tongues."

Connor groans, and I feel something nice and firm poking me now. "I've never tested it, but now I'd really like to find out."

"Great!" I proclaim. "It's decided then. We walk Nut and Juice, grab some water from the fridge, and get right down to work! And by work, I mean round one." I frown. "Wait, is it still round one if we had sex last night after midnight? What are the rules here? Should we count that since it was technically today, and this morning, because it was the same twenty-four-hour period? If so, we're starting round three and you're already doing great. Let's aim for . . . what do you think? Six? Ten?"

He blinks, and I hope he's imagining three through ten because I know I am.

"Unfortunately, work is going to have to mean actual work for us both," Connor reminds me. "You have a deadline. And so do I. And I don't want to have to save you from an angry agent."

He has a good point, but I feel like we're encased in one of those soap bubbles that float through the air, all shimmery and iridescent in the sunlight, and I'm afraid if I'm not careful, it'll pop and leave Connor and me falling back to earth only to splat gracelessly.

The splat is coming though because I want to ask about his work, about what he's going to steal. But I also . . . don't. I haven't forgotten what Connor does or how wrong it is. And he's said he's got prep work to do. So he's getting ready to steal something.

It's been ingrained in my mind since I was a child that stealing is wrong. Maybe there's some leeway for a hungry person stealing bread or something like that, but not swiping electronics at the first available opportunity. Even if he did help me get my laptop back. What about the other people who've lost phones, laptops, wallets, and more?

Can I be okay with that?

Connor strokes the back of my neck with a thumb, making me shiver with pleasure. "You went quiet."

I sigh, laying my head on his shoulder as uneasiness gnaws in my gut. "I'm worried about you."

"I'm fine," he says, but I can hear something in his voice, and I sit up more.

"Are you? I'm not telling you what to do, but what you do is dangerous. And hurtful. What if you take something from someone violent?"

Connor smirks. "Like you? You attacked me. Working out pretty well so far."

"I'm serious! I'm not saying everyone is innocent, but I don't want you getting hurt!"

Connor sighs almost sadly. "I've been waiting for this."

"You have?"

He nods. "I do what I do for good reasons. Ones I can't explain . . . not to you, not my family, not even to myself sometimes. But I'm fine. I promise."

"Can you promise that you'll be careful? That no one will get hurt, especially you?"

"That's my MO," he tells me, kissing me on the forehead. "You know I've been doing this for almost half my life at this point, and I've only been caught stealing twice? Once, the shoplifting as a kid . . . and then you. That's a pretty good track record."

He sees that's not what I wanted to hear, so he kisses my nose and adds, "I promise."

It's not enough, but it'll have to do for now. We finish our biscuits quickly, even though I'd still rather chill all day.

After a too-fast goodbye, I have to rush home to let Nut and Juice out to do their morning business. I tell myself it's not a walk of shame but rather a Walk of Fame. Let all the jealous neighbors watch me walk out in his T-shirt, letting everyone know exactly where *I* spent last night.

So I hold my head high and add a little bounce to my step, knowing that Connor is watching me walk across the small yard to my own place with my dress and heels in my hands. It's awkward at best, but then . . .

"Good morning, Poppy!" a voice calls out. I turn to see my neighbor, Jane, and a handful of other neighborhood residents on the sidewalk a few yards away. They're all dressed in workout gear, complete with water bottle belts, sun visors, and matching smirks.

"Hi, Jane. Ladies. How are you?"

"Not as good as you obviously are," Jane says, looking down her nose at me. But I'm not going to let her shame me right now.

"It was a great night," I reply, agreeing with her that I feel great, satisfied, and boneless with bliss.

"It certainly looks like it," one of the women with Jane says. "Too damn long since I had a good night."

"Can't hate on getting some of *that*," another voice says, and I follow their covetous looks, glancing back over my shoulder to see Connor leaning against the doorframe of his place. He's got his arms crossed over his bare chest, his coffee cup in his hand. Wearing only shorts, he exudes sex from his messy hair and scruffy beard to his bare feet. His eyes are heated, boring into mine and then scanning my body possessively. I flush, pushing the T-shirt down, mainly because I feel like I might flash him if he keeps that up.

"Come on, ladies. We've got a mile to go, though I think my heart is already racing," Jane says, patting her chest at a pitter-pattering pace. "You have a good morning, Poppy."

"Thanks," I tell them honestly. "Have a good walk. I'm gonna . . . go." I point toward my house, seeing Nut and Juice barking at the front window. "I've probably got a puddle to deal with."

"Yeah, he'd leave me in a puddle too," one says before waving to Connor. "And you have a good morning, Mr. Sexy Coffee!"

Everyone laughs as he lifts the coffee mug in a salute. But it's me that he watches as I go back to my house, feeling good. The whole neighborhood knows now . . . and nobody's trying to jump my claim.

Well, I mean, I can't 'claim' him like a seat at a movie theater, but yeah . . . he's mine. And I'm his, even if we've got things to work out.

I let Nut and Juice out to do their business and go back inside, heading to my bedroom. I consider taking a shower or actually putting on pants. But I don't want to. I like that I smell like Connor, that I'm wearing his shirt. So instead, I pull on some short shorts so my ass doesn't stick to my chair before I sit down and get to work.

First, I send Hilda an email update, letting her know that I am back on target. I don't tell her any details about how I got my laptop back, only that it's all good now and I'm working my ass off and making good progress. She replies instantly, telling me to keep at it and reminding me that the deadline is rapidly approaching.

"Yeah," I murmur as I pull out my flash drive, back up yesterday's work, and go back to my word processor. "No shit, Hilda. I'm foregoing multiple orgasms for this book."

But though I bristle at her reminder, I do get to work, and the words pour out of me and onto the screen.

There's a knock on the door a couple of hours later, and my heart jumps, hoping it's Connor coming over after all. Or at least coming over for one more kiss, so I hurry to the door, opening it with a smile. "Well now, I suppose I could—"

But it's not Connor.

It's Detective Jax Carter.

"Uh . . . Miss Woodstock?" he asks.

"What the fuck do you want?" I snap.

He recoils, his face going slightly pink at the less than friendly greeting. "Ahem. Like I mentioned on the phone, I want to discuss some new information about your missing laptop. Can I come in?"

"Are you fucking kidding me?" I ask, my hands on my hips and my tone getting more and more shrill. "I told you, talk to Hilda."

I literally shoo him, wishing Nut and Juice would get their lazy butts off the couch to bark or nip at his shoes or something. But they're fast asleep, so I block the door as best I can because there's no way in hell he's coming into my home.

I almost say that my laptop's not missing anymore, but I manage to bite my tongue. I don't want to help this jerk of an officer when he completely dismissed me when I needed his help.

"I'm afraid it's much bigger than that now, Miss Woodstock," he says, not moving. "It's come to our attention that your laptop wasn't the only thing stolen that night."

I stop, blinking. "What?"

Connor didn't say anything about stealing anything else. Just my bag.

Detective Carter nods, looking past me into my home like he still wants to come in. "*The Black Rose* was also taken."

I laugh in disbelief. "No, it wasn't. We all saw it on the stage. It was literally the first thing they checked after making sure J.A. Fox was okay. Remember? They left me spreadeagle on the floor, not giving a shit if I was hurt or flashing my kitty cat to the whole world?"

His eyes flicker to my legs, and I step behind the door, using it as a shield, but even with a slab of wood between us, I suddenly feel very naked. Holding up a hand, I reach over to my coat rack and snag the longest thing available, a knee-length red trench coat that I bought last year and haven't worn since. Pulling it on,

I step out of my house and knot the belt around my waist, crossing my arms over my chest to glare at him.

"Eyes up here, Detective," I growl, literally snapping my fingers in his face when he glances back down, seeming disappointed that I'm covered to my knees.

His gaze moves back up my body to meet my eyes, but he offers no apology. In fact, I think that smarmy smile is supposed to be charming. As if. "Of course. Actually, the painting you saw was a replica, a fake."

"Gee, thanks for the mansplain. If you'll remember, I write for a living, so it'd be reasonable to assume that I have a grasp on the English language. Although, I would expect a police officer to have observational skills to read people, and you apparently have none," I muse. Snidely, I tell him, "I know what a replica is."

While I'm busting his balls about his rude assumptions, my brain is twisting and turning over what he actually said. But he must've been hit on the head one too many times during car chases or something because he's making zero sense. The painting was right there the whole time. Unless . . .

"Are you sure it was the original on display in the first place? If it was a replacement, perhaps the original was taken before the dinner began?"

Detective Carter shakes his head. "We believe the lights going out was a cover for the painting to be replaced with the reproduction. And your laptop is somehow connected."

"Wait a fucking minute! You think I had something to do with it?" I say in shock. "How the fuck—"

He holds his hands out in a 'calm down' manner. "No, no. We don't think that. But you mentioned a security guard."

I roll my eyes, even though I feel like I'm quickly moving into the realm of pantomime as the rest of my brain whirls with the fears I'm developing. "Oh, now you want to listen to me?"

Everything clicks, and I realize that he's looking for Connor!

He's talking about Connor stealing *The Black Rose*!

Well, he did steal my laptop. He openly admitted that. Well, after I jumped on his back. But is that connected to his maybe stealing The Black Rose *too?*

No. No way. There's no way he would've done that. J.A. Fox must have had a replica on the stage, and someone stole it another time. Or she's lying. Or she never had it authentically. Or . . .

What if he did? a tiny voice whispers somewhere deep in the dark shadows of my mind where demons like fear and mistrust live. *One painting pays for a lot more townhouse living than a laptop. And he hasn't exactly been out picking pockets every day since you met.*

I have a mental flash of Connor telling me all sorts of interesting details about the art at the museum and realize that maybe . . . he could do that. Stealing my laptop when he didn't want the manuscript never did make sense, but I somehow didn't think about that too deeply.

Because you were too busy fucking him . . . and falling for him.

Detective Carter is looking at me expectantly. Shit, he must have said something else. "Sorry?"

"The security guard?" Carter says, probing. "He's a person of interest."

"Uh, yeah. The Kyle, Chad guy? Did the other security guards figure something out about him?"

In mere seconds, I've gone from thinking there is no way Connor could've stolen the artwork to realizing he might have and then pumping Detective Carter for information because I'm scared . . . for Connor.

Petty theft is one thing. A major art heist is quite another.

He's in some serious shit here, and so am I.

Carter shakes his head, sighing. "Not really. I wondered if you maybe remembered something that could be helpful? Or you said you were going to continue your own . . . investigation."

He makes it sound like I'm Nancy Drew trying to play with the big boys. It's insulting, but I'm too damn scared to be insulted.

What do I say? What do I do?

I have all these feelings for Connor, and I know he has them for me too. They're in the way he looks at me, the way he strokes my neck. The way he only had eyes for me as he toasted the neighborhood walking group with his coffee. I saw it in his eyes, even in that dark truck. I know that for sure.

My gut struggles with what's right here, though. At first thought, I should tell the truth, the whole truth, and nothing but the truth and let the chips fall where they may. Lying is wrong. But I can't bring myself to do it. I want to protect Connor, save him, even from himself.

So even though I'm not sure it's the right thing, I cover for him. "No. I never found out anything useful."

Carter blows out a breath. "Sorry to hear that." While it's a good huff of disappointment, he doesn't seem sorry. It's like he expected that I would be useless at tracking someone down.

"Are you looking for him now?"

Carter nods. "Of course. Don't worry, Poppy, we'll find him."

Poppy? When did we start going on a first-name basis? "Good luck with that," I say just as condescendingly.

"Thank you. I'll definitely let you know as soon as we have more information to share." When I don't bow down, thanking him for the kindness, he asks, "Hey, how's your book going?"

I blink at the sudden subject and tone change. "Uhm, good?"

He pauses, clearly looking for more information for some reason. When I don't offer anything further, he adds, "Glad to hear that. I'd love to read it sometime. What'd you say the title is?"

"*Love in Great Falls*. I'm working on the sequel, which I should probably get back to . . ." I trail off, suddenly very uncomfortable with this whole conversation. I can't decide if Detective Carter is flirting . . . or if this is still a conversation about the stolen property.

It's a lot to take in, and I need to process all this.

Because I've fallen in love . . . not with a petty thief but an art thief . . . who's been lying to me all along.

But Carter seems willing to drop it for now. "Sure thing. I understand. I'll be in touch."

I nod slowly. "Bye, Detective Carter," I manage to stammer out, sounding mostly normal. But going back inside, I'm freaking the fuck out.

What if they figure out that it's Connor who stole my laptop and the painting? What if they track him next door? What if they realize that we're dating . . . and telling people that we're engaged? They'll think I'm in on it. Especially after I lied to the police about seeing him again.

"What the fuck am I going to do?" I whisper, peeking out my fisheye lens like a total paranoid nut to make sure he's left. "Oh, fuck. Oh, fuck. Oh, fuck . . ."

I start pacing the living room, which wakes up Nut and Juice. They look at me worriedly, probably wondering why the hell their mama's gone crazy this time. They're the ones who're supposed to run in circles, not me.

"What do I do?" I ask them, but all Nut does is yawn and lie back down. "Thanks for nothing, you fuzzy little monster!"

Juice climbs off the couch, coming over to lick my foot. It tickles, and when I wiggle my toes, Juice thinks I'm playing, but this is no game.

I start my pacing again, panic rising and thoughts scrambling around faster than a cow in a tornado.

What the hell am I supposed to do?

CHAPTER 21

CONNOR

I've done all the internet research I can, and now it's time to get eyes on my target.

I've adjusted my features some, like I normally do. First, I put in colored contacts, making my eyes look brown, then hid them behind a pair of designer, slightly gaudy nonprescription glasses. A small insert between my gum and upper lip adds a subtle amount of weight to my face, and a clip-on earring in my left ear pulls attention away from the rest. All added to my black suit with a purple striped tie that's an attention grabber, I'm a much different version of myself.

I look . . . flashy and expensive. But also like I belong at the upper-crust auction house, either to purchase for myself or perhaps as a personal assistant to someone wealthy enough to purchase things here.

At the front desk, there's a woman at a computer, typing in a desultory way that tells me she's not enjoying her job right this moment. The rest of the place is deserted, as planned.

"May I help you?" she says in a bored voice, not looking up from her screen.

I clear my throat, putting on an accent that I've practiced for years. I've got three, but this one is perfect for this situation—slightly British, but indistinct enough to sound American influenced. "Yes, I represent a potential buyer for several pieces coming up for auction. I've been sent to examine and authenticate the pieces he . . ." I dip my chin like I've misspoken and add, "or *she* . . . is interested in."

The woman's eyebrows lift as she looks me over, suddenly alert and attentive. Just as planned. "Do you have an appointment?" She knows good and well that I don't, but this is part of the game.

"My employer isn't the type to advertise interest. It tends to be bad for the purchase price. I'm sure you understand." I scrub my chin with a hand, framing a charming smile and exposing my expensive watch. Her memories should be centered around the bling and flash and not the man in the suit.

The woman is hesitant, understandably so considering she works with a wide variety of expensive merchandise. But she also works with wealthy, and sometimes eccentric, buyers. And their representatives.

When she still pauses, I reach into my inner pocket and remove a small envelope, which I slowly place on the desk. It's obviously got something in it, based on the subtle thickness of the package.

She looks at the envelope carefully, her eyebrows lifting and then lowering.

"Well, I'm sure a little peek wouldn't hurt, right?"

"Exactly," I respond, straightening my suit jacket. Actually, I'm slouching some, but again, I've learned exactly how to do this to the point of making it look natural.

I follow her down the hall, looking for weaknesses in their systems or protocols. I already know a lot about the site's security, but I double-check my data on the alarm system and badge scanner, comparing it against what I know as she places an ID against a solid black panel with a small company name engraved on the top. It's top-notch, as is the sprinkler system. No opportunity for a false fire alarm, no getting in without an ID badge, either stolen or reproduced.

So far, the only obvious flaw in their system is the woman letting a complete stranger in to view upcoming auction merchandise. But a distract and snatch won't work this time. Their monitoring includes cameras in every room, including this hallway. Hopefully, the fake glasses will do enough to disguise my appearance. As an added bonus, my glasses have a small pinhole camera hidden behind a rhinestone, and I'll review the footage later, frame by frame.

She scans her ID badge once more and opens the door into a large storage room. The tables are long, set up in labeled sections and filled with treasures. A weaker man would start stuffing his pockets and make a run for it. But that has never been my style.

"Which pieces do you want to see?" the woman says, businesslike but nervous. "We need to be quick. People will be returning from lunch soon."

"Of course. There are three pieces." I tell her the titles of the pieces, and she leads me to the first one.

The painting is dramatic, a Viking ship with tattered sails in tumultuous seas backed by thunderous clouds. I pull a magnifying loupe from my pocket and lean forward to examine the signature.

The woman tells me about the piece, a consummate salesperson, but it's information I already know. After a quick but thorough examination of the brushstrokes, frame, and small chipping along the side edge, I nod.

She smiles and rushes me to the second piece, but again, it's not the one I'm here for. It is, however, next to the one I'm interested in. I narrow my eyes, scanning the Japanese piece as the woman gives me the details on it while actually looking past it to a rustic stone figurine.

The female figure sculpture is remarkably robust, the weight apparent by the full curves of the stone. Past that, it's small, roughly the size of my forearm, and primitive in design. Through my surreptitious looks, I verify it's the piece I want, noting its most unique feature, the well-documented fault line where the figure's left arm broke off sometime in the last four hundred years.

"The last one?" I ask, straightening up. I want to cast all suspicion away from me when I do steal the stone figure. That's why I'm looking at three pieces and making sure I show no awareness of the one I'm actually interested in.

I'm a ghost on the breeze, never to be suspected or even considered.

The woman's anxiousness is ramping up, judging by the way she's nibbling at her lip now. Whether it's the elapsed time or a return of her conscience, I don't know. "You have to hurry."

I nod, and she leads me to the third one. Another painting. I do a cursory examination, not truly interested and only finishing my casing of the room, but something in the layers of paint catches my eye.

I look again in another spot, and then another. The crackling of the paint is all wrong. This piece should have aged out with spiderweb-style cracks, and while they're there, the cracks are too pronounced in some areas and nearly indistinct in others. Storage in non-climate-controlled areas might cause that, but this piece has been in a documented private collection for generations. It would have been cared for diligently.

I'd have to do a deeper examination, but I'm reasonably certain this is a forgery. That it's for sale by a reputable auction house tells me that fact is unknown, and I muse mildly about how long the original's been gone. For all I know, the forgery could have been passed off for a generation or more. Or it might be a new development by a family who needs funds but is unwilling to sell off an important heirloom.

But I don't tell the woman who's looking toward the door and then at her watch. I save that information for myself. Instead, I push my glasses up my nose and dip my chin. "Thank you."

"You're welcome. We need to go now."

I nod and follow her back out. I consciously don't look back at anything, not wanting to show my hand in the middle of the game. Anyone who reviews the tape would think I came, I saw, I walked.

There's a man coming back in the door as we return to the front desk area. At the sight of him, the woman with me freezes like a deer in the headlights, stammering. *You'd make a terrible criminal.* "Oh, hi . . . Randy. This is . . ."

I step forward to help, taking charge before she blows the whole fucking thing up without even meaning to. It's for her good as much as my own. "Mike. I'm a . . . *friend*." I say the word with a hint of allusion, letting Randy fill in what that might mean. Boyfriend, side piece, truly just a buddy. "How's it going?"

The woman steps closer to my side as Randy gives me a surprised nod. I fight the urge to bristle at her closeness and instead look down at her, faking fondness to sell the cover story. "I'll see you later?"

Implication drips heavily from the question, and Randy's eyebrows go up another inch. Perfect. At this point, it'd take an act of God to get this woman to tell anyone about what she just did. She pushes her hair behind her ear. "Yeah."

I move toward the door, glancing back once to make sure Randy bought the whole thing. He's already striding down the hall, not paying the woman any mind. But she picks up the envelope and mouths, "Thank you."

I smile in answer, but as soon as the door closes behind me, the fake smile falls away instantly.

I've got more work to do.

It's late afternoon before I get back home, changing clothes into comfortable jeans and a T-shirt before going next door. I knock and hear Nut and Juice go crazy on the other side. "It's me, you little monsters. Go get Poppy."

A moment later, the lock slides, and I'm ready to press inside and get Poppy back in my arms as soon as possible. It's been a long day of prep, but as soon as I lay eyes on her, I know something's wrong. First, her mouth is a thin line, lips pressed tightly together. Second, she doesn't jump at me like one of her overly hyper dogs who are swirling around my ankles.

"Get your ass in here."

Damn. What happened since this morning? The flatness in her usually bright tone guts me.

"Writer's block back?" I ask, hoping it's only that and not something much more dire. If it's that, I'm more than up for naked muse time and pep talks and whatever else it takes.

No such luck. She shakes her head and sits on the far end of the couch, her legs curled up in front of her, putting a literal wall between us. I sit down on the other end, turning toward her and laying an arm across the back of the couch, intentionally choosing an open posture that invites her to crawl into my lap.

Poppy doesn't take the invitation and looks at me evenly. "Tell me about when you took my laptop."

"We've covered this," I point out.

"Not everything," she says, and I feel my stomach clench.

No. Not yet. I want to tell her, but this isn't the time. I glare at her, hoping she'll let this go. I need her to, just for a little while.

She glares back. In fact, she reaches out with one leg, digging her big toe into my thigh. "I'm giving you a chance to come clean here. Don't fuck it up, mister. Last chance . . . tell me about when you took my laptop."

Fuck. How could she know? There's no way she could know. No way she should know. But there's knowledge in her eyes.

Somehow, she found out why I was there.

"I don't know what you know or how you found out, but yes," I tell her, keeping my voice calm, "there was more to it than your laptop."

She growls but retrieves her toe as she sits up fully, listening intently. "Spill it. I want all your guts laid bare on this couch, right here, right now, or so help me God, I will do it for you. Gut you like Rambo in the middle of a jungle, but I'll use a dull, rusty pair of scissors and make it slow and painful." She makes a stabbing motion, but thankfully, her hand is empty for now.

"I don't doubt that." I sigh, scrubbing at my face and looking at the ceiling. There's so much to unpack, and I haven't had a chance to figure out how to tell this story, where it begins, or where it stops.

So I'll have to wing it. "I did steal your laptop, obviously. But I wasn't there for that. I was there to steal something much more valuable."

Was it just last night that I told myself I'd have to tell her? Back then, it felt academic, easy. Now, I'm scared shitless to tell her the whole ugly truth. I don't want to see her look at me with disdain, with the same disgust I've become too familiar with. Or worse, disappointment. I saw that on my parents' faces for so long, so many times. When I was younger, I enjoyed being the hellion who challenged their beliefs. But as I've gotten older, I've realized how unimportant that is. The way I live my life only truly affects me. Until now.

"The Black Rose," Poppy fills in when I don't say it. "You snatched it, replaced it with a fake."

I grunt an agreement. Not much else to do.

Poppy leaps from her end of the couch to where I'm sitting, landing in my lap, but not in a good way. Her palms swat and slap at my chest, more annoying than painful. What hurts are the barbs she's spitting as she does it . . .

"You son of a bitch!" *Swat.*

"Why didn't you tell me?" *Slap.*

"Lying asshole!" A yank of my ear, which actually does make my eyes water in pain.

She starts pounding at my chest, each fist punctuated with the same word. "Why . . . why . . . why?"

I take it all, not fighting or even protecting myself, which somehow enrages her more. She pokes me in the chest, right over my heart, with a jagged fingernail that she's obviously been chewing on in her worry. "Why didn't you tell me? You lied to me!"

She goes for another slap, and this time, I catch her wrist gently, hugging her flailing arms tight against my chest. She struggles, but I quiet her with a growled plea. "Poppy. Listen to me."

When she stills, I can see the glitter of tears in her eyes. Quieter, and less sure, she asks, "Was it all a lie?"

I cup her face, releasing her hands slowly as a sign of trust. "No. It's not all a lie. I swear it."

She sniffs, pouting and hurt, and I can see the deep pain beneath the puffed-out lip. "I don't believe you."

I swallow and let it all drop. I have to now. "If it was all a lie, I wouldn't be here now. You've got your laptop back, and you more than covered for me with my family. If this wasn't real, I would've already moved on."

I run my thumb over her lip, hating the pain I've caused. Her eyes narrow, scouring my words for half-truths and lies. She's looking for loopholes, the way she does her book plots, making sure every nuance is sealed.

"What do you mean?"

"I mean that next door is a cover home, a place to hole up away from my actual house so I don't leave a trail. I've lived in a dozen or more places like that over the past few years. Poppy, I stayed because of you. If not, I would have blown out of here a week ago."

She huffs. "I hate it when you use logic on me, especially when I've got a good fit happening. For a damn good fucking reason," she reminds me with one last love pat, this time to my cheek. Even as she snaps at me, her anger is waning. She sags, slipping off my lap to the couch beside me. "Tell me the full story. All of it, every detail."

That's hard, and I sit silently for a moment before I get up and start pacing her living room, one way and then the other, as I try to put my thoughts into words. Nut and Juice follow me the first lap, but then they lie down in their bed and watch me walk, occasionally looking to Poppy for a clue about what's happening.

I wish I knew too, but I'm as lost as they are about how we all got here.

"What I told you before wasn't a lie, except by cutting the tale short. I did get started with pickpocketing and petty theft stuff. I got caught once, as a juvenile, for shoplifting, but my parents helped me get out of it. There was lots of volunteer work to make restitution. But they never let me forget it. From that point on, I was the black sheep. A criminal. Ungrateful for all they'd done for me. I could've chosen to be better, prove myself worthy to them. But I didn't. I figured if they'd already written me off, then why bother trying to prove otherwise?"

I clear my throat, mentally staring off into the past. "Ironically, it was during all that community service that I met people who appreciated me. There were other juvenile delinquents, and they accepted my point of view and taught me things. They gave me some new connections. I fell further and further."

"Connor, I know it's going to sound bitchy, but right now, I don't care about your spoiled rich kid problems," Poppy says, rolling her hand expectantly. "Get to the art heist part."

"I'm getting there, trust me. After I got those connections, I had a corner I'd hang out on, pickpocket the tourists. One day, I overheard this guy in a suit talking on his phone about a gallery showing. He said he was prepared to pay $10,000 for this painting if he could get his hands on it. I don't know why I did it, but I followed him, saw where he worked and the name on the door."

I think back, shaking my head at my stupid luck at my first art job. "The next day, I went to the gallery he mentioned and looked at the art. I'd been to museums on field trips, but that was the extent of my art knowledge then. But I had balls bigger than my brains and figured I could swipe it. So, I watched, waited, and in the end, it was easy."

"Easy?"

I shrug. "You have no idea how slack security can be at galleries. They don't even realize it because most of the customers are law-abiding, good people who aren't going to swipe things. In the end, I literally slipped it right under my sweatshirt and walked out. Later that day, I showed up at that guy's office, told him I had something for him."

"You should've seen his eyes," I continue with a shake of my head. "They were big as fucking saucers. He was so excited, didn't even care that I'd obviously stolen it. He gave me ten grand cash right on the spot like it was chump change, and I walked out feeling like a god."

"That had to be a high," Poppy murmurs, and I hum in agreement.

"Some, but when it faded, I didn't feel like a god. I felt like . . . like a devil. I was exactly what my mom and dad thought I was. So I decided to revel in it, stupidly thinking that by rebelling against them, I could lessen the impact of disappointing them."

"Then what?"

"Well, I started chasing that high. I did it again, and again. But I was smarter than most. I learned about art, moved from pickpocketing to breaking and entering, and then to more complex methods. I got good. So fucking good. Word spread, and I got hired on for jobs. It would've been fine, except . . ."

I swallow thickly, running my hands through my hair as memories of my high-flying days turn sour.

"My grandfather died unexpectedly. I was out of town on a job, and Mom and Dad couldn't reach me. I didn't know, so I missed the service completely. My dad was furious, and he's never forgiven me." I haven't forgiven myself either, but this is not about my absolution.

"Dad hasn't been the same since my grandfather's death. He . . . retreated, became what you've seen of him. Maybe if I'd been here, I could've helped somehow. We'll never know."

I sigh, leaving behind the pain of those dark days, the solitary visit I made to the gravesite of the man who'd taught me magic tricks as a kid by pulling quarters from behind my ears. Those sleight of hand tricks came in useful in ways he never imagined. In a twisted way, I feel like my stealing is an homage to him, using the things he taught me, though not exactly in the way he'd intended. I wonder sometimes if he'd be ashamed of me or proud of me.

"In one way, it saved me. I stopped stealing for the rush and became a professional in all aspects. So, when I was at the dinner, it was for a job—stealing *The Black Rose*. It was all set up, the replacement, the bag to take the original piece, the trigger on the lights. Everything."

Poppy takes a deep breath. "Until me?"

I look at her, wanting her to see the honesty in my eyes. "No. The plan was to swipe it during the one on ones. I'd set it up that way because people don't remember who was where as accurately when there's so much movement. It wasn't personal. Not then. In my prep, I'd gotten a custom bag, something that would allow me to protect the artwork as I made my escape. Then, just as I pulled it out to do the swipe . . . the goddamn thing split in half. I needed something to hide the original in to get out of the ballroom. I grabbed the closest thing to me. Your bag."

Shame washes over me, wishing I hadn't gotten her tangled up in all of this. It does seem like fate intervened, though. If the bag hadn't torn, I wouldn't have needed one. If she hadn't been on stage getting her picture taken, I wouldn't have grabbed her bag. If Hunter hadn't placed me next door, we never would've seen each other again. But all of those things happened precisely to get us where we are now. And that, I wouldn't change.

"I was collateral damage."

I wish I could deny that, but it's the truth. "I was buzzing so much, so focused on getting out of that hotel, I didn't even notice the weight of the laptop. It was just a bag until I delivered *The Black Rose*. But as soon as you told me about it, I wanted to help you get it back. I did help you get it back."

"Yeah, you did," Poppy admits. "But what about *The Black Rose*? Where is it?"

I shrug, knowing she'll be disappointed in my answer. "I don't keep anything I swipe. The last I saw of it was less than two hours after I took it. Handed it off to my contact, and it's his problem from then on. "

"So that's it?" Poppy asks in disbelief. "You took it and then nothing? Just dropped it off like a pizza? Ding dong, Dominos." She rings an imaginary doorbell, looking skeptical.

"That's the reality of my life. I do the work, assume the risk, but ultimately, the prize is someone else's. I'm on to the next job with deposits in my account. Poppy, it's what I've done for almost a decade. I live and work in the shadows, disappearing and reappearing at will."

It's a harsh summary of my life. One that I thought I was comfortable with . . . until now. Because I want Poppy to see me, to accept me, even if it's the worst version of myself. It's an impossible request, especially of a woman like her. But I'm asking anyway.

Slowly, I drop to my knees, taking her hands in my own. "Poppy, you . . . I . . . can you understand?"

"Understand that you're not a petty thief who swiped my laptop but some super-skilled mega-art-thief come to life?" she asks, sounding impressed, not horrified. And still a bit in denial, even as I admit to the truth. "You do realize how bad boy sexy that makes you?"

I shake my head, blinking hard to keep myself from falling apart. "Don't romanticize it, Poppy. This is serious. You said it yourself. You don't want or need a bad boy. You deserve a good man."

"I know. And I know that you, Connor Bradley, are both a bad boy and a good man. If you'd told me I was crazy or tried to lie your way out of it, I would've kicked your ass and told you to get the fuck out. But your honesty is unexpected, especially after *so many lies*."

There's still a hard edge to her words, a reminder that lying to her is not okay. But otherwise, she seems . . . accepting?

"Seriously?"

She should be throwing things, screaming and calling the cops on me. Part of me wants to shake her and rattle that sort of drama from her so I can write all of this off as a bad idea.

Logically, I should be grabbing my go-bag and getting the fuck out of here. But she's got something I can't leave behind. My heart.

Whether she knows it or not, it's hers.

But maybe she does because her eyes soften and her hands clasp mine tighter. "Maybe. I haven't decided yet. I'm still mad."

She waits a long moment, letting that sink in, and then she leaps at me, shoving me backward onto the floor before climbing on top of me and clinging to me like a koala on a eucalyptus tree. I wrap my arms around her, my hands cupping her ass, gripping her tightly and never wanting to let her go.

She bites me on the chin but soothes it over with a gentle kiss, and relief washes through me like a tidal wave. I don't deserve her, never have and probably never will, but I'll fuck up anyone who tries to take her from me. For now, though, I cuddle her, letting her cling to me no matter how much Nut and Juice want to sniff around our heads wondering what the hell we're doing at their level.

She lifts her head, and I kiss her lips softly. There's still fear in my heart, still disbelief that this can be real or long-term. Most of all, though, I'm terrified that the darkness in my life will tear her away from me.

"Are you sure, Poppy?" I ask. "There's . . . a lot of crazy shit in my life."

Poppy shrugs, petting my chest lightly as though she can wipe away the small, and well deserved, swats she leveled there before. "As sure as I ever am."

I wish she could say with absolute conviction that she's sure, but it's a lot to take in, so that'll have to be enough for now. I'm still worried about losing her. I'm honestly not sure if I even have her in the first place.

Carefully, we sit up, and I lean back against the front of the couch with Poppy in my arms. The floor is less comfortable than the couch, but at least in this position, the dogs aren't sniffing my ear anymore.

"How did you figure it out?"

Poppy shifts in my lap, perfectly content to be where she is for the moment. "That fucking asshole detective came by today, asking questions like I would help him out after he blew me off about my laptop being taken."

I freeze, stiffening. Poppy feels it and leans back, looking me in the eyes. "Connor, it's okay. Really."

"Somebody came by?" I ask, praying I misheard her. "Asking questions? Who?"

That's more questions in a row than I've probably ever said, and Poppy's reaction shows that. Her brows drop down in concern. "Relax. I didn't tell him anything."

I take a deep breath, knowing that if she were going to turn me in, she'd have done it already. I would have been greeted at the door by the cops, and not her.

"Okay. Tell me what happened."

She wiggles, getting up on the couch again, and I follow, the two of us facing each other again in almost the same positions we started this conversation in. But we're together, I can sense that.

She starts her story, her hands waving wildly as she recounts the details. "His name's Detective Jax Carter, and he's what happened. He's the guy who was so fucking condescending the night you took my laptop that I flipped my shit right there at the station."

I lift a brow wryly, having seen what a shit-flipping Poppy looks like.

"Yeah, yeah, it was stupid but completely warranted," Poppy admits. "He called a few days ago too, said he had a lead, but we were already working on it, so I knew he couldn't know more than we did, and so I told him to go fuck himself. Anyway, he showed up today, started saying they were suddenly interested in what I had to say because *The Black Rose* was replaced with a replica."

I wince, knowing that was the weakness in the whole plan. Honestly, I didn't think anyone would discover the reproduction for a long while. It wasn't perfect, but it was good enough that it should've escaped detection for years.

"Fuck," I spit out, suddenly much more worried. "What else did he know? What did you tell him?"

At my poorly worded question that could be taken as accusation, she glares at me angrily. Sarcasm drips from every word as she ticks off on her fingers, "Well, you know, just that I knew who'd stolen my laptop, so he's probably the art thief too. Oh, and that you live next door and would be home shortly. The SWAT team is in my laundry nook waiting to arrest you."

First, I know Nut and Juice would be going apeshit if there were strangers in the house. So the rest of that's probably lies too. "Poppy. This is serious."

"No shit," Poppy says, going serious again. "But Connor, I didn't tell him anything. Actually, I tried to get information *for you*. The other security guards you worked with don't remember your name, so that's a dead end. I told him that I hadn't had any luck finding the security guard myself. There's no reason for Detective Carter to link my next-door neighbor to the stolen laptop or *The Black Rose*. So unless you did a shitty job handing off the painting, you should be in the clear."

"Other than the bag and the laptop, my part went as planned," I tell her. "What the other guy did . . . well, he's even more smoke in the wind than I am."

Poppy holds her hands out wide. "All good, then?"

That should be the case. But it's too much to risk, both for me and for Poppy.

I know what I have to do. I have to leave, at least for now. It's the only way we can both be safe. And above everything, I won't risk

Poppy. She has a life, one that was good and happy before I fucked it up.

"Poppy," I say slowly, standing up. "I need to go."

Her eyes narrow, scanning mine for what's going on in my head. "Why? You can trust me."

I take a deep breath. "I know. But you can't trust me. I'm a liar. An asshole. A thief."

Poppy snorts and gets up to face me again. "You say that like I didn't know that from the beginning. I've known since the day I tackled you that you weren't exactly Mr. Rogers."

Though I just told her not to trust me, I contradict myself. "I need you trust me and believe that there's a good reason. I need to go."

"Go, go or . . . go?" she repeats, her voice tight and worried.

I want to lie to her that this is temporary.

But no more lies.

Not with Poppy.

"I'll try to come back," I tell her, hoping that it's enough.

It has to be.

CHAPTER 22

POPPY

My house smells like pine and lemons.

Connor left, and I didn't crumble. I am furious, stomping around my place and cursing his name with every other breath. And when I get mad as hell, I clean. I take out all my conflicting emotions on the tiles in my shower, nearly scrubbing the finish off them.

I vacuum until nearly midnight, to the point where I doubt there's a single Pomeranian hair anywhere but on my dogs. Every dish gets washed to squeaky clean, my stove shines like glass, and by the time I sit down with my angry-weepy jar of peanut butter and a spoon, I think you could do surgery on my kitchen table.

I eat half the jar until the angry little demon in my belly is quieted, and then I curl up with Nut and Juice. I barely cry, but it doesn't feel right going to sleep without having Connor's arms around me.

I'm sure that I do fall asleep at some point, but it can't be much more than a short nap before bad dreams have me up just after the crack of dawn. I can't go back to sleep with the worry and nervous energy pulsing through my veins like I've got a Red Bull IV going, so instead of fighting it, I grab a granola bar and sit down behind my computer, pouring myself into my work.

Time crawls, but my fingers fly. By the time the sun sets, I've cranked my way through three whole chapters in record time. After stopping for a bowl of microwave ramen, I go back to work, only crashing out on the couch after Nut and Juice dramatically go to bed on their own at three in the morning.

By nine the same morning, I'm back up, back to writing. The only time I take breaks is to take Nut and Juice out to wee, and I spend most of that time looking at Connor's house, his driveway. His truck is gone, the windows dark. Mostly, I know he's gone because of the void I feel inside. It's like my heart can feel that he's too far away, wherever he's gone to.

That's my routine for five days. I've ignored Hilda's calls, simply sending emails that I'm working, skipped a W3AS library session with the girls, and basically just kept my head stuck in the sand to write and then pop up every once in a while to check for Connor.

The only places I go to are the front yard for the boys, the bathroom to take care of myself, and the couch because I don't want to sleep in my bed if I can't have Connor. Oh, and the front door once to pay for pizza delivery since I can't spare the attention or time to actually cook for myself.

The knock on the door doesn't give me any hope, though. The melodic *thunk-thunk-thunk* isn't Connor's style. But I open the door, just in case.

It's not Connor or another pizza delivery but my girls. W3AS.

"What are you—" I ask as Daysha reaches for a hug.

She instantly recoils, wincing and pinching her nose. "Damn, woman! You smell like sweaty feet!" She fans the air between us with her other hand, subtly pushing me back so the rest of the girls can come in. "What the hell have you been doing?"

Aleria doesn't speak, just reaches into the organic hemp burlap tote that she uses as a purse. Out comes a bundle of green herbs, and she goes into my kitchen to look for a lighter.

"Aleria, what are you doing? I don't want my house smelling like patchouli-perfumed skunks!" I call out, but Jasmine puts a hand on my shoulder.

"Uh-uh. Daysha's right. This place smells. Bad. And so do you." I turn my attention to her, ready to say something snappy, but Jasmine has the decency to soften the critique with a caring question. "Are you doing okay?" she asks.

"Fine," I tell her.

In the corner of my eye, I see Becca happily playing with Nut and Juice, who are always excited to have human attention. She might also be sneaking them treats, but I do know that I've fed them, even if I haven't taken care of myself much the last few days.

"It's been days. How's the book coming?" Daysha asks.

Aleria comes back in, waving her smudge bundle, which smells woodsy and floral and not at all unpleasant. Still, I go over and open a window.

"I haven't showered, I've barely eaten, and my dogs are getting cabin fever," I admit. "But I'm pouring myself into these pages and making progress."

"That's good!" Becca says. "Tell Mommy 'good job', sweet boy." She holds up Nut's paw, high-fiving herself with it because he certainly doesn't know any tricks.

"No, it's not," Jasmine says. "Look at her. No offense, babe, but I'd burn that T-shirt if possible."

"She's right," Daysha says. "Go shower, let us make you some real food, and you can tell us what else is going on."

I shake my head, my stubborn streak popping up. And I don't smell that bad. I sniff my right armpit to prove my point. Okay, I smell. "No time, I have to finish."

"You won't be finishing shit if you kill yourself in the process," Daysha says. "Now go. Becca, think you can take care of the pups?"

"Of course!" Becca cheers, in love with my dogs. She looks at Nut and Juice, who are staring up at her like she's their new favorite person. "I'll take care of these adorable babies. Who wants to go for a walkie-walk?" she says, baby talking to them.

"I'll finish cleansing the house's energy," Aleria says. "After your shower, I'll cleanse your aura too, and then you'll truly have a fresh start." She begins to walk around the room, chanting, "Release, renew, reside in respect." And then her whispers become too quiet for me to hear as she closes her eyes. I hope she doesn't walk into the coffee table, but she seems pretty sure-footed.

I can see that I won't get these women out of my house without swinging Gary around. Sighing, I agree. "Fine, but I'll be back in a flash."

I go to the bathroom and hop into the shower, sighing in unexpected pleasure as the pulsing hot water hits my shoulders.

I try to rush, but the feeling of shampooing my hair and letting all the sweat, funk, and dirt sluice their way from my body is refreshing. Getting out, I catch a blurry glimpse of myself in the foggy mirror. I wipe the condensation away and am surprised at what I see. The circles under my eyes are deep purple, and my bags have carry-on luggage that would require an oversize fee. And when I pull on fresh clothes, they're a bit baggier than usual.

Back in the living room, I find Jasmine's happily puttering around the kitchen, watching over something on the stove that smells delicious, while Daysha and Aleria wash and put away the dishes. I guess Becca's still out with Nut and Juice.

As I pad in, Daysha gives me a much more welcoming smile. "She's alive."

"Barely."

"Well, Jasmine's making her famous spaghetti sauce, so you'll be refueled with yummy carb-a-licious goodness soon enough," Aleria says, leading me back over to the couch where she pushes me down, forcing me to sit.

"Fill us in. Is it the book?" Aleria asks, perching on the edge of a chair across from me. It feels vaguely like therapy, and I expect her to ask me how I feel next.

"No, it's not the book," I reply, taking the silently offered hairbrush and getting to work. There are a lot of tangles, but I work at them carefully as I answer her. "The writing is actually going pretty well. But that's only because I've been floating on cloud nine while I was writing the characters' relationship building right along with mine and Connor's."

"While you were hunting the laptop down."

"Yeah," I agree. "It's all seamless now, and I'm working on the last chunk of plotline."

"That's good," Aleria says positively. "A few weeks ago, you couldn't write a single scene, so that's progress."

"But now that I'm mad at Connor, I'm writing the characters blowing up too. I've been taking out my anger on Ryker and having Amber say all the shit I want to say to Connor. Like, 'How could you? Were you using me the whole time?'"

"I take it that's not going well?" Jasmine asks from the kitchen.

"Or it's going really well?" Daysha adds, drying a glass I don't remember using. "Turmoil makes for good books. But I can't tell if you're using your real life as inspiration in a good way or in a 'you're gonna get sued for defamation' way."

"Maybe both," I confirm, sighing. "I'm just . . . I'm mad because he's had to leave for a little while."

"Why?" Aleria asks, and I see Jasmine and Daysha give each other a pointed look. But before I can answer, Becca comes back with Nut and Juice, who are panting hard alongside her.

"Hey, ran them *hard* to get out some of their pent-up energy," she explains, grinning and pink-cheeked. "Ooh, that smells good, Jasmine!"

"Becca!" Daysha shouts. "You were saying, Poppy? Something about Connor leaving?"

"Oh, shit," Becca hisses, plopping onto the other end of the couch. Nut and Juice, the traitorous fiends, curl up at her feet.

"Yeah," I reply, not mentioning the details. They know he swiped my laptop, but fine art theft? Nope, I promised Connor I wouldn't tell, and I'll keep that promise no matter what. Even with the girls. Even when he's pulled a disappearing ghost act.

Right now, I wish I hadn't told them about his stealing the laptop because that could get sticky. Especially if they hear about *The Black Rose* going missing from the same event. It wouldn't take any of them longer than a split second to put that together and come up with Connor.

This is fucking complex. And dangerous.

"Look, I need you girls to promise me something," I tell them quietly. "About Connor . . . what I tell you is a secret. You gotta swear."

Bless them all, my friends immediately all swear without even questioning. Aleria even places her hand on her heart, a signal she doesn't take lightly since she follows her heart always.

"Okay," I whisper, taking a deep breath. "He's had some trouble. And I don't know where he went, how long he'll be gone, or even if . . . if he's coming back."

I expect pity, maybe even a bit of blame for losing my heart to a criminal. What I don't expect is the universal anger around the room.

"Men are pigs."

"That's why I write aliens!"

"That's why we all write fictional heroes."

"True that."

It helps, even if I think they're wrong. Or at least I'm hoping they're wrong. Because I believe deep in my heart that Connor is worth this pain . . . and not lying to me about a secret wife and kids he's got hiding out in another town, which was Daysha's twisted thought.

For the rest of the afternoon, the girls help out. Jasmine makes me a delicious bowl of spaghetti while Daysha and Becca go through my rough draft with a fine-tooth comb.

My backup computer and thumb drive come in handy as I get into the swing, sprinting through scenes and chapters while my W3AS sisters help.

"Open wide," Becca orders at one point, popping a donut hole into my mouth. "Good girl!"

"What's that for?" I mumble around the mouthful of donut.

"Every ten pages, you get a reward," Becca tells me, patting my head. "Now back to it!"

"You know you're treating her like the two rug rats," Jasmine says, looking over at Nut and Juice. "You going to take her for a walk later, too?"

"If I have to."

THE MOONLIGHT SHINES THROUGH MY WINDOW AS I SIT ON MY couch. It's long after the girls have left, and I'm sipping decaf. Frankly, stripping coffee of caffeine is an affront against nature and downright evil as far as I'm concerned, but the bitter coffee suits my mood and I do want to sleep tonight.

Suddenly, Nut and Juice go crazy, growling and barking at the door. I didn't hear anything, but they're obviously riled up at something.

"Connor?"

I peek out and see a vehicle in his driveway, but it's not his big King Ranch truck. This one is a black Suburban. And the front room light is on, glowing warmly.

"Fuck no. I will destroy you before I let you hurt him," I vow to the empty room. Surging off the couch, I don't bother tying my robe or putting on reasonable shoes. Nope, I run right over in my fuzzy slippers with my robe flying out behind me like a cape. I'd look like an avenging angel if I weren't wearing cartoon character PJ pants and carrying Gary the Golf Club.

I don't knock. I swing the front door right open, Gary on my shoulder and ready to swing as I stomp into the living room.

"Who the fuck is in here?"

A man, tightly built with blond hair and all black clothing, whirls, aiming a small handgun at me. "Freeze."

"Back atcha, asshole." Gun versus golf club doesn't put me in the winner's column, but I've got fury and concern on my side. Plus a considerable lack of self-preservation. "Who are you?"

"Hunter."

Well, we're on first names, it seems. "Poppy."

The gun doesn't move, but his eyes scan down my body and back up. It feels like an assessment, not particularly personal. More like an android scanning a human to compare to their data banks or something. "You're her, the woman he met."

"I can neither confirm, nor deny, that allegation. Until you tell me more than your first name."

I'm afraid he's an officer sent by Detective Carter, though I don't know how he would've linked all that together. Carter's all badge, no brains. And he definitely would've come himself if he got a hot tip on *The Black Rose* thief's location. He'd want all the credit and wouldn't want to share it with anyone. After all, the hero gets all the good press.

But Hunter scoffs and gives me a wry look. "I'm the closest thing to a friend Connor's got. I help him with . . . his work." His brow lifts at that, questioning what I know.

"You work with Connor and he told you about me?" I repeat cautiously. When he nods carefully, I throw caution to the wind and unleash wildly, "Where is he? He hasn't been here in days. Is he okay? Tell me where he is."

Okay, so maybe I get a tad bit hysterical and bossy. And I might be screeching loudly.

Hunter holds up a hand, telling me to be quiet. Seeing his gun still in his hand, he slips it back into a holster at his side. "He's taking care of a job," he tells me. "For some very dangerous people."

"Where?" I beg. "I need him!"

"What's wrong?" he demands, instantly serious. "Are you in trouble yourself? Threatened? Or . . . uhm, pregnant?"

I whirl, walking around in circles as I rant. "What? No, I'm not pregnant." I repeat his last thing, shaking my head. "But what isn't wrong? He dumps all this heavy shit on me and then ghosts like fucking Casper. No, not Casper. He's a *friendly* ghost. Connor disappeared like a fucking poltergeist, leaving me jumpy and terrified."

As I pace, spinning one way and then another, Hunter ducks away from the golf club resting on my shoulder. Finally, he puts a hand on my shoulder, stopping me and making me face him. "What heavy shit did he dump on you?"

He's parroting my words back meticulously, which makes me suspicious as hell. Maybe he is one of Carter's flunkies. Surely, somebody at the police department has half a brain and one ball between their legs.

I lunge forward, shoving the head of the golf club to Hunter's neck, wishing it were a fat, chunky driver instead of an iron. "What do you know about Connor? You say you're a friend, but what if I don't believe you?"

He freezes, though I have every belief that he could push the golf club away easily. "He stole your laptop but helped you get it back. It was an . . . unfortunate collateral damage to another job. You got the jump on him, and somehow, he ended up taking you to his sister's wedding. I'm still not sure how you managed that one."

I sigh, weighing his words carefully. They're all true, but I'm trying to make sure there's no other way he could know that other than Connor telling him. Hunter pushes the golf club away slowly. "Believe me now?"

"Yeah. But you still haven't answered my main question. Where is Connor?"

"If I tell you, I'm going to need your word that you won't hurt him. How ride or die are you?"

"If he's at a strip club, I will rip his balls from his body and stuff them down his throat until it's so swollen he looks like a bullfrog," I state flatly. I'm dead serious. "If he needs help, I'll bring hell with me to protect him."

Hunter chuckles, his smile turning his hard face into something much warmer. "I can see why he likes you. No strip club, I promise."

"Then I'm totally riding, no dying."

Hunter takes a big breath and points to the kitchen table. "I'm gonna need to hold you to that. Have a seat, let me fill you in."

CHAPTER 23

CONNOR

*D*ifferent coffee shop, same routine. Hunter and I never meet at the same place more than once every few months, but it's always the same. Same franchise chain, same code phrases, same beverages just to make sure we're in the clear to discuss things.

Once we've jumped all the old, familiar hurdles and I sip at my black coffee, I lay it out for Hunter. "I've got a problem, man. The five-oh sort."

Hunter sips at his coffee, wincing. "How in the hell do they mess up black coffee? Shit, bitter is one thing. Burnt is another." I agree with him. The coffee at this particular shop is terrible compared to some of the other places we've met. But that's not really the point I want him to focus on. Finally, he sets the mug down, staring into its depths before scanning me up and down. "You've got more problems than that, but let's start there."

I'm pretty sure that's a dig, but I don't have time to volley back and give him shit in return. I dive right in and tell him about Detective Jax Carter, his behavior, especially his coming to see Poppy, and that they've linked the missing laptop to the missing painting. "They shouldn't have even realized it was a fake yet. Seriously, what happened?"

"Word is Fox tried to get it insured right afterward. Guess she hadn't done it before, and the lights-out deal scared her into doing it pronto, and Lloyd's of London knows their shit."

I snort. "But how do they know it was a recent switch? It could've been that way for months, years, no telling how long."

"The ownership change was documented when Fox took possession, so the assessment of it was recent enough that they could narrow it down. Especially since it doesn't go many places, mostly just hangs on the wall in Fox's office as a trophy of sorts. Easy to pin down then." Hunter shrugs, well aware that he's telling me things I already know from my prep work research.

Everything he's saying is why it was best to steal the painting at the dinner, and if things had gone according to plan, I'd be in the clear. But the fake being discovered so soon makes things extra messy. "I don't like it."

"I don't either, but what are you going to do about it?" Hunter asks.

I've been racking my brain for the last few days, doing more planning and recon on the statue job while looking into this Detective Carter. It's been tough, with my mind working in two directions at once. It's more than tough, it's risky. I've always been single-minded before.

Not now.

"I don't know. I'm so close to getting Mr. Big, but it doesn't seem as important now. She's all I can think about."

Hunter leans back in his chair, stretching his legs out. He looks me in the eye, but I feel like he's looking deeper into my soul. Can he see that my heart's not in this anymore? That whatever gaping wound I've been trying to fill with stealing stuff has been filled with Poppy now?

Finally, he says, "You've lost focus. I never thought I'd say that about the great Connor Bradley, but it's the fucking truth. You should've walked away a long time ago, but out of some misguided sense of obligation, you got the laptop back for this woman. But now, it's time to drop her. Bitches get you stitches."

His voice is dead cold, and realistically, I know he's right. But I shake my head, running my fingers through my hair. "I can't. I don't want to. She's it, man. I don't deserve her, but I want to. Whatever it takes."

Hunter's voice doesn't thaw a bit as he leans in, hissing sharply. "You know you can't simply walk away from this. There are consequences to what we do! If you lose focus or fail at your mission, it won't just be you paying the price. It'll be her too."

"Don't you think I know that?" I growl. "But desperate times call for desperate measures. I have to figure out a way to walk away and to protect her at the same time. Things have changed too much now."

"Bullshit," Hunter spits out, unswayed by my desperation. "You've changed too much, lost your edge, and a man with no edge in our world is a man on his way to a shallow grave. You know too much, have seen too much, and have done too much."

We meet eyes once more, the silence growing long as the truth sinks in for both of us. This very well may be the last time I see Hunter. He has a job to do, a role to fill in this madcap world, and if I'm stepping off our conjoined path while he stays on its rocky road to wherever he goes next, we may never see each other again.

Hunter holds a hand out, and we shake firmly. "Honor among thieves, brother. If you need me, you know how to find me."

"Same, brother. Eyes open."

I don't turn around as he leaves the coffee shop, but I do watch his reflection in the window in front of me. Both because I'm sad to see him go, but also to make sure he doesn't double-cross me once he's behind my back. *Honor among thieves* is a common motto, but the reverse phrasing, *no honor among thieves*, is just as prevalent. But Hunter is out the door without a glance back, joining the small crowd of people on the street outside.

Once he's gone, I finish my coffee, thinking and planning.

My body is relaxed, my mind comfortable with my plan to steal the stone sculpture, but my senses are still on alert as I sit in the gathered audience at the auction. I've already scanned the crowd, noting two prominent millionaires who are known collectors, four assistants, and a small number of unfamiliar faces who are probably lookie-loos who won't bid on anything. There are also a few people off to the side at a table, some on computers and some on phones to take bids.

I see the woman who let me in for an impromptu preview as well. She offers a polite smile of recognition, which I return. But I'm shocked when I hear a voice behind me say, "You'd better stop smiling right the fuck now, mister, or I will knock every single one of those Colgate white teeth out of your head and leave you looking like a blow-up doll ready for a dick in your mouth."

My back goes ramrod straight, and I turn quickly. Poppy . . . looking amazing in a skirt and silk blouse combo, her thick red hair pulled back into a professional bun, and wearing black-framed glasses I've never seen her wear before.

"What the fuck are you doing here?" I hiss quietly.

Poppy smooths back a nonexistent stray hair and adjusts her glasses. "If I say checking up on you, would you find that adorable or stalker-y?" She flutters her lashes at me innocently.

"You can't be here. You need to go," I growl. "Now."

She looks at me evenly, completely unfazed by my aggression, which is somehow so damn sexy. If I weren't scared shitless that she's going to get hurt simply by being here, I'd want to kiss the fuck out of her.

"Hmm, nope."

She smiles, but it looks more murderous than congenial, and her butt is still sitting in the chair, not moving a bit.

"Poppy, this is serious business," I plead, trying a different tactic. "Dangerous. I don't want you to get hurt."

"Yeah, I know. That guy over there" —she points to a local millionaire who collects everything from primitive pottery to midcentury velvet clown paintings— "looks *super* sketchy."

She nods like she knows things, but she doesn't have a clue. She doesn't even know that I'm here for a job. I mean, me plus an art auction doesn't take a genius to figure out, but she doesn't *know*.

"Is there any chance I could talk you into sitting here and being quiet? Let me do what I need to do and don't interfere."

Before she answers, someone slips into the empty chair next to me. Fuck my life when I see who it is. "Hey, man."

If it wouldn't make a scene, I'd throw my hands up in the air. "Fuck, why don't we hold a whole damn board meeting? The gang's all here," I mutter. "JP, what're you doing here?"

JP looks cool as a cucumber, completely unfazed by this impromptu meeting between him and me, which makes me leery as fuck. Especially when he straightens his already straight tie. "It's your lucky day. Boss man is ready to meet."

"Today?"

JP levels me with a stare. "Now."

"He's here?" I say incredulously. "I'm in the middle of a job!" Not that it's going to plan, by any means, but I'm not going to tell JP that. Or Mr. Big, for fucking sure.

"No shit. Now."

My heart starts to race in excitement. This is what I've been waiting for, laying eyes on the infamous Mr. Big, the man nobody sees, nobody meets. He's virtually a ghost while simultaneously buying and selling the bulk of the art black market. I look around again, considering the people I wrote off as lookie-loos, deciding whether they might be Mr. Big.

"Come on," JP says. "Follow me."

JP stands, and after a second's consideration, I do too. "Where are we going?

JP angles his head, indicating a door off to the side. Once his back is turned, I give Poppy a hard look, silently begging her to stay put. I don't want to leave her out here unprotected, but I don't have a choice. I grit my teeth and follow JP.

Through the door, we're in the back hallway. It's ironic because this was exactly how I planned on swiping the statue, taking advantage of the post-auction hubbub to slip right in and do the deed.

JP knocks on a door I know well because I've already been on the other side of it. I glance up at the camera as we pass through it, noting that the light showing it's recording is dark. In the room beyond, I see the familiar tables and shelves full of treasures. It should be crawling with people in here, ready to carry out the items for auction, return them for safe storage, and tracking each item precisely. But there's no one here except for one man.

"Mr. Big, I presume?"

He dips his chin one time, one time only. "Connor Bradley."

He's smaller and younger than I predicted, looking suave and flashy in a designer suit. For a man who's been the king of the art theft world and the region for almost two decades, he's exceptionally ordinary looking. Brown hair, brown eyes, and not particularly intimidating in appearance. You could pass him on the street and think him one of thousands of businessmen and then instantly forget what he looked like.

I take a closer look at his face, studying and memorizing the details I need to know, and it's only then that I recognize him. He's not a face known to all the public, but when you're part of the ownership group of our local minor league baseball team, you do occasionally make the papers.

It seems Mr. Big is a well-rounded scoundrel, deep in both art and sports.

And now I know his real name. Mr. Big is Shane Harris, but I'll smartly keep that info to myself. For now.

Mr. Big turns and runs his hand along the edge of a table, nodding to himself as he scans the pieces there. I keep my silence. Whatever he has to say, I'm not going to tip my hand to him yet. "Seems I owe you a debt of appreciation for the work you've done for me."

I shrug casually. "You've compensated me well. Paid in full after each job."

His face tightens, as if he's got a little bit of gas, and he turns back to me, looking stony. "If only that were true," he says sadly from between pursed lips. "If only."

"Excuse me?" I reply, alarm bells going off in my head. Something's not right here. Why the hell have me case the place to steal a statue, only to show up when he knows I'm doing the job?

Unless . . .

Oh, shit.

"Betrayal is a funny thing," Mr. Big says when he sees something change in my eyes. "You expect it to come from enemies, but it so rarely does."

I freeze. I don't know how he knows, or what he knows, but he does.

Mentally, my brain goes ten different directions at once . . . how to get out of here, how to make sure Poppy is safe, how Mr. Big could've found out, what JP's role in this is.

Before I can decipher anything, Mr. Big pulls a gun out of his jacket pocket. I fully expect a sharp crack and the impact of a round hitting me in the gut. I'm bracing for it already. But instead, he aims at JP.

"The fuck?" I exclaim, trying to keep my hands loose at my side.

JP throws his hands up high, rambling in Spanish. I catch something that I think is a prayer before he switches to English. "Boss—"

"I considered you trustworthy, Juan Pablo. I was very disappointed to find out you've been talking to the police."

I look at JP in surprise, but he's shaking his head wildly. "No, Boss, no, no."

"Wait, hold on. There must be some misunderstanding here. Why would JP talk to the police? He loves his work." I'm trying to diffuse the situation because I'm missing some major pieces of information.

"Why doesn't matter," Mr. Big answers me. To JP, he snarls, "It only matters that you did."

Mr. Big points the gun again, emphasizing his anger to a now-quiet JP.

Something behind Mr. Big catches my attention, and only experience keeps me from reacting to the flash of red I see duck behind a crate on one of the shelves.

Motherfucking shit! That's Poppy.

What is she doing? I told her to stay in her seat and let me do what I need to. Now I've got two people to save, JP and Poppy.

"Connor, you've done excellent work for me, and this is your chance to step up the ladder. This job, as you can guess, was a . . . test. Take out the middleman, and in the future, you'll work directly for me. Sound good?" Mr. Big cocks his pistol, and I recognize what the real test is. It's about either shooting JP myself or getting rid of the body. Either one will demonstrate my loyalty.

JP says something quietly in Spanish, but he doesn't move other than that. Personally, I don't want JP dead for a multitude of reasons and would prevent this if possible. "I appreciate the compliment on my work. Not sure about this whole situation, though." I wave a hand from the gun to JP. "Seems like a bad way to start off a new arrangement."

While I speak, Poppy is sneaking up behind Mr. Big. She mouths, "Keep talking."

JP looks to me with wide eyes. I definitely hear him say, *"Perra loca"*.

I agree with him, Poppy is a crazy bitch. But she's *my* crazy bitch and it's my job to warn her off. I glare at her, trying to tell her with my eyes to back the fuck off and get out of here. She responds by flashing me a thumbs-up and taking two more exaggerated tippy toe steps toward us.

Is she trying to save *me*?

Thankfully, the gods favor fools and redheads, it seems, and since Poppy's both, Mr. Big doesn't notice her. "I can understand your hesitation, but it felt necessary to show what I require of my people. I am serious about loyalty."

"I can see that," I reply, trying to keep Mr. Big's attention so he doesn't hear Poppy.

But I'm not surprised when that doesn't go to plan either. As she comes around the crate Mr. Big is standing next to, she trips over her own feet and stumbles right into the open.

Mr. Big whirls and aims the gun at her. "Who the fuck are you?"

"Oh!" she exclaims, completely ignoring the gun aimed at her chest in favor of adopting a ditzy airhead act, "I was looking for the bathroom and seem to have gotten a little lost." She holds her hand up to her mouth as though confiding top-secret intel. "Do you know where the ladies' room is? I swear I can't go more than a few minutes without having to tinkle. That's what my grandmother used to call it—tinkle. She said it was more ladylike than saying you had to piss. But really, we all do it, so why the need for code words?"

She's rambling, getting closer and closer as if she doesn't even see the gun. It's so off the wall, though, that it works, and Mr. Big somehow doesn't shoot her. "What? Just . . . stop moving. And talking."

Poppy stops as if she just realized what she walked into. Taking off her glasses, she wipes at the lenses, then puts them back on, doing a double-take at Mr. Big. "Holy shit." Her eyes are wide, and she covers her mouth with her hands. From behind spread fingers, she says, "What's with the gun? Did I walk in on something? I didn't mean to interrupt, sorry about that. Just needed to piss." She looks up to the ceiling, backpedaling. "Sorry, MeeMaw."

She backs away, her butt bumping into a table, rattling everything on its surface and sending a vase several feet away crashing over.

"Stop right there, woman," I yell in a last-ditch effort to keep Poppy safe. Maybe if Mr. Big believes she's a wayward attendee of the auction, he'll let her go. I hope that's true even as I know there's zero chance of that happening.

When Mr. Big glances over at me, Poppy takes advantage and grabs the closest heavy object, which happens to be the statue I was supposedly sent here to steal. Four pounds of stone make a hell of a club, and with Mr. Big's head half turned away, the statue catches him right in the temple.

Mr. Big drops to the floor like he was the one who got shot, and Poppy starts jumping up and down like she won the hammer strike game at the county fair.

"I did it!" Her shout of excitement reminds me of *Dora the Explorer*, loud and ridiculous considering what she's done. "That worked better than I thought! I saved you! With female ingenuity and . . . bewbies!"

She points at the statue's breasts, sounding proud of herself, but I'm pretty much flummoxed. "What? You didn't save me. I was about to do something to save you."

Poppy scoffs, holding up her impromptu weapon like it's completely natural for a woman to wield ad-hoc bludgeons like golf clubs and ancient stone statues on a regular basis. "*Sure*, you were."

My gut twists, the fear of losing her turning into hot, liquid fury as I look at the still stunned Mr. Big. Poppy, my woman, had a gun held on her, and I couldn't do anything about it. I couldn't save her.

Shame weighs on my soul.

She's such a bright light, one the world needs, and it was almost snuffed out too soon. Because of me.

But I can fix this. Moving quickly to Mr. Big's sprawled body, I pick up the gun from the concrete before plucking the statue from Poppy's hand, not wanting her to crack me over the head with it too.

JP, who realizes that somehow, he's been given the gift of life at the last moment, looks at me in shock. "Connor?"

I look him in the eye, trusting my gut. "Both of you, let's go. Now."

JP's eyes narrow, and I know what he's thinking. I pissed off a very valuable, very violent man. What's stopping me from doing the same to JP?

"Not a question," I tell him, tucking the pistol into my belt. "We've got some shit to talk about."

We go out the back door of the building and around the side to climb into my truck with Poppy in the back and JP in the passenger seat because I'm not entirely sure I trust him at my back just yet.

As soon as we're clear of the parking lot, I grab my phone and dial Hunter.

Despite how our last conversation finished, he answers on the very first ring. "Miss me already?"

There is no time for niceties or manners. Shit's hit the fan, officially and majorly. "Need a pickup team at the auction house. Mr. Big is unconscious in the back room. You'll recognize him. Shane Harris."

Hunter's tone goes serious instantly as he demands, "What? What did you do?"

"Not me, Poppy," I reply, glancing into the rearview mirror. Poppy still looks like she's pleased as punch about this whole thing. "She hit him over the head with the fucking statue."

Hunter unexpectedly barks out laughter in my ear. "She does like to hit things, doesn't she?"

"What are you talking about?"

"Oh, ask her. It's a funny story."

I glare at her, and she smiles like nothing is wrong in the world, even though she just fucked up everything I've been working on for months. And almost got herself shot in the process!

"I've got Poppy and JP. Mr. Big says he's been talking to the police."

Hunter's voice goes so hard I'm surprised he can unlock his jaw enough to answer me. "Fuck."

"Yeah," I tell him. "I'll be in touch."

I hang up and glance over at JP, who's looking at me in confusion. He usually bosses me around, but planning is my job, down to the exit strategies. Even when they're this fucked up.

CHAPTER 24

POPPY

Connor looks furious as he hangs up with Hunter.

I never thought 'mad' could be this sexy of a look. On Connor, or anyone, really. I thought it'd make him look scary. But instead, he looks like he could slay a dragon and then cook it over a bonfire for the whole town to feast on.

Maybe I can write that into my book somehow? Though it's not a fantasy period piece, so a random dragon showing up might be a stretch. But maybe a town barbeque? Hero dude just standing at a grill, wearing a plaid apron and holding a spatula. That's . . . not as sexy. Never mind, I think, scrubbing that idea off my mental possibilities list. But either way, all I want to do is rip that suit off and get me some Connor meat.

"Poppy."

"Connor," I return, still pleased with myself.

"Why does Hunter think you're aggressive?" he asks, meeting my eye in the rearview mirror.

"Huh?" It takes me a second to leave behind my barbeque scenario and return to this one where Connor is gritting his teeth so hard, the muscle in his jaw is popping. "Oh, because I introduced him to Gary, up close and personal. *Real* personal. In my defense, it was absolutely warranted."

Connor glances back at the road, his eyes tight. "When?"

"When he was at your house last night. I demanded to know where you were. He didn't want to tell me at first, but with a little persuasion from Gary" —I hold up my thumb and finger an inch apart— "he was singing like a canary. Tweet, tweet! He told me where to find you, what the dress code was, and he gave me these cool glasses as a disguise."

JP looks at Connor warily. "Who's Gary?" When Connor doesn't answer, he turns around to look at me as if he can't decide which of us is the larger threat to his well-being. "Who's Gary?"

"My golf club," I tell him proudly. "He's a three iron."

Connor isn't as amused, though. "Shit! I saw him this morning." He slams a hand to the steering wheel. "That motherfucker played me. He was testing me by telling me to ditch you."

"He what?" I screech, leaning forward over the seat to snatch Connor's phone so I can redial Hunter. I'm going to give that guy a piece of my mind. "That asshole! I'll kill him. Oops, maybe we shouldn't discuss urder-may in front of the olice-pay informant-ay," I tell Connor, tilting my head toward JP, who scoots a little closer to the door as if the extra inch or so might protect him.

Connor doesn't stop me from grabbing his phone, and a few seconds later, I understand why as his phone stays locked. "It's fingerprint, as well as swipe pattern, locked," he growls. "And nobody is murdering anyone."

"Well, not now, when you told him the plan." I roll my eyes and flop back in the seat. "And fingerprint? Really? As your fiancée, I should have your code. It's happy marriage rule 42. Or maybe 24? I forget, but it's one of the big ones." I'm totally making that up, but I've seen enough late-night TV to know that if your man is locking his phone, he's got a side chick in his DMs, and I don't share.

"I'm a criminal with a phone. It's that or constant burners," Connor points out. Looking over, he says, "JP . . . what the fuck?"

He sounds tired. Maybe today has been a long one for him, but I can help with that. Maybe after we figure out the JP issue, we can eat pizza in bed and relax. I can give him a massage and rub all that stress right out.

After that, he can rub my stress out too.

"I had to," JP pleads with Connor.

He sounds like he's still not sure what the hell's going on. Join the club, man! But the important thing to remember is that we're safe now because I saved us. But does either of them thank me? Of course not. They're going on with their conversation like I'm not sitting in the back seat.

"I got picked up by a man, a police officer. He said my fingerprints were on a painting, a fake one. He was going to charge me with grand theft unless I agreed to help them." He shakes his head. "I didn't want to, but I had to . . . for my wife and kids. My daughter is pregnant, and Manuel is still young. He needs me."

"Aw, congratulations, *Abuelo*!" I interject, patting JP's shoulder gently. He jumps like I scared him for some reason. Meanwhile, Connor glares at me like what JP said isn't important, but I disagree. Family is very important.

"Did you tell this police officer about me?" he asks JP in a hard tone.

I can tell this answer is important. JP can too. There is definitely a right answer and a wrong one. "No, I swear it!" he promises. I'm no expert, but I believe him. Connor grunts, so I think he does too. Either that or he's the one making murder-y plans now. "Just the boss. Though I guess that won't matter now, since he's dead."

The words hit me by surprise, and my heart stutters in my chest. "Did I kill him? Oh, my God, did I kill him?"

I'm suddenly not proud at all, I'm freaking out, my eyes wide as I beg Connor to tell me I didn't murder someone. A bad guy with a gun, so I'll probably get off on a self-defense rap, but still . . . I don't even have plants because it makes me feel guilty when I forget to water them and they die in my windowsill. I love Nut and Juice because they will never let me forget or ignore them.

I will definitely have immense guilt if I killed a man by hitting him with an old statue of some curvy woman. Reminded of it, I look at the statue in the seat beside me and scoot another inch away from it like it might fly through the air on its own and knock me upside the head.

"No . . . you didn't kill him. I don't think." Connor shrugs like it's no big deal either way. "He was breathing when we left, and Hunter will keep him alive. Probably."

"Probably?" I repeat vacantly.

Connor meets my eyes in the rearview mirror again. "If anyone dies, I'd rather it be them than you."

Can talking about death and murder be romantic? Apparently so, because I'm melting back here. "Aww, that's so sweet."

"*Perra loca*," JP whispers.

"Watch it," Connor warns JP, though I don't know what he said since the only Spanish I speak is to order tacos and nachos. JP holds his hands up in apology. "The police officer . . . what's the name?"

"Carter," JP says immediately. "Jax Carter."

I gasp, and Connor slams a fist to the steering wheel again. "Of fucking course!"

"Have I mentioned that I hate that guy?" I growl through clenched teeth. Seriously? "He's such a Paul Blart shart."

"Shart?" JP asks, and I can't help it, I smirk. I don't know Spanish, and he doesn't know Poppyish.

"Shit plus fart . . . shart."

JP snorts as he covers his mouth with a hand, but he nods his agreement with me.

That particular bridge crossed, I look back to Connor. I know more than he realizes now, but I can't tell him that until we're alone. "What are we going to do? We need a plan."

Connor keeps his eyes on the road, driving in a roundabout, meandering course to keep us safe, but we're generally heading back to the house. "I'm thinking."

"While you're thinking, can we go home? I need to let Nut and Juice out."

He doesn't say anything, but it means something to me that Connor speeds up. He's probably worried about my puppers too.

JP turns to looks at me with a furrowed brow, his brain working overtime behind his brown eyes. "Uhm, English is not my first language. Not even my second. But did you say 'nut juice'? That means uhm . . . the kids call . . ."

I laugh at his stilted question. Some people just don't get me. "Yeah, they're my two Pomeranians. Named after exactly what you think. It was funny at the time. There might've been a bottle of wine involved. And since I'd drunk-shopped for specially engraved name tags, it stuck."

JP looks at Connor, even more confused after my perfectly reasonable explanation. "This is your woman?" He mutters something in Spanish that has Connor clenching his jaw, and JP sighs.

Connor growls. "Yes. She's my woman, so watch what you fucking say."

Connor's claiming of me in such a caveman way makes my whole body light up with warmth. I'm usually more of the Cinderella meets her Prince Charming and gets romantically swept off her feet type, especially in what I write. None of my heroes are the growly, possessive, asshole sorts, but I am definitely rethinking my main characters. It's too late to change the characters and plotline of *Trouble in Great Falls*, but maybe I can use these last few chapters to introduce a new character with a bit of asshole-itis?

"You are so sexy," I purr, leaning forward to wrap my arms around Connor from behind. But the seatbelt pulls me back sharply, and I have to settle for only touching his shoulder. "Have I told you that?"

I feel JP looking at me like I've lost my mind, but my eyes are locked on Connor. His eyes drift up to the rearview mirror and he smiles. Well, his eyes do. His lips don't lift, but I know he likes that I think he's sexy because those gold flecks in the center of his eyes are flashing like fire. I move the boob separator seatbelt strap beneath my arm so I can lean forward again, lifting out of the seat to press a kiss to Connor's cheek.

One of his hands leaves the wheel and cups my head as he turns to kiss my mouth. But before our lips meet, I scold him through a smile. "Ah, ah, ah! We are safe drivers first, so eyes on the road, mister! We can't get into a wreck while we're making our getaway."

He growls as I pull out of his reach and fix my seatbelt but places his hand back on the wheel.

"You are going to be the death of me," he groans.

"That's how you know it's true love. It is like this with my wife too," JP says with a soft laugh. "A wise man once told me . . . if you're not at least a little scared of your woman, she's not the one."

Connor snorts. "You're scared of your wife?"

"Absolutely," JP says without a second thought. Looking back at me, he holds his thumb and finger an inch apart but slowly spreads them wider and wider until he's spreading his hands apart like he's measuring a fish. His laugh is louder and deeper, coming from his belly now. "You do the same to him?"

"Trying my best," I boast, perking up and trying to look as boss as possible. "She sounds like my kind of girl. Maybe we can meet sometime?"

Connor clears his throat, sounding amused but getting back to business. "Forgetting something, Poppy? We've got to figure out what to do about Carter first."

My smile fades as the crazy little bite of normalcy gets chewed up by the situation we're in. "Ugh, don't remind me about him. He ruins my good mood instantly."

"That's why we've gotta to deal with him," Connor says, putting on his turn signal to make the next to last turn on his way home. "So you never have to frown again."

I'm still not convinced but trust in him and in my heart. I'm just eager to see what Connor has up his sleeve.

CHAPTER 25

CONNOR

I don't really like the idea of bringing a man like JP to Poppy's home, but she's right about the dogs. They'll probably destroy the place if they're ignored too long. As soon as we reach the door, they're barking and scratching at it in anticipation.

"Yes, my babies," Poppy calls, shimmying a little herself. "Mama's coming. Hold your bladders one more minute!"

She unlocks the door, and the two white pompoms rush out past our feet, tearing circles in the grass before Nut squats in the corner of the grass that's 'his.' JP makes a noise of surprise that turns into a laugh.

"Ah, I get it . . . Nut Juice."

Poppy tuts gently to correct him, pointing at one dog and then the other. "Nut and Juice."

Juice finds his spot. He's more of a wandering pisser with his business. Once he's done, the two trot happily back inside, ready for a treat from Poppy.

While she feeds her monsters, I gesture for JP to sit on the couch. He does so slowly, legs tense and elbows braced on his thighs to stand quickly if need be. He's ready to fight for his life, to battle me or anyone else who threatens him or his family. That, I can definitely respect because I'm ready to do the same thing.

But if this conversation goes the way I hope, it's not going to come to that between us.

JP gives me a wary look, still not relaxing. "Are we . . . good, my friend?" he asks carefully. "No problems?"

I sit in a chair across from JP, keeping my hands on the arms and in the open to show I don't intend harm . . . at the moment.

"Men like us will always have problems, but hopefully, we won't have any between you and me. But I need you to tell me everything about Mr. Big and Detective Carter. All of it. The more I know, the easier I can get us out of this shit. You showed me a lot of trust in telling me where your son worked, and I'm showing you the same by bringing you here."

I look to the kitchen where Poppy is sitting on the floor with both dogs in her lap, their dinner forgotten. Poppy's heels lay askew from where she kicked them off, and she's totally oblivious to what she's doing to her skirt in the moment. All three of them are making these happy yipping sounds as she pets them, Poppy working in, "I know, Mama's been gone so long. I missed you too."

Of course, she's one of those people who baby talk to their dogs. And yips with them because she speaks fluent Pomeranian.

JP follows my gaze then turns his eyes back to me, nodding once. In the silence, a bond is solidified. One I hope we will both honor.

He leans back, crossing his legs to assume a comfortable, almost conversational body posture like we're about to sit around discussing the weather or our favorite sports teams. It's an intentional shift he's offering, showing his willingness to work with me.

"I've worked with the Boss for five years. It didn't start out like . . . this." He doesn't need to explain what 'this' is because it's obviously this clusterfuck. He glances up, probably wondering just where things went wrong. That's something I can understand. "Believe it or not, he hired me to be his personal assistant, above board and clean . . . at first. It was good work for a man like me. I know how to get things done but don't have the sort of corporate resume that's accepted here." He levels a stare at me, making sure I understand, and then, with a sigh, he continues. "I could manage his calendar, talk to business contacts all over the world, drive him places, things like that. We worked well together, and he began to trust me to do more. He'd confide in me, though we weren't friends. He made sure I didn't forget my place—to serve him. Over time, he would send me to pick things up or meet with people to relay messages." He waves a hand in my direction.

"Like me," I fill in.

JP nods. "Yes. At first, I didn't realize he was doing anything illegal. He's a businessman, so he buys and sells things, and nothing seemed out of the ordinary. I don't know anything about art." He holds his hands out wide, inviting me to look at him as if art knowledge is a visible trait. "There were others before you, of course. I'm not a stupid man. I soon knew he was doing something he shouldn't be. But by then" —he shrugs— "my family . . . we have a home, a life."

"I understand."

Once that wouldn't have been true, but now, since meeting Poppy, I can understand how someone could unintentionally become caught up in something and feel like they couldn't do anything to jeopardize what means the most to them.

"I told myself that no one was getting hurt," JP continues, looking disappointed in himself. "It's pieces of paint on canvas or statues. Stealing from the rich, who cares? I'm not taking food out of someone's mouth . . . at least, that's what I said before he had me making arrangements with 'cleaners'. And when that detective grabbed me, I realized that I was the one who was going to be hurt. Me and my family. The Boss? He would replace me and go on like nothing had happened."

I tilt my head. "You told Carter what you had to."

"I did, but only about the Boss. He asked me where *The Black Rose* painting was, and at first, I played dumb. Nobody expects me to know art," he says dryly. "But the police officer kept asking questions, saying they knew I'd touched the replacement, and eventually, I told him I didn't know where the original was because it had been sold by my employer. That made him very interested."

"Always better to catch the big fish, not the minnows." I point from him to me, acknowledging that we're not the criminals the police would be most interested in when there's a chance at catching a true black-market powerhouse.

We're quiet for a moment, both of us lost in our thoughts. I'm trying to decide what Carter's move would be. He's got an inside man in JP and will want to maximize his chances of catching Mr. Big.

"Did Carter know about the auction today? About Mr. Big coming to meet me?"

JP shakes his head, narrowing his eyes. "No, I didn't have time to tell him. It was a last-minute meeting. The original plan was for you to steal the statue as a final test of sorts. If you could get past Boss's own security . . . well, it doesn't matter. When he told me, I was surprised, but now I understand. He didn't want me to know that he'd found out about my betrayal."

"You didn't betray anyone," I tell him honestly, feeling for the man. "Except maybe yourself. We'll fix this."

Hope and fear mix in his dark eyes. "I need to call my wife."

He's asking permission, and I want to say no. It's a risk we shouldn't take, but I was only gone for work for a few days before Poppy was swinging golf clubs at Hunter's head. I wonder how long it'd take JP's wife to do the same?

"You said Poppy would like her," I point out. "Is she a *perra loca* too?"

For the first time in the last hour, JP smiles. "Absolutely. And I wouldn't have it any other way."

I smile back, acknowledging everything he's shared by giving permission. "On speakerphone, please."

JP nods in understanding and pulls out his phone and dials. A woman answers in Spanish, already talking fast and furiously. I catch enough to know that JP's in trouble for skipping dinner and in even more trouble when he tells his wife that he has to work overnight again.

She stops cursing him out, but I can hear the intensity in her voice. Like her son, I suspect she doesn't know everything her husband does, but she knows enough.

She knows not to ask questions.

I give them as much privacy as I can, stepping into the kitchen with Poppy and the dogs while still keeping an ear on JP's conversation.

But I need Poppy. Standing over her, she looks up at me. Her eyes are full of worry, her bottom lip red and puffy from where she's been chewing on it, and her hair is no longer tucked up into her professional, tight bun but disheveled and half escaped.

"Is everything going to be okay?"

She wants me to say yes. She needs me to. But the truth is, I don't know. And I've already lied about so much and there's still so much she doesn't know. I don't want to add this to the pile I'm accumulating.

I reach down, taking her hand to pull her to her feet. She instantly falls into my arms, her cheek pressed to my chest and arms wrapped around my waist. I hug her back, holding her tightly as I memorize everything about her—the smell of her shampoo, the press of her breasts, the sound of her breathing, and even the way she makes me feel. Like I'm enough.

"I'll make it be okay," I vow. "Just give me time, and I'll make it okay. I promise."

"I believe you."

Those words mean a lot after all the lies.

"I will also always believe *in* you," Poppy whispers.

Another sentiment, but equally important. It means so much and actually brings us back to something approaching normalcy. Poppy tries to work a bit, but she's too amped and winds up telling JP all about her book. He even reads some of the draft, making comments. "You would make a very good *telenovela* writer. That's a compliment."

"Thank you," Poppy says graciously.

A couple of hours later, I'm still trying to decide what to do when there's a knock at the door.

I go to answer it, but Poppy waves wildly at me, shooing me away.

"My door, I'll answer. What if it's Carter?" she whispers, not nearly quiet enough. "He can't find you two" —she points at me and JP— "hanging out in my living room."

She's got a good point, but I don't like her answering her door alone. Who the fuck would be coming over this late, anyway? "Take Gary."

She winks, and I know she's thinking that I've come around to the brilliance of having a golf club handy. Even though I'm not a gun man myself, I wish Gary were a Glock right now.

She picks up Gary from beside the door, laying it over her shoulder casually. I stand behind the door just in case, and she cracks the door ever so slightly. I hear a familiar voice ask, "Gonna take another swing at me, Tiger?"

"Maybe," Poppy teases as relief rushes through me. "Depends on whether you kept Mr. Big alive or not, Hunter."

I hear him chuckle, and I want to rush the door, both to hug Poppy and to yank Hunter inside. It's pretty clear that I need to hug him too . . . right before I kick his ass.

"The bad thing is," Hunter continues, "I'm honestly not sure if you'd prefer for him to be alive or dead."

"Let him in, Poppy," I call, keeping myself as calm as possible. "We've got some shit to figure out."

She opens the door in invitation but lunge steps at Hunter as he passes by her. He doesn't flinch away but rather lunges back at her, both freezing before I can hurl myself between them. They both smile like they shared a secret handshake, and I slowly feel my heart loosen up in my chest. "You two . . ."

Poppy grins. "Well, you boys have a seat. I'm pretty sure I've got a bottle of wine tucked away somewhere, and I think it's time to pour a few glasses. Oh, and pizza. I'm the best at ordering pizza."

As she goes into the kitchen once more, Hunter side-eyes me and quietly says, "I get it, man. I'll back your play, whatever you need."

CHAPTER 26

POPPY

The next morning is too bright and too early, especially when my belly is unhappy with the amount of pizza, wine, and stress I subjected it to last night. But when Connor wakes me up with a kiss and says it's time to go, I slowly rise to my feet. But I refuse to shine. Yet.

Shuffling into the living room, I see all three men up and ready to go, apparently having already helped themselves to coffee. "Where are we going? Are we going on the run? We'll have to pick up JP's family too before we leave the country. Oh, wait . . . I'll have to find my passport. And get Becca to take care of Nut and Juice until we can bring them with us. We'll have to do one of those adorable reunion videos when we get them back."

Hunter sighs from the couch, rubbing at his stubbled cheek. "Is she for real?"

Connor chuckles, which is an amazing sound that draws me into his side so I can feel the vibration of it against my skin. He wraps an arm around me easily, nodding before kissing the top of my head. "Amazingly, yes. She is. If you don't know, the craziness is just camouflage for a very sharp mind."

"Aww, thanks, babe," I tease, skipping the coffee to go straight for the hard stuff. I've had to 'self-medicate' before in order to wake up after a late night of work, so I know exactly what I need. Grabbing a sugar-free Red Bull out of my fridge, I use a corkscrew to poke a hole in the can before popping the top and shotgunning the whole thing in one long swallow.

"Ignition in three, two, one . . ." I drone. "Blast off." I shake my whole body, sending the caffeine through my bloodstream. Eyes clear, I look at Connor. "Let's do this."

Connor's eyes are wide, and I realize what he just watched me suck down. Grinning, I playfully, and obscenely, lick my lips. He growls, taking the can from me to drop it in the trash. "Go get dressed."

"It's a good thing you're sexy when you're grumpy," I tell him, scooting back down the hallway to pull on jeans and a T-shirt. I also choose tennis shoes in case I need to make a run for it. At this point, I'm planning for any and every thing.

Once Connor assures me I won't need a passport, we load up in his truck. JP and I are relegated to the back seat this time so that Hunter and Connor can sit up front. As we pull out, I see the walking club women making their rounds. They stop, wide-eyed and staring.

I wave as I roll down the window. "Hey, ladies! Beautiful morning, isn't it?"

Jane, who once surreptitiously asked me to sign a copy of my book for her, sees three handsome men and blinks. "Uhm, hi, Poppy. Aren't you gonna introduce us to your friends?"

She points to JP and Hunter, striking a flirty pose with one hand on her hip as she pushes her hair behind her ear. But before I can say anything, Connor rolls my window up and pulls away.

"That was rude," I comment. "I was about to tell them I'm researching a reverse harem story with some real first-hand experience!"

Connor doesn't laugh, but his lips do twitch. Like I could ever need another man after him? Pssh. "JP's married, and Hunter's a bigger asshole than I am."

I lean forward, looking at Hunter, who merely shrugs.

"I'm sorry for Connor," I tell him very seriously. "I've met his family, and manners aren't exactly a strong suit. *Words as weapons* is more their style."

Hunter smirks, and I think he'd like to laugh at my humor but is as unfamiliar with laughter as Connor was before I came around. "Maybe so, but Connor's not wrong. I'm definitely an asshole."

We drive in silence for a few minutes until I realize where we're going. "The police station? That seems like a bad idea, guys. A really bad one."

Connor seems self-assured, turning on his blinker as he comes to a stop at a red light. "Trust me. We talked this through last night after you crashed."

I look at JP because he seems to be the one who hates Detective Carter as much as I do, but he smiles encouragingly. I cross my arms over my chest, pouting. "Okay, but I'm not looking to be on the next episode of *Orange is the New Black*."

When we get to the station, Connor parks but leaves the truck running. He turns around, pinning me with a serious look. "I'm going in with Hunter. I want you two to wait here."

"Like we're the getaway car? I'll move up to the front seat then."

Thank God Connor realizes that at least half of my silliness is a way to deal with stress and nerves because he doesn't yell or anything. He just takes me seriously and responds evenly, "No, not a getaway car. We want to talk to Carter and settle some things. While you wait here."

That last part sounds dangerously like an order. There is only one place I like to be bossed around, and this isn't it. Well, Connor was kinda bossy when we got back from fucking on the same seat I'm sitting in now, but that was a deliciously good way. Other than that . . . nope. Naked and making me come is the only time someone can boss me around. Even Connor.

I stay silent, not agreeing but not disagreeing either while I think about what he's 'asking' of me. I am definitely in over my head here, and Connor and Hunter obviously have some mastermind plan they agreed on after I fell asleep last night.

It pisses me off, honestly. What am I, some sitcom housewife? Good for a laugh when I'm swinging a golf club but not able to be filled in on the real details of things? Nah, that's not going to continue.

Connor and I will discuss that later.

And I'm worried about him. He's walking into a police department where that asshole Detective Carter is actively looking for *The Black Rose*'s thief.

My best guess is that Connor plans to leverage Mr. Big's reputation as someone Carter shouldn't mess with, but how tough is the guy really if I could take him out with one swing of a statue?

As Connor and Hunter go inside, JP and I are left alone. I twiddle my thumbs patiently for about two minutes before I turn to him and ask, "So, are you supposed to keep me here?"

JP smiles kindly. "No, but we are supposed to stay here. Let Connor and Hunter talk to the police."

I nod, considering my options and still not sure what's best. After a minute of squirming, I look back over at JP, who's still cool and collected. "But if I were to get out, you won't stop me?"

JP looks concerned and glances toward the police department door. Just to test him, I open my door and stick a foot out.

"Poppy?" he says uncertainly. "*Por favor.*"

I give him a mega-watt smile to ease his nerves. "It'll be fine."

I'm not sure if I'm telling him or convincing myself. But either way, I get out, closing the truck door and striding toward the station door with as much guts as I can manage. Nothing bad happens, or at least nobody swarms out to arrest me for attacking Mr. Big, and I get braver.

Inside, I see the same desk officer from before, and she smiles warmly. I think she remembers me and my anger-induced loud dismissal of Detective Carter the first time I was here, but hopefully not my dramatic tirade when I was forced to wait while freaking out. Her response gives me confidence, and I stride up to her desk with my head held high.

"I'm here to talk to Detective Carter."

The desk officer gestures toward the chairs off to my right. "He's with someone at the moment. Would you like to wait?"

I can't wait. I will lose all my courage if I sit in one of those chairs. And I'm already not doing what Connor asked of me, so why would I follow what this woman wants me to do? I'm in for a penny, in for a pound, so I keep my composure and give her a casual smile. "Two growly-sexy dudes, one who's walking sex on a stick and the other, an asshole? I'm actually with them too, so I'll see myself back. This is urgent."

I don't wait for permission, preferring to ask for forgiveness or flat-out ignore that I might need permission in the first place, and walk into the back room of desks. Connor, Hunter, and Detective Carter are all standing at one of the desks. Carter looks murderous, his palms on the desktop as he leans forward to snarl at Connor and Hunter.

"No way. You're not taking this from me. I worked this case. It's mine." He thumps his chest with a fist, and I'm reminded of a posturing gorilla trying to warn off a potential threat.

Hunter looks totally unrattled. "Federal trumps all in this field. It certainly trumps some city dick looking to make a name for himself," Hunter sneers coldly. "Would you like to get our bosses involved with this?"

"I've been working this fucking case for months," Connor grits through clenched teeth, his jaw looking like carved stone he's so tense, "and you stroll in here like some goddamn rookie and fuck everything up. You'll be lucky if you still have a badge when my superiors get done with you."

Wait . . . what?

How would Mr. Big take Carter's badge?

Connor turns and sees me. I see the 'oh, shit' reaction cross his face as he realizes that I heard what he just said. It's still processing, pieces falling together in my mind like plot points in my book wrapping up through twists and turns to a surprise ending. "Poppy."

Just my name on his lips brings it all to a sharp point of focus. "You . . . how long were you going to lie to me? You're a fucking liar."

I knew that, but stupidly, I thought he wasn't lying to me anymore. But once a liar, always a liar because Connor isn't a petty thief. And he's not an art thief.

Based on what he just said and how he said it . . .

He's an undercover federal agent.

He didn't want me to find out, didn't want me to know. He's been hiding it this whole time.

Rage ignites in my veins, and my feet move of their own volition. I'm going to attack him again. This time for stealing something even more precious than my manuscript. My heart. That foolishly trusting organ that's pumping way too fast in my chest now.

"Miss Woodstock?" Detective Carter interrupts, clearly not getting the full story from Connor and Hunter to this point. That smug fucking smirk curls his lips. "Let me guess, the whole 'stolen manuscript' thing was some sort of PR stunt tied into *The Black Rose*'s theft?"

He does air quotes with his fingers when he talks about how I lost my book, just as condescending as he was that first night when I tried to report it stolen. That look on his face is the push over the edge I didn't need.

With a Valkyrie yell, I lunge at Detective Carter, clawing and scraping my stress-induced-chewed nails down his face. "What the fuck?" he shouts, trying to push me back.

"You should've helped me that first night! None of this would've happened!" I'm screaming, pain pouring out with all the anger.

Connor and Hunter grab me, pulling me off Detective Carter and telling the officers who have appeared to stand back. But they're not listening to two random men, and before I know it, arms have grabbed me and ripped me away from my target.

They push me back a few steps, and Connor roars, pulling an officer's hands from my arms. He tries to wrap me up, holding me and telling me to calm down and that everything's okay, but I fight him too.

I fight them all.

I fight until I have nothing left. Until I'm a ragdoll, empty with tear-stained marks down my cheeks and someone is holding me up.

An officer says, "In here."

Before I know it, there's a sliding sound and a final clang as they lock me in some sort of holding cell in the corner of the room.

With nothing left to hold me up, I collapse to the floor, curling in on myself.

Connor's on the other side of the metal grate, crouching down until we're only separated by a few millimeters of steel. "Poppy, baby," he says softly, "I'm so sorry."

I glare at him, wanting to hurt him the way he's hurt me with his lies and betrayal. "A few weeks ago, I was fine. Look at me now," I whisper, angry and heartbroken and all sorts of fucked up all at once. "All because I'm a klutz who bumped into you. You're not a black sheep. You're fucking poison."

He tries to reach me through the mesh, even as the barbs of my words pierce him. But I recoil, not wanting him to touch me. His touch would only be lies, anyway.

It's all lies.

Detective Carter, who's watching and swiping away blood from my scratches, decides to chime in. "Crazy fucking bitch."

Connor whirls in place as he stands and pops Carter square in the nose. Blood splatters over Carter's cheeks in a gush of red, and his hands fly up to cover his nose.

Hunter grabs Connor, manhandling him to get him away from Carter and away from me. He pushes him several feet back, growling that Connor needs to get ahold of himself. "Let it go, man. Let it go."

Detective Carter sounds more nasally than he did before when he whines, "You broke my fucking nose."

Even in my empty, soulless state, I take sick pleasure in that. Detective Carter deserves that and so much worse. Connor does too. And even Hunter. They all deserve to feel pain like I'm feeling, but life isn't fair and that wish isn't granted. I curl up on the floor, comforting myself.

A loud voice bellows with authority, "What is going on in here?"

Everyone freezes, eyes turning toward the man who's exited an office off to the side.

Except me. After a quick glance, I look at the floor, trying to figure out where everything went wrong. Dimly, I hear Connor tell me, "I'm going to fix this. I promise."

But I don't react to that either.

I wait until the office door closes behind Carter, Hunter, and Connor before I let the tears fall.

I don't know how much time has passed when a man in a black suit walks through. I wonder if he's my lawyer when he glances my way, but he doesn't say anything before going into the office with Connor.

Fine, fuck you too, I think. *Fuck everyone and everything.*

But the rage is short-lived, burning hot and fast and then leaving me weighed down with inner darkness. I sigh and curl back up. I stare at the wall until the officer from the desk appears sometime later with a paper bag of food. "Hey, honey. Thought you might be hungry, so I brought you some lunch."

"Not hungry."

"Okay, I'll leave it right here in case you change your mind. Just do me a favor, don't go chucking meatloaf sandwich all over the place?" She sits there for a minute, looking uncomfortable. When she glances over her shoulder for the second time, I glare at her.

"What?"

"I know this is an awful time, but I'm a really big fan," the officer says, biting her lip a little. "I've been kicking myself for not asking last time. Do you think you could sign my book?"

She holds out a marker and a copy of *Love in Great Falls* that's obviously been read multiple times. Even with everything falling to shit, I can't be rude to her. Not when she's been nothing but kind. It's not her fault I'm where I am.

It's Connor's.

And mine.

I scoot over to the slot in the mesh, and she holds out the marker. I reach for it, but she moves the marker back slightly to ask, "You're not going to stab anybody with this, are you?"

I lift an eyebrow, silently asking 'seriously?' and she smiles. "Didn't think so."

While I sign the book she's holding open, she clears her throat. "So . . . your social media said that you've got a new book in the works. *Trouble In Great Falls?*"

Oh, God, that. Hilda is going to kill me. There is no way I'm going to make my deadline, and if word gets out that I'm in the slammer for going full assault force on a police officer, I'll be done for. "Uhm, yeah. Who do I make this out to?"

The desk officer smiles excitedly. "Penelope. Everything's going to work out for Ryker and Amber, right?"

I look across the office, where the men are all mansplaining the shit out of everything to each other, doing what men seem to do best. "I might kill Ryker off."

Officer Penelope follows my line of vision and frowns. "I hear you, honey. Maybe don't take out what that one did on my Ryker, though? He's my favorite book boyfriend."

"We'll see," I tell her. "You know, no promises and all that."

But everyone knows that's just a kinder, gentler way of saying no. Officer Penelope leaves, and I must fall asleep at some point because the rattle of keys wakes me. I open my eyes to see Hunter and a uniformed officer standing at the cell door.

"You sure you can handle her by yourself?" he sneers. "I can call the pound if you need it."

I glare at him, clacking my teeth together.

Hunter sighs and rolls his eyes in exasperation. "Poppy, could you not? You have no idea what we just went through to get you out of here. And you," he says, looking at the officer, "be a fucking professional."

That melts my orneriness a bit. Hunter's right on both counts, I bet. "I'm free to go?"

Hunter holds out a hand but frowns, which doesn't make me feel any better. "Not exactly. You've been released to my custody. As a witness for our case against Mr. Big." He stares at me hard, his eyes telling me to listen to what he said carefully. "I'll have to cuff you until we get to the car. Seems you scared the shit out of Carter over there, and he's considering pressing charges for assault on an officer. He's not much a fan of being told to stand down and back the fuck off."

I glance where he points to see Detective Carter glaring at me from across the room. If looks could kill, I'd be goo on the floor. I return the same glare, wishing I could do the same to him too.

"Fine." I stand up and turn around, placing my hands behind my back like I've seen on television shows.

The officer unlocks the door to let Hunter in to cuff me, but he mutters, "Your funeral, man."

The idea that he thinks Hunter can't cuff me by himself gives me a small bit of twisted joy. Even down and broken, I'm strong.

CHAPTER 27

CONNOR

*P*oppy is asleep on the floor of the cell when we come out of the captain's office. Hunter tells me to trust him and that he'll do right by her, but I know I'm not going to see her for a while. I have to take a step back while Hunter handles things. That's his job . . . he's my handler when I'm undercover. And closing this huge case could be career-making for both of us. But that doesn't matter when I see Poppy curled up on her side, fast asleep.

She's right. I did that to her.

Before that dinner, she was a successful writer with a little bit of writer's block, living her best life. And now . . . she's fighting to stay on steady ground at every turn and still getting blind-sided.

By me.

Worst of all, I know she still hasn't finished her fucking book. At least I could have let her do *that*.

I've wanted to tell her the truth for so long. Since that first night over pizza, I wanted to let her in. I knew I could trust her, could confide in her. But that's not the gig, and I know it. This isn't my first rodeo, dealing with the stress of this life. I've lived a series of lies for so long that sometimes it's hard to remember where the truth ends and the lies begin . . . or if they're all the same thing.

All I've been able to focus on is the job and the adrenaline. And then I found her. I remember every smile and frown, every secret shared, and everything I felt. Feel. Everything I . . . feel.

I hate to do it—it physically pains me—but I walk out of the police station to my truck and leave her there. I have to trust that Hunter will stick to his word and get her out of there.

As I walk up to my truck, I remember something . . . or *someone*.

JP was supposed to be waiting in the truck with Poppy when we got here, but he didn't come in with her and the truck is empty. My gut sinks, and I scan the parking lot, looking for any sign of trouble. Cautiously, I open the door and get in, checking to make sure he hasn't lain down in the back seat to hide and fallen asleep like Poppy did. But no.

I don't see JP anywhere, but I find a scribbled note on the back of a receipt sitting on the console.

Do not look for me. I told you what I know. I am taking my family somewhere we can be safe. We have started over before, and we can do it again. Be well, my friend.

I clench the note in my hand, crumpling the paper. I look around once more, hoping to see JP somewhere nearby. The truth is that people will keep looking for him. Men like Hunter, who deserves his first name in many ways. But part of me hopes that there are always going to be bigger fish to fry than Juan Pablo. I meant it when I told him that men like me and him are minnows, and the people in power want the big fish.

When I don't see him, I say out loud, "You too, my friend. Be well."

I hope that somehow, he hears me.

I go to Poppy's place to let Nut and Juice out. They jump on my legs, but when I give them a few pets, they do eventually piss in the grass. Back inside, I get to work. I have a lot to do while Hunter closes this case.

Poppy

"Are you sure he's gone?" I ask Hunter. I pat my pockets, but I'm out of gum, and my mouth feels nasty. "Gimme some gum."

Hunter fishes a few pieces out of his pocket and passes a stick over. He pops one into his own mouth too and nods silently.

He does that a lot. If Connor is the King of the Glare, Hunter is the Silent but Deadly sort. Kind of like a fart, but way worse because when Hunter stays silent, I talk to fill the space, and I think he's annoyed with me to the point of tuning me out.

Three days of one-on-one supervision in a hotel room will do that to a person. The only time he leaves my presence is when one of us has to pee. It's getting pretty creepy at this point.

The rambling is what prompted him to offer me gum the first day, and it's become a fast habit. Nervous? Gum. Talking nonstop? Gum. Mad at the situation? Gum. Bored as fuck? You got it, gum.

But while I'd been going stir crazy, now, with us driving to my place, I sort of want to return to the safety of the hotel room. I feel vulnerable out here. And alone. "He's been taking care of Nut and Juice?"

Hunter nods again but this time adds, "I've been keeping him updated on closing the case. Mr. Big, aka Shane Harris, is going away for a long time with all of Connor's intel and what JP told us. Well, once he gets out of the hospital, and how he got there isn't going to be investigated any further." Hunter smiles an evil grin at that, having already praised and lectured me on my actions and assured me that it was an absolutely appropriate use of force to save JP and Connor.

"Harris has already lost all credibility with the business people in town, his assets are frozen, and the conglomerate that owns the baseball team bought him out and kicked him off the board. You're clear on the assault on Detective Carter." He pauses, holding up a finger to stop my argument before it starts. "Yeah, I know he deserved it. The statue is back where it should be. Hell, we even got a lead on another forgery from Connor's recon. It's basically a blue-ribbon winner of a case as far as the bosses are concerned."

"And *The Black Rose*?"

"Recovered and returned to J.A. Fox. Harris had actually kept that one for himself. He's a fan, I guess, and it was hanging in the panic room at his penthouse." Hunter drums his fingers on the steering wheel and looks at me. "It's over. If you want it to be."

Over? Nothing's over until I know the answer to one question. "Where is he?"

He shrugs, silent again. I swear it's like he uses his word allotment of the day in one minute and then, *poof* . . . nothing for hours. It drives me insane.

"Will I see him again?"

Hunter levels me with an even look, not so much a glare as a piercing gaze. "Do you want to?" There's no judgment or pressure in the question. He's truly only curious, but I feel a heavy weight on my chest that makes my breath catch.

This time, I'm the one who goes silent. I've had a lot of time to think and learn about what Connor does when working undercover by pumping Hunter for information. Connor broke a lot of rules to spend time with me, letting me into his real life and history. Hunter confided in me how much that means to a man like Connor, who's been betrayed and plays with loyalties like a toddler with a toy. But once I'd calmed down and gotten over the shock of Connor's being an undercover federal agent, I didn't need Hunter to tell me that everything between Connor and me couldn't have been a lie. Nobody lies that well. I felt it, and I know Connor did too.

I nod slowly, not trusting my voice.

"Give him some time then," Hunter advises me. "He's pretty fucked up too. You know he's got issues packed away like a damn squirrel storing nuts."

We get back to my place, and I get out of Hunter's SUV and go inside. Even though Hunter just told me that Connor isn't here, a small part of me still hoped to see him sitting on the couch waiting for me.

But it's only Nut and Juice. Their ears perk up at the door opening, and when they see me, they go wild. Nut leaps from the couch, running to greet me, and Juice does laps on the couch, back and forth while barking like mad.

"Hello, babies," I greet them, not letting them know how messed up I am right now. They've had enough bad days. I can at least give them a reasonable return to normality. "Yes, Mama missed you too. Are you okay?"

I pet their soft fur, feeling their round bellies, and know that Connor took good care of them in my absence. He fed them, he took them out . . . smelling Juice, I think he even bathed them.

A wave of sadness washes through me. I miss him.

I SIT AT MY DINING ROOM TABLE, WANTING A CHANGE OF SCENERY AS I work. My ass went numb hours ago as I try to power through the last bit of my book, but I can't stop. I won't stop. This book and my deadline are the only things keeping me functional right now, which I know is dysfunctional as fuck.

I'm drinking Red Bull from Connor's 'seven ways to kill you' mug instead of the can, purely for the comfort of having his things nearby. I found it in the sink when I came home a few days ago and have been using it ever since. I hope it's a sign from him that he'll be back and not a token for me to remember him by.

I haven't heard from him, though. Hunter isn't responding to my messages either, and I feel like maybe it was all a con to wash their hands of me.

I read back over the last page of what I've written, making tweaks as I go. It's good, but it needs to be great. After everything I've been through to get this book to fruition, it needs to be the best thing I've ever written, which means I need help.

I open a new tab and text the group chat for the W3AS gang, asking them if they can meet at the library for a sprint session and hype huddle.

Everyone replies in the affirmative, with Becca even promising donut hole rewards since that worked so well last time to motivate me. They're the best friends I could possibly have, helping me on the fly even after I disappeared and went radio silent for the days in the hotel with Hunter.

I chug the rest of my Red Bull, making a sour face at the liquid that's gone warm. I'm drinking too much of this shit. My kidneys have to be half pickled by now. After the book's done, I'm going to need a detoxing or something.

But that's a problem for Future Poppy. Right now, nothing matters but finishing *Trouble in Great Falls*. And Connor.

My hair is piled in a messy, days-dirty bun, I'm wearing clothes that I slept in, and deodorant that's been applied in layers, so I take the quick ten minutes to shower. I want the girls to think I'm doing okay for once, even if it's only a façade. I head to the library with my laptop in a bag. This one is a brand-new cross-body bag with an extra security strap that attaches around my waist. I'm not taking any chances.

And I've still got my flash drive in my pocket with my backups. No fucking around anymore.

I get to the library, and the girls are all here already, gathered and waiting for me. They go silent when I enter, making it obvious that they were talking about me while they waited. After a bit of fuss and a spritz of homemade essential oil body spray from Aleria that she swears is beneficial for mind clearing but makes me sneeze, we gather around the table and get our tech out.

"So, what happened?" Jasmine asks before I can type a single word. "You've been MIA for a few days. Working?" she prompts hopefully.

I rub my overly tired eyes, shaking my head. "So much has happened, I can't even explain it all."

Really, I can't tell them anything, per Hunter's orders. I can't risk messing up their court case.

"Your aura is full of static," Aleria says knowingly. "You need to bathe in sage."

"I'm just glad you bathed," Daysha says, sniffing the air in my direction. I make a face at her, knowing that I don't stink this time. Especially after the body spray spritz.

Becca glares at Daysha, changing the subject. "How's the book going? Tell us what you need other than a sprint session."

I sigh heavily. "It would be great if you could read over the last few chapters and see if I've missed anything," I admit. "I know it sucks to ask you guys to be beta readers, but I need the assist badly. I think I've got the loose ends tied up, but I want to be sure because I'm heading into the happily ever after. And the cliffhanger."

"Cliffhanger?" Jasmine says with a wrinkle of her nose. "Readers hate those. Unless you're explicit that it's supposed to be that way."

"I know, but I was totally upfront about it. It's a three-book series, already plotted out and contracted that way," I remind them. "So the cliffie is a necessary evil, but I need there to be some resolution that feels good."

"Then let's do this shit," Daysha says, opening her laptop. "Gimme a copy."

I give her my thumb drive, and Aleria places a hand on my shoulder. "Let me clear some of the static first. I truly think it'll help."

She's done an aura cleanse on me before, so I know it won't hurt, and at this point, anything that might help is fair game. I nod my agreement, and Aleria stands behind me, humming softly as she traces over my skin with her palms a few inches from connecting with me.

"Allow creativity to flow freely, unrestricted by worldly concerns. Release stressors and bring only warm light to Poppy's soul. Blessed be," Aleria intones. Her voice is soothing, even if the words don't actually do anything.

"Thank you," I tell her, appreciating the thought and support more than anything.

Daysha passes around my thumb drive, and within a minute of everyone's opening the file, we're all going at it. They're reading the last few chapters, making notes for discussion or tweaks, and I'm writing forward from my last stopping point. New hope blooms that I might be able to do this and do it in a quality way that will make this book my new favorite thing I've ever written.

I'm so thankful that we all help each other this way. All five of us are better writers since we started calling each other on our shit, pushing us to do more and be better.

While they read, I put on my earbuds with my hand-selected inspirational playlist for these characters and pour the story in my mind onto the computer screen. I'm down to hours, not days on my deadline, it seems, and the situation is so tense that even Hilda's leaving me alone simply because she knows that the minutes she wastes yapping my ear off are minutes I can't work.

I'm furiously working until I feel eyes on me. I glance at the computer clock to see if I finished a sprint, ready for the donut hole, but find that I still have six minutes left on the timer. I look up from my screen questioningly to see all four women with their eyes looking just beyond me.

"What?" I turn around, not sure if I'm expecting it to be Hilda demanding the book, Hunter telling me I fucked up, or Mr. Big coming back to take his revenge. All of those options are terrifying.

It's none of those people.

It's Connor. Finally.

I stand up, my knees quaking as I walk over to the door, not quite believing what I'm seeing.

"Are you real?" With a hesitant smile, I poke him in the stomach, which is rock hard beneath his black T-shirt. Seeing him, alive and in the flesh, relieves so many worries and fears. Ones that have been keeping me awake at night and distracting me from my writing. Ones that have kept my breath tight in my chest and my heart feeling hollow.

"I'm real," Connor says, his voice insistent, his eyes burning. "I'm here for you."

Tears sting my eyes, and I cover my mouth with my hands to keep from squealing too loudly in the library. But a pretty loud, high-pitched sound still gets out through my fingers, and the librarian shushes me.

I should tell her to stop interrupting my big romantic moment, but I can't take my eyes from Connor. He's really here. We have a lot to figure out still, but that he's here means it was real. I'm not crazy, not wrong about that.

I leap into his arms, quickly wrapping my legs around his waist in what he calls my 'koala maneuver'. Without even waiting, I pepper his cheeks with kisses, feeling his hands squeeze my ass tight.

"Does this mean you've forgiven me?" he asks uncertainly. My lips are pressed to the corner of his mouth when he asks, so I feel the slowly blooming smile on his lips.

Daysha interrupts, slyly inquiring, "Forgiven for what, exactly?"

I don't answer. All my attention is on Connor. I want to hold on to him and never let go, or crawl under his skin and write my name on his heart, or both.

"Of course!" I reply into his neck, trying my best not to lick it like a lollipop yet. But I give in and swipe my tongue over his skin just a little, tasting the salty musk that's uniquely him and thinking, 'I licked him, he's mine.' "If you forgive me too."

Aleria hums, apparently hearing that one. "Ooh, she fucked up too. Must be why she needs the sage. But her aura is already looking better."

"There's nothing to forgive, Poppy," Connor says, holding me tighter to whisper in my ear, "I love you."

The words are quiet, meant for just me and him, but my girls hear him clearly in the otherwise quiet room, and they gasp. I do too, especially when he slowly rubs the tip of his nose against mine in a tender move that makes my inner romantic sigh in blissed out delight.

He lays a soft kiss to my jaw, my cheek, and then my earlobe before saying it again, his breath hot against my skin. "I love you."

Then he nips my earlobe with his teeth, claiming me and making me yelp in happy surprise. That's the Connor I know. "I love you too!"

That was definitely too loud, but even the librarian is looking at us in wide-eyed wonder since we're basically making out in the historical fiction section.

"Oh, my gawd! Did you hear that?" Becca squeals as she claps her hands enthusiastically, grinning like a fool. "They're in love! I'm swooning! It's like a book to real-life adaptation right in front of us." At the librarian's glare at the noise, Becca clasps her hands under her chin, looking ridiculously happy and near tears. "Where is Netflix when you need them? I vote for Julia Roberts to play Poppy because of the red hair."

Daysha holds a finger to her lips, telling Becca, "Shh, maybe they'll forget we're here and we'll figure out what the fuck is going on with some decent context clues. And Julia Roberts is too old to play Poppy, but she could play her mom."

"Emma Stone?" Aleria suggests.

Slowly, Connor puts me down, but he keeps me curled into his side, his arm around my shoulders like he can't bear to not touch me. Or maybe like he's afraid I'll end up doing something crazy again.

But I only have one thing on my mind.

"Uh, thanks, ladies, but I gotta get going now."

"But your book!" Jasmine reminds me before rolling her eyes. "Fuck it, you'll get it done."

"Yeah," Connor growls. "I'll make sure she finishes, but we've got some shit to straighten out first."

Daysha snickers. "Just make sure she can form a coherent thought when you're done, and maybe still type, or else you're going to be the one taking dictation!"

"*Dick*-tation!" Becca repeats, putting a lewd emphasis on the first syllable. "I'm stealing that one!" She holds a finger out, implying an erect penis, and then makes a tapping motion as though someone could actually type with their dick.

"All yours," Daysha tells her easily. "That's not really my style in my books."

While Becca and Jasmine encourage Daysha to introduce an occasional light moment into her super dark, twisted stories, Connor shoves my laptop into my bag and slips it over his own head to carry it. Holding his hand out to me, he entwines his fingers with mine and kisses my temple. It feels special and intimate, as though I'm precious to him.

"Let's go home."

CHAPTER 28

CONNOR

*A*s soon as the door to Poppy's place opens, all hell breaks loose. I'm swarmed by a duo of fluffy, white-furred hype machines who yap and jump and smile big, pink-tongued doggy grins when they realize I'm back. All the while, they completely ignore Poppy, who's watching the whole scene with a pouty lip. I can almost see the thought bubble over her head reading, 'what about me?'

"I see how it is, you ungrateful brats," she scolds them. She's amused more than anything else, her eyes smiling even if she sounds disgusted by her pups. "Was Connor feeding you more biscuits than I do?"

I give Poppy a chance to drop her computer bag on the dining table, then snap my fingers, and both dogs calm instantly and sit at attention, their eyes on me. "Settle . . . good boys."

Poppy's jaw drops open, and her eyes go wide as Nut and Juice sit still as stones, although Juice's tail is wagging so hard his butt's going side to side on the carpet. "Show off!" she says, grinning. "Okay, Mr. Dog Whisperer, how'd you do that? Teach me your ways."

I lower my hand, 'releasing' the boys from their pose as I kneel down and start to scratch them under their chins. After a ridiculously tiny amount of affection, both dogs lie down to give me their bellies. I scratch them there too, praising their excellent behavior. "I had several days to work with them. That and a bag of treats goes a long way. Nut is easy, wants to learn, and Juice wants to do whatever his brother does."

I got to know both dogs pretty well during those lonely days while I was separated from Poppy. At first, I'd tried to stay at my place next door and only come over to take care of the boys. But I missed Poppy so much and wanted any connection with her that I could have, so I needed to be in her space. Sitting on her couch, smelling her shampoo, and hugging her pillow were the only things that kept me sane. And kept me from scouring the hotels I know Hunter uses as safe houses to find her.

When I stand up, Poppy's eyes are on me and she looks uncertain. I can feel it too. The excitement of the moment we saw each other again is passing, and the questions are rising once again. It helps to know that we're in the same place emotionally, the declarations of love real and spontaneous, but there's a lot for us to share. Not all of it is going to be easy and comfortable.

"Let's sit down," I offer, pointing toward the couch. "I know you need to work, but if you can give me a few minutes, I want to tell you everything." I shake my head. "No, I *need* you to know everything," I rephrase, baring my soul with the words. I've never been able to tell someone everything, but with Poppy, it's something I have to do. For myself, and . . . "You deserve that. I want this to be your happily ever after, and that means doing the hard things too."

Poppy already looks near tears, but she lets me take her hand and lead her to the couch, where we both sit. Her legs are crisscrossed in front of her, her hands clasped in her lap. She takes a big breath and resolutely says, "Okay, I'm ready. Hit me. All of it."

I smile gently, knowing this is going to take fits and starts to get through. I'm not even sure where to begin.

"First, I want to say I'm sorry," I begin, getting the most important thing out of the way. "I never meant to lie to you. I need you to know . . . I'm me, the same man you've known all along. I told you more than I have anyone in a long time, maybe forever. More truth, more me." I pause, realizing, "The me that maybe I even forgot existed."

"I'm sorry too. I was so . . . blindsided and scared and mad," Poppy admits. "I felt betrayed, like you'd been using me."

I try to interrupt her, but she doesn't let me get a word in edgewise. "I know you weren't. Hunter filled me in on some stuff, which is how I ended up at the auction. But not all of it. He let me think you were still . . . your cover." Her jaw clenches at the memory. "Believe me, I bitched him up one side and down the other about that. Told him if he wanted to keep fucking around, he was gonna find out what'd happen when I shove Gary up his ass. After that, he was much more forthcoming, and I learned a lot when I was waiting for him to close the case." She sounds proud of herself for intimidating Hunter, and honestly, that's a scene I would've liked to have seen.

I wonder exactly what Hunter told her, but we can get to that later. That's probably a conversation I need to have with Hunter, anyway, because Poppy doesn't have clearance to know about some of our previous work together.

But beyond the details of every case, I need to make her understand everything that's happened to bring me to this point, to her.

"The case," I continue before I shake my head. In my mind, I go back years. "It started way before that. What I told you was true. I started with petty theft shit as a teen. Then I phased up to art, for real. I was on a job, and Hunter found me. He stopped me."

I remember back to that job. I was stealing a post-modern work, one of those ink blot type things that look like something shrinks show their patients. There was a guy who wanted it for his office, so he hired me.

I was good then, and could've done it, but Hunter was watching the guy and knew about his hiring me. He played it cool, waited right until he could observe my skills, and put a hand on my shoulder literally seconds before I was about to make my move.

"He stopped me and offered me something else—to work with him. Not as a special agent or anything, but as . . . well, a freelancer of sorts, I guess? It's complicated. But on the right side of the law. I laughed at first, but every time I turned around, there he was. Job after job, he was there, stopping me or frustrating me. I went months without a successful gig. He wore me down, and I agreed. I was a cocky bastard, but he taught me so much. We've been partners for years, through dozens of cases. This one, catching Mr. Big, was supposed to be a career-maker. Probably will be for Hunter."

Poppy's brows furrow. "Not yours?"

I shake my head, not delving into the likely limitations to my career path. That's not the important part. Poppy is. "That's what I've been working on the last few days. I gave them my notice. I'm out of the field. No more undercover, no theft. Not even for the good guys. Things are different now . . . with you. I don't want to leave you, to risk us for some old painting."

Her mouth drops open in surprise, and then she scrambles into my lap, straddling my hips and holding my cheeks so tightly she's smushing my lips into a misshapen pucker. "I love you so much," she says excitedly. "You growly bastard, I love you!"

The weird, almost insulting nickname is surprisingly cute in its accuracy, and I growl against her mouth as I kiss her back. "I love you too."

Poppy and I exchange a long, deep kiss, and when she pulls back, she's dancing in my lap and grinning. "What are you going to do then? Because I'm no sugar momma!" She taps my nose and lifts a finger to correct herself. "Except to Nut and Juice."

I don't really mind sharing her with the dogs. They are . . . kind of adorable, in a slobbery, wild fluffball sort of way. And currently watching us from the dog bed in the corner after hearing their names.

"Ironically, I'm moving into a consultant role. For the FBI when they need me, but mostly as a private contractor, planning and evaluating security protocols for museums and collectors with valuable collections."

"That's awesome, but are you okay with that?" Poppy asks. "I don't want you to regret giving up something you love for me. Whether that's really stealing or doing it for the FBI."

I hold her tighter, not believing my good fortune with Poppy. Not that I would, but I believe I could tell her I've decided to go private and truly steal for a living, and she'd tell me to chase my dreams. Acceptance like that is more valuable than anything I've ever known. I squeeze her hips, feeling fortunate to be the man she loves. "You're worth it. And I've been thinking a lot." I swallow thickly, not used to spilling my guts like this and not liking it one fucking bit. "All this started . . ." I search for words. "There were days where I felt empty. I was holding on too tightly, the line getting too blurred again. I lost sight, had no anchor. I needed something. A purpose."

That was hard to say, but I'm glad it's out there now because the truth is . . . "But I'm not anymore. Empty, I mean. Because of you."

Poppy considers my words for a moment, then says, "But I am."

I freeze.

She's empty?

Am I not enough? Even after all this? Giving up everything I've worked for to be with her?

Even when I love her with all my heart?

And then she smiles softly and leans in to whisper seductively in my ear, "But we can fix that."

When she grinds against me, I can't help it, I groan, but before I can say anything, she fixes me with a serious gaze. "That was hard for you to say. I know that. I want you to know that I see you and what you're doing. I appreciate the courage it takes to be that honest, and I love you for it."

As she speaks, she lifts and lowers her hips, rubbing her pussy against my thickening cock in delicious torture.

I growl, thankful for the change in direction. I want her again, need to claim her, and don't want to talk about this shit anymore.

I'm a man of action, and I can show her everything she needs to know by worshipping her, fucking her hard until she comes all over me again and again.

I push her back to the couch, laying her down and climbing over her. She feels good writhing beneath me, her nails tracing over my chest through my shirt. "Connor."

"Poppy." I look her in the eye, pinning her bucking hips with a firm grip. "I'll answer any questions you have for the rest of our lives. But right now, what I need is something beyond words."

"Good . . . I need more than words too," she agrees, pulling me down. We kiss, tenderly at first as we let the rift of the past few days dissolve, then warmth and heat and desire flow through our every touch.

I press into her, letting her feel what she's done to me, maddeningly close to what we both want considering the layers of fabric between us. "You know," I tell her as I reach down, pulling her thigh up to cup her ass, "you look great in jeans."

Poppy wraps her leg around my back, digging her heel into the globe of my ass. "So do you. But you know what makes you look even better?"

"When you're out of them!" we finish together, giggling. I stop, stunned. Me, giggle?

I can't even remember the last time I legitimately giggled at *anything*.

Poppy recognizes it too, and she traces my lower lip with her thumb before pulling me into another long, lingering kiss. I push the hem of her shirt up, ready to feast on her tits when she suddenly stiffens, swatting my chest. "Wait! That's it!"

"Already?" I ask. But then logic returns, and I lift up in confusion, barely having time to get off her before she sits up, jumping off the couch and running to her laptop bag. Yanking it out, she sits at the dining table and begins typing at a furious pace, her fingers almost a blur as she hammers at the keys.

My cock aches, but I understand what's gripping her, and watch in awe as she writes. Within moments, her lip disappears behind her teeth as she focuses on the screen. It's so fucking sexy to see her brilliance in action.

"I've been struggling to get the ending right," she explains. "But this just inspired me. It's perfect."

I make my way to her side to read over her shoulder, adjusting myself in my jeans.

"Take your cock out," Poppy says, her eyes not leaving her screen.

My heart stutters, and my dick goes as hard as steel. Normally, she wouldn't have to tell me twice, but she seems pretty involved in her book for her order to make sense. "What?"

"You heard me. Do it."

Her fingers keep typing. Mine go to my shirt, pulling it over my head to drop to the floor, and then to my jeans, unbuttoning and unzipping them. Once I have room, I shove my underwear down and fist my cock, giving the shaft a long stroke.

Poppy tears her eyes from her work and licks her lips as she watches me, so I do it again.

"Feeling inspired?" I growl, my voice getting rougher with need.

"Fuck my mouth," she tells me. "While I write this scene, I want it to be ours. Their happily ever after and ours, at the same time."

I search her face, and she gives me a temptress's smile. I run my fingers into her hair, gripping her bun to guide her mouth to my cock. She licks around the head, moaning as she tastes the drop of pre-cum gathered there. "Open," I order.

She opens her mouth wide, sticking her tongue out instantly. I slide over her tongue, dipping further and further into the wet warmth of her mouth, and she closes her lips over me, sucking me even deeper.

Our eyes meet, hunger and love mixing in equal measure. I pull my hips back and thrust in again, watching as her eyes flutter closed. "That's it. Suck me, but keep typing, Poppy. You're on a deadline."

She whimpers faintly, her hands returning to the keys. They're moving slowly now, but the words still pour onto the screen. I go quiet, only releasing an occasional grunt when I slip into her throat, so she can think. My eyes flick from the sight of her mouth on me to the screen.

She's writing the final sex scene of *Trouble in Great Falls*. It's from Amber's point of view, and I think the thoughts of Poppy's character are what she's thinking too. It's a unique perspective, allowing me to read exactly what's on Poppy's mind. On the screen, Ryker pulls Amber's hair as he thrusts faster into her mouth, and I do the same. Poppy cries out in pleasure, her fingers jumping across the keyboard now.

Come in my mouth. Come now. Make me yours forever.

As soon as the words appear on the screen, I'm a goner. "*Fuck*," I grit out, pushing my cock deep into her throat to release. She swallows every jet of my cum hungrily.

My brain is mush. My cock is softening. I have no idea how she can still be typing, even as she licks me clean.

I take a shuddering breath, leaning over the table to hide how badly my knees are shaking. Poppy grins in satisfaction and then holds up one finger.

"Almost done."

I huff out a laugh, still panting. "Take your time," I tell her, slipping my cock back into my jeans.

She types easily and quickly, fully focused on wrapping up the story. She's got Amber and Ryker together again, with a secure happily ever after, though there's a hint of more story that'll obviously be the next Great Falls book. But the best part is when she taps the *Enter* key twice, centers her cursor, and types . . . *The End.*

"Congratulations," I tell her as she leans back, cracking her knuckles. "You going to send it in to Hilda?"

"Not quite yet," Poppy says, turning around to look up at me with shining, happy eyes. "I want to read it in the morning and see what the girls say about what they're reading for me. But yeah, Hilda's going to get it by lunch. Barring a spell check, though . . . I'm done!"

"You deserve a reward," I say suggestively.

"Got any donut holes?" she asks.

I have no idea what she's talking about. Maybe it's a writer thing? "Sorry, no. But I have something even better."

"Better than donut holes?" Her nose wrinkles cutely, making it obvious that she's seriously doubting my reward skills. "A cupcake?" she guesses.

"Better than donut holes or a cupcake," I vow. "Come here." I take her hand to pull her from the chair. As soon as she's standing, I scoop her up, holding her ass while she wraps her arms and legs around me. Against my bare abdomen, I can feel the wet heat of her pussy through her pants. I carry her down the hall to her bedroom, kicking the door closed to keep the dogs out.

"Three . . . two . . ." I throw her to the bed before I get to one. She keeps me on my toes, so it seems only fair to return the favor. Poppy bounces, her laugh bright and happy.

"Connor!"

"You like it. Now, strip and lie down," I tell her, one brow raised, daring her to disagree or argue.

But she's more than agreeable, instantly shuffling around to send her clothes flying all over the room carelessly. Her pants go one way, her shirt another, and her panties end up hanging off the ceiling fan. She wasn't even wearing a bra. I drop my jeans and underwear too, climbing onto the bed to loom over her.

From my propped-up position, I watch as she wiggles happily, ready for more. I force my own smile to fade, giving her straight-faced look. "I was here for a few days, you know," I tell her. "I missed you . . . a lot."

Her brow wrinkles in sadness, and she reaches for me, her hands going to my waist. "I missed you too." She tries to pull me down onto her, wanting the skin-on-skin contact, but I'm not guilting her.

"You called me your muse, but I found some inspiration being here in your space." Sex drips from the words, and her eyes glow with fire.

"Did you jack off in my bed?" she guesses.

I shake my head. It hadn't felt right to invade her space that much, though I did steal her pillow to sleep with on the couch. "No, but I did do a little . . . recon work. Target—Poppy Woodstock. Mission—learn everything I could about her so I would have half a snowball's chance in hell of making her mine."

She interrupts to say, "I am yours."

"I know. But I found some rather interesting things out about you, Poppy." I reach for her nightstand, and she squeals, pushing me away from it.

"Oh, my God! You did *not* go through my drawers! Did you?" A pretty pink blush has risen on her cheeks, but she's grinning.

"Of course, I did. And I read *Love in Great Falls* to find out more about those fairy tale prince types you claim to love. It was all very informative." It should be a simple declaration, but it's not. It's a threat, and she knows it because she knows exactly what's in her nightstand. And I did learn a little about grand romantic gestures, hence the drop-in to her writer's group.

I go for the drawer again, and this time, she doesn't stop me. If I'm not mistaken, she's breathing a little faster, actually. Inside, I pull out one of the toys I discovered. At first, it'd scared the shit out of me because I thought it was a dildo. A really *huge* one. But a little research told me it's called a 'magic wand'.

"What're you gonna do with that?" Poppy asks breathlessly.

"You'll see." I run the still silent head along her thigh and over her mound, enjoying the way her hips lift, trying to get the toy to touch where she wants. Her lips are slick with juices, perfuming the room with her desire, and I dip the head over her pussy to gather the wetness.

She moans, "Please, Connor. Turn it on."

With an evil grin, I do. And though she asked me to, she jumps in surprise before moaning in disappointment when I lay the buzzing device against her thigh again and not her clit.

Slowly, I drift up her leg, over her hip, and across her mound, getting closer and closer. When I finally let the vibrations hit her clit, she cries out in relief. "Yes, right there."

I hold the vibrator against her, watching her core pulse as I trace my nose along her inner thigh for an up-close view of her heaven. "So fucking sexy, Poppy. I could look at your pretty pussy all day, drink you down until you soak me, and then do it all over again." I punctuate the words with soft nibbles and kisses along her skin, dipping down to lick and trace her lips.

Suddenly, her whole body goes tight, the orgasm taking her faster than I expected. Her hands fly to the wand, holding it tight, and together, we ride out her pleasure, her fucking the toy and me pumping against the bed mindlessly. But when she releases her grip, I don't move it. I keep it right where it is and slide two fingers inside her.

She's drenched with her own cum, slippery with it, and I use it to fuck her with my fingers. In and out, slowly at first, letting her get used to the added sensation.

"Again," I demand.

She whimpers, her head thrashing against the pillows and her hands clawing at the sheets. "More . . . more . . ." she begs.

I stroke my fingers in faster, harder, deeper, bending them to hit that spot on her front wall that makes her fight me. Not to make me stop, but so that I *won't* stop.

She's close. I can feel her walls clenching down on my fingers tightly, and her whole body is frozen on the edge of release. And then an animalistic sound comes out of her throat, and she spasms wildly. Fresh juices soak my hand, and I keep fucking her with my fingers through the orgasm, but I have to set the wand down, needing to taste her as she comes.

She's sensitive to my tongue, bucking against my mouth as she grabs my hair and holds me to her. I suck her clit past my lips and batter it with my tongue, and she cries out. "Oh, my God, Connor. I can't."

"Yeah, you can. It's been days since I've had you."

"Then take me," she bargains. "I want you inside me."

I have to squeeze my cock hard and fast to keep from coming right then. "Turn over."

She flips over quickly when I give her space, pulling her knees up beneath her but dropping to her elbows to present herself to me. I kneel behind her and lewdly pull her ass cheeks apart to see all of her. She sways her hips to tempt me, but I'm already hers.

She owns all of me. Always.

I line up with her entrance, and with one driving thrust, I fill her. She arches her back to take all of me. I don't give her any mercy. I need to fuck myself onto her soul. All I can offer is the ugly stain of who I am, both past and present, but I hope it's enough. Because I can be better for her. I already am. She's changed me, somehow turning what was supposed to only be one day into forever.

I grip her ass, spreading her to watch my cock disappear into her pussy. It's a gorgeous sight, one I will never take for granted. I'm on a hair trigger, but I want her to come once more. I want her to come with me.

I slip my finger down, teasing along her lips to gather her juices and smear it up over her tight pucker. "Poppy?" I ask, wanting permission.

She nods against the pillow, and I slow my strokes, focusing on gently slipping my finger into her ass. Once seated, my cock in her sweet pussy and my finger in her tight ass, I move in tandem, filling her and then retreating.

"You okay?"

Poppy lets out a deep moan of pleasure, so I pick up the pace. I watch her carefully, reading her sounds and movements to learn what she likes in this new way. I learn she doesn't want it fast the way she wanted my fingers. Instead, she likes it slow and hard, so I slam into her again and again, watching the globes of her ass jiggle with every hammering thrust.

It doesn't take long before we're both hovering on the edge of release. Stars start to flash in the periphery of my vision, but I need one last thing from her. Keeping my punishing pace with my finger and cock, I reach forward with my other hand, gripping her hair. "Tell me, Poppy. Please."

It's not an order or a demand. It's a begging plea for her to tell me that this is enough. That I am enough. That she believes me, forgives me . . . loves me.

"I love you."

The response is instant, and I fly off the ledge into floating space, growling out, "I love you, too."

I feel her pussy milking me as she comes, both of us experiencing so much at once . . . together. Jets of my cum explode from my balls, rushing down my shaft to fill her, and she takes it all greedily.

Our cries are loud, and distantly, I realize Nut and Juice are singing along with us. But I don't give a single, solitary fuck about disturbing the neighbors. All that matters is Poppy. All that matters is us.

Once we're spent, I lay a soft kiss to her back, and she looks over her shoulder at me. "I do love you, Connor. Exactly who you are and how you are."

I pull out of her, guiding her to flip over onto her back. I want her eyes for this. On my elbows over her, I look at her with all seriousness in my eyes. "I love you, Poppy. Maybe even *because* you're crazy and wild and impulsive."

She laughs, her eyes dancing. "Damn fucking straight, you do. And don't you forget it."

I fall to the side, lying on the bed, and then rearrange her to lie on top of me. Sprawled out across me, her legs askew and laced through mine, she traces her fingernails over my chest.

I feel a peace and acceptance I never thought possible sweep through me. A future I never dreamed of. All because of Poppy.

After a few minutes of quiet, she rests her chin on my chest and smiles up at me. "Hey, remember that time I finished a book and you gave me like a gazillion orgasms as a reward?"

I laugh, the vibration bouncing her. "Yeah, I vaguely remember that."

"Yeah, that was awesome, but you know what I want?"

Holy shit! She wants more? I'm basically a bag of bones, and not the one I think she's after, but for her, I can rally. There were some other toys in that drawer, and I've got my fingers and tongue still.

"What?" I say slowly.

"Donut holes," she says seriously. "Donut holes are the best."

I shake my head. "Seriously?"

She shrugs, but she's giving me better puppy-dog eyes than either Nut or Juice are capable of.

"Not a cupcake?" I ask, curious about the hierarchy of her treat reward system.

She hums, thinking. "Donut holes sound better. We could get some delivered," she suggests.

Hell, feeding her donut holes will let me recover for a little bit before we go for the next round. And I could use a sugar rush too.

"Let me get my phone."

Poppy leaps from the bed, obviously nowhere near as exhausted as I am, and skips from the room. Yeah, she literally skips. She returns with both of our phones from the living room, her tits bouncing with every little hop. Standing there naked, she twists and turns as she clicks around on her phone, ordering delivery donut holes.

I watch, falling even more in love with her by the second. I think it'll always be like that, falling for her again and again every day, my love deeper and bigger than I imagined and still growing.

"Delivery ETA is thirty minutes. What should we do until then?" she says, a gleam in her eye.

I reach down to my cock, giving myself a stroke. I'm already starting to harden from watching her joy at the thought of donuts. "I don't know, but I'm sure you'll think of something."

"You know it!" she exclaims with a big grin, jumping onto the bed to straddle me. "Challenge accepted."

"Fair warning, you are not answering the door nude, so we'd better make it more like twenty-five minutes to be safe."

She winks. "No fun in that. I'll just send you to answer the door naked."

"What if it's a female delivery driver?" I ask.

Poppy growls, instantly jealous. "I'll dig her eyeballs out with a spoon."

"Twenty-four now, my little jealous minx," I say.

She lifts her hips and settles onto me easily. Suddenly, I don't give a fuck about donut holes.

CHAPTER 29

POPPY

"Stop messing with your tie," I tell Connor as he fidgets again, and I have to reach up to tug his hand away. "It looks perfect."

It's not only the tie. He looks perfect, wearing a black suit that shows off his broad shoulders and long legs and a blue tie that highlights his beautiful eyes. He's fresh-shaven, a fancy watch gleams on his wrist, and his jaw is clenched in a way that makes him look strong and in control. Other than the nervous squirming, he looks sexy as fuck.

"Tell me again why we're doing this." He sighs heavily, looking back at the truck in the driveway.

"You wouldn't make it two steps before I tackled you to the ground. And if you get my dress dirty before dinner, I will be madder than Nut and Juice combined when I promise them a trip to the dog park and then take them to the vet."

"Understood." I don't think he'd really make a run for it, but he is anxious about tonight.

He jerks at the tie once more, setting it ridiculously off-center. I growl, and with more force than is needed, I adjust it one last time. "Leave it alone for two whole fucking minutes. After that, fuck it. I won't care if you take it off and wear it around your forehead. Two minutes, that's all I'm asking for."

Standing here on the front porch of his parents' house, where we're having dinner tonight, I want to make a good first impression for the night.

After all, this was Connor's request, of all things. It probably blew their minds that he asked, and I'm sure they think it's to inform them that he's going to prison for something or another. I bet they think this is a goodbye meal before he turns himself in.

Me? I'm looking forward to tonight because I want to see the looks on his family's faces when they find out how wrong they've been for so long. I figure it'll go one of two ways. First option, they're apologetic for how awful they've been, which has a chance at leading to some rebuilding of bridges. I figure that'll be Caylee because she seems like that sort of person. She loves her big brother, and while it'll be a shock, she'll be over the moon to realize he is the good guy she's always believed him to be.

Second option, they don't believe Connor, and I'll get to watch while he eviscerates them. Which may or may not happen with his parents. If so, I'll probably even help because while he'll go all grunty-angry, I'm good at slapping together some spontaneous word diarrhea that'll make them regret every mean thing they've ever said to him. That one might be more fun, but it'll have worse consequences in the long run because it'd leave Connor hurting even more later.

So, like the responsible, good-hearted person I am, I'm hoping for option one. For Connor's sake.

"Just remember, you're a good man, and you can live a life of honesty now." I smooth his lapels and then pat him a bit too hard. Tough love before I lay on the compliments. "And you're sexy AF."

He ignores the compliment, and with an evil twist to his smirk, he clarifies, "Honesty. So I can say anything I want."

I roll my eyes, pushing his tie knot up high and tight, choking him a little bit in warning. "No, not insults and mean shit. That's what we're trying to stop, remember? You can be honest, but not to a fault. No barbaric, grumpy asshole shit."

I let go of the tie slowly, daring him to disagree, but he tilts his head and adjusts the knot back to a less constricting position before taking a deep breath. "Conan once said he preferred barbarians to polite society because a man's a lot more respectful when he knows he might get an axe to the head."

"Well we don't have an axe," I remind him, "and Gary's at home. But how about this? If they start it, you finish it."

The very idea of the possibility of unleashing on his family seems to help with his nerves, and more confidently, he says, "Let's get this shit over with."

But I see the slight hesitation before he rings the doorbell. Underneath the curmudgeonly act, he's nervous that even the truth won't be enough to satisfy his parents or change their long-held opinion of him. The huge bell *ding-dongs* with echoes, and dimly, I think that doorbell sounds like a fucking funeral dirge. Hopefully, that's not a bad omen.

Debra opens the door, her smile a bit trembly as she steps back to let us in. "Hi, kids! Come on in!" Her tone is overly bright and chipper, falsely so. "You look so nice."

"Thank you, Debra. You do too," I reply, not even looking her over. I'm too busy focusing on how she's looking at Connor. There's a darkness in her eyes, a worry she's carried for a long time. Hopefully, what Connor has to say will help alleviate some of that.

Caylee calls out from the living room, "We're in here."

We follow Debra into the living room to find Caylee and Evan sitting on the couch, their thighs pressed against one another and Evan's arm thrown over the back of the couch surrounding Caylee protectively. They look comfortable, happy, and very much in love. And a bit tan from their honeymoon.

For his part, Robert is sitting in a leather club chair, his scotch glass looking freshly poured. And despite our being right on time, it feels like we're interrupting something.

"You decided to get together early to gossip about me," Connor guesses, reading the room. I can feel his weight shift as he prepares to bolt, so I squeeze his hand tighter. It's a reminder that we're here, we're doing this together, and he'd better not make me run in my sexiest heels. I'd probably break an ankle, end up falling to the floor, and then Connor would have to decide if was leaving me behind to the wolves or taking the time to scoop me up and carry me to safety.

Hmm . . . wait, that would be good for the next book. Maybe Ryker could save Amber? Or hell, she could save him. I'm not trapped in gender roles. Amber can be the knight in shining armor.

"No, of course not, dear. We're just . . ." Debra says, pausing as she searches for the right words, "uhm, excited about what news you might have to share with us."

Caylee doesn't play along with Debra's lie, laughing and telling Connor, "Mom's bet is that Poppy is preggers. You got yourself a little Poppyseed muffin in the oven?"

"Caylee Marie!" Debra shouts. She looks to me, horror in her eyes, not at the thought but at it being laid so plainly bare. Quieter, and aiming for some semblance of manners, she asks, "Uhm, but since Caylee mentioned it . . . are you?"

"No, Mom," Connor snaps, not seeing the humor in it all. "I didn't knock her up."

I shake my head and tell Debra a bit more gently, "Not pregnant, though the practicing is fun. But we're safe. We stretch before and after to prevent pulled muscles."

Whatever relief she felt from finding out that I'm not pregnant is dashed at the mention of Connor's and my sex life, but hey . . . ask personal questions, get personal answers.

Connor, though, is still a bull in a china shop with almost no relaxing despite my attempts at humor. "I'd bet Dad's guess is that I've been charged with something. What about you, Caylee?"

Caylee rolls her eyes but doesn't look upset. "Right on Dad." She snuggles into Evan's side and adds, "Our bet is that you two eloped and you're here to tell us that there won't be a wedding because you're already hitched." She sighs. "I wouldn't blame you. I wouldn't change a thing about our day, but damn, that was stressful. All the planning and work, the expenses, and the people. If I'd known, I might've considered running off to a beach somewhere, just the two of us, to get married. The wedding costs alone would have snagged us a down payment on a house, you know that?"

"We'll get there with our next quarterly bonuses, honey," Evan says, looking at his bride with so much newlywed love that it inspires me.

That's definitely a better muse for book three. I got Ryker and Amber back together after their trouble, but I'll need fresh drama, and then maybe I can find a way to have them renew their commitment to each other in some sweet, private way.

Fresh drama . . . maybe a kidnapping? Or what about a coma? Meh, a bit soap opera . . . but I'll figure it out.

"Thank you, you guys. Eloping is an awesome idea," I tell them as I tap my forehead, storing that idea away for later consideration. Connor glares at me, and I assure him, "For a story. I'll explain later."

Closing his eyes, he pinches the bridge of his nose for a long second before striding over to the bar. He pours a double shot of scotch and drinks it in one swallow without making a face despite the burn that must be searing his throat right now.

I sit on the other couch and point at the chair next to Robert, telling Debra she should sit too. "This is about to get good." Slowly, she does, but she's tenser than a virgin asshole lubed in lemon juice.

Connor turns around, leaning on the bar. When his eyes meet mine, I expect to see resolve, excitement, maybe even some gloating, considering he's about to throw his family's preconceived notions about him in the gutter and piss on them. But what I see is doubt, uncertainty, and an overwhelming amount of fear. We talked about this before asking for this dinner, and I know he's worried that even the truth won't be enough.

But I believe in happily ever afters, and I have enough faith for the both of us. Hell, if I can forgive him and he can forgive me, surely, his parents will understand if given a little time and the whole story.

"Connor," I tell him, "hit 'em with the biggie first. I wanna see their faces when you tell them."

He grits his teeth, and before my eyes, I see him gather his courage. Slowly, so slowly I hope to not be noticed, I pull my phone out. But Connor, always aware of everything, sees. "No filming it, Poppy."

I want to argue, to explain that right now I'm more in awe of him than ever before, but that wouldn't help Connor. So instead, I crack a grin. "Spoilsport. I think it'll be funny . . . later. Much later."

He growls, and I shrug an apology, putting my phone down on the coffee table so it stays in plain sight before placing my hands on my crossed legs and smiling innocently.

"I've been lying to you for a long time," Connor starts.

Robert interrupts with a snort. "Is this supposed to be news?"

Debra places a staying hand on Robert's arm, hissing his name.

"What? Like that's headline worthy?" He moves his arm away from Debra to swipe it through the air like he's reading a newspaper headline. "Connor's a liar. If you remember, I was the one who had to go bail him out when he got picked up. And this whole 'consultant' shit? Like you believe that either."

Debra pales, letting us all know that Robert's telling the truth. Connor's parents have assumed he's been a crook this whole time.

Caylee interrupts her parents' arguing, hoping to save this disaster before Leonardo DiCaprio signs up to play the lead in the movie adaptation. "Connor, I'm hoping there's more to this big announcement?"

Anger swirls in the room, from Connor to his parents and back again. And I know that I need to help Caylee get this back on track.

"Tell them the rest.," I encourage Connor. "Just do it."

Connor snorts, much like his father just did. "They don't even deserve to know."

"Maybe not," I concede, "but you deserve to tell them. And besides, Caylee should know the truth, if nothing else."

Our conversation has at least shut Robert and Debra up as they look from Connor to me, realizing that there might actually be something they don't know. Connor inhales deeply and looks at his sister, then me, and continues on.

"You're right. Okay, here it is. I've been lying to you for a long time, and no, I'm not a consultant. I work for the FBI, mainly undercover. Or well, I was until last week when I essentially retired."

The room goes so still and quiet that we could be filming one of those mannequin challenge videos. No one breathes or moves a muscle. Suddenly, Robert starts laughing. Debra tries to smile, not sure if this is some elaborate joke we're playing.

Robert looks to me, his eyes bleary with disbelief and scotch. "Girl, you'd best get away from that one. He's no good. Worse than I thought if that's the line he's telling you."

That's when I crack, and I'm on my feet, angrily snatching the tumbler away from Robert. I only mean to take it, but the momentum of the movement and the slick crystal make it slip through my fingers, and I accidentally throw it across the room to shatter against the stone fireplace. "Oops!" But however unintentional, the dramatics work, getting all eyes on me. I decide to act like I totally meant to do that and hiss at Robert, "He's telling the truth, and you're too much of an asshole to believe him. Just because you decided a long time ago to write him off doesn't mean everyone else should."

"Poppy!" Caylee protests, but I keep going.

I point at Connor. "I loved him when I thought he was a petty thief. I loved him when I thought he was an art thief, and I love him now that I know the truth . . . that he works undercover for the feds. What a pity that his own flesh and blood can't love him the same as someone he met only a few weeks ago." My voice has gotten louder with each ugly accusation until I'm yelling at them all and standing in front of Connor protectively, ready to fight for his honor.

Debra's eyes are wide, likely not used to anyone talking to her like this. Or maybe it's that she's not accustomed to having a screaming banshee in her living room? She stands up, not moving toward us but not able to stay in her seat either.

"Wait, what? I'm lost . . . petty theft, art, FBI? What do you mean you only met a few weeks ago?"

Connor sighs behind me, wrapping his arms around my waist. His voice is flat and hard as he tells his mom, "That's what you got out of what Poppy told you?"

Debra blinks rapidly, still stunned. "Well, give me a minute. This is a lot to take in."

Robert huffs. "You're not actually believing this, are you?"

But when Debra looks from her husband to her son, something happens. She sees the truth, that Robert is a shell of his former self, the good man Connor has told me he once was, and that her son is standing in front of her with all his walls down, simply asking his mother for love.

"I do, Robert," she says quietly, turning away from her husband one last time to focus on her son. "Please tell me, Connor. I think I need to know. And Poppy's right, I think you need to tell us."

She gestures to the couch with an open hand and pleading eyes.

I can feel Connor trying to decide, his heart pounding against my back. I won't make this decision for him or even encourage him one way or the other. It's his call.

He can keep throwing grenades, precisely aimed to do the most damage, or he can begin to truly explain, with softer words and truth.

But when he moves toward the couch, taking my hand to bring me with him, I'm relieved. I think he's got a chance at repairing things with his mom. His dad is an entirely different issue, but if he can get his mom to listen, I think it'll help them both.

Sitting down, Connor takes a steadying breath.

"It started in high school. I was doing stupid shit, shoplifting and pickpocketing. The reasons . . . don't matter now. Some of the stuff you know, and some you don't. That's when I got busted and you bailed me out. After that, I was hurt, really hurt, so I moved on to bigger and better jobs—stealing art."

"Art?" Evan asks, and Connor nods. "Like *The Thomas Crown Affair?*"

"Something like that, I guess, but a lot less sexy," Connor answers, which I disagree with, but I'll keep that to myself for now. Connor looks back at his mother. "I got good. Really good."

Debra is listening intently, and though he's not looking at Connor, Robert is paying close attention too.

"I worked my way up, starting with pieces worth thousands of dollars, then hundreds of thousands of dollars, and worked for some really shady people."

Caylee pales, her chin trembling. "That sounds dangerous, Connor."

He nods. "It was. A few times, I figured I'd had it."

Debra lets out a soft cry at that and takes Robert's hand.

"About ten years ago or so, I was on a job, and an agent found me. He could've arrested me right then and there, but he saw an opportunity for both of us. I'm not bragging, but I'm good at stealing. I feel like Granddad's watching over me every time."

That gets Robert's eyes to focus on Connor. "Dad?"

Connor nods, addressing his father for the first time. "You remember, he taught me all those magic tricks as a kid? Those skills, they're like the foundation. This is a way I can honor that, feel close to him."

"By stealing?" Robert says harshly, offended. "How dare you."

"At first, you're right. But later, by using what he taught me for the good guys. By being one of the good guys. The agent I work with? We've taken down businessmen who think the rules don't apply to them, black-market masterminds who use their funds to bankroll terrorist groups, and caught scammers who steal thousands of dollars in fake auctions and insurance claims each year. So yeah, I think Granddad would be proud of what I do with what he taught me."

"An undercover FBI agent that steals art?" Robert asks, and I can tell he's starting to believe Connor too.

"Not quite, I never went to Quantico to become a special agent . . . and I'm retired," Connor points out, "but basically, yeah." He takes my hand, much like his mother took his father's, and holds it tightly. "As for us, I met Poppy on a job recently, and she changed everything."

Debra still looks confused. "What about Scarlett?"

Connor shrugs one shoulder, not ashamed and simply admitting the truth. "Another lie. I don't date, Mom. Relationships are impossible when I can't exactly explain why I'm gone or what I'm doing. My work is all-consuming, but I didn't want you to worry."

Debra smiles sadly. "I . . . I'm sorry."

"Look, I know this is a lot, and you're not going to understand everything all at once. You're going to have questions, but I wanted you to know that I'm not still the black sheep of the family you've made me out to be. Once upon a time, yeah, that was true. But not anymore. And now that things are changing, I want to fix this." He moves a hand from his chest to his parents and then to Caylee and Evan. "If you want to."

Debra speaks for her and Robert, saying. "Of course, we do."

Robert is still holding Debra's hand, though, and also nods, so he seems on board too. "It'll take some time."

Connor presses his lips together, looking stern and stronger than ever, but I think . . . is he fighting off a smile? "I know it will. But we can do it. Poppy's taught me that anything is possible." His lips do tilt up slightly at that, and I can see how pleased and relieved he is at his parents' reactions.

He looks at me with love in his eyes. I might've pushed him to talk to his parents, and he wasn't sure it was such a good idea, but now, I can feel that he's glad I made him. They have a chance at a relationship again. A happily ever after for their family.

Debra gets up and approaches Connor slowly. He stands too, and when Debra wraps her arms around his middle, hugging him like he's the baby boy she's known and loved all along, he relaxes into her. He's a foot taller than Debra, but make no mistake, in this moment, he's a boy getting hugged by his mom, something he needed more than he would've ever admitted to.

When they're done, she turns to hug me. She whispers in my ear, "Thank you for bringing him back to us. I didn't know how much we'd lost him and how much of it was our own doing."

Robert, who needs a little more time to unleash the tears, it seems, still searches for a good step forward. Clearing his throat, he says, "How about we eat some dinner? Debra made a roast chicken and vegetables that have smelled good all day."

The compliment from him is unexpected, and Debra smiles at her husband in appreciation. Caylee and Connor lock eyes, their brows raised as they silently question, 'What just happened?'

"Sounds good . . . Dad."

Robert clears his throat at the term of affection, and we make our way into the dining room. Debra brings in the serving platters from the kitchen, setting them on the table, as Evan opens the wine for us all.

We're just about to raise a glass in toast when the phone rings. Debra pauses to look at it, a plate of dinner rolls in her hands. But instead of answering, she rolls her eyes and says, "It's Audrey. I'm not letting her interrupt our family dinner with her narcissistic bullshit."

As Debra rearranges a few plates to make room for the rolls, Robert, Caylee, and Connor all look at each other in shock.

"Uh, Mom?" Caylee asks as she sets down her wine glass, "Where did you learn about narcissism?"

Debra blushes slightly. "Well, things have been rough lately. Like you said, the wedding was a lot of stress, and there's been . . ." She trails off, looking at Robert and Connor before the words rush out in one breath, "I started going to therapy. It's only been a couple of sessions, but I'm learning a lot."

Caylee smiles widely, seeming bowled over. "Wow, Mom. That's great."

"You think so?" Debra asks hesitantly. "You don't think it's stupid?"

"Welcome to the new generation, Mom. Everyone goes to therapy now," Caylee says. "There's nothing to be ashamed of. I had a few sessions when I needed help in college, stressing out. And Evan and I did premarital therapy to help us define boundaries and learn to communicate better. Therapy is a good thing."

Debra straightens as she sits down next to Robert. "Oh, well . . . yeah. I think it's a good thing too."

We eat, honestly complimenting Debra on the delicious meal, and somehow, conversation turns to Connor's grandfather. Robert seems particularly interested to hear how his dad's old magic tricks, which were apparently not that great to begin with, could've possibly helped Connor steal a well-protected piece of art.

"He taught me that sometimes, you have to roll with it. I can't tell you how many quarters he dropped before he'd pull one from behind my ear. And he'd sell it as my ears being so full that he couldn't even catch them all. But later, he could do it easily. I learned to practice from him too. The theories he taught me are sound, regardless of a few dropped quarters."

The memory is a good one, bringing a smile to Connor's face and even a small one to Robert's.

"He used to do card tricks when I was a kid, basically play three-card monte with me," Robert recalls a little wistfully. "This was when he was younger, and his skills . . . well, he could frustrate me all day if he wanted. But eventually, he'd let me win the pot. I'd eat all the candy I won but save the strawberry candies for him because they were his favorites."

Caylee perks up, smiling. "I remember that. He always had strawberry candy in his pocket." She pats her chest, right over her heart, and I get a mental image of a miniature Caylee digging in her Granddad's pocket for sweets every time she saw him.

Connor told me that Robert wasn't the same after his dad died, and I wonder if a part of that is because nobody talked about him anymore. He's been living with all this sadness and grief inside and no one to talk to about it. Hopefully, today will be a new beginning for us all, one with open lines of communication.

Over dessert, Connor places his napkin on the table and says, "There is one more thing."

I look at him in surprise, and wary concern steals the smile Debra's been sporting all through dinner.

"Uh, what are you talking about? That's everything." Connor raises a brow questioningly, and I pale. "Isn't it? Oh, shit, is there something else I don't know? It'd better be something good because I'm all out of patience and understanding right now. I've got zero fucks left to give, Connor, so choose your next big reveal carefully."

He smiles, not the least bit scared by my threat, and stands. "Poppy, I met you a few weeks ago and could've never predicted what your running into me at that dinner would do to my heart. Or my foot. Those heels of yours left a bruise for days."

I interrupt, grinning. "You deserved it." I look to Caylee, Evan, Debra, and Robert, pleading my case. "He did!"

Connor chuckles and drops to one knee. "Are you seriously going to show them the bruise?" I ask. "It's healed. I know it is because I saw you walking around naked, swinging your dick like a helicopter this morning. And there was no bruise on your foot."

Connor cocks an eye at me in mock anger. "If my dick is out and you're looking at my feet, we have a problem."

I shrug, ignoring the occasional shocked gasp from Debra. "Fair point. But what are you doing down there?"

Caylee gasps, getting it before anyone else does. "Connor, didn't you already do this?"

"Do what?" I ask, still confused.

Connor smiles and looks around the room. "About that . . . Poppy voluntold me that she was coming to that dinner with me. She was only supposed to be a one-day fiancée. But I want a whole lot more than that. I want her to be my wife forever."

It hits me, and my cheeks puff up from how big I'm smiling, and my eyes burn from unshed tears of happiness.

"Is that a question?" I ask him, knowing that he never asks things. He's getting better, but he's still grumpy and statement based. Questions are like gold coins for him.

But this time, he nods and in a rough voice filled with emotion, he asks, "Poppy Woodstock, will you be my wife?"

I launch myself at him, tackling him to the floor. Thankfully, the rug is soft and breaks our landing as I smother him with kisses. *Mwah–mwah–mwah.*

He laughs, the vibration in his chest making my own happiness bubble up too, and our teeth clack together as I kiss him once more, not letting a little thing like laughter get in my way.

"I'm taking that as a yes."

"Yes, yes, yes." I cup his face, grinning. "You, big bad thief. You stole my heart."

I hear snickers from the table and realize that might've sounded a bit like bedroom talk, but I'm too happy to care. Especially when Connor plays along, growling, "I didn't steal it. It was mine all along."

Oh, fuck yeah, my next male main character is going to be a growly-possessive sort inspired by Connor because my baby makers are exploding like fireworks right now. Can it be possible for sound to trigger ovulation? Right now, I'm pretty sure it can.

In fact, the story is already writing itself in my mind . . . an asshole not looking for love and a spontaneous, crazy girl who believes in fairy tales. There should be twists and turns, with someone almost dying. Oh, and a lovey-dovey scene on the beach where they express their deepest, sweetest emotions. Yeah, that sounds like a bestseller!

"Poppy?"

I come back from my mental journey into my next book to see him looking at me with worry marring his brows. Relieving his stress, I smile and kiss him. "Can we elope to the beach like Caylee said? I think it'll be good research for my next book."

He shakes his head, his brows rising in question. "Anything you want."

"Even if I say I want the *Mona Lisa*?" I tease, making it an impossible job.

He shrugs as if I just asked him to get me a Slurpee down at the corner store. "The one in the Louvre is already a replica. The real one is stored away for safekeeping. Which one you want?"

We all laugh, but I'm not sure he's actually kidding. I guess it doesn't matter because my art thief is retired, and his one-day fiancée is going to be a forever wife.

EPILOGUE

CONNOR

"Put it on speakerphone!" I tell Poppy.

Finally, the call's here. I don't think I could stand the stress any longer. I've handled numerous thefts, done business pitches now, even mock stole something from the freakin' *Pentagon*.

But I can't take this any longer. She's been waiting on this call all day. I've tried to keep her distracted, but now that the phone is ringing, I'm nervous too.

She answers, her hand shaking slightly. "Hello."

Hilda's on the other end of the line and is panting with excitement even before the first words come out of her mouth. "Poppy Woodstock! Are you sitting down?"

Poppy sinks to the coffee table, the nearest flat surface. I sit on the couch in front of her, framing her knees with mine and placing my hands on her thighs. I believe in her, and Hilda's voice is encouragement . . . but sometimes, you just gotta hear the words.

Poppy, too. "I am now."

"*Trouble in Great Falls* is officially a *Times* bestseller! Better than book one, even, which is rare for sequels. It's at the top of the charts, and sales are still going strong. You did it, Poppy!"

Poppy's eyes are as wide as saucers, her jaw is hanging open, and a strange 'ahh' sound is coming out of her mouth. After a few moments of this continuing, I clear my throat. "Ah, I think she's excited, Hilda. She's frozen, but in a good way. Let it go, Pops. Let it go."

"Oh, hi, Connor!" Hilda greets me like a casual bar buddy, which is funny since we've only ever met face to face twice so far. "Well, when she comes to, tell her the publisher wants to discuss what's next . . . after the conclusion of the Great Falls trilogy. I think they'll consider anything she wants to write at this point. I'll just need something to pitch, and I bet they'd be sending over a contract before you know it."

"Will do. Thanks, Hil. We'll call you tomorrow." I hang up the phone and cup Poppy's face in my hands, running my thumbs over her cheeks soothingly. "Honey? You okay?"

"Uh-huh. Did Hilda say better than book one?" she quotes vacantly.

"She did. Did you hear the rest?"

Poppy nods, and her whole face lights up from within as everything sinks in. She squeals, jumping into my lap in excitement.

"Oh, my God!" she gushes, pumping her fist in the air. "I did it! We did it! Aaaahhh!"

Her words turn to gibberish and sounds of joy as she shakes me by my shoulders. At our feet, Nut and Juice are barking and howling, feeding off our energy. After all, if Poppy's going crazy, then everybody's going crazy.

"We should celebrate," I tell her when she pauses to take a breath. "Get dressed, and I'll take you to dinner. I'll even call the girls and have them meet us."

I expect her to jump from my lap and run to get ready. This is a celebration-worthy moment. But she doesn't. She leans in and kisses me.

"Or we tell the girls tomorrow at lunch, and tonight, we get naked and celebrate," she says. "Just the two of us."

There's only one answer to that. "I like the way you think."

I pick her up as I stand and carry her to the bedroom, kicking the door closed to lock Nut and Juice out. I've come to love the rug rats, but I do not have sex with an audience.

Instead, I spread Poppy out on the bed—our bed now—and we truly celebrate.

Just the two of us.

Her and me, celebrating her success, my new career, and most importantly, our life together.

Happily ever after.

ABOUT THE AUTHOR

Big Fat Fake Series:
My Big Fat Fake Wedding | | My Big Fat Fake Engagement | |
My Big Fat Fake Honeymoon

Standalones:
Drop Dead Gorgeous | | The Dare | | The Blind Date

Bennett Boys Ranch:
Buck Wild | | Riding Hard | | Racing Hearts

The Tannen Boys:
Rough Love | | Rough Edge | | Rough Country

Dirty Fairy Tales:
Beauty and the Billionaire | | Not So Prince Charming | |
Happily Never After

Get Dirty:
Dirty Talk | | Dirty Laundry | | Dirty Deeds | | Dirty Secrets